THE MANIPULATOR

DAN BUZZETTA

Copyright © 2025 by Dan Buzzetta.

All rights reserved.

No part of this book may be reproduced in any form or by any electronic or mechanical means, including information storage and retrieval systems, without written permission from the author, except for the use of brief quotations in a book review.

Severn River Publishing
www.SevernRiverBooks.com

This is a work of fiction. Names, characters, businesses, places, events and incidents are either the products of the author's imagination or used in a fictitious manner. Any resemblance to actual persons, living or dead, or actual events is purely coincidental.

ISBN: 978-1-64875-633-7 (Paperback)

ALSO BY DAN BUZZETTA

The Tom Berte Legal Thrillers

The Manipulator

The Winter Verdict

System of Justice

Join the reader list at

severnriverbooks.com

I dedicate this book to the men and women in law enforcement – those who carry guns and badges, and those who carry briefcases. And to my wife, Justine, and my children, Anthony, Michael, and Elizabeth. Thank you for taking this journey with me.

PART I

1

The *M/Y Vulcania* chiseled its way through the churning seas of the western Mediterranean near the coast of Malta. Winds howled and rain pelted the double-paned blast-resistant windows. Nino steadied himself in the dimly lit salon as enormous swells crashed against the vessel's gleaming steel hull. Almost three football fields long, with a crew of eleven and only two passengers, the massive floating palace had been at sea for more than three months without touching land. In the bridge, the captain maintained a watchful eye on radar, while making visual sweeps of the horizon at regular twenty-minute intervals using night vision binoculars.

At 5:40 a.m., the encryption-keyed satellite phone in the *Vulcania's* study chimed, interrupting the lonely silence. Nino placed a tumbler of iced amaretto on the marble side table and glanced at the clock sitting atop the credenza. He pursed his lips. The caller was ten minutes late. He slowly raised the receiver and heard the sound of labored breathing before he heard the caller's quivering voice.

"Nino, my apologies for the delay. I was having difficulty connecting to your line. Perhaps you were out of range."

Nino leaned back on the white leather sofa and imagined the caller sitting alone in his high-rise palazzo thousands of miles away.

"Are you prepared to assist me?" Nino asked coldly, disinterested in exchanging pleasantries.

"I have studied your plan in detail," the caller said after a moment's hesitation. "Are you certain this is the best way to accomplish your goal, or the right circumstance?"

Nino sensed fear in the caller's voice. He had correctly assumed the caller's first instinct would be to protect his young ward.

"What you're asking will be very difficult to achieve. Perhaps even impossible," the caller continued. "So much needs to fall precisely into place for your plan to succeed. I beg you to reconsider. We can work to devise a different strategy. Please."

Nino was unaccustomed to having his orders challenged, and the caller was becoming a source of torment. But at the same time, Nino needed the caller's power and prestige. Few others could accomplish what the caller could. For now, Nino would need to remain patient. The caller's compliance was critical to the success of his plan. The stakes were too high, and he risked losing too much if he gave up now.

"Your job is not to question me, but simply to do as you are told," Nino said calmly. "If history has taught us anything, it is that even the impossible can be achieved with overwhelming power. I assisted you in your time of need and invested much time and resources to rescue you from certain disgrace. I did so willingly, and I will continue to provide for those closest to me. In return, I expect you to heed my instructions and carry out the plan I've laid out. There is no alternative."

The caller had counseled titans of industry and thugs in white collars with his keen intellect and influential connections, but Nino knew he would be powerless to resist the demands being made of him now. He was confident the caller could be persuaded to see things his way.

"I am resolute in my commitment," Nino added firmly, "and I will not allow anyone to interfere with my plan. I must discover what they know and how they'll attack. I am certain the *Ragazzo* will provide the necessary assistance when the time is right."

The caller had his instructions. There was nothing left to say. It was time to execute.

"I wish you and all of us Godspeed," the caller said in a muffled whisper as he pressed the end call button.

Nino reached for the amaretto and peered out the salon's windows at the vast reaches of ocean that lay ahead. Moments passed. He barely heard his closest confidant, Totto Nessa, enter the salon.

"Is the plan in motion?"

Nino nodded slightly. "Just as I envisioned it. I've waited too long to reclaim the most important thing in my life."

As blustery winds continued to roil the seas, stray wisps of faint light leapt from the sun's edges as it slowly pierced the eastern horizon. Time would tell if it would rise to glisten brightly or fade behind darkening clouds gathering in the distance.

2

The pursuit of justice is the bedrock of a civilized society.

C. Thomas Berte read those words carved into the ornate wood paneling high above the judge's perch as he sat at the defense table in the ceremonial courtroom in downtown Manhattan. Three weeks had passed since opening statements in the trial against AMX Corporation, the giant manufacturing company that for decades had produced the chemical centuron in a sprawling quarter-acre, four-story factory in the Bronx. It was centuron, the plaintiffs' lawyers claimed, that caused everything from sterility to pulmonary distress and lung cancer. Based on the look on jurors' faces as they stared daily at the plaintiffs in the courtroom, some of them in wheelchairs breathing with the aid of oxygen tanks, and at least one lying on a full-size gurney connected to machines that intermittently hummed, beeped, and chirped, it appeared they had already made up their minds: Centuron was deadly and AMX was liable. Tom, too, spent time looking at the plaintiffs and recalling what his ethics professor at Harvard Law School would say about lawyers. Something about attorneys "being foot soldiers of the Constitution and the army protecting the citizenry's rights and liberties." As he surveyed the plaintiffs' faces and heard the devastating effects centuron had on their lives, Tom wondered whether he was doing battle on the right side of justice.

The hour of the day, coupled with the stifling heat in the courtroom, made it too much for Judge Vernon E. Simons to bear. From the bench, he surveyed the crowded courtroom. "Counselors," the Judge said in a gravelly voice, "let's end here for today. We'll pick up with Dr. Millon's testimony tomorrow morning promptly at nine." Turning to the jury he said, "Ladies and gentlemen, you are excused. I remind you not to discuss this case with anyone, including among yourselves. And please avoid any media stories or internet postings about the trial. Finally, please arrive no later than eight forty-five in the morning." With that, Judge Simons headed for his chambers and an afternoon martini.

This wasn't Tom's first trial, but it was his longest so far. He was a rising star at Balatoni, Cartel & Colin, BCC for short, one of the oldest, largest, and most prestigious law firms in the world. With more than thirty-five hundred lawyers, including five hundred partners, and offices in every major city and capital across the globe, BCC was at the top of its game and the law firm everyone else tried in vain to beat. Tom was sitting second chair for the trial, there to assist Troy McDonald, a BCC partner and AMX's lead lawyer.

"Jesus, what the fuck was Millon saying up there?" Troy said as he let out a deep breath. "I couldn't keep my eyes open. How the hell am I going to cross him tomorrow?"

"What are you worried about?" Tom said, cracking a smile. "You'll review the transcript tonight and wing it tomorrow—like you always do."

"Very funny," Troy said with a slight grin. "Maybe I should make you handle the cross."

"Any time. Just give me the word."

As Troy and Tom walked out of the federal courthouse in Foley Square, they were greeted by the oppressive humidity of the late June day. The forecast had called for temperatures in the eighties, but with heat radiating off the pavement and trapped by the downtown buildings, it felt hotter. There was no breeze coming off the bay, and the air was stale. Fortunately, awaiting the two lawyers was an air-conditioned Lincoln Town car, one of the many perks enjoyed by BCC lawyers and happily paid for by AMX. While the plaintiffs' attorneys scurried to find taxis or lugged briefcases down to the heat chamber of the New York City subway, Troy and Tom traveled back to their offices in style and comfort. Even the paralegals and clerks who assisted them at trial were escorted to and from the courthouse each day in a luxury travel van.

After a twenty-minute ride, they pulled up to BCC's headquarters in the Americenter Tower in midtown and made their way to the elevators.

"I assume the direct testimony will be over in the morning, so we need to be ready to cross after lunch," Troy mumbled while yawning. Tom nodded respectfully, knowing they had little chance to undercut the rock-solid testimony of the plaintiffs' expert, and even less chance of persuading the jury he was a hired quack.

"Let's meet tomorrow morning in the conference room at seven again," Troy said as the elevator doors opened on the fifty-sixth floor. He nudged himself around messengers and delivery folks bringing food to the tired and weary BCC lawyers who didn't have time to go out for lunch hours earlier.

Tom nodded while remaining in the elevator for the ride up to his office on the fifty-ninth floor. As the doors closed, he yelled out, "I'll be here at 6:30."

Tom was a seventh-year associate, and his job was to stay alert, take notes, and know the facts, documents, and deposition testimony cold, like the back of his hand. If he was lucky, he'd get to question a witness or two. He'd worked hard to get where he was in his young career, and he truly believed his successes and accomplishments were the result of his persistent dedication and commitment to everything he set out to do.

Tom shuffled into his office and realized he was exhausted. The papers piled high and strewn across his desk were a testament to the countless hours he'd spent preparing for trial over the past few months. Drafting motions, reviewing thousands of pages of documents, and reading hundreds of cases were the chores that had contributed to Tom billing over three thousand hours so far this year.

He pulled back his black leather chair, slung his jacket over its high back, and let himself fall into it. He reached down to the mini-refrigerator to the left of his desk which was always stocked with the finest *Yoo-hoo* money could buy—in bottles, not cans—and pulled out a frosty one. Twisting off the cap, Tom took a long swig while logging onto his computer. He had eighty-five unread emails in his inbox. As he began scrolling through them, he noticed the handwritten note on BCC stationery tucked below the flat screen monitor. He picked up the note and began reading, his eyes widening with every word.

Dear Tom,

Please come to my office as soon as you return from court. It is important.

IB

Tom's heart raced and his palms began to sweat. In seven years at BCC, Tom had never been called to Ignatius Balatoni's office. He first met Ignatius, BCC's sole surviving founding partner and Chairman Emeritus, when he interviewed at the firm for a summer associate position as he was beginning his second year at Harvard Law School. And it was Ignatius who came to his office at the end of that summer to deliver the letter inviting him to join the firm as a full-time associate after graduation. But now the great Ignatius Balatoni, one of the most revered attorneys in America, and the man everyone affectionately called The Pope, was requesting to see him in his office. Tom had never heard of another associate being summoned in this fashion.

He jumped up and sprinted for the door, only to realize he'd left his jacket draped over his chair. He grabbed the jacket, straightened his tie, and darted for the elevator, but took the stairs at the last minute hoping to shave off a few seconds. As he made his way up the three flights, Tom thought back to his first day at BCC when Ignatius invited him to a meeting with a lawyer from another large firm who represented a competitor of Ignatius's client.

Ignatius had called the meeting to explain to the lawyer why accepting his client's offer was in the competitor's best interest. The lawyer, in his mid-thirties, was a pompous hot shot who kept interrupting Ignatius's presentation by saying "with all due respect" every time he disagreed with Ignatius. The negotiations had dragged on for hours with no resolution in sight. Although Ignatius allowed the young, arrogant lawyer to interrupt him multiple times, as the sun was setting and day turned to night, Ignatius had had enough.

He'd risen from his chair, removed his glasses, and slowly walked over to the large window in the far corner of the conference room on the sixty-ninth floor of the Americenter Tower. A hushed silence fell over those assembled in the room. After a few seconds, which seemed more like an eternity, Ignatius, with his back still turned to his prey, began speaking with a steely edge in his voice.

"A smart judge once told me that every time he hears a lawyer utter the words 'with all due respect' in his courtroom, he suspects that what the lawyer is really saying is he considers himself the smartest person in the room and everyone else is as dumb as horse excrement." It was only his first day at the firm, but Tom guessed someone of Ignatius's stature would never utter the word 'shit' in public. Ignatius had slowly turned toward the lawyer. "So, with that in mind, let me be perfectly clear so even you understand me. I've tolerated you interrupting me for the last time. Your client will either agree to the deal I've outlined, or we'll wage a proxy war that will cost your client millions and which it will eventually lose. My client has unlimited resources and the will to fight this battle to the bitter end. At the end of the day, your client will either thrive as a subsidiary of my client, or we will bleed it dry in a war it cannot win, with you representing a worthless company, and its carcass being picked apart by a long line of creditors in bankruptcy court. So, I suggest you get your client in line to sign the deal we're offering, or this meeting is over. With all due respect, of course."

The room was still. The Pope had made his point without ever raising his voice. In fact, his last sentence was barely above a whisper. Ignatius Balatoni had a reputation as a gracious and elegant elder statesman, but the daggers in his eyes that night had made it clear to everyone seated around the table that he was prepared for a legal brawl. The young lawyer sat motionless, his mouth agape like a supplicant begging for mercy. By 8:00 p.m., the lawyer and his client had come to their senses, and the deal was signed just before ten.

With that memory of Ignatius's fierceness and cunning power fresh in his mind, Tom quietly said a little prayer as he approached The Pope's office door and prepared to knock.

3

"Thomas, good to see you, please come in." Ignatius waved Tom into his office. "I appreciate you coming up to see me, considering the late hour and that you've been in trial all day. Please have a seat." Ignatius motioned Tom to one of the two wingback chairs opposite his desk while he remained seated. Even at eighty-eight, Ignatius Balatoni looked spry and in good health, and Tom thought he could pass for a man in his early seventies. Although he had transferred day-to-day management of BCC to an executive committee over a decade ago, everyone knew Ignatius still ran the firm with a tight grip and would for as long as blood coursed through his veins. Seeing Ignatius again reminded Tom why he was called The Pope. He had a small frame and was bald, except for a semi-circle of snow-white hair on the sides and back of his head, and he wore glasses carefully resting on the tip of his nose.

Tom strode purposefully toward the chair and took a seat, nervously looking around the cavernous space. He noticed Ignatius's desk was completely bare, unlike his own cluttered mess. The corner office was immense compared to Tom's. Long shelves stacked with books lined the wall opposite the floor to ceiling windows with sweeping views overlooking Central Park to the north, and the Hudson River, the Palisades, and the far reaches of New Jersey to the west. Orange and yellow flowers arranged in crystal vases placed around the office provided a pop of color.

The wall to the right of Ignatius's desk was covered with framed photos of him with every president since John F. Kennedy, as well as every sitting U.S. Supreme Court Justice. Also hanging on the wall behind Ignatius's desk were two color renderings by sketch artists of a young Ignatius Balatoni during oral arguments before the Supreme Court, along with two framed quill pens, mementos given to every lawyer who argues a case in the highest court in the land. Behind the desk, on the large antique-looking cellaret, were photographs which Tom presumed were of Ignatius's wife, a distinguished white-haired woman, who looked devotedly to the man standing next to her. Curiously, though, Tom saw no pictures of children or grandchildren.

"Mr. Balatoni," Tom said as he tried to settle himself, "it was a very nice surprise to receive your note, thank you for inviting me to your office." As he uttered those words, he realized how foolish he sounded. *Thank you for inviting me to your office.* What a stupid thing to say, he thought. So much for his ability to think and speak on his feet.

"Please, call me Ignatius. It's what all my friends call me. It sure beats *Ignazio*, my birth name, don't you agree?"

Tom let out a nervous laugh, relieved at Ignatius's down-to-earth style, and surprised to learn his given name.

"Yes," he said. "This is a beautiful office, and the view is spectacular."

"It is. The view is one of the reasons BCC chose this space for our headquarters. Jacob Cartel always said it provided us with a way to keep an eye on our enemies," Ignatius said with a gentle smile as he gazed wistfully out the window. Jacob Cartel was a BCC co-founder, along with retired New York State Court of Appeal Judge John Colin. Both had died before Tom joined the firm, and he recalled reading about Cartel's death in a mysterious plane crash that had made headlines in both the legal and mainstream press.

"The view of the sun setting over the Hudson River is particularly spectacular, especially on a cloudless day like today," Ignatius said after a few seconds of awkward silence. "Would you like a drink, Thomas?" He rose from behind his desk and walked over to the large credenza on the opposite side of his office, motioning for Tom to join him and take a seat in one of the leather club chairs encircling a glass-top coffee table.

"Club soda would be fine," Tom said, noticing an acrylic box, perfectly centered, on the glass table. In it was a miniature copy of a *Time* magazine cover from 2010 with Ignatius Balatoni's picture on it. He had been named one of the 100 most influential people in America that year by *Time*. The article described his many accomplishments and noted that he was regularly called upon by captains of industry, movers and shakers, and Washington insiders for his sage advice and his ability to accomplish things for his clients no one else could. It was required reading for every lawyer who joined the firm.

The caption on the cover under the photograph read *Rainmaker for His Firm, and Fixer and Confidant for His Clients*. The article detailed Ignatius's leadership of BCC after the Great Recession of 2008-2009. In one famous passage, Ignatius was asked about the secret of his success. His answer: "Make your friends your clients and your clients your friends." One of Ignatius's life-long friends was quoted in the article as saying, "With a friend like him, you don't need any more friends." Tom smiled as he recalled reading the article.

"Perhaps you should try something stronger than club soda. It could help you to unwind after a tough day in court," Ignatius said with an impish grin as he sipped cognac from a snifter. "Tell me, Thomas, how was the AMX trial today?"

"Well, sir, you know the ebb and flow of trials better than I do. Some moments you think you're winning, and the next you're back on your heels playing defense. There is a tremendous amount of technical data to convey to the jury, but Troy has an excellent mastery of the details. The real problem is the courtroom is full of sick and disabled plaintiffs, which undoubtedly is prejudicing the jury against us. Not that the facts are favorable to our side, either. You know them, I'm sure. Centuron is lethal." As Tom finished speaking, he noticed Ignatius was barely listening.

"This experience is good for you," Ignatius said, sounding wistful again and looking out the windows into the distance. "You won't win all your trials and losing a couple in your early years just makes you savor all the more the victories that will come later."

Tom lowered his head and cracked a soft smile, knowing Ignatius Balatoni had won his fair share of trials in his day.

"How do you like working at BCC?" Ignatius asked after taking another sip of cognac.

Tom was surprised at the question. "I enjoy it very much. The work is incredibly interesting, and it keeps me on my toes, and the people here are wonderful. I'm very grateful for the opportunity to work at such a wonderful firm," he said, pleased with himself for giving the firm such high praise.

"Good, good," Ignatius nodded. "Keeping our attorneys happy is a commitment BCC is always proud of maintaining."

After a few more seconds passed in silence, Ignatius spoke up again in a gentle voice. "How is your lovely wife? Brooke is her name, as I recall, is that correct?"

"Yes, it is. She's doing well."

"Is she still working with children?"

"Yes, with the Paulsboro Group. She really loves kids, and it gives her a great sense of accomplishment knowing she is helping children who come from broken homes or have parents who are incarcerated, drug addicted, or who abandoned them."

"It is such important work, Thomas. I believe you know my wife was involved for many years with the Paulsboro Group and other charities assisting children. I call it God's work. You've met my wife, Helen, haven't you?"

Tom remembered hearing about Helen Balatoni and knew she had been involved with the Paulsboro Group for many years, chairing several successful fundraising events and helping to raise millions for various children's charities.

"No. I've never met your wife," Tom said, sipping his soda.

"She spends most of her time in Florida now and doesn't get out much anymore. She hasn't been at the firm's holiday party in quite a few years, ever since her fall several years ago. She's a remarkable woman," Ignatius said, glancing at the photograph of his wife. "Sixty years we're married, and I still get tongue-tied every time I see her. Sixty years. She is the single greatest gift God has ever given me."

Tom sensed Ignatius was becoming emotional, and he quickly looked away for fear he might stare.

"How many years have you been married to Brooke, Thomas?"

"Six years. We were married after my first year at the firm. But it seems like only yesterday."

"Cherish her," Ignatius whispered. "For only with a great woman supporting us can we mere mortals achieve success," he said with a lingering smile. "You don't have children yet, is that right, Thomas?"

Tom was taken aback, but quickly surmised Ignatius was simply trying to get to know him better. "No, not yet. Brooke and I want to wait to start a family. She is really enjoying her career and doesn't want to interrupt it now. And frankly, I don't think we're ready to be parents." Tom decided to leave out Brooke's hesitancy to start a family while Tom was working long hours.

"Ah, well, when you are, seize the moment. Children are the second greatest gift God can bestow upon us."

All the references to God and his gifts made Tom wonder if there wasn't more to Ignatius being called The Pope than just his looks. Tom wanted to ask Ignatius if he had any children, but it didn't feel right.

"You know, Thomas, I clearly remember the first time I met you. It was right before your second year at Harvard Law School, when we flew you to New York to interview with us and to see BCC in action."

Tom recalled that visit vividly. He was amazed at the regal elegance of BCC's offices, and even more amazed that a firm as prestigious as Balatoni, Cartel & Colin was courting him.

"We wanted you. Of all the summer associates we hired that year, and there were twenty-seven of you as I recall, you were my number one choice. I wouldn't be surprised if we wanted you more than you wanted BCC."

"Oh, well, Mr. Balatoni...I mean Ignatius, sorry. I'm not sure about that," Tom began, fumbling for the right words. "I long hoped to work at BCC. Believe me, I was more than honored that this firm was interested in me. Perhaps also a little surprised and overwhelmed by the opportunity. I know I made the right choice to accept your offer, and I will forever be grateful to you and the firm for allowing me the privilege to practice law here."

Tom knew he sounded like a brown-nose, but he meant what he said and was both humbled and proud that BCC considered him worthy of a position at the firm.

"I know you are. But we're the ones who are honored. You had quite the resume even before law school. Outstanding academic achievement as far back as high school, including valedictorian of your class, and then graduating Summa Cum Laude from Harvard University, and then of course Harvard Law School where you were on the Law Review and moot court, followed by the clerkship with Chief Judge Harrington of the First Circuit Court of Appeals. And aside from your leadership positions and very impressive academic achievements, you had this unspoken quality I caught onto right away."

Ignatius cleared his throat and took another sip of his cognac.

"It is your quiet reserve, your humility, combined with a sense of confidence and self-assuredness, but without a shred of arrogance. You have demonstrated an energy and appetite for hard work that matches your passion for being a lawyer. There's no false pride with you, and I admire that. You have an uncommon intellect, an unparalleled work ethic, and you're unwavering in the principles you hold. You possess the qualities that make BCC attorneys the best in the world."

Tom felt himself blushing. What can you say after The Pope blesses you with such a compliment?

"Thank you, Ignatius," he said, realizing it didn't begin to express the depth of his sincere gratitude for the praise.

"I knew then that you would make an outstanding attorney, and I'm even more convinced of it now. Not only has Troy commended you repeatedly for your work on the AMX case, but your annual reviews since you first joined the firm have been stellar. And the work you've done for my clients over the years has been superb. Our gratitude, Thomas, will be reflected in your mid-year bonus."

"Thank you," Tom said, as he felt himself choking up. He never sought out compliments but appreciated the recognition of his hard work and dedication to the firm. "But I'm not here for the money, sir. I mean the money is welcomed, but I truly love being a lawyer, and BCC is a great place to practice law." Tom shifted in his seat, uncomfortable talking about himself. "Becoming a lawyer and practicing law at this firm is the fulfillment of a dream."

While he appreciated the salary—Tom stood to make $475,000 this year before a six-figure bonus—it wasn't the money that drove him. He wanted to make a difference and thought from a young age that becoming a lawyer would give him the best chance to create the world he wanted to live in, one that gave everyone a level playing field to achieve their dreams based on hard work and determination.

"I know you are committed to BCC because you believe in what you're doing, and you recognize the law is an honorable and noble profession. Don't ever change that about you." Ignatius spoke the last few words with his head bowed. Tom wondered how Ignatius was able to read him so accurately. When Ignatius finally looked up, his eyes were glistening. After a few seconds, he cleared his throat again and continued.

"Thomas, this year Balatoni, Cartel and Colin will be doubling its annual gift to the Paulsboro Group in recognition of all the wonderful work servants like Brooke do there."

Tom didn't know what to say. He paused for a moment to collect his thoughts. "That's wonderful news. Brooke will be extremely happy to hear that."

"I'm delighted you think so. If there was ever a worthy cause, the Paulsboro Group is it." It was Ignatius who paused now. "I'm sure your parents are very proud of you, Thomas."

Tom froze.

"Are you all right, Thomas?"

"Yes." Tom tried hard not to convey his discomfort. "My mother is very proud of me, and I assume my father would be. He died when I was very young."

"Yes, I recall that. Very unfortunate."

A chill ran down Tom's spine and he suddenly felt cold. He rarely spoke about his parents at the office and didn't remember the subject ever coming up when he interviewed at the firm. He certainly never discussed the situation with Ignatius Balatoni. But just as quickly, Tom thought BCC must have done a thorough background check on him before he was hired, and the firm knew everything about him. A small price to pay to work at BCC.

Tom regained his composure and relaxed a bit. "I wish I had met him. I always wondered what he was like. My first initial C is for Charles, my father's name."

"I see. It's unfortunate you never met your father. You know, fate always seems to be a step ahead of us, doesn't it? I believe everything always happens for a reason. It is not for us to question fate, Thomas. One day everything will make perfect sense and all our questions will be answered."

After gazing out the window again, Ignatius continued, "I'm certain wherever your father is, he is very proud of you. Be assured of that." He closed his eyes and let out a soft sigh. "I'm certain he's very proud." He rose from his chair and walked back to the credenza to refill his glass with ice.

"Thomas, I asked you to come to my office this evening because there's something I'd like to ask you. And," Ignatius said, turning and looking straight at him, "your answer may change your life forever."

4

Realizing he was slouching, Tom sat up.

Ignatius was on a roll and continued speaking, his eyes now squarely trained on his audience of one.

"As you know, Attorney General Bradley Mitchelson was a partner of this law firm before he was elected to the Senate. He and I have been friends for over thirty years, and I encouraged him to accept President Ferguson's invitation two years ago to lead the Justice Department. We had lunch recently and he shared with me that his right-hand man, the Executive Deputy Attorney General, will be leaving at the end of the month. Bradley is looking to hire his replacement. He asked me to recommend someone for the position. I immediately thought of you."

Tom was stunned into silence.

"This isn't a ceremonial position. The Executive Deputy Attorney General runs the day-to-day operations of the Justice Department. In a very real sense, the person holding that position oversees the entire Department and reports directly to the Attorney General. Bradley also shared with me that his office has a top-secret investigation it's working on, and he needs to fill the position as soon as possible. Your administrative and leadership abilities, not to mention your brilliant legal mind, integrity, and judgment make you ideally suited for this position."

Tom swallowed hard. For a second, he considered whether this was a ploy by the partners to push him out of the firm. But the DOJ was a step up, not a step out. He was unsure where to begin.

"I...I don't know what to say," Tom stammered. "I'm perfectly happy here, as long as you'll have me, and I'm not looking for another position." He was surprised Ignatius was speaking to him about a job offer outside the firm.

"I know that. Believe me, the other partners and I would like nothing more than for you to stay at the firm, build a practice here, and join us as a partner in a year or two. But this is a once in a lifetime opportunity. I think you should give it due consideration. The experience you'll gain leading the Department of Justice cannot be replicated elsewhere. You'll be leading a dedicated group of men and women who are committed to the pursuit of justice, and you'll have a front row seat over some of the most important and highly consequential legal matters concerning our nation. Public service is a big part of the culture and DNA of our firm, and BCC has a long and rich history of sharing our finest attorneys with government agencies and public service organizations to promote justice and equality, and to protect our country and its citizens. It is the core belief in shared responsibility that led the Attorney General to depart BCC and engage in public service."

"Do you really think I'm the right person for this job?" Tom wondered if his face betrayed the surprise and confusion swirling inside him.

"Thomas," Ignatius leaned forward, his voice growing excited. "The Attorney General is looking for someone with the highest moral character and superior legal skills. Someone who is a natural leader and who can rally others to pursue the cause of justice. You have those qualities in spades. You are the best-qualified candidate to take on this incredibly important role. Never doubt that. And, of course, your time in Washington will not hinder your place on BCC's partnership track. When your service to our nation is complete, we will welcome you back with open arms. Your time at DOJ will be viewed quite favorably by the firm's Executive Committee, and a seat at the partnership table will be waiting for you when you return."

"I don't know what to say." Tom was relieved to hear this was a promotion in recognition of his hard work and talent. "I'll need some time to think about this and to speak with Brooke."

"Of course," Ignatius said, reassuringly. "I understand this is a monumental decision. But I would not have recommended you for the position unless I thought this job was in your best interest." Ignatius paused and took a deep breath while bowing his head and looking away from Tom. "For you and for your family," he said in a whisper.

Tom thought there was something odd in the way Ignatius uttered the last few words, but he was too numb to think clearly. First the glowing accolades from The Pope, and now an endorsement to run the daily operations of the Justice Department.

"I'm truly speechless," Tom said, searching for something else to say. "Don't get me wrong. I'm honored and grateful you think highly enough of me to recommend me to the Attorney General. But it's something I've never thought of. My dream was always to be a partner at this law firm."

"Certainly. Take your time. I have, however, taken the liberty of arranging for you to fly to Washington on Thursday to meet with Attorney General Mitchelson and members of his staff for a formal interview. We've taken care of all your travel plans. Give this serious thought, Thomas. Offers such as these, if they come along at all, come rarely."

"Thank you. But, what about the trial?"

"Don't worry about that. I'll take care of it. Troy is on board with all of this, and we'll assign someone else to take over for you for the next few days. And hopefully for the remainder of the case," Ignatius said with a hearty laugh. "As we discussed earlier, it is unlikely the trial ends with a favorable verdict for AMX, even with your considerable legal talents working hard for our client." The two men shared a brief, but uncomfortable, smile.

"Seriously. This is an opportunity of a lifetime. The partners of BCC would like you to be in Washington. You deserve it."

"I promise you Brooke and I will give this opportunity the consideration it deserves. Is it all right if I get back to you when I return from Washington?"

"Of course," Ignatius said, nodding and rising from his chair. "Now go home to your lovely bride and tell her the good news."

"I will, sir," Tom said, as he, too, rose from his chair. "I certainly will." The two men took a step toward each other and for a moment Tom thought Ignatius would embrace him. But at the last second Ignatius extended his arm and shook Tom's hand. Tom turned to make his way to the door, truly touched by Ignatius's confidence in his ability. Life, he thought, was full of amazing surprises.

As Tom reached for the handle to open the door, Ignatius spoke up again.

"Thomas," he said softly. "I was never blessed with children, but if I had, I hope they would have been like you." Ignatius's voice quivered, and the words *like you* were almost inaudible. Ignatius's eyes filled with tears.

Tom looked down at his shoes as his eyes also moistened. The lump in his throat came back, and he could barely speak.

Ignatius Balatoni walked over to the window, gazing at the evening sky. "Go in peace," he said as Tom walked out of the office and closed the door behind him.

Ignatius wiped his eyes and walked over to the desk. The request he received several months earlier from his most important client had become his greatest challenge yet. It consumed him night and day. Refusal was not an option, and failure could be deadly. He picked up the phone and dialed the number he'd called so many times before when matters involving Tom were concerned.

"Offer delivered. The *Ragazzo* was surprised, of course, but I'm sure when the shock wears off, he'll realize the immense value of this opportunity and the lasting benefits to his career. He's flying to Washington the day after tomorrow to meet with the Attorney General. I hope for your sake, and for the sake of the *Ragazzo*, you know what you are doing."

5

"That's incredible!" Brooke said. "And the gift to the Paulsboro Group is so generous. It couldn't have come at a better time."

Tom had met Brooke when they were both undergrads at Harvard. He was a junior and she was a senior. He'd walked into the History of Women in Power class and immediately spotted the tall blonde sitting at the end of the third aisle. He'd dropped back from his friends and asked if the seat next to hers was taken. She had looked up, looked at the empty chair, and said sarcastically, "I don't think so, unless the person's invisible." Tom fell instantly in love.

She was a few inches taller than Tom, slender and beautiful, in a natural, no make-up kind of way. During classes Tom would continually ask her if he could look at her notes, telling her he couldn't write as quickly as the professor spoke. In reality, he was too busy imagining his future with her to take notes.

At first, Brooke paid little attention to him. She would smile an occasional greeting and quickly duck away. He tried small talk, but her answers were short and to the point. He wondered if she even knew what flirting was. Despite her apparent lack of interest, he persevered, figuring he could charm her into going out with him. Two weeks after they first met, he got up enough courage to ask her out. He walked over to her dorm room, but she wasn't there so he left her a note, along with a bouquet of wildflowers.

May I have the honor of your company for dinner one night this week at the restaurant of your choice. Feel free to respond by carrier pigeon, smoke signal or skywriting.

Tom signed the note "Your History of Women in Power classmate and note-borrower," and he included his phone number and email address.

The nerdy Tom was in full bloom. He sat anxiously every night waiting for her to call or email. He couldn't stop thinking about her. Finally, after letting him squirm for a few days, Brooke accepted his invitation—by hiring a messenger to deliver a singing telegram.

That was eleven years ago, and they'd been inseparable ever since. Brooke remained in Boston while Tom attended Harvard Law School and then clerked at the First Circuit Court of Appeals. She studied child psychology and received her master's degree from Tufts University and later worked at Boston Children's Hospital. When he joined BCC, they moved to New York and rented an apartment. By then Tom had proposed by using his summer associate's bonus to hire a vintage WWII fighter plane to skywrite the proposal against a cloudless blue sky high above Manhattan's skyline.

"What happens now, tell me everything," Brooke practically shouted, unable to contain her excitement.

"Nothing until the day after tomorrow." Tom was trying to play it cool. "That's when I fly to D.C. and meet with the Attorney General's staff, and at some point, I assume I'll meet with the Attorney General himself. And if he likes me, I guess he'll offer me the job. Would you be willing to move to Washington for a few years?"

"Are you kidding me? Absolutely. I haven't been this excited since... since...since our wedding day. Of course I'm willing to move. I can't wait to go. We'll be close to my sister in DC, and the Paulsboro Group has a sister organization in Crystal City, Virginia, that's doing amazing work." Brooke was talking so fast she ran out of breath.

"Okay, okay, but slow down a second, Brooke. Remember, I don't have the job yet, so let's not start packing," he said, trying to contain his own building excitement for the opportunity he'd been given.

"Yeah, right. Of course they're going to hire you. Mr. Balatoni wouldn't recommend you for the job if it wasn't already yours. I'm going to call my mom." Brooke got up and started walking toward the spare bedroom. Her tight jeans hugged her slim hips and long legs, highlighting her every curve. "I'll be right back Mr. Executive Deputy Attorney General," she said cheerfully as she sauntered away.

Tom allowed her words to hang in the air for a few seconds. The reality of the last few hours began to sink in. Instead of preparing for trial the next day, all he could think of was the possibility of working at the DOJ for the next few years. He was tired and overwhelmed but couldn't rest. Thoughts crashed in his head. Could it really be that he was so close to being hired as the second in command at the Justice Department? He loved law and politics, and this could be a tremendous steppingstone in his career that could open so many doors for him down the road.

Tom reclined on the couch and closed his eyes. He thought about how fortunate he'd been throughout his life. He worked hard in high school and was class valedictorian, but he was still surprised when he was accepted to Harvard even though he scored 1560 on the SAT. No one turned down Harvard, and neither did he. He made the most of it and worked hard, making the Dean's list every semester. He once got a C- on a final exam, which threw him for a loop, but after pleading his case the professor agreed to change his grade to an A, allowing him to ultimately graduate summa cum laude at the top of his class. He was also stunned when he received a perfect score on the LSAT and was accepted to Harvard Law School. Tom knew he was smart, but the perfect score still amazed him.

And his good fortune kept coming when he landed the clerkship in the First Circuit and then an associate position at BCC. He had led a charmed life to this point, and good things always seemed to fall in his lap. He didn't feel privileged or entitled, just grateful he'd been so fortunate and had accomplished so much. He'd developed quite the resume, but he still questioned whether he was worthy of all the accolades and achievements. It was as if a guardian angel was looking out for him. Maybe it was his father, he wondered. Tom often found himself asking if the many blessings he'd been given were to make up for the one person missing from his storybook life.

He thought back to his conversation with Ignatius a few hours earlier.

Fate always seems to be a step ahead of us, Ignatius said. *Everything always happens for a reason. It is not for us to question fate. One day everything will make perfect sense, and all our questions will be answered.* Those words comforted Tom, even though he had no idea what the future held for him. Succumbing to exhaustion, he drifted away.

"I guess I need to begin respecting you now, Mr. C. Thomas Berte, don't I?" Troy said as he walked into the conference room the next morning at 8:10. "After all, you're not a lowly BCC associate anymore, but practically the attorney general of the United States. I'm very impressed."

Tom knew this was Troy's way of congratulating him. "News travels fast. But it's only the Executive Deputy position. I'll need to wait for you to become president so you can appoint me as the attorney general before I can claim that honor."

"Just give me a few years, Tommy," Troy said, as the two men laughed. "I'll turn Washington, D.C. upside down and finally get rid of all those liberal bloodsuckers once and for all," Troy was waving his hands as if he were clearing smoke from the room. "Seriously, Tom, Ignatius called me the other day and asked my thoughts about recommending you for this position. I understand the vote by the Executive Committee was unanimous, and Ignatius almost cried when the votes were tallied. No one had ever seen him so emotional before. What did you do to make Ignatius love you so much?" Troy wiped a mock tear from his eye.

Tom recalled how sentimental Ignatius became last night but was surprised to hear he also became emotional in front of his partners. Perhaps he was beginning to sense his long life was coming to an end and this was one last chance to influence the career of another young lawyer, something he'd probably done scores of times in the past.

"At least you're off the hook on the AMX trial now," Troy said, grinning and not waiting for a response from Tom. "We'll find someone else to be my caddy going forward. Just put in an honest day's work today, and then you can go home and rest up for your big day tomorrow. Just one thing, Tom.

Remember me when you become the big shit in Washington." Troy grinned and offered Tom his outstretched hand.

"Absolutely. After all, you've taught me a very important lesson."

"Oh, and what might that be?"

"You've taught me not to take you so seriously," Tom said, as he broke into laughter.

"Screw you, buddy, screw you." The two men embraced.

"Come on, " Troy said as he headed out the room. "Let me show you how to lose a case and still look good."

6

Tom's phone rang at five the next morning. The voice on the other end announced that an SUV would arrive in forty-five minutes to take him to the airport. Tom could barely manage a grunt. He had set his alarm for 5:05 a.m., but now wished he'd scheduled the pick-up for 7:00. He rolled over and snuggled into Brooke, wishing he could stay in bed with her all day. But when his alarm finally chimed, he gave Brooke a peck on the cheek and headed for the shower, anxious about the long day ahead.

The ride to LaGuardia Airport took about thirty minutes from his apartment on the east side of Manhattan. Even at that early hour, traffic was building. As the black GMC Yukon inched along the Grand Central Parkway, Tom allowed himself a few moments to close his eyes.

He thought back to the many times he'd made this early morning trip to LaGuardia in the pursuit of justice for his clients. In his seven years at BCC, he'd been dispatched dozens of times to cities across the globe to interview witnesses, meet with clients, take depositions, and attend court hearings and conferences. On a few occasions he'd arranged for Brooke to join him, but even when she did, she wound up touring cities by herself or spending countless hours alone in museums or the gym while Tom billed away the time. If they were lucky, they managed to have dinner together once or twice, but often Brooke would order room service and eat alone.

It wasn't a perfect life, and Tom felt guilty about the long hours he worked and the lack of quality time he spent with her. They talked often about starting a family, but Brooke was hesitant to do so with him working so much. She didn't want to raise a child as a single parent like Tom's mother raised him. Deep down Tom knew she was right. His plan was to work hard at BCC for a few more years and make partner, all while saving his bonus money every year, so when the time came for them to start a family of their own, he could slow down at work and spend more time at home. He hadn't planned on making a switch now to a lower paying government job when his savings account balance was still below what some BCC partners paid in annual dues to swanky country clubs.

After arriving at LaGuardia and wading through long lines at the TSA checkpoint, Tom finally boarded the plane and was settling in when he heard the words every air traveler dreads. Due to approaching thunderstorms, take off would be delayed. Ironically, Tom was relieved. The butterflies in his stomach had been churning since he woke up. He considered again whether to call his mom, Mary, and share the news with her. But each time he thought about it, he decided it was best if he waited to see whether he actually got the job before telling her. He took a deep breath as the pilots powered down the engines to wait out the passing storms.

Ever since his meeting with Ignatius, he had been reflecting on his childhood and thinking a lot about his mom. She had told Tom his father died in a motorcycle accident when he was very young but rarely spoke about him. The only picture Tom ever saw of his father was a grainy black and white wallet-size photo of a young man with black slicked-back hair straddling a motorcycle with a cigarette dangling from his lips. His name was Carlo Berte, but his friends called him Charlie. All his mom ever said about Charlie was that he was born in Italy and came to America with his parents when he was a young boy. He enlisted in the army when he was eighteen but served only two years before being honorably discharged, never seeing combat. Whenever Tom asked his mother more questions about his dad, she became tense and looked uncomfortable, so he stopped asking. Whenever she did bring him up, it was only to say he was a good man who provided for her while he was alive, and that Tom shouldn't worry about anything because she would take care of him and make sure he always had what he needed.

Mary was a bookkeeper for Harding & Glasgow, a two-person accounting firm in Jericho, Long Island. They lived in a small, but comfortable home in Roslyn, less than a mile from the catholic elementary school Tom attended. As far as he knew, his mother had worked at the accounting firm since about a year after he was born. She was smart, organized, and efficient. Her bosses were so appreciative of Mary's dedication and hard work that they arranged for her to start work at 8:30 in the morning and leave by 3:00 p.m. so she would be home when Tom got off the school bus at 3:30.

Later, as Tom grew older and had friends whose dads lost their jobs or had to move in with relatives because they couldn't afford their homes, he would ask his mother if she had enough money for the two of them to live in their house. She told him Charlie had bought a life insurance policy before he died to provide for her and Tom in case anything ever happened to him.

That made sense to Tom and explained how his mother was able to afford a new car every few years and take him on vacation every summer, including cruises and visiting Disney World. One summer, Mary even took him to Paris, and he rode the elevator to the top of the Eiffel Tower. Tom figured it also explained how his mother was able to pay for his college and law school without applying for financial aid or student loans.

Mary always filled the house with laughter, games, and adventures. Their house was the prettiest one on the block, something Tom came to appreciate as he got older. Flowers bloomed in the garden from spring through fall. The red brick, rich stone façade, and tall white columns made the house look bigger than it was, and the manicured lawn, always meticulously cared for, looked like an emerald-green carpet. And the best part was that cutting the grass and maintaining the flower beds was not one of Tom's after-school chores. While most of his friends' dads mowed the grass, a landscaping crew came to Tom's house every week to take care of the lawn, pull weeds, and make sure the flower beds were bursting with color. They would clean the yard in the spring, pick up leaves in the fall, and even shovel the walkway and plow the driveway when it snowed. Tom loved hearing compliments from neighbors about how their house always looked neat and tidy.

Although his mom was loving and caring, Tom knew she could be one tough lady. He recalled an incident one summer when he was about six or seven. He was on the swing set in the backyard and saw Mary get into an argument with one of the landscapers. Tom couldn't hear everything the man said to his mom, but he saw the worker touch his mother's back and lean in close just at the same time she shouted for the man to keep his hands off her and pushed him away.

She didn't look scared, Tom remembered, but he could see the anger in her eyes and the fierceness in her voice when she told the man to back away. Tom started running toward her but stopped when she put her arm out and told Tom to stay where he was. He remembered hearing the man hissing and saying what sounded like, *oh, come on baby, I know you'll like it.* Mary walked over to Tom, took his hand in hers, and walked him inside the house, while keeping an icy glare on the landscaper. She sat Tom on the sofa and turned on the TV for him. She then picked up the cordless phone and walked down the hall into the kitchen. When she came back, Tom asked if she was ok. She hugged him and kissed his forehead. She whispered they were both fine and safe and for Tom not to worry about anything. She reached over for a coloring book and crayons and the two started doing what Tom enjoyed most. Coloring. Tom loved using the brightest colors and was meticulous about staying within the lines.

For the rest of that summer and fall and winter, and for as long as Tom lived in that brick and stone house with his mother, he never saw the landscaper again. He didn't ask his mom what happened to him. In his mind, Tom figured she called the man's boss and got him reassigned to work somewhere else, or worse, he'd been fired.

That was probably around the time Tom began to realize he didn't need a father to feel safe. His mother was always there for him, and when she tucked him into bed at night she would always say as long as they had each other, they wouldn't need anyone else.

That sense of security allowed him to excel in school, especially high school. He was proud he made the dean's list each semester and never received a grade below an A- in any class. He was on the student governing body all four years, and in his junior year he was inducted into the National Honor Society.

He also loved playing sports. Soccer in the fall, basketball in the winter, and baseball in the spring. He was named captain of his baseball team in his junior and senior years and had the highest batting average both seasons.

From a young age Tom had a knack for never getting too emotional during tough games. Win or lose, he always maintained his cool, and he tried hard not to get too excited or too dejected. Sure, he celebrated a win or a game-changing play and was upset when his team lost or if he didn't play well, but his reaction, gloom or glory, never lasted more than fifteen minutes. He would only celebrate for fifteen minutes if his team won before he'd settle down and get ready for the next challenge. And when he lost, or played poorly, he was only gloomy for fifteen minutes before turning the page and wiping the slate clean. His high school coach liked that rule and adopted it for the team: players were allowed fifteen minutes of gloom or glory no matter what happened.

As Tom's games moved from the ball field to the courtroom, and became more competitive, he learned to keep his emotions in check even more. His fifteen-minute rule served him well and proved to be an important tool. He was a steady hand and even keeled, and never allowed judges, clients, or even his adversaries to get him too worked up. Tom tried to find the bright side of any situation and always gave everyone around him the benefit of the doubt.

But if anyone ever mistook his approach for apathy or lack of caring, they'd be sorely mistaken. He out-worked other associates at the firm and out-hustled his opponents. Fortunately, the partners at BCC took notice, and in their annual reviews of his work they repeatedly complimented him for his demeanor and attitude. He was rewarded with plum assignments on high profile cases for the firm's most important and prestigious clients, along with hefty annual bonuses.

The plane's hard landing jolted Tom. He had fallen asleep and didn't even remember taking off. He opened his eyes, and it took him a few seconds to realize he'd just landed at Reagan National Airport in Washington, DC. He caught his bearings and felt energized and excited. Although he was still apprehensive, he felt he could run laps around the airport.

As he walked out of the terminal and into the waiting black sedan that would take him to his interview at the Department of Justice, Tom felt invincible. New opportunities were awaiting him.

Little did he know at that moment he was dutifully following a plan devised for him long ago by someone he'd hardly met.

7

The sedan came to a halt in front of the entrance to the Robert F. Kennedy Department of Justice Building, or Main Justice as it was known to insiders, an enormous building covering an entire city block in downtown Washington, D,C. along Pennsylvania Avenue, midway between the White House and the U.S. Capitol Building.

In preparing for his interview, Tom learned the Department of Justice employs thousands of lawyers across all fifty states and tens of thousands of support personnel from secretaries to paralegals to clerks. If it were a private law firm, it would dwarf every other firm, including BCC. He looked up at the gray limestone exterior standing seven stories tall. It resembled a fortress. He read the inscription above the entrance to the building. *Justice Is Founded In The Rights Bestowed By Nature Upon Man. Liberty Is Maintained In Security Of Justice.*

Tom recalled the inscription he'd read in the courtroom during the AMX trial. He couldn't help but wonder if the DOJ's mission today was still draped in the idealism of the Founding Fathers. Since he'd started working at BCC defending mega corporations, boards of directors, and individuals rich enough to pay BCC's exorbitant hourly rates, Tom learned justice wasn't always administered fairly and not all men and women were equal. The rich were given opportunities poor defendants could only dream of. While the wealthy and biggest corporations were able to afford the best and smartest lawyers, the poor and indigent were often relegated to being represented by overworked and understaffed legal service agencies lacking sufficient resources to compete with the big boys and girls, like the lawyers at BCC. Stepping into the cool lobby, Tom believed he could make a difference and even the playing field. All he needed was the opportunity.

After entering through the rotating doors, checking in at the security desk, and passing through the metal detector, Tom was escorted by a staffer to the elevator and brought to the third floor where he entered a large conference room at the end of a long corridor. The staffer offered Tom coffee, told him to make himself comfortable, and said his meeting would start in a few minutes. As the staffer walked out, Tom stood in the corner of the room and gawked out the window, marveling at the view of the Capitol dome. Tom noticed the thickness of the windows and quickly realized he couldn't hear traffic noise or the cars honking three floors below. He wondered if the windows were bulletproof, or perhaps even blast resistant. Not even a truck bomb was going to deter the work of defenders of the Constitution, a thought that made Tom proud. As he waited, he still couldn't get over the fact that a kid from suburban Long Island, who grew up in a single parent home, was about to interview for the second highest position in the United States Department of Justice.

The sound of a door opening at the opposite end of the room startled Tom. He turned to see Attorney General Bradley Mitchelson stride into the room. He was stunned and for a moment thought Mitchelson must have entered the wrong room. He wasn't expecting to meet the Attorney General until he had been vetted by this staff through multiple rounds of interviews.

"Good morning, Tom, it's a pleasure to see you again," AG Mitchelson said, as he reached out his hand and greeted Tom warmly. "I hope you had a pleasant flight. Thank you for coming in on such short notice."

Tom could barely react. He reflexively put out his hand and immediately sensed the Attorney General's firm grip on his, but he was at a loss for words. After a few awkward seconds he licked his lips, trying to clear what felt like gauze in his mouth. "Ah, thank you Mr. Attorney General. I'm sorry, I wasn't expecting to meet with you. I'm...I'm...ah...here to interview for the position of Executive Deputy and I didn't think..." Tom's voice trailed off, and he realized he sounded like a lost kid looking for his parents.

AG Mitchelson, being ever the politician, rushed to place a comforting hand on Tom's elbow. "I'm sure you weren't expecting to meet with me so soon, Tom," his smooth baritone voice betraying a hint of southern accent. "But since you work at BCC and came highly recommended by Ignatius, I thought we would dispense with the preliminary rounds of interviews with my staff, and I would meet with you directly."

"Thank you, Sir. I very much appreciate that. Thank you for this opportunity."

"Don't thank me. We're the ones who are grateful to you, and to Ignatius, and to everyone at BCC, for recommending you for the job. We have a lot going on here, and filling the position of Executive Deputy AG is a priority."

AG Mitchelson invited Tom to take a seat at the long oval conference table to the right of the head of the table where Mitchelson sat. Tom noticed Mitchelson's silver-gray hair, which looked richer than it did on TV he thought. It was perfectly cut and short, like a military buzz, but still long enough to be gelled and slightly combed back without a hair out of place. His white shirt was crisp and starched and contrasted nicely against his tanned skin and royal blue tie. Even Mitchelson's navy-blue suit framed his tall, athletic build like a glove. And his shirt cuffs peeked out from his jacket sleeves the perfect length, revealing his embroidered initials, and white, silk pocket square stuck out above the lip of his left breast pocket, with one corner barely hidden behind the jacket's lapel which had an American flag pinned to it. If Tom didn't know better, he would have thought he was on a movie set with a character out of central casting playing the role of Attorney General.

"I remember meeting you a few years ago at BCC," AG Mitchelson said. "I guess you were just about to start at the firm back then."

Tom remembered the meeting well. BCC held a retreat for incoming first-year associates in BCC's Los Angeles office. Mitchelson was a Senator at the time, and the firm invited him to the retreat to impress the incoming associate class just in case their sky-high salaries and the glitz and glamor of the LA office weren't enough.

Each year during the last weekend in August, BCC flew its incoming associates to a city where BCC had an office, rotating cities every year, to meet members of the partnership and Executive Committee. Tom's year it was Los Angeles. BCC arranged for these young, wide-eyed lawyers and their significant others to spend a long weekend at the Ritz Carlton. Tom and Brooke were giddy when they stepped into their room. Never had they seen such opulence. The bathroom was bigger than their Manhattan apartment, the oversized king size bed was the largest Brooke had ever seen, and the room had a separate living room with two deep-seated sofas, a writing desk, and a large armoire. The highlight was the fully stocked mini bar with imported candies, Dutch chocolate, cookies, and liquor. And the best part was that the entire weekend was paid for by the law firm of Balatoni, Cartel & Colin.

"Tom, I'd like to get right to it if you don't mind," the AG began. "We've taken the liberty of having the FBI run their standard background check on you and, as we expected, there are no issues. The position of Executive Deputy AG is an extremely important one on our team, and the person holding the position essentially runs the day-to-day operations of the Department and leads several of our most sensitive and important investigations and prosecutions. I need to fill it right away so we can move forward with those cases."

Tom listened intently, nodding as AG Mitchelson spoke.

"Your credentials and achievements to date are nothing short of spectacular. Double-Harvard, top of your class, law review, moot court, clerking for the Chief Justice of the First Circuit. Those are all wonderful accomplishments. Ignatius shared with me that you've been the lead associate on large cases at BCC over the last several years. He says you have one of the sharpest legal minds he has ever seen, you have excellent judgment, your analytical skills are first rate, and you're a natural leader."

Tom nodded and smiled.

"I'm sure my mother would agree with Mr. Balatoni," Tom said. "But I just try to do the best I can. I take my responsibilities seriously and I rely on a great team of lawyers around me." Tom tried to sound modest but was pleased his hard work and the long hours he devoted to BCC, sacrificing time with Brooke and with family and friends, was again recognized and appreciated.

"Teamwork is key, Tom," Mitchelson said. "None of us in this office could succeed unless we all work in tandem with others, leaning and pushing each other to achieve the best results we can while ensuring our freedoms are protected and our laws are enforced, without fear or favor, in every corner of our country."

"Mr. Attorney General, I believe I speak for all Americans when I say our democratic ideals and the economic and social stability of our country is dependent on the fair and just administration of justice, and this office under your leadership rightfully enjoys the trust and respect of the American people." Tom had prepared that line the night before. He'd figured the importance of the job he was interviewing for called for a grand statement praising the Attorney General for his service to the country, and he'd hoped for an opportunity to use it during his interview. He'd just been given one.

"I appreciate that, Tom. Very kind of you to say. But there's more this Administration and I want to accomplish. And that's where you come in."

Mitchelson reached for the phone in front of him on the table. "Please ask Special Agent Young to join us." Turning to Tom, he picked up where he left off without missing a beat. "We're all stretched thin here and I need a leader who can step in and take the reins from day one. This office is at a pivotal point. We have a top-secret investigation we're about to kick off. The FBI Director and I, with the President's blessing, are about to unleash the full powers of the United States Government with the goal of bringing down, once and for, one of the largest international criminal syndicates that has endured for a very long time, despite law enforcement's dogged pursuit with almost limitless resources."

Tom was intrigued. His mind was racing. What was the criminal syndicate? International terrorists? Drug cartels? Cyber hackers? As if on cue, there was a quick knock on the door followed by a short man with red hair, a red beard, and a wide paunch, walking confidently into the conference room. He stood next to the Attorney General with his hands in his pants pockets.

"Tom, this is FBI Special Agent Bruce Young who's been detailed to our office to get us organized for the major investigation we're about to kick off.

Tom rose from his chair and was about to extend his hand when he noticed Special Agent Young remained expressionless and made no effort to remove his right hand from his pocket to shake Tom's. Agent Young looked down at Mitchelson and barely looked at Tom.

"Special Agent Young has been working on this top-secret mission for a few months now. Since you both would be working closely together if you accept the offer to join the Department, I thought it made sense for the two of you to have a quick meet and greet."

Tom nodded respectfully and sort of half smiled as he looked again at Agent Young, but received a blank, disinterested gaze in return. Maybe these FBI types are trained to always keep their game face on and try to look indifferent no matter the circumstance, Tom thought.

"Tom," Mitchelson continued, inviting Tom to sit as Agent Young took a few steps back. "I'm asking you to join our team and have a seat at the table to ensure that all Americans can feel safe and secure in their businesses and in their homes, and that our economy continues to be the envy of the world, untainted by fraud and corruption."

"Mr. Attorney General, I'm honored you have such faith in me and my abilities. I've always believed it's every American's responsibility to do his or her part to serve their country." Tom thought he saw a faint smirk cut across Agent Young's face. At least he isn't a robot, Tom thought.

"It's that sense of duty I'm appealing to. Ignatius and many of the other senior partners at BCC have long seen a leadership quality in you. They said you understand that service is most valued when it's for the greater good, be it for BCC, its clients, or in this case, for our country. That's the kind of leader I want on my team. I've been in public service a long time, as you know. And I can say without a shred of doubt there is no greater honor than to stand up in court, or in the court of public opinion, and represent the United States of America. You can have that honor. I'd like to invite you to join the Justice Department as the Executive Deputy Attorney General of the United States."

Tom hesitated for a split second. Was this really happening? "Thank you Mr. Attorney General. I'm humbled and honored by your offer."

"It's yours, Tom. All you need to say is 'I accept.' Now, it comes at a serious pay cut compared to what Ignatius is paying his associates at BCC,"

Mitchelson said with a sly grin, "but the experience you'll gain, and the good you'll be doing, can't be measured in dollars and cents."

Tom thought it was easy for Mitchelson to be so noble when talking about trading in a hefty salary for the honor of serving his country. It was public knowledge Mitchelson had amassed a small fortune as a BCC partner for nearly twenty years. His nest egg, and those of his children and even grandchildren, were well feathered with the millions in profits he had earned over the years.

He glanced around the room, a surge of nervous excitement rushing over him. He noticed Agent Young had turned his back and was staring out the window. Just as Tom was about to accept the offer, Agent Young interrupted him.

"Sir, excuse me," he said, looking only at Mitchelson. "I need to get back to my office for a scheduled call. Is there anything else you need from me?"

"No, thank you, Bruce, for coming in and meeting Tom. Hopefully you two will be working together soon."

Special Agent Young let out a short sigh, smirked again and tilted his head. While shifting his weight to his heels he turned slightly toward Tom. "It was nice meeting you. Have a nice trip back to New York." Tom was about to thank him, but Agent Young turned and headed for the door as quickly as he'd come in, never removing his hands from his pockets. That was odd, Tom thought, but he was too focused on the job offer he'd just been given to be concerned with Agent Young's boorishness. There'd be time for that later.

Without waiting for Agent Young to close the door, AG Mitchelson turned to Tom. "So. What do you say? Are you willing to join our team and represent the most important client you'll ever work for?"

Dumbstruck, and in awe at how quickly things transpired, Tom blurted out, "I accept." Catching his breath, he continued. "I will work my hardest every day to protect the interests of the United States and to justify the faith you're placing in me. Sir," he added quickly, but earnestly. He was truly honored, and humbled. "I'll need a few days to tie up some loose ends on my cases and prepare them to be handed off to others in the firm, if that's okay."

"Of course," Mitchelson said, "but as I mentioned, we need to kick off our major investigation immediately and I'd like you to start right away. I'll speak to Ignatius after this meeting and I'm sure he'll agree to forego the customary two-week notice period. And Ignatius mentioned BCC would be willing to make one of its apartments at the Watergate complex available to you for a month or two, at a reduced rent, of course, in keeping with your new government salary," Mitchelson said with a hearty laugh, "while you and your wife find suitable living arrangements. So, if it's at all possible, I'd like you to start a week from Monday."

Tom understood an offer he couldn't turn down when he heard one. Rising from his chair he said, "I think that will be fine, Mr. Attorney General. I can't thank you enough, Sir, for this opportunity. You won't regret it. I give you my word."

"Good, Tom, good. I look forward to you joining our team," Michelson said as he stood. "My staff will be in touch with you about the forms you'll need to fill out. Have a safe flight back to New York."

With that, the Attorney General of the United States shook Tom's hand and walked with him out of the room.

Tom made his way to the elevator, down to the lobby, and across the marble floor to the rotating doors. He couldn't help but feel a mix of excitement and apprehension. As he headed for the black sedan that had waited for him during his meeting with the AG, Tom noticed the sun, which had been shining brightly that morning when he arrived in Washington, was now hidden behind dark clouds. Tom hoped his return flight to New York wouldn't be delayed by storms like his flight earlier that morning. He slid into the back seat and pulled out his phone to call Brooke. He had a lot on his mind. He loosened his tie and began making a mental note of all the things he needed to do before he and Brooke moved to Washington to start their new life together.

Fifteen minutes had passed since his meeting with the AG ended. As the black sedan maneuvered its way toward the airport, the satellite-linked encrypted computer whirred to life halfway across the globe. The one-line text that appeared on the screen was succinct and to the point: *Il Ragazzo ha accettato la offerta.* The young man has accepted the offer.

8

Brooke and Tom drove to Long Island Friday evening after he returned from Washington to share the good news with Tom's mother.

"Your mom is going to be so excited," Brooke said as Tom slid the BMW into the eastbound lanes of the Long Island Expressway. It was the start of the long 4th of July weekend and traffic heading east was at a virtual standstill.

"I hope so. Although with us moving to Washington, mom will be alone in New York. And she is getting older."

"Oh, stop," said Brooke laughing. "Your mother has more friends than days in a year. She's hardly ever home and always has something planned. She has a more active social life than we do. She'll be fine without her little baby boy. Besides, she can hop on Amtrak and be in Washington in about three hours. She can visit us as often as she wants, and we'll come up to New York for holidays and other occasions."

Tom knew Brooke was right, but ever since he was a small boy he'd felt the need to protect his mother and be there for her even though she was strong and independent. He worried about her. All his life he'd wanted nothing more than for his mom to be proud of him, and he tried hard to never disappoint her. Tom would do anything for her. When he was accepted to Harvard University, he told her he was thinking of going to school closer to home so he could be there for her. But she would hear none of it and made it clear that he needed to do what was best for him and his future, which meant going to Harvard. He did as he was told.

They pulled into the driveway at 7:30 p.m. Mary greeted them at the door. The sweet aroma of her homemade sauce filled the air. At sixty, she still had striking features that made men's heads turn, just like when she was in her twenties. Her hair was full and naturally dark, and she worked hard to stay healthy and maintain her shapely figure. Between Pilates, yoga, and regular workouts at the gym, Mary was in the best shape of her life.

Both Tom and Brooke noticed how men looked at her when they were all out together, and they knew a lot of eligible bachelors and widowers who would love Mary's company. They both wondered why she never dated, and Brooke once mentioned it to her. She assured them she was perfectly happy being single and enjoying her friends. She had no need for a man in her life she said. It was the last time Tom or Brooke brought up the subject.

They moved into the dining room where Mary had set out her fine China and adorned the table candles and fresh flowers. As she served the pasta course, she asked "So, to what do I owe this wonderful surprise of you visiting me on a Friday night?"

"I have some news about my work we want to share with you, Mom," Tom began.

He noticed his mother sink into her chair at hearing the news had to do with Tom's work—no doubt because she'd long hoped they'd announce that Brooke was pregnant.

"Tell me."

"You remember Mr. Balatoni, from the firm? He called me into his office earlier this week. It turns out there's an opening at the Justice Department in Washington, DC for someone with my skills. Mr. Balatoni and the other partners at the firm recommended me for the position."

Tom noticed his mother's eyes narrow. She looked confused. "So, you're leaving the law firm?"

Brooke jumped in. "What Tom is trying to say is the Attorney General of the United States is looking to hire his right-hand man at the Department of Justice and asked the partners of BCC for a recommendation. Tom was unanimously recommended for the job. He flew to Washington yesterday and met with the Attorney General who offered him the job on the spot. And your son accepted. He starts his new job as Executive Deputy Attorney General of the United States a week from this coming Monday. That means we'll be moving to Washington."

Mary looked stunned. Tom expected his mom to be excited and to congratulate him for this step in his career. Instead, she looked sullen and stared at her plate. Tom was surprised at his mother's reaction and shot Brooke a look.

"Mom, this is an incredible opportunity for Tom," Brooke offered hesitantly. "It's a promotion in recognition of Tom's hard work and his talents. Tom so impressed the Attorney General he was hired for the second highest position at the Department of Justice, second only to the Attorney General himself. And Mr. Balatoni assured Tom that when he returns to the law firm in a few years, he'll be welcomed back as a partner. This is fantastic news, mom. It's cause for celebration."

Mary sat silent for a long moment. Finally, she said flatly, "That's wonderful news. Congratulations, Thomas. But how did this come to be? Were you looking for a new job? I thought your goal was to become a partner at the law firm."

"It was," Tom said. "I mean it is. I didn't apply for the job. I didn't even know there was an opening at the Justice Department. I was just going about my day when Mr. Balatoni left me a note saying he wanted to see me. He said I'd be perfect for the position and he and the other partners recommended me to the AG. I decided to go through the interview process just to see what it was all about, but instead of rounds of interviews with the AG's staff as I expected, I met only with Attorney General Mitchelson. And he offered me the position."

"I see," Mary said after another long pause. "And Mr. Balatoni recommended you for the position? He must think very highly of you."

As far as Tom knew, his mother met Ignatius once or twice when she came into Manhattan to have lunch with him. They were just chance encounters while they walked down the hallway or exited the elevator. Ignatius was always extremely courteous to his mother and sang Tom's praises.

"He sure does," Brooke jumped in. "He and the other partners recognize Tom is an amazing lawyer, and their recommendation was instrumental in Tom being hired. I'm so proud of your son."

"Yes, of course, so am I," Mary offered. "I'm just a little surprised, that's all. It seems like since your first day at law school your plan was to become a partner at a law firm. I never heard you mention anything about working in Washington for the Justice Department."

"I know, mom, that's what's crazy about this whole thing. Just a few days ago I was working on a trial that was going to last another month, and now I'm heading to Washington and working for the government. I never planned for this to happen, but I think it's a great opportunity for my career, and it can only enhance my resume when I come back to BCC."

"Brooke already has several job opportunities in Washington, and since we don't have children yet, this seems like the right time to make this move. It really is a once in a lifetime opportunity, mom."

He saw his mother furrow her brow and look away while she reached for her glass of wine. He was still confused by his mother's lack of enthusiasm.

"Aren't you happy for us?" Tom asked.

"Yes, of course," Mary said vacantly. "It all sounds wonderful. I just worry what a high-stress job could mean for you, and with all the political squabbling going on in Washington, is this really what you want to do?"

"Oh, mom, I'll be stressed no matter what job I have. An associate position at BCC isn't a walk in the park, you know. You see how hard I've worked all these years. And unlike the Attorney General, my position isn't a political appointment. I'll be insulated from all the political parlor games. I'll be managing the day-to-day operations of the Justice Department, and leading teams of lawyers and investigators in large, mostly criminal cases. It's a demanding job, but I'm excited about the challenge."

He noticed Mary wince when she heard him say he'd be working on criminal cases. It was obvious that none of this made any sense to her.

"That's wonderful. I know you'll do a great job, and the Attorney General will be lucky to have you by his side," Mary said softly.

"Those criminals better watch out with my husband chasing them. There's a new sheriff in town, and he's going to clean up the place. " Brooke laughed as she raised her wine glass to toast Tom's success.

Mary stiffened. She was the last to raise her glass, but finally did, and the three clinked in unison. After taking a sip, she cleared her throat. "I'm very proud of you son. And I'm very thankful for you, Brooke."

"We can't wait for you to visit us in Washington," Brooke told her. "Promise us you'll visit as soon as we get settled in."

"Of course, I will. I can't wait."

On the drive back to Manhattan Brooke started to doze in the passenger seat.

"Don't you find it odd the way my mother reacted to the news?" Tom asked, interrupting Brooke's nap. "I mean, my whole life she's been my biggest fan and loudest cheerleader and was excited about everything I did. But tonight, she sounded downright morose and even scared. I don't get it."

"She told us why she reacted the way she did, honey. She was surprised, that's all," Brooke said, still drowsy and sounding cranky. "She never heard you talk about leaving the firm or moving to Washington, and I'm sure she was just shocked by the news. We probably should have told her before we arrived, so she could have processed it and let it sink in. By the end of the night, I thought she was fine, and she seemed genuinely happy for you. And for us. Don't fret about it." Brooke curled her long legs under her and turned slightly to her right side.

"I guess you're right, honey. Close your eyes and rest. I'll wake you when we get to the garage."

Mary sat quietly in the darkened living room after Tom and Brooke left. She was puzzled. What was this about? Why was Ignatius recommending

Tom for a job at the Justice Department? Did *He* know about it? Or was *He* behind it? None of this made any sense to her. She wanted answers but was afraid of what she might learn. Would she wake a sleeping giant or find out it was just another move in the master plan of Tom's life?

She couldn't help but fear the worst.

9

The going away party Balatoni, Cartel & Colin hosted for Tom was classy and elegant, exactly what you would expect from a firm like BCC. Ignatius Balatoni arranged for the event to be held in the Rainbow Room at the Top of the Rock, on the 65th floor of 30 Rockefeller Plaza, surrounded by the glittering lights of Manhattan's sparkling skyscrapers. Brooke had even received a hand-calligraphed invitation delivered to her apartment by a BCC messenger.

Every partner in the New York office attended, as did most of the associates, except for the unlucky few who had to man their battle stations and keep the billing meter running, doing last minute research for a brief due the next day, or performing due diligence on a mega merger or a headline grabbing hostile takeover. The firm even flew in heavy hitters from BCC's other offices. The heads of the Los Angeles, Cleveland, Chicago, Washington, Atlanta, and Houston offices were there, as was the head of the antitrust practice group, for whom Tom had done some critical research during a trial a few years ago.

Even the heads of the London, Hong Kong, Berlin, Paris, Madrid, Rome, Toronto, and Mexico City offices attended, as did almost every member of the Executive Committee. It likely wasn't lost on any of them that having one of their own second in command at the Justice Department might come in handy for their clients one day. By the looks of the empty liquor and beer bottles filling up the garbage can behind the bar, everyone was enjoying themselves.

Waiters wearing black tuxedos, white shirts, and yellow bow ties were everywhere, offering trays of hors d'oeuvres to tipsy lawyers. In true BCC fashion, a four-piece band, accompanied by a pianist, played soft jazz and easy listening classics just loud enough not to drown out partners regaling their eager, wide-eyed associates with war stories of cross examinations that left witnesses whimpering, or late-night negotiations that allowed BCC's clients to acquire multimillion-dollar companies for pennies on the dollar using other people's money.

As with most gatherings of two or more lawyers, with a sufficient amount of alcohol and a captive audience, the boasting grew more fanciful by the gulp. By the end of the evening, cases that had only seen the inside of a small claim's courtroom at night became the trial of the century making the OJ Simpson murder case seem like a law school mock trial exercise. Tales of BCC lawyers steamrolling witnesses and forcing them to recant on the witness stand, juries returning multi-billion-dollar verdicts in favor of BCC clients, and judges readily granting game-changing motions written by BCC lawyers could be heard being recounted again and again, with the stakes growing exponentially higher with each successive sip. While most of the stories had a grain of truth to them, the wins were rarely so one sided. Even a firm as prestigious and respected as BCC lost a case or two every now and again.

Partners kept coming up to Tom and Brooke to offer their congratulations and wish them well. And associates were both proud and envious that one of their own had not only survived BCC, but hot-skipped a few rungs on the career ladder and made it all the way to the number two job at the Justice Department. For them, a position at DOJ was seen as a meal ticket to partnership, or a cushy in-house general counsel position at a Fortune 500 company of their choice, with hefty salaries that could buy McMansions in the suburbs, beach houses in the Hamptons, or slope-side ski chalets.

After a few hours and a few hundred handshakes, Tom and Brooke were drained. Their mouths hurt from smiling and their feet hurt from standing. It was the first quiet moment they had all night when Brooke tugged on Tom's arm. "I still can't believe it. All these people came here to see you off. We're moving to Washington tomorrow. This is crazy. It's all happening so fast."

"Oh Brooke, don't tell me you're having second thoughts," Tom said with a fake pout. "Just give me the word, and I'll turn this into a 'staying at the firm party' instead of a going away party."

"Not on your life, C. Thomas Berte. Besides, all my clothes are packed, and I can't wait to live in DC and be closer to my sister." Brooke paused. "I also can't wait to start our own family, babe, just as we're starting the next chapter in our lives together." Brooke's eyes watered as he pulled her in tight for a hug. Tom loved Brooke and loved the idea of having kids of his own one day and being the kind of father he'd always wanted but never had.

They had talked a lot about what life would be like when they had kids. He didn't want Brooke working, even though she insisted she wanted to keep her career and contribute as much as she could financially to their family. Tom thought back to how hard his mother worked at the accounting firm so she could provide for Tom. He wanted his kids to have everything they wanted, especially doting parents who were always around.

Tom and Brooke were still in their embrace when Ignatius walked up and smiled at them. "Ah, the happy couple. You're a blessed and lucky man indeed, Thomas, to have such a beautiful and loving wife."

"I count my blessings every day, sir," Tom said, as he gently kissed Brooke's cheek.

"Brooke, you remember Mr. Balatoni, don't you?"

"Of course, it's wonderful to see you again, Mr. Balatoni. Thank you for this wonderful send-off. Tom and I are so appreciative for all you have done for us. And the firm's gift to the Paulsboro Group was incredibly generous. I can't thank you enough."

"I am delighted to hear that, dear," Ignatius said. "This is a wonderful occasion."

"It is, but in response to your comment a moment ago, I'm the lucky one, Mr. Balatoni," Brooke said, looking into Tom's eyes. "Tom has worked so hard and I'm so proud of him."

"We all are," Ignatius responded. "But as I've always said, behind every successful man is an even more successful woman who nurtures and gives her husband the sustenance and strength to succeed. I know I could not have accomplished half as much as I accomplished in my lifetime without my wife Helen by my side for sixty years."

"That is so beautiful." Brooke reached out to grab Ignatius's hands.

"Thank you, Brooke. Thomas is so very lucky to have you."

Brooke blushed and smiled at Tom.

"My dear, would you mind if I had a word with Thomas alone for a few moments?"

Surprised, Brooke paused before recovering. "Oh, of course, of course. I was just on my way to the ladies' room," she said haltingly.

"Thank you, Brooke, we won't be but a minute."

"I'll meet up with you, sweetie," Tom said as she walked away.

Ignatius gently placed his hand on Tom's elbow and guided him toward the corner of the room. "I meant what I said, Thomas. You are a blessed man."

"I know I am. In more ways than one. I mean, Brooke is terrific, and so supportive. But I've also been very lucky to work at BCC for the last seven years, and now with this opportunity you've given me, I just don't know how to express my appreciation to you and to the partners of the firm."

"We know how grateful you are, and this party is just our little way of saying thank you for all your hard work and dedication over the years. You're an excellent lawyer, and the things we said to the Attorney General about you are all true. We are all so very proud of you. I wish I could live another ten or twenty years to see all the great things you'll accomplish." His voice trailed off.

Tom looked away and felt a lump in his throat. He knew he would get choked up when it came time to say goodbye to Ignatius.

"I have some thoughts I'd like to share with you. I've been thinking a lot about what this new job will mean for you and Brooke."

Tom looked up, wiping the corner of his eye, as he eagerly prepared to listen to The Pope.

"I am thrilled for you. At the same time I'm also apprehensive about what the future holds for you, and for your family."

Tom took in a breath and waited for more.

Ignatius looked around, making sure no one was within earshot, and then turned to look back at Tom.

"Ever since I first interviewed you all those years ago, I've felt a strong connection to you. You are an excellent lawyer with superb judgment." Ignatius's voice was shaky, as if he was about to cry.

"I don't know what to say. I've always tried to do my best and be humble and learn as much as I could."

"I know and it's all about to pay off. But this new chapter in your career is going to expose you to things you would never imagine. You'll likely learn of threats to our country's national security that will cause you sleepless nights and cause you to question our country's ability to endure in the face of them. You'll be leading investigations into organizations whose goal is to destroy America and the pillars upon which this magnificent country has stood since its founding. You'll learn about plots that will cause you to question whether advancements in science and technology have benefited our society or hasten its demise.

"You'll encounter criminals who are pure evil, who have no soul, and whose self-proclaimed purpose is to destroy everything they come into contact with. And you will also learn of people whose avarice knows no boundaries, and who will let no one stop their desire to enrich themselves at everyone else's expense."

Tom listened intently and dared not interrupt The Pope but couldn't fathom where this conversation was going. After a short pause Ignatius continued.

"The work can wreak havoc on a man's character, to say nothing of his soul. It will test your fortitude. You'll be challenged to maintain your integrity and to stay true to yourself and your values. I've seen countless people before you who were exposed to these realities who made poor choices because they were weak and unprincipled. They were selfish, and envious, and jealous, and secretly lusted for power and money, instead of glory that comes from pursuing justice and honoring the rule of law." Ignatius bowed his head as his hands trembled.

Why was Ignatius telling him this? Was he having second thoughts about recommending Tom for the job? Was he giving him a pep talk, or sending him a message? What was he driving at?

"Few can withstand that kind of pressure. Our Attorney General is one of them. But flawed men have succumbed to it." He paused again and took a breath. "They sacrificed honor and integrity for power and wealth."

"Sir, if you're concerned whether I can rise to the challenge and maintain my honor at the expense of financial gain, you have nothing to worry about. I know who I am, and I would never do anything to jeopardize my career or my reputation. I would never put my personal interests above the interests of our nation," Tom said, surprised he needed to explain his character and values to Ignatius on the night of his farewell party.

"I know. I'm not questioning your integrity. I know you're different. Still, I was conflicted about recommending you for this position, not because you don't have the abilities. You have them in spades. But because it means exposing you to truths that may have been better left entombed in secrecy. But it wasn't my choice to make." Ignatius's voice trailed off again, and he appeared to mumble the last few words.

Tom still didn't understand why Ignatius was saying this at the eleventh hour. What truths were better left hidden? And what choice was he talking about? Tom wondered whether Ignatius's age was finally catching up with him, and whether he was taking leave of his senses.

Ignatius cleared his throat and continued, "I know you're taking this job for all the right reasons. I know your moral compass is unshakeable. Remember that when you're challenged. Remember that when you're faced with monumental decisions requiring you to stand in judgment of those you're pursuing. Remember that good does triumph over evil. Be vigilant against feelings that may seek to sway you against doing what is right.

"Maintaining your values and ethical rectitude will be paramount for a person in your position. You can and should be aggressive and forceful for your clients, be they corporations or the United States of America, but you must remain vigilant to never cross that line. You may never cross back. The pursuit of justice by lawyers is the only thing standing between a democratic society and tyranny. The rule of law is dependent on lawyers. We are the foot soldiers of the Constitution, and the army that protects rights and liberties granted to all of us by the Almighty. Never forget that."

Tom had heard that phrase before. His ethics professor at Harvard said that once, and the words stuck with him. Tom wondered whether his professor had heard it from Ignatius first.

"When it's all said and done," Ignatius continued after a short pause, "history has shown that those who nobly pursue justice are rewarded with much more treasure than those who are motivated by lust for greed and power."

Tom nodded, not quite sure what to make of The Pope's sermon.

"My faith in justice and the rule of law will never be shaken. No matter what they throw at me, no matter the challenges I'll face, and no matter the evil I'll see." Tom said, his voice rising as he stood ramrod tall, just like he did when he was arguing in court. "Nothing will deter me from doing what's right for me and my family. Too many people have worked too hard and invested too much in me to allow me to get to this point, including you, and I owe all of you a tremendous debt of gratitude.

"I know how much my mother sacrificed for me, and how hard I've worked to get where I am. And I think of Brooke and the family we want to have one day. I promise you I will use this opportunity, or this challenge, or whatever it is I've been given, to make all of you proud, and to show you the faith you have all placed in me is warranted. On that, I give you my word."

Ignatius let out a sigh, as if he was comforted by Tom's words. "I know you will. Stay true to yourself and to your values and to your family." Ignatius leaned in and put his arms around Tom. He hugged him gently, and Tom welled up. As they released from their embrace, Ignatius lightly kissed Tom's cheek. Tom was startled but tried not to show it.

"I'll miss you, Thomas," Ignatius whispered. "I have great affection for you. As I told you the other day, I never had children of my own. That was God's plan. But if I had a son, I would have wanted him to be like you." Ignatius wiped the tear rolling down his cheek. "I would tell you to go and make us proud, but you already have. May God protect you and watch over you."

The founder and leader of one of the richest and most powerful law firms in the world was overcome with sadness. Ignatius held him firmly before pulling back and slowly walking away. The Pope had given his blessing.

Tom took out a handkerchief to wipe his eyes. He knew deviating from his true north was not an option. Although he was emotional, his spirits were buoyed. He was calm and confident, and ready to enter the ring and fight like hell to show everyone around him how strong he was.

10

I will support and defend the Constitution of the United States against all enemies, foreign and domestic; that I will bear true faith and allegiance to the same; that I take this obligation freely, without any mental reservation or purpose of evasion; and that I will well and faithfully discharge the duties of the office on which I am about to enter. So help me God.

With those words, recited in a private ceremony in Attorney General Bradley Mitchelson's executive chamber on the seventh floor of Main Justice on a cloudless Wednesday morning in mid-July, with Brooke holding a bible that had been in her family for several generations, C. Thomas Berte was sworn in as the Executive Deputy Attorney General of the United States.

Invitations had already been printed and sent for a ceremonial swearing-in to take place later in the summer before Tom's family and friends, including Ignatius Balatoni, and his former colleagues at BCC. But given the urgency of the work awaiting him, this private and abbreviated ceremony would have to do for now.

The plan was in motion. The only question was whether Tom would do his part.

With his investiture behind him, AG Mitchelson kicked off Tom's first meeting on his first day at DOJ at precisely 9:30 a.m.

"Good morning, everyone. Let's please get started. I know you've all had a chance to meet Tom. We're excited that he's joined our team, and humbled knowing that, in doing so, he left behind, for the time being anyway, a lucrative partnership track position at one of the world's most respected law firms."

Those attending the meeting gave Tom a respectful and welcoming round of applause.

The Attorney General sat at the head of the long oval table in the same room where he and Tom had met barely two weeks earlier for his interview. The room seemed different now, smaller, and less ornate. The floral arrangements that sat on the table when Tom was first there were gone. The curtains framing the dozen or so tall windows along the side of the room facing Pennsylvania Avenue looked dingier and duller. The rug under the conference table was worn and tattered in the corners, something Tom hadn't noticed when he anxiously waited for his interview. He was amazed at how many details he'd missed. AG Mitchelson, though, was again impeccably dressed in a starched white shirt, deep gray pinstriped suit, and baby blue tie. His hair was again perfectly coiffed, and Tom wondered whether he visited a barber every morning.

Seated around the table were Fred Johnson, Chief of the Fraud Division of the DOJ, Marilyn Lewis, Chief of the Securities and Commodities Division, Bill Levey, Chief of the Organized Crime and Domestic Terrorism Division, and Rachel Robinson, head of the Narcotics and Drug Trafficking Task Force, who reported to Levey. Also joining the meeting were FBI Director Emanuel Greevey, and liaisons from the Drug Enforcement Agency, Securities and Exchange Commission, Interpol, and CIA. Mitchelson also invited other heavy-hitters from President Ferguson's Administration, including the Secretary of the Department of Homeland Security, Director of the National Security Agency, First Assistant Secretary of the Treasury, Director of the Secret Service Money Laundering Unit,

Director of the Financial Crimes Enforcement Network, Chief of the US Marshall's Service, and the head of US Customs and Border Protection. At the opposite end of the table was FBI Special Agent Bruce Young, whom Tom met briefly during his interview. Agent Young barely looked at Tom and had the same expressionless mien as he did the first time Tom saw him.

It took a moment for Tom to collect himself given the potent firepower assembled in the room. These men and women represented the brain trust of the Department of Justice, together with the immense resources and power of the Executive Branch. They had the authority to investigate whomever they wanted for any or no reason. Collectively these individuals, and the agencies they led, had brought down kingpins and king makers, leaders of foreign governments and their military apparatus, terrorists, drug cartels, and executives of some of the biggest, richest and most well-known and most well-connected banks, brokerage houses, and Fortune 500 companies in America.

This is where the real power of American law enforcement resided, and damned be the person caught in their crosshairs, Tom thought. He looked toward the windows and recalled the thick-paned glass he noticed the first time he was in that room. He realized now why the government needed to protect these assets.

"Thank you," Tom said as the clapping died down. "As I said to the Attorney General, I'm honored to be here and eager to roll up my sleeves, to work with all of you, and to assist the Department of Justice in carrying out its mission. If there's anything I can do to assist any one of you, please let me know."

"Thanks, Tom," Mitchelson said. He looked like he was about to launch into a stump speech. "That's a perfect segway to why we're here this morning. We're about to commence an extremely critical and important investigation that will affect scores of Americans. The Department of Justice has been coordinating for months with the FBI, the CIA, and the rest of the departments and agencies represented in this room, as well as with the White House, to line up the legal authority and political backing to undertake this operation.

"Now that Tom is here and this office is fully staffed with the resources it needs in place, we can finally kick-off the investigation which will be led by Tom under my direction and supervision."

As he gazed around the room, Tom noticed that Special Agent Bruce Young had turned his chair around and appeared to be looking out the window, his back to Tom and the AG. Although it was disrespectful, Tom was too caught up in the moment to let it get to him. Just then, the AG spoke up again. "I'm going to turn the meeting over to FBI Director Greevey to brief us on the particulars of the investigation and the scope of our mission."

With that, FBI Director Emanuel Greevey welcomed everyone to the meeting and thanked the Attorney General for his leadership, his vision, and for bringing together the august group of men and women assembled in that room from the various government agencies who would work together on the investigation. After uttering exactly forty-six words, the Director introduced his colleague, FBI Special Agent Bruce Young to lead the meeting and brief the attendees.

Tom wasn't surprised the Director punted. During his years at BCC, he learned it was rarely the person at the top who knew all the facts or did the heavy lifting. While the ones with the titles got all the attention, commendations, and made the big bucks, it was their deputies who always did the grunt work that allowed the leaders to shine. That was certainly true at BCC, where partners received accolades and were rewarded with multi-million-dollar compensation packages, while the workhorses, hordes of associates and paralegals who shouldered the burdens and stayed up all night researching, writing, and reviewing documents, paved the way for partners to make brilliant legal arguments and negotiate deals that made the front page of *The Wall Street Journal*.

"Thank you, Mr. Director," Special Agent Young said as he stood and walked over to a large flat screen. He pressed a button on his hand-held remote and up popped a color picture of a middle-aged man wearing glasses, with salt and pepper hair. The man looked fit and trim, with a tanned, handsome face, rugged features, a receding hairline and a prominent nose. The man wasn't looking directly at the camera and likely didn't even know he was being photographed. To the experienced crime fighters in the room, it was obvious the picture was taken using a telephoto camera and long-range surveillance technology.

The man was leaning back in a chair, possibly in a lounge or club, wearing a red shirt opened halfway down his shaggy chest exposing a gold crucifix on a chain around his neck. Standing next to the man was a topless woman in heels, holding a glass of what looked like champagne. If a picture tells a story of a thousand words, a few dozen quickly raced across Tom's mind.

After a few seconds, and without uttering a word, Agent Young pressed a button on the remote in his hand and a second color picture filled the screen. This one was of an older man, perhaps in his eighties. He had a cane and wore a cap with long stringy hair poking out the sides and back covering his ears and neck. The man's face was unshaven and looked swollen with deep circles under his eyes and a reddish bulbous nose. He wore an unbuttoned raincoat and appeared heavy in the midsection. Tom wondered whether the coat could be fastened over the man's belly. He appeared to be walking with a stoop. The photo looked down on the man as if taken from above.

After another ten seconds or so, and again without saying a word, Agent Young pressed a button on the remote and a third photo appeared on the screen. This picture was in black and white and grainer than the other two. It showed a shirtless man, perhaps in his thirties or forties, sitting on the rear of a boat in the middle of a harbor or bay. A skyline with what appeared to be two tall towers and perhaps a bridge was barely visible in the background. Were those New York's Twin Towers? Tom wondered.

It looked as though the boat was moored, although no anchor was visible. The man was holding a drink, and a cigar dangled from the corner of his mouth. He had a full head of bushy hair that matched his hairy chest. Sitting next to the man, but with her head turned away, was a young woman in a flowing sundress, resting her head on the man's shoulder. The woman's arms were crossed against her rounded midsection. Given the angle of the photo, Tom thought the woman looked pregnant. Watching the screen, Tom sensed familiarity with something in the photograph but couldn't pinpoint anything in particular. Suddenly, the screen went blank.

"The person you've just seen in the three photos is the same man,"

Agent Young said, puncturing the silence in the room. The photos were taken many years apart by FBI surveillance teams in Florida, Italy, and New York. At the time the earliest photo was taken, in the 1980s, all that was known about the gentleman was that he was an associate of the Gambino crime family in New York.

"Today, we know the man's name is Cosimo Benedetto. To his few close friends and associates, he's known as Nino. But he has used at least a dozen aliases over the last quarter century, including Vincenzo Balsamo, Alberico Damiano, and Stefano Duce. Not many people have heard of Cosimo Benedetto, and that secrecy, and the many disguises he's used over the years to alter his appearance, are his calling card. Based on the scant information we have developed, we believe for the last twenty years or so, Cosimo "Nino" Benedetto has covertly led a sophisticated global criminal Syndicate that has grown hugely profitable and immensely powerful. We believe the Syndicate is responsible for unspeakable, heinous crimes. Forget everything you've ever read, heard, or learned about organized crime or La Cosa Nostra. That play book is out the window. This is not your grandfather's mafia." Tom had never heard of Cosimo Benedetto or the existence of the Syndicate before today and he was rivetted by the presentation. Agent Young paced the room to let those words sink in as he made eye contact with everyone seated around the table, except Tom. He seemed much more animated than when they first met, Tom thought, as if he actually had a pulse and could maintain a conversation.

"We have a lot of conjecture and suppositions, and a lot of circumstantial evidence concerning his criminal empire, but very little concrete evidence linking Benedetto to the Syndicate, let alone that he is the leader of it. That's our job." Special Agent Young pivoted to a summary of Benedetto's biography based on scant information the Bureau had on him.

"We believe Cosimo Benedetto was orphaned at a young age and raised by a middle-aged couple in the town of Monreale, Sicily, located in a mountainous region east of Palermo. The boy's adopted father was a local mafia chieftain who controlled a large swath of Sicily's agricultural trade. Cosimo wasn't raised as a typical son of a mafioso, however. He was sent to the finest schools in mainland Italy, and by the age of fifteen was fluent in English, French, and Latin, in addition to his native Italian. He later studied at universities in Milan and London and holds degrees in economics and political science. After graduation he returned to Sicily and started his career as an accountant in Palermo. He was smart, shrewd, and sophisticated."

Tom mused that he would fit right in at BCC.

After a brief pause, Agent Young continued his presentation. "When Cosimo was twenty-two his father, or adopted father, was gunned down in a raid on a farmhouse in the Sicilian countryside. The raid was conducted jointly by the US Bureau of Narcotics and Dangerous Drugs, or BNDD, the precursor to today's DEA. The CIA and the Italian Ministry of Justice and Drug Enforcement also took part in the raid. Reports at the time said it was a US BNDD agent who fired the fatal kill shot cutting short the man's life."

Tom looked around the table. He was trying to read everyone's face. But while he was sitting on the edge of his chair and hung on every word Agent Young said, he noticed everyone else sat expressionless and looked calm and relaxed. He'd hate to play poker with this crowd, he thought.

Agent Young looked down at his notes for a few seconds. "After his father's death, we believe Cosimo Benedetto stepped in and took control of his family's business, but in a more sophisticated fashion. Based on his contacts in the Ministry of Economics both in Palermo and Rome, Benedetto began funneling millions of dollars in government contract money into Sicily and into the hands of various mafia dons. He proved himself quite capable at fundraising and made many in Sicily very wealthy. His success eventually caught the attention of the Commission in the United States, the governing body of the US mafia, and in 1983 Cosimo Benedetto illegally entered the United States, we believe through Canada, and took up residence in New York working for the Gambinos. But despite his book smarts and extensive experience perpetrating financial frauds and manipulating financial markets, the gangsters in New York didn't quite know what to do with him. Benedetto was relegated to forming dummy corporations used to win construction contracts issued by municipal governments that allowed New York's Five Families to create hundreds of no-show jobs for their capos and associates.

"Through those companies, the Gambinos strengthened their hold on the construction industry and several labor unions, especially the trucking, machine operators, and drywalling unions. Beyond creating phony companies, Benedetto was also tasked with setting up wire rooms for bookies and laundering proceeds from the families' extensive loan sharking operations. And, occasionally, we believe Benedetto carried out a hit or two. But his true talents were never fully utilized. The wiseguys in New York were too focused on their bread-and-butter rackets of extortion, , prostitution, hijacking, loan sharking and gambling, and they didn't know what to do with a guy like Cosimo Benedetto. On the flip side, Benedetto was able to evade immigration officials and the long arm of the law, and he had no arrest record, despite running with the Gambinos for many years."

Tom looked up and noticed he was the only one taking notes. It was a habit he picked up in college. He learned best when he took copious notes that he re-read at night and again before exams. Tom wondered if everyone else in the room had a photographic memory and learned just by listening.

"In the late 80's, Benedetto began freelancing by arranging drug smuggling operations through the marine ports and airports around New York. But drug dealing wasn't an officially sanctioned activity of the Gambinos at the time, and he risked severe punishment by the bosses of his own family if he was caught. After almost a decade as a criminal in New York, Cosimo Benedetto was making a nice living, but was bored," Special Agent Young continued. "He was frustrated that he wasn't given opportunities to realize his full potential and angry that the New York goodfellas didn't understand the extent of his talents and what he could do for them. With New York being the financial center of the world, Cosimo tried to also push his bosses to increase their influence on Wall Street and to use his connections in Italy to control commerce and trade between the two countries. But his efforts fell on deaf ears, and he was heard on wiretap in 1991 lamenting that the "New York goombahs couldn't see past the mulberry bush on Mulberry Street." The room stirred to life, and everyone politely laughed.

"By late 1991, after our office turned Sammy "The Bull" Gravano, the underboss of the Gambino's and highest-ranking member of the US mafia ever to cooperate with law enforcement, leading to the conviction of John Gotti, we had the mafia on the run. Cosimo Benedetto's opportunities in New York were shrinking just as his luck ran out.

"Immigration and Naturalization Services detained him in the summer of 1992 after they raided a backroom gambling parlor on Staten Island. Benedetto was deported and eventually returned to Sicily. But even there he was limited in what he could do. Recall the mafia in Sicily at the time had suffered major setbacks and was in disarray as a result of the Maxi trial and testimony of Tommaso Buscetta, the highest-ranking Italian mafia leader to cooperate with the authorities. As a result of Buscetta's testimony, over four hundred mafiosi were sent to prison, some for multiple life sentences."

Agent Young surveyed the room, probably to make sure everyone was still awake, before he continued with his next sentence.

"1992 was also the year that two of our law-enforcement colleagues, Italian judges Giovanni Falcone and Paolo Borsellino, who devoted their careers to prosecuting the Sicilian mafia, went to their untimely deaths fifty-seven days apart. They were killed in Palermo by bombs set off by what was left of the Sicilian mafia after the upheaval caused by Buscetta's defection."

Agent Young paused again, which Tom thought appropriate as a way to mark the solemn memory of two fellow crime fighters, a brotherhood Tom was now proud to be a part of.

"I knew those men well," AG Mitchelson offered. "They are heroes and giants in our collective efforts to make the world a safer place. We stand on their shoulders." He bowed his head and appeared his eyes.

Agent Young cleared his throat and continued with the briefing. "We largely lost track of Benedetto after he returned to Italy. But we now have reason to believe that since then Benedetto filled the void created after the mafia in Sicily and the US was decimated, and he quietly built a criminal Syndicate the likes of which international law enforcement has never before seen. We're dealing with *La Cosa Nostra 2.0.*" The gravity of the moment sank in as those words hung in the air.

"Cosimo 'Nino' Benedetto is rarely seen in public, and we only have a few minutes of audio recordings of him despite a life of crime spanning more than forty years. The three photos I showed you earlier are the only pictures we have of the man. He's currently in his late sixties with no family of his own. He spends most of his time on an opulent mega yacht, a floating fortress really, named the *Vulcania*, that is almost three football fields long, sailing between Florida, the Caribbean and the Mediterranean with a small crew and a female companion."

Agent Young pressed a button on the remote and brought up a photo of an immense, sleek vessel. It had a glossy black hull, with gold-plated accents and gold trim on the upper decks. A wide white sash encircled the hull below the first rail, like a star-studded designer belt cinching the waist of a high-class super model. She stood fourteen decks high, with eight open decks over six enclosed ones and dozens of large portholes and massive tinted windows. On a landing pad on the topmost deck sat a silver and black helicopter. Two red speedboats were hoisted over the yacht's sides. A large swimming pool replete with a waterfall was visible on one of the rear decks. Limassol, Cyprus, its port of registry, was stenciled in white block letters below the name *M/Y Vulcania* in cursive script on the stern of the enormous craft.

Agent Young gave everyone time to digest the photo of the vessel. "Based on confidential information we've been able to piece together so far, we believe the *Vulcania* was built in 2018 by Fincantieri S.p.A in Monfalcone, Italy, and then dry docked in Israel for four months for retrofitting with the latest state-of-the art gadgetry that makes worldwide communications instantaneously possible, and detection by the outside world practically impossible. For a hefty price tag, a little-known Israeli company headquartered out of a mail drop box in the port town of Ashdod, designed and installed inertial synchronization global positioning satellites, wireless infrared encryption, and an AI-interfaced electronic data system that makes its communications with anyone anywhere in the world virtually indecipherable and undetectable. We also believe a subdivision of the Russian intelligence service outfitted the yacht with satellite location-jamming robotics, diffused counter-illumination technology, and stealth radar diversion meta surfaces that, at a push of a button, makes the 825 ft floating enclave practically invisible to conventional and sonar radar. This latest technology, coupled with a biodefense air purification system, ion exchange membranes to desalinate and decontaminate water, ionic-hydro nutrition propagation to grow foods and nutrients, and solar and nuclear powered, carbon-neutron fuel regeneration bio cells that power the yacht without ever needing to refuel, makes the *Vulcania* a self-sufficient ecosystem which could remain at sea, fully sustainable, for an infinite period without ever having to touch land. The *Vulcania* is an engineering marvel."

The silence in the room would have been deafening had it not been for the Organized Crime and Domestic Terrorism Division Chief's long whistle. "Too bad Gilligan didn't have a yacht like that." Nervous laughter filled the room, but Tom was too focused on what he'd just learned to join in the levity. Looking around, he noticed others in the room staring at him. He wondered whether they were jealous that he'd be leading the Benedetto investigation—or pitied him.

"Based on records we've uncovered," Agent Young continued, "we have reason to believe the *Vulcania* also boasts a state-of-the-art anti-missile defense shield, blast resistant windows, Russian-made Buk-M2E and Pantir S vertical launch weapons systems, and a nuclear-powered submarine in a watertight hull compartment used for deep water exploration, or...," Agent Young paused, "for clandestine escape from enemy forces. At last count, we estimate Cosimo Benedetto has spent upwards of $2.5 billion on his massive sea castle, where he lives in extreme extravagance and complete isolation."

Tom was amazed at what he had heard. He almost had to remind himself to breathe.

"Benedetto wasn't on our radar until we picked up chatter among Afghani warlords about six months ago. The chatter made repeated references to a Sicilian who was financing the explosion of poppy fields in Iraq and Afghanistan, with refineries scattered throughout Sicily. From there we began tracing the movement of large shipments of drugs, mostly heroin, cocaine, and opiates throughout Europe, North America, and Asia, and we learned of the existence of a worldwide criminal Syndicate bigger than any criminal organization we've ever investigated. Based on what we know thus far, the Syndicate controls a vast portion of the international drug and opiate trade, including fentanyl, and is responsible for the addiction and overdose deaths of hundreds of thousands of people worldwide. It is also involved in everything from cyber warfare and ransomware attacks emanating from Russia, Israel, and China to arms sales. It holds controlling and well-hidden interests in banks and financial institutions in Cyprus, Isle of man, Lichtenstein, and a half dozen European capitals, and even brokerage houses on Wall Street. We suspect the Syndicate is behind several stock manipulation and pump and dump schemes, and penny stock scams, costing investors billions. Also left in the Syndicate's wake is the murder of scores of rival gang members, as well as some high-ranking government officials who apparently refused to play ball with Benedetto and his organization. Cosimo Benedetto is calculating and ruthless, and a cold-stone killer."

Agent Young slowly made his way to the front of the room. "Ladies and gentlemen, we have reason to believe the Syndicate is responsible for funding terrorists in the Middle East, cyber warfare and ransomware attacks, exponentially increasing the distribution of illegal narcotics around the globe, and increasing the cost of international trade by billions of dollars for goods as varied as computer chips and soybeans. In the name of profits and power, the Syndicate is responsible for untold murders and has destroyed the lives of countless others. Let me repeat that: the Syndicate is a killing machine responsible for the death of untold numbers of people around the world. In short, we believe this criminal organization impacts the health, safety, and economic welfare of over half the world's population. With all due respect to South America's drug cartels and to scourges like El Chapo, their antics pale in comparison to the catastrophic destruction, both in terms of lives killed and treasure lost, at the hands of this criminal enterprise. The threat posed by this new, international mafia, makes old timers like John Gotti, Carlo Gambino, Lucky Luciano, Bugsy Siegel and the like look like child's play.

"And," Agent Young said before pausing one more time, "we have reason to believe the mastermind and leader of this criminal enterprise is one Cosimo "Nino" Benedetto."

Tom saw AG Mitchelson squirm in his chair.

"My job…I'm sorry, our job is to gather and piece together evidence to indict, prosecute, and convict Cosimo Benedetto and the entire leadership structure of the Syndicate." Looking directly at Tom and letting out a sly smirk, Agent Young took in a breath. "Our mission is to bring down the largest and most sophisticated criminal organization we have ever gone up against, and once and for all eradicate the mafia and its tentacles from ever taking hold again—anywhere in the world."

Agent Young turned to a side table stacked high with folders. "We will distribute to each of you and your staff a top-secret dossier containing all the information we have uncovered thus far about Cosimo Benedetto and the Syndicate. It is just a start, and no doubt there will be much more we will learn in the weeks and months to come. Effective immediately, our work will proceed under the code name Operation Eradicate Aifam. Thank you for your attention."

AG Mitchelson slowly rose from his chair, let out a deep breath, pursed his lips, and surveyed the room.

"Ladies and gentlemen, this will be no small undertaking. Years from now, decades from now, the work we begin today, together, will be discussed and dissected and studied across the globe. What we do from this day forward will define our country's security and law enforcement's ability to control the flow of drugs, secure and protect our financial markets, and allow for the free flow of goods and services around the globe. The importance of our task cannot be understated. I spoke again with President Ferguson this morning and she asked me to convey to all of you that she is praying for us, deeply appreciates our courage and our resolve, and our commitment to the rule of law."

Turning to Tom, Mitchelson said, "Tom, I look forward to your steady leadership as we undertake this investigation, and what I hope will culminate in criminal convictions that will rid us of Cosimo Benedetto and the reach of his Syndicate around the world. Godspeed to us all."

After a few seconds, all Tom could muster was a muted "thank you" as the magnitude of the task that lay ahead settled in. "And, yes, Godspeed to us all."

It was almost 11:00 a.m. by the time Tom returned to his office, and he was already exhausted. He scheduled a meeting for the next morning with the strike team that would handle the day-to-day operations of the investigation and detailed the lines of reporting and a timeline for status reports and meetings of the larger task force. Boxes were still piled high in his office, and he had yet to unpack any of his belongings.

As he slumped back in his chair, Tom turned and gazed out the window. The deep blue sky was a perfect backdrop to the Capitol dome framed perfectly by the window in his office.

He had an uneasy feeling about the investigation and the information he'd learned earlier that morning but chalked it up to rookie jitters. Soon, Tom would discover he had good reason to fear the future.

11

At a few minutes past midnight, as the *Vulcania* sailed toward Rhodes, Greece, the satellite-linked telex machine in salon whirred to life. The printout confirmed the software company Cambridge Logistics, which began trading just six months earlier on the Nasdaq electronic exchange, had been awarded a five-billion-dollar contract by the Kyrgyz Republic to upgrade the country's national healthcare computer network infrastructure. The news, coupled with the algorithmic trading program launched earlier in the month, would soon cause Cambridge Logistics' stock price to skyrocket.

That was just enough time before the press and SEC began investigating the dramatic price increase and discovered the news release was fake, revealing Cambridge as nothing more than a shell company used in a pump and dump scheme. But by then, Cosimo and the Syndicate had flooded the market with their custodial shares, resulting in over $400 million in profits being wired to several clearing firms. Cosimo's team of hackers in Israel then launched codes instructing the clearing firm's computer servers to immediately funnel the money to secret numbered accounts in banks in the Isle of Man, Isle of Jersey, Lichtenstein and, yes, in the Kyrgyz Republic, which would be used to handsomely compensate the minister of finance for his troubles. The instructions instantly vanished the moment the transfers were executed, making it impossible to trace or to find the whereabouts of the money.

This was all in a typical day's work for Cosimo and the Syndicate. They would acquire a shell company and take it public, announce dummy revenue that would inflate its stock price enough to interest investors who would begin bidding up the stock's price. The market would be systematically enhanced by algorithmic trading programs that magnified the shares of stock traded. After a few days they would release a phony press release leading to more interest in the stock that caused the stock price to soar even higher.

Cosimo and the Syndicate then sold off their entire holdings, with the proceeds transferred through clearing firms whose servers would be hacked with untraceable instructions, and the funds ultimately transferred into secret bank accounts controlled by the Syndicate. By the time the fraud was uncovered, investors would be left holding worthless stock. A barrage of investigations would be launched, and a flurry of worthless lawsuits would be filed.

But what was almost never reported in the press was the computer hacking activity by Cosimo's team of engineers. Red faced and embarrassed that their supposedly foolproof systems were so easily hijacked, the clearing firms and brokerage houses they relied on managed to keep details of the hacking under wraps for fear it would lead to mistrust by investors and a collapse of US financial markets.

After the funds were securely deposited in untraceable accounts, Cosimo and the Syndicate used the proceeds to finance their drug trade, whose deadly products were sold throughout North America, Europe, and Asia. Despite the ravages caused by his narcotics distribution empire, Cosimo gave little thought to the young kids overdosing in the streets of small towns and cities, or to their grieving parents left behind. This was the empire he had created, one that gave him untold riches and extraordinary powers that allowed Cosimo Benedetto to exact revenge on tyrannical governments and corrupt institutions that had taken so much from him.

In the dimly lit salon aboard the *Vulcania*, Cosimo reclined on the leather sofa and read the telex. He smiled in satisfaction.

The irony of his life was not lost on him. Although he lived aboard an opulent vessel that transported him to far reaches of the globe, with immense wealth that could easily place him in the company of royalty, tycoons, and world leaders, Cosimo was consumed with measures to protect his identity and conceal his very existence. That included sailing with a modest crew of his most trusted associates and loyal confidants, one that was far smaller than the *Vulcania's* size and amenities would otherwise suggest.

At the helm of the *Vulcania* was a man from Licata, Sicily, who began working in Cosimo's organization at a young age before being promoted to captain. Cosimo rescued the young man from certain death at the hands of a deranged Sicilian drug addict who suspected the man of inappropriate dalliances with the drug addict's girlfriend. After Cosimo's intervention, the drug addict went missing and was never heard from again. As for the young man, he married the drug addict's girlfriend and he now served as head chef and director of the *Vulcania's* housekeeping staff, which included the woman's sister and niece.

Also on board was Salvatore Nessa, known as Totto, the Chief Engineer, First Mate, and head of security who commanded Cosimo's army of warriors. Upon Cosimo's return to Sicily after he was deported, Totto was the first person he hired when he began to build the Syndicate. Although Cosimo kept his own counsel, and liked to play things close to the vest, Totto was his most trusted friend and consigliere. Cosimo didn't make a move without Totto Nessa by his side.

Totto was born in Sicily but educated in the United States. When he completed his studies, he returned to Italy and joined the highly regarded *Guardia di Finanza*, the Italian law enforcement agency under the authority of the Minister of Economy and Finance and rose to the rank of Captain.

Disillusioned by the graft and corruption he witnessed in the Italian government, Totto began using his authority to help Cosimo arrange drug shipments. When other members of the *Guardia* uncovered Totto's extracurricular activities, they demanded protection money and threatened to expose him unless he split his take with them. Rather than give in to their extortion, Totto refused. Members of the *Guardia* arrested Totto, and he was savagely beaten and tortured. They placed him in solitary confinement for three months with little to eat or drink to persuade him to testify against the head of the drug smuggling operation.

But doing so would have meant testifying against Cosimo, something Totto would never do. He withstood the beatings and torture, and after lawyers hired by Cosimo bribed prosecutors and the judge, Totto's indictment was thrown out and he returned home. But not before his wife, who was overwrought with depression at the thought of Totto spending the rest of his life in prison, took her life by hanging herself in the family's olive grove. After Totto's exoneration, Cosimo ordered his men to find those who blackmailed and beat Totto while in their custody and deprived him of food and water. The men were kidnapped, and with extreme care, their legs and arms were severed and their body parts, including their torsos, dissolved in vats of acid and lye. From that point forward, Totto pledged his undying loyalty to Cosimo, the only family he had left.

Alongside Cosimo wherever he went was his trusted bodyguard, Gino Terranova. Gino was born in America and started his criminal career as an associate, and later a made man, in the Gambino crime family in New York. He stood almost seven feet tall and weighed a hefty 375 pounds. He was a hulk of a man who once dead lifted a 500-pound slab of marble and smashed it over the head of a deadbeat who made the unfortunate mistake of failing to pay vig on a loan underwritten by the Gambinos. Legend had it Gino weighed almost twelve pounds at birth, and due to difficulties passing through the birth canal, his face became elongated which led to his nickname, Gino the Horse. Cosimo despised the use of nicknames by the American mafia, a practice he viewed as unbecoming an organization with an honorable history of protecting the working class in Italy against overreach and subjugation by fascist governments.

After the FBI arrested the leadership of the Gambinos in the early 1990s, Gino the Horse fled to Italy and took refuge in Cosimo's organization. Gino was tasked with eliminating a number of competitive barriers presenting obstacles to Cosimo's strategic growth plans, and as his reward for a job well done, he was given the awesome responsibility of protecting Cosimo's life.

The final passenger aboard the *Vulcania* was Cosimo's constant companion and girlfriend, Fabiana Parides, a Cypriot woman Cosimo met when she was twenty-five and working in a Nicosia nightclub. At the time, Cosimo traveled frequently to Cyprus where he had founded a base of operations for his growing narcotics business outside the watchful eye of European regulators and law enforcement. Fabian's voluptuous breasts, long legs, and dark, supple skin instantly caught his attention and desires. For her part, she found the older, wealthy businessman exciting and dangerous. Fabiana fell in love with the handsome jet setter, and Cosimo relished the attention and devotion showered on him by the young, gorgeous woman.

Fabian's loyalty to Cosimo, the trait he treasured most, was apparent in everything she did. She never questioned his business affairs and was always eager to celebrate his successes and stand with him through his battles. And after what started out merely as a relationship built on physical attraction and a means to satisfy his carnal lust, Cosimo began craving Fabiana's tenderness and compassion.

But while Cosimo showered Fabiana with gifts and affection, he refused to give her what she wanted most, to bear his children. His business came first, he would say repeatedly, and he didn't have time to raise children or be a father. In their moments alone, Fabiana asked him to reconsider, but he would grow sullen and withdraw, never willing to discuss the matter further. In time, Fabiana came to accept she would never have a child of her own.

Cosimo cared deeply for Fabiana, but he could never bring himself to feel love. He knew love once, but it was a distant emotion, a feeling he left behind in New York when he was deported to Italy. Now, decades later, as he sailed across the globe on the *Vulcania*, Cosimo had settled into a familiar relationship with Fabiana that was at once comforting and safe.

A quick knock on the massive door to the salon caused Cosimo to sit up, as he wiped away drowsiness from his eyes. Standing there was Totto Nessa with two glasses of amaretto on the rocks.

"Please come in, Totto."

Totto handed one of the glasses to Cosimo before falling into a chair across from him.

"I trust you read the telex?" Totto asked.

"I have. We have been blessed with good fortune. But we must remain ever vigilant against forces that will try to destroy what I have created." Cosimo sighed heavily and gazed out the large windows of the salon toward the bow of the *Vulcania* where the nighttime sky descended to the edge of the shimmering moonlit waters of the Mediterranean. He slowly sipped the iced amaretto, savoring the sweet liquid.

"Nino," Totto began, "I've noticed you have been preoccupied with the state of your affairs and whether efforts are underway by law enforcement authorities to investigate the Syndicate's operations. I can assure you there is no reason to believe you are under any imminent threat. You are safe, and soon you will know if the plan you have put in place will succeed."

"I appreciate and value your advice, Totto." Cosimo paused and seemed to measure his words carefully. "As a matter of pure logic, we must recognize we're playing a game against time and that one day the world's tyrants, with their vast resources, will attempt to take what is ours. All I've built and nurtured could evaporate in the blink of an eye. That's why I need powerful warriors, like you Totto, whose loyalty is beyond doubt. And hopefully, soon, we'll add one more loyal soldier to our ranks who will protect us and tell us about *their* plans."

Cosimo longed for a future that embraced his past. A past taken from him decades ago with the brutal killing of the only father he'd ever known. The slaughter was ruthless. Hunted and cornered like a caged animal, his father was bever given the opportunity for a dignified surrender. That was the beginning of his anger, his hatred, his mistrust, his need for revenge. Against authority. Against governments. Against tyranny. Against power. It was the same power that deprived him of his future and the family he so desperately wanted. The one that took away his legacy and denied him the one thing he loved and cherished most. He learned long ago that to conquer such power he had to attain power of his own.

Totto harbored doubts about the Cosimo's plan and whether it would succeed. But because of his love and affection for Cosimo, and his unyielding loyalty, he did not dare question Cosimo about the wisdom of it.

Cosimo rose from the sofa, walked toward Totto, and gently placed his hand on Totto's shoulder. "When should we expect the next update on the progress of the *Ragazzo*?"

"Tomorrow," Totto responded. "He and his wife will be viewing several apartments in the Washington area that have been wired, so whichever one they choose we will know their every move."

"Excellent." "Please continue to update me on all developments. And please ask the captain what time we'll be arriving in Rhodes."

Cosimo slowly walked over to the etched glass windows on the back wall of the salon overlooking the illuminated pool which cast an eerie glow against the darkened horizon. He stood tall, squared his shoulders and set his jaw. "Today is the day I reclaim my legacy and lay the foundation to secure the future."

PART II

12

"Good morning, everyone. I hope you all enjoyed reading the dossier about Cosimo Benedetto as much as I did," Tom said as he convened his first meeting of the strike team in the conference room adjacent to his office. "I have a few ideas on what our initial tasks should be, but this is a joint effort, and I encourage each of you to share your thoughts and suggestions, both today and in the days to come. I am a big believer that no one has a monopoly on good ideas, and the only way we're going to succeed is if everyone in this room works together as one to accomplish our mission.

"My style is to have an open-door policy, and I am always available to discuss possible investigative leads, analyze an issue, or run through alternate scenarios. I believe in sharing all information with the group, so we don't wind up with silos of information being hoarded by a select few. As the judge I clerked for many years ago in Boston liked to say, 'if each of us works hard to make everyone else look good, we'll all shine.' To kick things off, I suggest we go back through the prosecution files of the Gambino family in the late 80s and 90s to see if we missed something when Cosimo Benedetto wasn't our target."

FBI Special Agent Bruce Young shook his head with a sour expression on his face. "Excuse me, Tom, but with all due respect, I don't think what you're suggesting makes much sense. Those files have been poured over a million times. We're not going to find anything new or useful there. I mean, my team and I do a deep dive on those files every time we arrest a wiseguy and we've scrubbed them clean. There's nothing else we can mine in those files."

Tom shifted in his chair when he heard Agent Young say the words *with all due respect*, recalling what Ignatius Balatoni said about blowhards who use that phrase.

Bruce Young hated government bureaucracy. Every time the FBI joined hands with the DOJ to start a new investigation, the same playbook was used. Everyone always wanted to start with a review of old files, which led nowhere and wasted precious time and resources.

Bruce had been with the FBI for twenty-eight years—the last six as Special Agent in charge of the FBI's National Security Division, a title that put him in the company of at least sixteen other Special Agents who led sixteen other divisions. It was a nice title, but he wanted more of the limelight and felt he deserved more recognition. He was always one rung below where the real power resided. Sure, he was told he had authority, but his main function was to act as a layer of insulation protecting the top echelon from criticism. His job was to take the heat and incoming fire, while the power-hungry guys at the top kept their hands clean. He had the knowledge and experience, and battle scars to prove it, but because he didn't have political backing, or muscle, he was relegated to riding the bench, grinding out work without ever getting praised.

He came close to being named Special Assistant Director of the FBI three times, was twice considered for the position of Deputy Director, and there were rumors he was once on the short list for the top job of FBI Director. But politics always got in the way. He didn't have the right connections or the right pedigree. He didn't graduate from Harvard, Yale, UVA, Tufts, Duke, Georgetown, Stanford, or Princeton, and he did nothing to ingratiate himself with his home-state senators or members of the Senate Judiciary Committee or their staffs.

He was naive enough to think his dedication to the Bureau, and the results of his hard work, would be enough to capture the brass ring. But so far, all it got him was a slightly larger office and direct command over a couple dozen agents. On the high-profile Benedetto investigation, like so many others he worked on in the past, Bruce Young would ride shotgun, this time to a hot shot DOJ lawyer who never carried a gun or slapped cuffs on a thug and couldn't fight his way out of a paper bag.

Tom was concerned before taking this job that members of his team, with years of law enforcement experience under their belts, would resent someone like him with no background in criminal law, and from outside the ranks of the DOJ and law enforcement, coming in to headline the show. But the DOJ historically ran the investigative phase of cases. The powers that be believed lawyers were best equipped to design the scope of investigations because they knew how far they could go to get evidence without crossing the line into violating a suspect's due process rights. The tool of choice for law enforcement officers was a gun and that's all they knew. But even the most powerful automatic assault weapon, in the hands of the most experienced law enforcement agency, could be muzzled by the US Constitution. That's why lawyers were routinely chosen to lead investigations. At least that's what Tom was told.

"I appreciate that, Special Agent Young," Tom said, "but Cosimo Benedetto worked for the Gambinos for almost a decade, providing many valuable services that made the organization a lot of money. It's possible he was caught on wiretaps or surveillance photos back then, but because he was never a suspect or even a target of those earlier prosecutions, the investigators may have overlooked something that makes more sense to us now that he is the focus of our investigation. Besides, we need to start our investigation somewhere and starting at the beginning of Benedetto's criminal career in the United States seems reasonable to me. So please have someone on your staff analyze those files. And it's best if you select someone who wasn't involved in a prior review. Having a fresh set of eyes and ears looking and listening to everything for the first time may turn up something new. Please pay particular attention to any audio files that were inaudible back then and see if our special ops team can help decipher them. Thank you."

"Fine, *Boss*. I'll have Special Agent Ann Leonardo look at those files for the umpteenth time and we'll report back if we find anything." Bruce said the words, but inside he was giving Tom the middle finger. He had spent more years fighting crime than Tom was out of diapers. And yet, once again he was taking orders from a lackey whose only qualification for his job was getting into Harvard Law School.

"Thanks, Agent Young. I appreciate that. Now, as a second step, we need to consider whether we can find a mole inside the Syndicate. I realize this will be extremely difficult given Cosimo's penchant for secrecy, but at the same time an organization this vast, with so many far-reaching tentacles, must have a weak link somewhere. Let's figure out where that weak link is so we can exploit it. If anyone has any suggestions, please share them."

After a moment, Madeline Kelly, a new member of the National Security Administration's staff who had been detailed to the strike team, spoke up. "I think we ought to consider what role our partners in Afghanistan can play in this investigation. We first learned about Cosimo Benedetto when he was mentioned in conversations picked up by intelligence officials in Afghanistan. Based on those conversations, Benedetto appears to have established a base of operations in that country. Given the assets the United States has developed there over the last dozen years or so, I believe Afghanistan may be a fertile ground to try to find our mole."

"Good idea. Please run with that and coordinate your efforts with the CIA." Madeline looked pleased that her suggestion caught immediate traction with Tom.

"Next," Tom said, "let's set up multi-disciplinary teams of accountants, forensic financial investigators, and computer whizzes to follow the money trail. Cosimo was an accountant by training, and it appears he had a sophisticated knowledge of international currency transfers and financial markets. Let's look at the largest securities frauds over the last ten years, and the largest computer hacking schemes, to see if we can decipher any patterns or clues that might shed light on where the hackings originated, and where the money flowed." Turning to the liaisons from the Treasury Department and Secret Service, Tom asked them to work with the FBI's Office of Asset Tracing and report their findings to the group.

After another thirty minutes spent checking off action items on his agenda, Tom looked at his watch. His meeting with AG Mitchelson would begin in an hour and he needed time to prepare. He thanked everyone for their time and told them he looked forward to their next meeting and the results of their initial investigations. As the group filed out of the conference room, Tom motioned to Agent Young to join him in his office.

"Bruce, I really appreciate all you've done so far in putting together the background information for this investigation."

"Just doing my job, *Boss*."

"I know you are, and I just want you to know I appreciate your efforts. It's not lost on me that you're the senior most person on the strike team and you have far more experience than everyone else in that room, including me. I'm going to rely on you a lot throughout this investigation, and your input and judgment will be invaluable to me and to the Justice Department as we put this case together and hopefully bring charges against Benedetto and other leaders of the Syndicate."

"I'm happy to help. I figure I've seen a thing or two in my day, and in my time working for the FBI I've learned experience is an invaluable weapon to have in your toolbox. With all due respect to you and the other lawyers at the DOJ, there's no substitute for learning the basics from the ground up by chasing bad guys out of the holes they crawl in."

Tom tried not to react to Bruce's use, for the second time, of the phrase *with all due respect*. "You're absolutely right. And I'm going to count on you and your experience as we proceed with the investigation. But I would appreciate it when we're in the large group setting like we just were in, that you don't criticize a suggestion I make, or any other member of the group makes. Debate is welcomed, and I encourage a free exchange of ideas, but let's do it in a way that respects each other's opinions and points of view."

"Understood, Mr. Executive Deputy Attorney General. I agree none of us has a monopoly on great ideas, as you said earlier. I'll be sure to save my misgivings or disagreements with an approach you're taking for when we meet in private."

Tom smiled. He knew Agent Young was being a condescending prick, but decided to let it go. "Great, thanks," he said as he slid behind his desk. "I appreciate your time."

Tom sat in his chair as Agent Young walked out of the office. He made a mental note to keep an eye on his new buddy. Bruce Young seemed to have a big ego and fit the mold of people he had dealt with before, Tom thought. You can't work at a firm like BCC and not bump into a couple dozen lawyers who compete with each other for the biggest jerk award. But Tom was determined to foster a different culture at the DOJ. It would take time and require some work, but he was up to the challenge, or so he thought, and looked forward to building a top-notch team to go after the world's most notorious criminal.

What Tom didn't know was just how much of a challenge Special Agent Bruce Young would become.

13

"Can you get out of work early tonight so I can show you the apartment I found? It's amazing. It's just a few blocks from the Potomac in a brand-new building. We'll be the first ones to live in it."

Tom leaned back in his chair, cradled the phone on his shoulder, and smiled at Brooke's excitement. "I don't know, sweetie. I'm already knee-deep into the investigation I'm leading, and I have a ton of documents I want to sort through tonight."

"Which reminds me, you still haven't told me anything about the case you're working on, except that it's crazy intense and is going to explode in the press at some point. So, maybe you can share more details when I see you tonight at the apartment?"

"Nice try, babe. You know I never share details with you about any of my cases. Attorney-client privilege, remember? The cases I'm working on are strictly confidential. Besides, I want you to get the full impact of the story when you read about it in the papers and see me being interviewed on CNN."

"Oh, so now you're going to be on TV too, huh," Brooke teased.

Ever since Tom became a lawyer he never talked about his work with Brooke. It drove her crazy. She had considered a career in the law, but chose to study psychology instead because she thought all the lawyers she'd met were nuts. But she loved the law, especially criminal law. She was always trying to analyze the minds of depraved criminals she'd hear about in the news to understand what drove them and what was missing in their lives that led them to turn to a life of crime.

She loved analyzing motives so much that Tom hated watching crime shows on TV with her because she'd figure out "who'd done it" within the first fifteen minutes, and then incessantly psychoanalyze their behavior. All Tom wanted to do, on the other hand, was unwind and watch a mindless show that didn't require him to think. That's why they had two TVs in their apartment. Tom learned early on that multiple TVs made for a happy marriage.

"But what about the apartment? The broker said four other people are interested and we need to move quickly if we want it. It's really a great apartment, with a separate bedroom and bath for when your mom visits or when my parents come to town."

"I thought your parents would stay at your sister's place when they visited," he said, only half-kidding.

"Ah, nice try, babe," Brooke parried back. "Can you please give me just thirty minutes and come see the apartment? It would make me so happy."

"Yes, okay, honey. But can we see it at seven-thirty?"

"Perfect. That's the time I told the broker we'd meet her. I know you so well. Love you."

"Love you too, Brooke. Text me the address and I'll see you there."

It wasn't a problem for Tom to leave the office before seven. The DOJ wasn't like BCC where if an associate left before ten at night, they'd be branded a slacker. There was one partner at BCC who would roam the hallways at ten-thirty every weeknight to see who was still in the office. He'd take mental notes and then share the information with other partners. His office was closest to the elevators, and whenever he saw anyone leave before ten, he'd sarcastically yell, "Going out for lunch?"

Associates on his floor would purposely leave the lights on in their offices and drape a jacket over the back of their desk chairs whenever they left before ten to make it look like they just stepped away and would be back momentarily. They would also take the stairs up or down a floor to another set of elevators just to avoid passing his office. What the associates never realized, though, because they were too busy working during the day to notice, was that the partner didn't show up to the office on most days until one or two in the afternoon, so even though he worked late into the night, he spent far fewer hours at the office than they did.

Tom often stayed at the office until at least eight, even in his new role, and he wanted to work late that night to review documents. Old habits were hard to break. As a result of Mutual Legal Assistance Treaties, known as MLAT's, between the Unites States and dozens of countries, the strike team had received thousands of documents and electronic records concerning Cosimo Benedetto and the Syndicate from around the world. Plus, the SEC and Office of the Comptroller of the Currency in the United States also searched their files for bank transfers suspected of being connected to Benedetto's vast business network. Those documents, which filled at least ten bankers' boxes along with four CDs, had been delivered to the strike team that morning.

Although he had a team of paralegals and investigators ready to catalog, analyze, and cross reference every document, Tom wanted to take the first crack at looking through the information. Document review was what associates at firms like BCC cut their teeth on, and Tom had become an expert at deciphering forensic clues and detecting patterns from what looked like gobbledygook to the untrained eye.

As Tom waded through the reams of paper and electronic data, the enormity of the task of investigating an organization as vast and complex as the Syndicate began to set in. There was a labyrinth of companies incorporated in at least a dozen countries that did business with one another, on paper at least, but their ownership was shrouded in secrecy. They were formed by anonymous professional incorporators with bearer stock certificates. This was a tactic the FBI and DOJ were very familiar with, but Tom was still learning the tricks of the fraud trade. Even the foreign law firms that helped form the corporations were nothing more than a PO box run by crooked attorneys who made a living starting law firms, forming shady corporations, shutting down the firms, and moving on to another law firm to do the same thing, all while collecting a handsome fee for legal services rendered.

Come to think of it, Tom thought, those were the really smart lawyers, not the associates who billed a hundred hours a week at big New York City firms and pulled in only half as much as these dodgy lawyers made in a few hours. There was that old saying from the *Godfather*, Tom recalled, "One lawyer with a briefcase can steal more than a hundred men with guns."

Tom clicked open a file on his computer marked Cambridge Logistics. It had its IPO six months earlier as a Special Purpose Acquisition Company, a public shell corporation that didn't make or sell anything, but instead raised money with the expectation it would acquire a target company and build on that company's success. As he read through the file, Tom learned that just four months earlier Cambridge Logistics acquired a company that had developed an artificial intelligence technology capable of reviewing thousands of medical records in seconds, thereby helping healthcare systems minimize the cost of retaining millions of pages of documents.

According to the company prospectus, the technology could reduce the cost of delivering medical services by hundreds of millions of dollars annually, which would provide huge savings for countries with nationalized health care systems. As Tom read more, he learned that recently the SEC began seeing unusual trading volume in shares of Cambridge Logistics, at just about the same time the share price of the stock began ticking up. Two weeks ago the company announced a five-billion-dollar contract with the Kyrgyz Republic to revamp the government's electronic healthcare filing system, causing its stock price to jump from five dollars per share to over sixty-five dollars in just a matter of days. Exactly four trading days later, however, the stock price cratered when the *New York Times* reported the contract with the Kyrgyz Republic didn't exist. But by that point, company insiders had already unloaded over $400 million dollars' worth of stock.

Tom was fascinated by the brazenness and simplicity of the fraud. The proceeds from the pump and dump scheme seemingly vanished into thin air. But authorities strongly suspected the money landed in the Syndicate's coffers. As he continued clicking through the documents, something caught his attention. When Cambridge Logistics acquired the AI company four months earlier, it was represented by lawyers at BCC. BCC also defended Cambridge when it was sued by a competitor claiming Cambridge stole its technology. And when Cambridge acquired that competitor, BCC was again at the table negotiating the deal. Tom wasn't completely surprised BCC crossed paths with a company suspected of wrongdoing. Afterall, BCC was one of the largest law firms in the world, with over three thousand lawyers, and tens of thousands of clients. It was certainly possible some of the gaggle of BCC lawyers represented a corrupt client or two. That's the business some lawyers sign up for.

But what he found most interesting was an SEC filing disclosing that Cambridge Logistics replaced BCC with new counsel just a week before the pump and dump scheme was uncovered. The timing could just be coincidence, Tom figured, but the fact that BCC wasn't counsel of record when the shit hit the fan was a big deal and saved BCC from embarrassment when news of the fraud broke. Sure, BCC's name would eventually surface and be linked to Cambridge Logistics, but that would be days or maybe even weeks, and several news cycles, after news of the fraud made headlines. By then, public attention would have moved on to the next headline-grabbing news story. Luck, maybe. Tom considered the alternatives for a moment but considered it fruitless unless he had more evidence.

He looked at his phone. It was already seven. If he left now and there were no delays with the Metro, he'd be at the apartment by seven-thirty. Just in time to make Brooke very happy.

The *Vulcania* arrived at the secluded port in Rhodes just before two-thirty in the morning. Cosimo was awake and watched from his stateroom balcony as the captain maneuvered the massive vessel into its berth. He rarely slept more than four hours straight, and which four hours depended on the location of the deal he was working on.

On this day, he was awaiting confirmation of a large shipment of high-quality cocaine across the Baja peninsula into Southern California. It had a street value of over $500 million, and he personally promised his friends in South America that delivery would happen on time and without interruption. A significant payment had been made to certain employees of the US Border Protection Agency and US Customs. This was America after all, and the entrepreneurial spirit was alive and well. Trump's wall hadn't made its way yet to this part of the Mexico-US border. But it wouldn't have mattered. The wall was no match for the greed of those border agents.

Fifteen minutes later, Totto Nessa called Cosimo on the *Vulcania's* intercom. "The *Ragazzo* and his bride are in the apartment and will sign the lease tonight, if you care to take a look."

"Excellent. Send the live feed to the monitor in my stateroom."

Cosimo watched Tom and Brooke as they toured the apartment and signed their names on the lease. This building turned out to be a sound investment, Cosimo thought. After watching the couple in BCC's Watergate apartment over the last month, he would now continue to have an uninterrupted front row seat into their daily lives.

But hopefully their stay wouldn't be long.

14

Tom's cell phone rang at 6:30 a.m. FBI Special Agent Bruce Young was getting an early start to his day.

"Tom, this is Agent Young. Can we meet first thing this morning? There's been an interesting development in the Benedetto investigation I want to share with you."

"Sure. How about ten? There are a few things I need to tend to before then."

"Uh, okay. If that's the earliest you can do, I guess I'll see you then."

"What a shithead," Bruce said to himself. "He's running what's likely the most important investigation in the history of the FBI but can't even make time for me." Bruce was still steaming that he was taking orders from Tom Berte. As far as he was concerned, Tom was just another wanna-be, smart enough to earn As in law school, with a privileged upbringing, but clueless how to catch bad guys on the streets.

Bruce had wanted to go into law enforcement since he was a kid. He planned to become a police officer right after high school in his hometown of Rushville, Indiana, but his mother begged him to go to college. Bruce's father was constantly being laid off from whatever odd jobs he could find because he liked to drink more than he liked to work, and his mom cleaned houses, but never earned much and used food stamps to buy groceries. She thought that having her son go to college might break the family's cycle of poverty. Bruce received financial aid and took out loans to pay for it.

He went to the University of Indiana and graduated with a degree in criminal justice. Although his grades in his major were fine, he barely passed his other classes. His criminal studies professor, a former FBI Special Agent in charge of the FBI's Indianapolis Field Office, persuaded him to apply to the FBI Academy instead of becoming a cop. The day after he graduated college, he drove to Quantico, Virginia, for FBI boot camp. It was there that Bruce flourished and became a star student. He always credited his college professor for setting him straight. Throughout his career Bruce often repeated the mantra his professor would use to motivate his students: "don't let today be your best day, because you can always be better." Bruce took that advice to heart, worked hard, and became a highly regarded agent.

Just three years after being sworn in, while stationed in the Indianapolis Field Office, Bruce was awarded the FBI Star for killing a suspected arms dealer in a gunfight, despite being shot in the abdomen. A cache of weapons, headed for several domestic terrorist groups, was recovered.

By the time Bruce celebrated his eighth anniversary with the FBI, he'd worked his way up to becoming the number four man in his field office. He also was second in command of the national cyber security task force for the Midwest region and had become an expert on cyber warfare and counter espionage intelligence. He was often detailed to strike teams investigating sophisticated hacking schemes, bank frauds, and ransomware attacks. By and large, he loved the FBI in those early days. He was drawn by its camaraderie, the discipline it imposed, and the power it wielded.

After his success with the cyber security task force, Bruce was detailed to investigate a group of Saudi nationals living in rural western Indiana suspected of being an Al Qaeda sleeper cell. When Bruce and his team intercepted communications between the Saudis and Al Qaeda leaders about a plot to blow up multiple transportation sites in San Francisco the following month, they executed warrants on the compound where the Saudis lived, arresting every member of the group and finding several steel containers loaded with explosives and detonating devices that could have killed and maimed thousands.

Because of the team's achievements, Bruce and his fellow agents received the FBI Distinguished Service medal for extraordinary and exceptional achievement in connection with a case of national security. After a hard-fought lobbying campaign, and despite the no-votes of several of his supervisors, Bruce was finally promoted to Special Agent in charge of National Security and Counter Espionage and transferred to FBI headquarters in Washington, DC.

But as time went on, he became disillusioned with the job due to interdepartment squabbling and his low salary. He felt he should earn more for risking his life everyday protecting liberties and freedoms most Americans took for granted. It was around that time that Bruce's wife, who had remained in Indiana after he took the job in DC, filed for divorce, after carrying on an affair with the family's dentist. She got the house and furnishings, as well as primary custody of their only child, a daughter, who was born a year after she and Bruce married. At the age of thirty-eight, Bruce Young was forced to piece his life back together. The divorce financially crippled him, and over the years he fell behind more and more on child support payments.

He eventually owed more in bills and back taxes than most people earn in a year. He could barely afford the one bedroom first floor apartment he rented in a dilapidated two-story home in a rundown part of Capitol Heights, Maryland. His ex-wife repeatedly took him to court demanding more financial support and slowly turned his daughter against him. Because she lived in Indiana, he only saw his daughter a few times a year, hardly enough time to build a relationship with her. He started drinking more and socializing less. His life was slowly crumbling. The only thing that kept him going was his secret sick addiction.

Despite his successes, medals and accolades, Bruce was always relegated to playing second fiddle. DOJ lawyers took the lead in major investigations, while the highly decorated and experienced men and women of the FBI were cast in supporting roles. Just once, he often mumbled, he wanted to lead a major case on his own from start to finish without a DOJ lawyer looking over his shoulder. Even now, despite being the FBI agent in charge of the Benedetto investigation, he was taking orders from a wet-behind-the-ears pencil-pusher who couldn't even design to make meeting him a priority this morning. "Asshole," Bruce muttered to himself.

Prior to meeting Brooke at the apartment the night before, something had caught Tom's eye while he was reviewing bank records linked to the Syndicate, and he wanted to follow up first thing this morning. He'd noticed a wire transfer confirmation for $100 million dollars from 2018 between Nedbank Douglas, Isle of Man, to Merchant's Commercial Bank in the British Virgin Islands. The wire was sent on behalf of CNB Limited, a Cypriot entity headquartered in Nicosia, Cyprus, with offices in St. Petersburg, Russia, and Beijing, China. CNB was in the business of brokering sales of rare earth metals, natural-forming elements vital to almost every piece of high-tech equipment, from automobile computer chips to cell phones, to precision-guided missiles.

Among the information secured by the DOJ through use of MLATs were multiple documents concerning recent thefts of metal shipments, including lanthanum, cerium, and neodymium mined in Asia. Authorities in the UK and elsewhere suspected the Syndicate was behind the thefts.

Tom looked up the phone number of Lindsay Crutcher, an investigator in the Serious Frauds Office in London which was working closely with the FBI and other US agencies investigating the Syndicate. Tom met Lindsay when he was at BCC working on a case representing a British company sued in the United States for allegedly defrauding the market for diamonds imported from South Africa. Lindsay was instrumental in locating key evidence confirming that a rogue employee had acted on his own and tried to implicate Tom's client. The information resulted in another victory for Tom and BCC.

He had emailed Lindsay when he awoke at six that morning and sent her a copy of the wire transfer slip. He wrote that he would call her at 9:00 a.m. Washington time to follow up.

"Good afternoon, Lindsay, thanks for taking my call."

"Of course, Mr. Berte. Anything for the Executive Deputy Attorney

General of the United States of America. Congratulations on the appointment."

"Thank you, but there's no need for such formality between us. You can continue to refer to me as Your Excellency," Tom joked, and the two shared a laugh.

"It's nice that you finally saw the light and decided to join the side of the good and brave against the forces of evil," Lindsay said. "Did the guilt of representing greedy corrupt corporations finally get to you, Tom?"

"Now, now, Lindsay, I clearly remember our conversation when I was last in London when you told me you were considering joining one of those greedy corporations and finally earning a living suitable to your needs. What happened? Did you get cold feet?"

Tom could hear Lindsay chuckling on the other end of the phone. "I don't know. Every time I make plans to leave, I get sucked into another investigation that's too good to pass up. I promised myself this case will be my last, but I've said that at the start of my last four cases."

"I'm glad we're on the same side of this investigation, and I'm really looking forward to working with you again."

"Likewise," she said. "Thank you for the document you sent me this morning. Our office has been independently investigating CNB Limited for about a year and looking into some very large financial transactions made through several British banks. We traced a number of them to companies and organizations we believe are linked to Cosimo Benedetto and the Syndicate."

The two discussed pooling their resources to trace the flow of funds from CNB Limited to various financial institutions in the UK, and Lindsay brought Tom up to speed on efforts MI 6, the British Intelligence Agency, was taking to track the movements of several additional rare earth metal shipments in hopes of catching the Syndicate in the act. They agreed to keep each other apprised of developments related to the investigation and to continue working closely together.

When Tom hung up the phone, he looked at the time on his computer screen. It was 9:52 a.m. Just enough time to grab another bottle of *Yoo-hoo* before Agent Young would arrive for their meeting.

He could hardly wait.

15

"Good morning, *Boss*," FBI Special Agent Bruce Young said, sounding obnoxious. Tom played it cool and didn't react.

"Good morning, Agent Young. You were up early this morning. How's the investigation going on your end?"

"We're plugging along. We've had some developments in the last twenty-four hours that I want to bring to your attention, and I have a recommendation on how we should proceed."

"Great, let's hear it."

"We received an alert from the National Intelligence Service of Greece at 1400 hours yesterday that three high ranking members of Columbia's Montavo drug cartel arrived in Rhodes, Greece. About two days ago, US DEA officials had eyes on a large shipment of cocaine heading across Mexico toward the Sea of Cortez. They lost track of the shipment once it crossed the border into Southern California. It disappeared without a trace. A group of border agents are suspected of being on the take and looking the other way."

"Excuse me, Agent Young, we're knee-deep in the Benedetto investigation. Why are you telling me about missing drugs in California and some rogue border agents? And what does that have to do with drug pushers in Greece?"

"I'm getting there, *Boss*. At 2200 hours local time last night, a DEA operative in Rhodes learned that a luxury mega yacht was expected in Rhodes overnight and would arrive in a secluded port owned by a Greek shipping magnate long suspected of involvement in the drug trade out of South America. Although we don't have confirmation of the yacht's arrival or whereabouts, we have reason to believe the yacht is the *Vulcania* and that Cosimo Benedetto is on board."

Tom perked up at the news. It could just be serendipity that Cosimo Benedetto would be in Rhodes at the same time as leaders of a Columbian drug cartel, and a day after a large shipment of cocaine went missing crossing the border into California, but given the Syndicate's expansive reach, Tom couldn't bet on it just being dumb luck. Rhodes isn't exactly the crossroads of the world, after all. Stock fraud, computer hacking, theft of rare metals, illegal arms sales, and drug trafficking. Was there any illicit activity Cosimo Benedetto wasn't involved in?

Still, Tom wanted to tread cautiously. "Tell me the evidence we have linking the Syndicate to the drug shipment."

"We don't have any yet, but I think it's a situation worth devoting resources to and pursuing."

Tom sighed. "I agree, but we need to be smart about deploying our assets. There are a lot of moving parts in this case, and we've already spread ourselves a bit thin on resources chasing a number of viable and potentially very fruitful leads. In this situation, the drugs are already missing and the most we're going to get is a meeting between Cosimo and known members of a drug cartel. That's hardly a smoking gun worthy of diverting scarce resources at this point."

What a spineless response from a windbag lawyer with no experience fighting crime, Agent Young thought. Unless evidence miraculously falls into the laps of these DOJ lawyers with a ribbon, bow, and instructions on how to use it, they don't understand what they're looking at. For twenty years he had built rock solid cases and got hundreds of scumbags off the streets with much less to go on than what he was bringing Tom, and yet he was still answering to this pretend cop who couldn't piece together a puzzle without watching a You-Tube video.

"With all due respect, if you allow me to finish, I'll give you my recommendation on how we should proceed, which just might answer the question of whether the Syndicate is behind the missing drug shipment."

Tom narrowed his eyes at hearing those trigger words again. He didn't say anything, though, and allowed the moment to pass.

"The FBI," Agent Young continued, "has an asset inside the Montavo drug operation. He's not an informant, but he's been providing us with bits of information for the last eight months or so, and much of it has checked out. I recommend we develop the asset into an informant and use him to get close to the Syndicate, maybe even get him inside and use the intelligence he gives us to bring down Benedetto and his entire organization."

Tom looked down at the papers on his desk and waited for more. Agent Young took the bait.

"The Bureau has done this a million times. We use a minnow to catch a shark. We'll nurture the asset, develop information that we'll threaten to use against him unless he agrees to cooperate with our investigation, and force him to flip against the Syndicate and testify in court. Depending on how close he gets and how deep he's in, we may even be able to catch Benedetto in the act on a wiretap incriminating himself. Then we can bring down the whole house of cards."

Bruce Young was proud of himself. This was a textbook plan right out of the FBI playbook, one that had been used with great success many times to bring down gangsters, drug dealers, and even a politician or two who were more interested in making a quick buck then serving their constituents.

He went on to recount the story of one of the biggest triumphs the FBI ever achieved. In the late nineteen seventies, FBI Agent Joseph Dominick Pistone took on the role of Donnie Brasco and infiltrated the Bonanno Crime Family in New York. Agent Young explained how the evidence Pistone collected, including hundreds of hours of wiretap conversations detailing the inner workings of the mafia, drug deals, and murders, led to over two hundred indictments and convictions of over one hundred made members of *La Cosa Nostra*. He envisioned a similar operation to take down Cosimo Benedetto and the Syndicate, but instead of having an FBI agent go undercover, he planned on developing an asset from the inside into an informant in order to decapitate the Syndicate and its leadership.

Tom sat there, eyes opened wide, with a bewildered look on his face. "So, if I understand you correctly, you want to use a gofer for a Colombian drug-cartel to infiltrate and take down the world's most wanted criminal, whose tentacles traverse the globe and is responsible for economic mayhem costing billions? Not to mention someone whose drug distribution network is responsible for killing tens of thousands of people a year, with the proceeds of those drug deals financing global terrorists? Is that right?" He shook his head. "Cosimo Benedetto is a master at avoiding electronic surveillance, and you even explained how his colossal yacht is an impenetrable fortress. I don't see how we'd get close enough to plant a bug or have this drug dealer wear a wire."

"I see you studied the notes you took during the initial briefing," Agent Young snapped, glaring at Tom. "Listen, I don't care if you're Cosimo Benedetto, Don Corleone, or Osama fucking bin Laden, we work our cases the same way every time, and a clandestine operation using a low-level informant is a proven and effective tool to take down a target." His voice rose in anger. "With all due respect to your comment about our asset being a gofer, may I remind you Donnie Brasco claimed to be a low-level jewel thief when he infiltrated the inner sanctum of the mafia and wound up taking down one of New York's five families.

"Maybe you never knew that since you weren't even born when the FBI, me included, made history ridding the streets of scum and getting shot at while doing our jobs." Agent Young Bruce was on a roll and spittle shot from his mouth. "When Madeline Kelly suggested that we look to develop an informant, you were all for it, but now that I'm recommending we do it, you think the idea sucks. The fact is you don't have the balls to take a gamble on my idea that just might blow the lid off the inner workings of the Syndicate."

He shot up from his chair with such force he almost kicked it backwards. "To educate you a little bit more, *Boss*, technology has come a long way since turncoats taped microphones to their hairy chests, or fake plumbers planted bugs in a target's home. For the last several years we've been working with MI 6 on Project Sana, a top-secret technology that uses a microchip surgically implanted below the scalp, behind the ear, and records everything the human ear hears."

Before Tom could respond, he continued his rant. "That's right, Mr. Executive Deputy Attorney General. Do you even know what micro stealth resin is? That's what the chip is encased in. It's biologically compatible with cells in the subdermal layer of the skin And it's completely fucking undetectable. No technology in the world is capable of ascertaining if someone has the chip implanted in them.

"Welcome to the twenty-first century Mr. Executive Deputy Attorney General. This isn't your grandfather's FBI. We've developed technology while you were living in your ivory tower at Harvard that would make your head spin. We can zero in on a pimple on the ass of a Taliban fighter sleeping under a fig tree halfway around the world based on satellite imagery. And an agent sitting behind a computer in Colorado using facial recognition software can scan millions of people in seconds during the annual Hajj pilgrimage in Mecca to identify a suspected suicide bomber with an IED strapped to his balls."

Tom took in a deep breath and waited a beat before speaking.

"Agent Young, I'm not here to get into a screaming match with you or to criticize you. I still think developing an informant could be a sound approach, I just don't think using a low-level drug dealer is the way to go about doing it at this time." He softened his voice and brought his hands together as if in prayer.

"Look, I appreciate what you've done to protect and defend America, and I respect your tenure with the Bureau. But the AG put me in charge of this investigation, and I'm going to conduct it my way, with due deliberation, while managing our resources and calculating the risk-reward ratio for every action we take. We need to slow down and continue building our case against the Syndicate before we start talking about using high tech eavesdropping gadgets."

If Tom was hoping to de-escalate the situation, he was mistaken. Agent Young leered at him with a venomous glare.

"You appreciate my service to my country? You respect my tenure with the Bureau? Who the fuck are you to appreciate anything I've done? You have no idea about the sacrifices I've made to get where I am today. While you were chasing tail in Harvard Square, I was getting shot for making America a safe place to live so one-percenters like you could keep your high-paying jobs sucking on the tit of corporate America. I didn't get to where I am today because of connections with power brokers, or because my boss paved a golden path for me and put in a good word with the AG."

Agent Young's words pierced through Tom like a hot dagger. His entire career Tom felt guilty that things always seemed to fall right in his lap. He was worried when he took this job that people would think he was hired as window-dressing, chosen solely because of his ivy league credentials or as payback for a political favor done along the way, especially since AG Mitchelson had been a partner at BCC.

He knew some thought he was too young and too green to be the Executive Deputy AG and to lead a group of experienced crime fighters trying to take down the world's most sophisticated criminal enterprise. But he had been assured, first by Ignatius and then by the AG himself, that it was his sharp legal mind, analytical ability, and sound judgment that were the reasons he'd been offered the DOJ job. They told him his background coming from outside the DOJ, and outside the Washington beltway, was an asset because he wouldn't be jaded by the old ways of doing things. He was expected to bring a fresh perspective and a new way of thinking about fighting crime, the world's second oldest profession behind crime itself. But Tom wasn't convinced.

Ever since he could remember he always questioned whether he was worthy of all the accolades he'd received and all the awards and successes he'd achieved in his life, and this time was no different. He'd risen to the second highest law enforcement job in the US Government, but Tom still worried he didn't have the chops to get the job done and didn't deserve the position he'd been handed, just like he doubted whether he deserved all his past achievements.

Now he was confronting his biggest fear. That people he'd been selected to lead would question his bona fides and challenge his judgment. But to back down now would play right into their hands. The question confronting Tom was whether Agent Young was waging a one-man insurrection, or was Tom facing an office-wide mutiny?

"Special Agent Young, maybe you're having a bad day, or maybe you didn't get a good night's sleep. Neither is an excuse for your insubordination and insolence, but at this point I'm not prepared to take this to the next level and formally reprimand you. Not yet. But let me tell you this: don't ever mistake my humility for lack of confidence or courage. I suggest you go back to your office and consider whether you want to be a part of this team, or whether you want to sit this one out. And while you're at it, I suggest you brush up on the DOJ handbook regarding your duty of professionalism and respect for the chain of command."

Agent Young moved sideways toward the door without averting his cold stare at Tom. He slowly reached for the handle while shaking his head and creasing his lips into an awkward grin.

"I'll think about it, and I'll let you know my decision, Mr. Berte. You have a good day now," he said as he walked out of Tom's office, the unconcealed smirk still painted on his face.

Tom followed Bruce with his eyes until he cleared the doorway. He exhaled a long breath and took a sip of *Yoo-hoo*. His adrenaline was pumping and he could feel sweat on his upper lip. At that moment he felt like he could sprint to the Washington Monument and back. He had his doubts when he took this job, but so many people were relying on him. He was torn between a lack of self-confidence and wanting to prove to his doubters he had what it took to succeed.

He turned and peered out the window. The sky was dark, and it looked like the skies would open up at any moment. He thought of Brooke. She was so proud of him. Then he thought of his mother. She was frightened that he'd trade in the comforts of BCC for the turmoil of Washington. Perhaps he should have questioned her more about her doubts. All he really wanted was for his mother to be proud of the man he'd become.

Tom also wondered about Agent Young, and whether he had the same lucky breaks Tom had growing up. Tom allowed his mind to drift. Was it normal for a man to doubt whether he was good enough to be a leader? Did experienced leaders doubt their ability to succeed? He immediately thought of Ignatius Balatoni. Did Ignatius ever doubt himself when he started BCC and built it into one of the most prestigious and richest law firms in the world?

It was times like these, when Tom was feeling sorry for himself, that he also thought of his father and wondered what kind of man he was, and what life would have been like if his dad was still alive.

Special Agent Bruce Young walked out of Main Justice and headed toward the National Mall. He needed to blow off steam. He was talking to himself. "Fuck Tom Berte. Fuck the DOJ. Fuck the FBI." For more than twenty years he'd devoted his life to the government, and what the hell did he have to show for it? He longed for the comfort of financial security and material trappings that had eluded him ever since his wife left him. He was practically broke and alone. He even dreaded his work, the one thing he used to care about.

Nobody knew this case better than he, and yet he was forced to take orders from that spoiled, naive prick. He reached into his inside jacket pocket and took out the flask. It still had some Southern Comfort left in it. He unscrewed the cap and took a long pull of the liquid gold. "Sweet honey," he said to himself. If he had another flask, he would have downed that one too. He was angry with his ex-wife, with his daughter whom he hadn't seen in almost a year, and with the hand he had been dealt. He was angling for a fight. "Fuck Tom Berte," he said to himself. "Today is not going to be my best day. My best is yet to come."

He picked up his pace, but his feet felt heavy, and he shuffled more than he walked. His head was in a fog. He hadn't noticed the two men following him since he left Main Justice. They were the same men who had camped out in front of his house for the last few weeks. He was oblivious that these men had put his life under a microscope, and that his unpaid child support and five figure tax liens had caught their attention.

He also had no idea they had discovered his secret obsession. The one that started with just some online videos but had grown over the years to encounters in parking lots, motels, and in the woods of Rock Creek Park on the outskirts of Washington. They got younger and younger over the years, just as he demanded. He knew he was risking his career and his freedom, but he couldn't stop. He craved their touch, their smell, and ever since his divorce and the loss of a real relationship with his daughter, he craved their attention and the way they made him feel. He was addicted to it. He convinced himself his training would allow him to avoid detection, and he would know if law enforcement was on to him. What he never counted on was that the men who were pursuing him would find out what he liked and who he liked doing it with before the police did. He had no idea the hunter had become the prey, and that he could be so easily exploited. In hindsight, he was an easy target.

The men caught up to him and tapped him on his shoulder. "Excuse us Mr. Young. Can we have a moment of your time? We could use your help."

16

Tom and Attorney General Mitchelson finished a two-hour marathon conference call with the ninety-three United States Attorneys right before noon. Tom had long heard the most dangerous place for a criminal was not prison but being caught between a prosecutor and a microphone. Prosecutors loved to call glitzy press conferences when indictments were returned to trumpet their tough-on-crime policies. Sure, convictions were nice, but the outcome was secondary since they didn't command the attention a splashy indictment did, complete with a perp walk and media blitz. Prosecutors would surround themselves with officials from all sorts of law enforcement agencies, and regale journalists with details of an exhaustive investigation conducted under their courageous leadership culminating in pre-dawn raids. Give prosecutors a microphone and a captive audience and they could drone on for hours. To Tom, US Attorneys were all wanna-be politicians, and the bloviating was on full display during the call.

Everyone thought Tom would become an Assistant US Attorney after his clerkship with the Chief Judge of the First Circuit. It was the customary path for graduates from top law schools, especially Harvard, on the career ladder toward higher office. But Tom wasn't interested. He wanted to go straight to a law firm. And not just any law firm. He wanted to practice at

BCC and would have happily stayed there his entire career had he not received an offer of a lifetime to join the Department of Justice.

As Tom entered his office, his phone rang. The last thing he wanted at that moment was to be on another call. He finally looked at the caller ID on the third ring. To his surprise he saw the name Ignatius Balatoni.

"Tom Berte," Tom said when he picked up the phone, unsure whether he'd hear Ignatius's voice or that of Arlene, his long-time secretary.

"Good afternoon, Mr. Executive Deputy Attorney General." It was the great Ignatius Balatoni himself.

Tom was happy to hear his voice.

"Mr. Balatoni, what a wonderful surprise. It's great to hear from you."

"You haven't called since you moved to Washington, which I can only imagine means you've been very busy, so I decided I'd call you. But I won't do it again if you address me as Mr. Balatoni. It's Ignatius, remember."

"Yes, of course. I apologize. I guess old habits die hard. Thank you for calling, and I'm so sorry I haven't called. I've been buried since my first day on the job, and then Brooke and I moved into our new apartment, and it's just been an incredibly busy few weeks."

"So I hear. Tell me, how is Brooke doing?"

"She's terrific, and she loves Washington. She found us a wonderful apartment about ten minutes from the DOJ building and we moved in this past weekend."

"I'm delighted to hear that, Thomas. And did she decide where she will work?"

"Yes, she is Managing Director at the Children's Advocacy Group which, as I'm sure you know, is affiliated with the Paulsboro Group. It's a non-profit umbrella organization that coordinates and distributes grant funds to children's organizations throughout the country. This is her second week there and she loves it."

"Splendid, just splendid. I had no doubt she would find a position that would be both fulfilling and rewarding. And your mother. How is she?"

The question set Tom on his heels. It was odd that Ignatius would inquire about her.

"She's doing well," he offered hesitantly. "I think she misses having Brooke and me visit her on weekends, but she's keeping herself busy with friends, and she still works a few days a week at the accounting firm she's worked at for many years. She's coming to visit us next week and will be spending a few days with us."

"Wonderful. I'm sure you and Brooke are excited to spend some time with her as well. And how are you?"

"It has certainly been intense. Whoever said government work is a piece of cake never worked at the Justice Department."

"I suppose that's true. I spoke with Attorney General Mitchelson yesterday and he shared with me that you have hit the ground running. He tells me you've taken the reins of the office and it's operating like clockwork. I'm elated by that."

Tom wasn't surprised Ignatius checked up on him, considering he recommended him for the job.

"Perhaps the AG is exaggerating a bit," Tom said, "but I have hit the ground running. It doesn't seem like I've stopped since I got here. There's so much to do and learn. But I'm very much enjoying it. For the most part."

"Ah, do I detect a note of regret in your voice?"

"No, no, I don't have any regrets. I'm thrilled to be here, but it's just...I guess it's the bureaucracy. I'm still getting used to it. The people here are generally wonderful. They're devoted public servants and consummate professionals who truly believe in the work we're doing and in protecting liberties and freedoms of all Americans, while adhering to the rule of law. But there are some people, or at least one person in particular, an FBI agent, who's been detailed to the team I'm leading, who's very protective of his territory and pushing back on my leadership in a way I didn't expect."

Ignatius let out a chuckle. "Ah, yes, turf warfare. It's as common in Washington DC as cherry blossoms in the spring. I understand it has replaced baseball as the national pastime within the beltway."

"I'm sure it's nothing new," Tom replied. "But I wonder sometimes if some of the people working here, who have spent their entire career in law enforcement and have decades of experience, resent taking direction from me. I mean, I have no experience, and yet I'm expected to call the shots and tell them what to do."

"Thomas, remember, you were selected precisely because of your leadership skills and because of your keen ability to analyze the law and build rock solid cases that will withstand scrutiny. Certainly, those in the FBI have experience fighting crime and gathering facts, but they don't have the specialized legal knowledge and training you have to piece together evidence and present it to a judge or a jury in a way that most guarantees success. Let them do the job they're best at, and you do the job you're best at."

"But that's just it. Am I the best person for this job? I've never had operational responsibility for criminal investigations before and I wonder if I'm in over my head. Maybe someone with a background in criminal law, or someone who trained with the FBI would have been a better choice."

"Oh, that's nonsense. You were hired because you have the skill set to succeed. And certainly the AG has seen it for himself the last few weeks. It's okay to cross-examine yourself about weighty decisions you will need to make in your job. But don't ever doubt your ability to *do* the job, or whether you are best qualified to do it. You undoubtedly are."

"Thank you. I appreciate the vote of confidence. I guess I just needed a pep talk. I'm sorry to bother you with this. How's the AMX trial going?"

"I wish I could tell you Troy is winning, but you'd know that isn't true. The plaintiffs rested their case last week, and AMX's first witness has been on the stand the last two days. Poor Troy has been battling one motion after another to exclude AMX's experts, and so far, he's succeeded in defeating the motions, but only barely. Troy expects the case will go to the jury in about two weeks."

"Please give him my best and wish him well for me."

"I certainly will." Ignatius cleared his throat. "What about your cases? I'm sure you must have some interesting matters you're working on. Is there anything you can share?"

Tom was surprised by Ignatius's question. Surely, Ignatius knew he couldn't disclose any details about the cases he was working on. Much of the work was top secret and strictly confidential. In fact, federal law prohibited him from revealing any material facts about pending investigations or cases within the Department of Justice. It was like disclosing non-public information about a stock. Strictly forbidden.

"The work is very interesting, but nothing stands out as worthy of sharing. It's all routine investigations and just a matter of following the play book, or at least as routine as I'm aware of since this is my first month on the job."

Ignatius was silent for a few seconds, and Tom wondered whether he was still on the line. Finally, Ignatius spoke up. "I know you must be very busy, so I won't keep you any longer. Remember to remain confident and follow your instincts. And stay true to yourself, and stay true to the principles that led you to becoming a lawyer. Don't be swayed by anything or anyone other than doing what's right. It is unfortunate, but sometimes it's those closest to you that can betray you and hurt you the most. You'll need to be on the lookout for that. The gravest threat often comes from those closest to you."

There was another pause, and Tom didn't hear any sounds.

"Ignatius, are you okay?"

After a few seconds Ignatius cleared his throat again and spoke up, but barely above a whisper. "Yes. I'm fine. Take care of yourself, Thomas. And please stay in touch."

Tom sat back in his chair, not knowing what to make of The Pope's comment. Was this another message, or perhaps a cryptic warning, like Tom thought Ignatius sent him during his farewell party? Tom considered the alternatives, but he kept coming back to the same conclusion. Ignatius Balatoni was eighty-eight years old and likely confronting his own mortality. Tom heard that when people reach a certain age, they begin to prepare for death. For some, this may mean a period of profound sentimentality as they wait at death's door. He wondered if Ignatius believed the end was near for him, which is why he was so easily overcome with emotion. He recalled Ignatius becoming visibly emotional the last two times they saw each other. Tom's eyes began to glisten. He didn't want to think of Ignatius's passing.

The satellite phone rang while Cosimo was in the *Vulcania's* gym with Fabiana. The vessel was still moored in Rhodes but would depart that evening for Monaco.

"Pronto," Cosimo said, answering the phone.

The caller hated having to call Cosimo with an update. After a long pause, he spoke hesitantly. "The *Ragazzo* suspects nothing, and he is settling into his new position."

He debated whether to continue. He was torn. He was fond of Tom and cared for him. Deep down he believed arranging for Tom to work at the DOJ was a mistake. But he had no choice. His hand had been forced. After a few seconds he spoke up again. "I still do not understand why you would give him the power to destroy you. You are putting him in a very difficult position."

Cosimo listened patiently but grew angry when his plan was questioned again. He saw no reason to explain himself. "Thank you for the update," he replied. "I know exactly what I'm doing. And you should continue to do exactly what you're told. I'm well aware of the position I've put the *Ragazzo* in. And I'm well aware of the position I've put *you* in. Do not concern yourself with him. He will do what is right when the time comes."

The caller placed the phone on the cradle. His hands were trembling. "What have I done? What have I done?" he asked himself in a faint voice. "God, please, have mercy on my soul and protect Thomas."

He let his head fall into his hands as tears streamed down his face.

17

The memo announcing Special Agent Bruce Young's bereavement leave was circulated via email the following morning. Bruce's mother passed away late last night, the memo said, after a long illness. He would be taking a two week leave of absence to plan the funeral and tend to certain unspecified family matters.

Perhaps his mother's failing health explained Agent Young's meltdown yesterday, Tom assumed. While he felt sorry for him, maybe time away from the office would do him good and clear his mind. Tom knew Agent Young was an important resource, and his experience and encyclopedic knowledge of the inner workings of organized crime would be crucial if they were going to bring down the Syndicate. Hopefully, in two weeks' time he'd be ready to return to wage war on America's enemies.

Tom's computer pinged. He had an urgent email. *Breaking News. Do you have a few minutes?*

It was from Rebecca Morse, a senior DOJ staff attorney working on the Eradicate AIFAM task force.

Yes, I'm available now, Tom typed quickly.

B right there, immediately flashed on Tom's screen.

Within seconds Tom heard a knock on his office door. He looked up to see Rebecca. Standing next to her was Attorney General Mitchelson.

Surprised, Tom stood up from his chair. "Mr. Attorney General. Rebecca. This must be really urgent."

"It is," AG Mitchelson said, walking into Tom's office. "A little over eighteen hours ago, computers in the office of the Department of Veterans Affairs were hacked. The VA's medical records and payment systems were compromised. The entire system was disabled, except for a single email received a few hours later. It was from the hackers who go by the name My Legacy. They threatened not only to destroy the electronic record system of the VA, but also claimed to have accessed the VA's cloud-based backup data network. What's worse, the hackers threatened to sell the names, addresses and social security numbers of this country's eighteen million plus veterans to the highest bidder."

"Holy shit. You've got to be kidding me? Let me guess," Tom added quickly. "Unless a ransom is paid."

"You got that right," Rebecca jumped in. "In fact, it is the biggest ransom demand we've ever seen. $500 million. Unless it was paid by midnight last night, My Legacy said it would destroy the VA's network and disclose the private information of America's veterans."

"So what happened?" Tom asked.

After a moment, the AG spoke up. "The US Government paid the ransom at 11:59 p.m. last night. All $500 million dollars."

"What the fuck?!" Tom blurted out and quickly regretted it.

The AG didn't seem to mind. "I wish it wasn't so." Mitchelson said, taking a seat in the chair opposite Tom's desk and turning to Rebecca.

"Despite assembling the best engineers and computer scientists from the NSA, CIA, and FBI, and even NASA, we've been unable to track the location of the hackers," Rebecca said. "We traced the attack to servers in Israel, but from there the trail went cold and we hit dead ends everywhere we looked."

"I thought the US Government doesn't give in to terrorists' demands and doesn't pay ransom," Tom said to no one in particular.

"That's been the policy of the United States for as long as I can remember," AG Mitchelson said, "at least with respect to traditional terrorist activity of hijackings and kidnappings. But cyber terrorism is different.

Especially when the victims are more than eighteen million veterans who turn out to vote on election day." AG Mitchelson shifted uncomfortably in his chair and fidgeted with his tie.

"Not paying the ransom would be like playing with fire. No one in public office would risk that. President Ferguson was briefed on the matter at 9:00 p.m. last night and she consulted with the Speaker of the House and minority leader, as well as leaders in the Senate. Everyone agreed the risk to veterans, and embarrassment to the nation, was too great to refuse the hackers' demands. President Ferguson authorized the Treasury Department to follow the hacker's instructions and $500 million was wired to several numbered accounts in overseas banks." AG Mitchelson sat back, looking dejected.

For a split-second Tom wondered why he hadn't been read in on the incident last night when it happened. He still had a lot to learn about the DOJ's internal politics.

"The wire transfers vanished the second they were made," said Rebecca. "We were prepared to trace them and follow the money trail, but they literally disappeared. $500 million dollars vanished into thin air."

"That's the same M.O. used by the Syndicate in their pump and dump schemes," Tom said almost reflexively. "Do you think Cosimo Benedetto is behind this attack?"

"That's exactly what we think," AG Mitchelson responded. "The hackers sent an email to the VA after the funds were wired. They said they did this because of unending wars the United States started, instigated, or financed around the world. They said they would ensure the ransom money goes directly to benefit veterans instead of paying for the overbloated bureaucracy of the US Government. We've since intercepted communications in the Middle East suggesting the hackers are associated with the Syndicate. Rebecca will give you the details. Can you believe the balls on these motherfuckers?"

AG Mitchelson caught himself and apologized to Rebecca.

"No need to apologize, sir. I've been around here long enough to have seen a lot of balls," Rebecca said, trying to lighten the mood just a bit.

The AG didn't skip a beat and turned toward Tom. "If we're right, then

Cosimo Benedetto just committed one of the largest cyber-attacks in history, leaving behind nothing but digital pixie dust and the government scurrying like a blind cat, while he professes to be playing Robinhood."

Tom, who had been standing, allowed himself to fall back in his chair. From his crash course on the history of the mafia in the last few weeks he had learned that *La Cosa Nostra* often justified its killings, thefts, and extortion by claiming they were benefiting society and realigning wealth. Taking from the undeserving rich and giving to the under-served poor. He learned that was the rationale used by the Sicilian bandit, Salvatore Giuliano, who, after the Allied Invasion of Sicily in 1943, took to a life of crime, stealing from wealthy Sicilian land barons to feed poor Sicilian workers. Even in the United States, the romantic view of mafia lore was that it protected blue collar workers against harsh treatment by big business. It was no coincidence that labor unions in America became powerful when the American mafia was at its strongest.

But at that moment, motivation and justification were beside the point. The only thing that mattered was stopping Cosimo Benedetto.

"Tom," Mitchelson said. "I assured President Ferguson we will get Benedetto and the Syndicate. All of the resources of the United States Government and of our law enforcement partners around the world are at your disposal. Whatever you require. All you need to do is let me know and President Ferguson will authorize it. We're all counting on you. I know you won't let us down," the Attorney General said as he stood up.

"Sir, I gave you my word when I accepted this position that I would do everything possible to protect the interests of this country," Tom said as he stood tall as if he were about to salute his general. "I intend to deliver on that promise."

"Thank you, Tom. Give 'em hell." AG Mitchelson said as he rose and headed for the door.

Rebecca said she would get Tom a memo on the hacking incident, or something to that effect, but Tom wasn't listening anymore. AG Mitchelson's words still hung in the air. The President of the United States and the entire law enforcement community were counting on C. Thomas Berte to bring down the world's most wanted organized crime figure. Six weeks ago,

Tom was sitting second chair at the trial of a serial toxic manufacturer, preparing cross examination outlines, and taking notes. How do you go from that to an international crime fighter, Tom wondered. Even Harvard Law School hadn't prepared him for this challenge.

He needed a distraction. He wanted to be with Brooke. He phoned her and invited her to dinner that evening. A date night.

"I would love that, honey. Where do you want to go?" asked Brooke.

"I don't know. Let's walk around Georgetown and we'll find a quiet, out of the way place where we can just talk and laugh."

"Are you okay? You sound kind of down."

"Yeah, I'm fine. It's just this job. It's such a pressure cooker. It's nonstop. A colleague and I are locked in a power struggle at the office. And, I didn't mention this last night, but Ignatius Balatoni called me yesterday and I'm afraid his age may be catching up with him. He sounded weak. And he became emotional again toward the end of our call. I'm worried about him."

"I know you are. I know how much he means to you. Without him you wouldn't be where you are today."

Tom wondered whether he'd be better off being anywhere but where he was right now.

"Yeah, I guess. I'll meet you on the corner of Wisconsin and M at seven. Love you, sweetie."

"I love you, too."

Just as Tom hung up, his phone rang again. The name on the caller ID read "Lindsey Crutcher, UK Serious Frauds Office."

"Hello, Lindsay. That was quick. Did you find something more on CNB Limited?"

"Indeed we have, Tom. The account numbers on the copy of the wire transfer you sent me correspond to a series of numbered accounts maintained at a small private bank in Birmingham, in central England, in the name of Duce International LTD., headquartered in Gibraltar. Duce is a subsidiary of CNB Limited involved in the offshore on-line gaming industry and it appears to be quite profitable. So much so that in 2018, Duce International wired over $400 million dollars to an Italian company for an almost three-hundred-meter yacht christened the *M/Y Vulcania*. Duce is definitely linked to Cosimo Benedetto."

"Nice work, Lindsay."

Tom immediately thought back to the briefing Special Agent Bruce Young gave on his first day at the DOJ. He remembered that Cosimo used several aliases. The name Duce rang a bell. Tom made a mental note to go over his notes from that meeting.

"Don't congratulate us just yet," Lindsay said. "We have a lot more digging to do and are reviewing financial transactions and data for CNB, Duce, and several other entities going back multiple years. It will take us some time, but I hope to have more to report in a few days. In the meantime, we've uncovered something else I thought might interest you."

"Don't keep me in suspense, what is it?"

"It appears Duce International has in the past listed the London Office of BCC as its attorneys. In fact, we were able to find the original Certificate of Incorporation for Duce. It was issued by Companies House in 2008 showing Jacob Cartel of BCC as the company's incorporator. That information was removed from the file in 2009 and replaced with a foreign listed agent. Quite a coincidence that BCC somehow factors into your investigation of the Syndicate, isn't it?"

It took Tom a minute to process the information. "Yes, it certainly is. That's very interesting. Please let me know what else you find. I have another call coming in. Thanks. Speak with you in a few days," Tom said as he abruptly hung up.

Tom didn't have another call. He just needed time to collect his thoughts. Jacob Cartel formed Duce International in 2008? The same company which partially financed the fortress-like yacht Cosimo Benedetto was sailing on at that very moment? Unconnected to the information Tom learned a few days earlier about BCC's representation of Cambridge Logistics until right before it was identified in one of the largest pump and dump schemes ever perpetrated, this latest information might not be important. But taken together, BCC's close relationship to Cosimo Benedetto and the Syndicate was becoming suspicious and troublesome. By 2008, Jacob Cartel, a senior partner and one of BCC's founders, would have been in his eighties, Tom figured. He wouldn't have been undertaking such menial tasks as forming companies for his clients. Unless they were a very special client.

Tom didn't know what it all meant, but he had a feeling it wasn't good. He turned to his computer and started typing.

What he soon learned would shake him to his core.

18

Tom typed "Jacob Cartel plane crash" in the search engine. Within seconds, dozens of results appeared on his computer screen.

According to news articles Tom pulled up, Cartel was on an overseas business trip in March 2009 when the accident occurred. He'd flown from New York to Vienna and then on to Nicosia, Cyprus. For such a small country, Tom had heard a lot about Cyprus in the last few weeks, he thought. Based on what he'd read, after the fall of the Soviet bloc at the dawn of the 1990s, scores of wealthy Russian oligarchs and their patrons parked millions of Russian Rubles, most of it acquired by questionable means, in Cypriot banks. As a result, the Cypriot economy flourished in the late 1990s and early 2000s, with Cyprus becoming a popular destination for foreign corporate headquarters. At least on paper.

Jacob Cartel went to Cyprus to meet with a group of Russians who were interested in financing oil drilling operations off the coast of Africa. After spending several days in Cyprus, he was set to fly from Nicosia to Vienna on March 18, 2009, bound for his return trip to New York. Right before he boarded a private jet, a Falcon 2000X leased by his client and registered to a company headquartered in Moldavia, the flight path was changed due to severe storms in the northern Mediterranean.

The jet took off from Nicosia and landed a few minutes later in Limassol, Cyprus, where the Russians disembarked. When the jet took off again, Jacob Cartel was the only passenger on board heading for Vienna. But the jet never made it. According to the investigative report detailed in one of the articles, somewhere over the Mediterranean the plane lost altitude and began a nosedive lasting more than thirty seconds. The jet exploded in the twilight sky, raining fragments of charred metal and human tissue into the abyss below. Jacob Cartel's body was pulverized in the massive explosion.

Sailors on ships in the Mediterranean said they saw what they believed to be a parachute deploy moments before the plane exploded, but one was never found. Rumors swirled the pilot ejected from the plane, but those rumors were never confirmed.

The jet's manufacturer and its registered owner paid the Cartel family millions of dollars to compensate for Jacob's untimely death, and no lawsuit was ever filed, said one of the articles.

Official government inquiries in Italy, Cyprus, and France, where the Falcon 2000X jet was assembled, all pointed to catastrophic engine failure as the cause of the crash, resulting from a faulty hose connection that allowed fuel to penetrate the engine seals and turbo valves and ignite instantly. Three other Falcon 2000X jets suffered the same fate in the early 2000s, leading Messault Corporation, the jet's manufacturer, to finally pull the plane from the market in 2010.

Tom clicked on other articles. One said that BCC's partners and attorneys mourned the loss of their colleague and firm co-founder by shutting all of BCC's offices across the globe for two days in late March 2009. They also set up a scholarship fund at Yale Law School in memory of Cartel. From that time onward, in each of BCC's twenty-two offices worldwide, a conference room was designated as the Jacob Cartel Memorial Conference Room, which by edict of Ignatius Balatoni, was to be used only for ceremonial purposes and to celebrate major milestones.

Toward the bottom of one article, Tom saw a photo of Cartel and a link to his obituary. Ignatius and Cartel met at Yale, the obituary said. In addition to being best friends and graduating first and second in their class, they became family. The year after graduating Yale, Ignatius married Jacob's sister, Helen, something Tom never knew. Ignatius and Jacob were also hired by the same Justice of the US Supreme Court as law clerks, and both were later sworn in on the same day as Assistant United States Attorneys in the Southern District of New York.

Tom scrolled down and found an article entitled a "Brief History of the World's Most Powerful Law Firm." He read that Cartel headed the firm's financial operations since the firm's founding in 1960. It was apparently a rough start for BCC. But as the economy rebounded in the mid-1960s, and manufacturing started to boom in the United States and Europe, the little firm began gaining traction. By 1966, BCC had ballooned from three attorneys to twenty-five and outgrew its cramped space on West 34th Street. It moved to larger offices in a building on the corner of Wall Street and Broadway, and soon earned the reputation as a top white shoe Wall Street firm. By the 1970's, BCC's client roster included more than half of the country's largest and most successful corporations, including household names like Ford, E.I. Dupont, Bethlehem Steel, CBS, and the Firestone Tire and Rubber Company.

In 1986 the firm moved to midtown as more and more clients moved uptown from Wall Street. BCC continued its steady rise when, in 1989, retired Judge John Colin, the third named partner of BCC and a graduate of Fordham Law School, who was older than his co-founders, died after a long battle with lung cancer. Balatoni and Cartel were left in charge of the firm. Together they continued to grow BCC into one of the biggest, most respected, and most feared law firms in the world.

By the early 2000s, BCC's profits exploded, fueled by the dot com boom. In 2006, BCC took up residence on the fifty-sixth through sixty-fourth floors of the newly built Americenter Tower, a palatial edifice befitting BCC's preeminence, prestige, and power. Whether it was mergers and acquisitions, private equity financing, real estate, products liability, trademark and patents, bet the company litigation, or lobbying the Washington elite on behalf of its blue-chip clients' causes, BCC had experts among its army of lawyers, including professors, authors, former judges, three former governors, six former senators, a dozen or so former congressman, and a former vice president.

After 9/11, when other law firms were reeling and many laid off lawyers and shuttered departments and offices, BCC held its own and weathered the storm. But its period of fastest growth occurred during and immediately after the Great Recession of 2008 and 2009. While other firms shrank, BCC doubled in size and thrived. The article highlighted Ignatius Balatoni's steady leadership of the firm which not only allowed it to navigate those turbulent times, but to flourish and become the world's richest law firm.

As Tom kept reading, he vividly recalled being in college during the Great Recession and planning to attend law school, and he knew many law firms had dissolved during those troubled times. How BCC managed to stay in business was a huge mystery given its roster of clients, including some of Wall Street's biggest banks, mortgage finance providers, insurance companies, and other financial institutions, many of which went bankrupt from 2008 to 2010. Tom heard it was Balatoni's courageous actions that saved the firm from collapse.

But when he asked what Balatoni did to keep the firm afloat, he never got a straight answer. It's as if Ignatius Balatoni was imbued with otherworldly powers and miraculously willed the firm to survive and thrive, underscoring the appropriateness of his nickname, The Pope. BCC's revenue soared, and it grew bigger and more profitable with each passing year beginning in 2009. Its profits per partner, the benchmark by which every law firm is judged, increased by an eye-popping 55% from 2008 to 2013, with the firm reporting average profits per partner of more than five million dollars by 2015. But by then, Jacob Cartel was dead.

Tom sat back in his chair and thought how terrifying Jacob Cartel's last moments must have been. One moment he was a senior partner running the most prestigious law firm in the world, and the next he was likely holding on for dear life as the plane he was a passenger in plunged toward the Mediterranean before exploding.

Tom was curious about the registered owner of the jet. He picked up the phone and called Bill Schrager, a law school classmate who'd gone on to great fame and fortune as a personal injury lawyer. He was a fighter pilot in the air force before attending law school, continued to hold a pilot's license, and was an aviation history buff. He made millions going after Boeing on behalf of hundreds of families who lost loved ones in crashes involving the 737 Max airliner.

Tom found an article with a picture of the jet Jacob Cartel perished in. Clearly visible from the photo was the jet's registration number on the fuselage, right below the tail rudder. He sent the information to Schrager who called him back less than two hours later.

"I was able to locate the ownership information you're looking for on that Falcon 2000X jet. At the time of the crash in March 2009, it was registered to a company named Lugano Micro Technology, listed in the corporate registry of Moldavia. Lugano purchased the jet only three months before the crash from a sister corporation. The name of that company was Duce International, registered in Gibraltar. According to what my associate found, Duce is owned by an entity called CNB Limited."

Tom was stunned into silence.

"Tom, are you still there?" Schrager asked.

"Yeah...yeah, I'm...I'm here. Sorry about that. I think we may have a bad connection." Tom could feel blood rushing from his face and beads of cold sweat forming on his brow. "Thanks, Bill. This information is very useful. Let's get together the next time you're in DC."

Schrager started to say something, but Tom hung up. His heart pounded. He stared for what seemed like minutes at the photo of the jet that carried Jacob Cartel to his untimely death. A jet registered to a company ultimately owned by Cosimo Benedetto—the world's most wanted fugitive. And the man Tom was charged with capturing. Tom felt weak and unsteady.

The bile in his stomach inched toward his throat. He dry-heaved and knelt down close to the wastepaper basket next to his desk. Moments later his morning breakfast and the tuna sandwich he had for lunch, along with the *Yoo-hoo* he just drank, were involuntarily launched into the trash can. He was sweating but felt cold. His shirt stuck to his back. He gagged and retched up more vomit. The smell of acid stung his eyes. He wanted to crawl into a hole and stay there forever.

He looked at his watch. It was 6:05 pm. There was no way he could go to dinner with Brooke. Not after what he'd just learned. He still had to draft an important email, and then just wanted to go home and spend time with her. He picked up the phone.

"Brooke, is it okay if we order in tonight? I'm sorry about this, but it's been a rough afternoon, and I'm not feeling great."

"Oh, Tom, I thought something was wrong when you called me earlier.

I feel so bad for you. Yes, of course it's fine if we stay home. We can just veg out on the couch."

Grateful, Tom rushed to draft the email that had been weighing on him for several days.

Five thousand miles away, somewhere in the Mediterranean, Cosimo Benedetto saw the concern on Brooke's face and heard it in her voice. He also heard Tom's frightened voice. He had not yet been able to see much of Tom and Brooke in their apartment. They both left early for work and returned late, falling asleep as soon as they got home.

But tonight, Cosimo was looking forward to spending time with the young couple.

19

"Oh, honey, you don't look so good," Brooke said when Tom walked into their apartment. "How do you feel?"

"I don't know," Tom mumbled. "I've had a rough couple of days. Sorry about tonight, sweetie. I'm just too tired to go out. I need to spend a quiet night at home. With you. Is that okay?"

"Of course, don't be silly. I said it was fine. I ordered Thai food and it's in the kitchen. Are you hungry?"

"Not really. But you should eat if you are. I'm going to take a shower. I'll be out in a few minutes."

Brooke had never seen Tom like this. There were times when Tom was worked to the bone at BCC. He once stayed awake forty hours straight while working on a Supreme Court brief. Tom had also been on trial teams where he would barely get a few hours' sleep at night for months on end. The longest trial Tom worked on lasted twenty-three days. Between preparing for trial and writing post-trial motions, and spending every weekend at the office, Tom figured he'd worked a third of the year straight without a day off. He seemed to thrive on the excitement of trials and working on big cases. Lack of sleep didn't bother him. He was always cheery and ready to go.

But this was different. This time he looked haggard and drained. He'd broken his fifteen-minute gloom or glory rule. It was now all gloom all the time.

After Tom showered, he settled on the coach with Brooke, lying on his back with his head on Brooke's lap. The lights were turned low and Brooke muted the TV.

"Babe, what's going on? I've never seen you like this," Brooke whispered.

"It's this investigation I'm working on. It's a really big deal for the Department of Justice. There's this one FBI agent who's been a real douchebag and doesn't like that I'm in charge. And the AG said today he and President Ferguson are counting on me and my team to indict and convict the target."

"Get out! The President knows who you are? And she's counting on you? That's unbelievable." Brooke must have realized she was shouting because she softened her voice. "Sorry, honey. If anyone can do this, it's you. Devote as much time to it as you need."

"It's not the work I'm worried about," Tom said, looking up at the ceiling. "I've worked way harder on less important cases for worse clients. I know how important this is, and I want to see it through. The work I'm doing will benefit so many people and I'm so proud of what we're doing. I now know why people who work at the DOJ say it's the best job in the world. The work is so rewarding. And I love the people on my team. All of them except for the jerk FBI agent. They're committed to justice and to doing what's right. I'm in awe of them, and they inspire me to be a better lawyer.."

"OK, so don't let that one person bring you down. Can't you just reassign the agent?"

Tom didn't respond. He just lay there somber, staring into space.

"What is it? Why do you seem lost?" Brooke asked.

"Have you ever discovered something that just stunned you? I mean just threw you for a loop?"

Brooke thought about it for a moment. "No, I can't say that I have."

"You know I can't share any details with you about my work, but I've learned some information about BCC over the last few days, and if it's accurate, it's just shocking when you piece it all together. I still can't believe it's true."

"Is it related to the investigation?"

Tom winced. He wanted to share everything he knew, but he couldn't. His work was top secret, and he couldn't discuss it with anyone outside the DOJ.

"I know what you're trying to do," Tom said, a smile creasing his face. "You want to figure out who the bad guys are, just like you do when we watch crime shows."

Brooke giggled and brushed Tom's hair away from his forehead.

"It's just that I've revered BCC for as long as I can remember," Tom said. "Yeah, some of the lawyers there are full of themselves, and some are even assholes, but I never saw anyone do anything that was unethical or that crossed the line."

"And today that changed?"

"I don't know. Maybe. I still have a lot more questions than answers and I need to dig further. What I'd really like to do is speak with Ignatius about it. But I can't."

Brooke looked confused. "I thought you spoke with him yesterday?"

"I did. But it was after that call and then again today that I learned some of the most disturbing information. I don't know. Part of me is shocked and betrayed. And part of me is...scared."

"Scared of what? Maybe you should just ask Ignatius what you want to know."

"I'm actually afraid he might confirm my worst fears. When he called me yesterday he said that *it's those closest to you that can betray you and hurt you the most*. I have no idea if he was sending me a message or trying to warn me. Ignatius is one of the smartest people I know. But I'm starting to learn some things that worry me."

"Oh, honey. I'm sorry about this. But it sounds like you need to speak with him again and get answers to your questions. Knowing the truth will make you feel better."

The two remained quiet for a long time. "Ignatius also said something to me at my going away party. He said that if he had a son, he'd want him to be just like me. It was the second time he'd said that to me. Then he got teary eyed. I've been thinking about those words a lot recently. And about my father. I'd like to think my dad was like Ignatius. Respected. Courageous. Powerful. A man of integrity. Feared by some but loved by many. But now I wonder if I've been blinded or just disillusioned, and the truth is more...," Tom was searching for the right word. "More dark, more sinister."

His whole life Tom had imagined what his father was like. When other kids played ball with their dads or told stories of going fishing with their fathers, Tom would turn glum that his dad had died before he got to know him. And whenever something good happened to him, he caught himself wondering whether his father was watching over him from heaven and was proud of him. Tom often found himself asking whether he'd give up all the successes he'd had in life if it meant having his father by his side. He thought about that question again now. And just like the other times, Tom struggled with the answer, knowing he'd never have the opportunity to see his father again.

"Oh, honey, I wish I could help you with this. The worst experience with the kids I've worked with is when they realize someone they've trusted their whole life won't be there for them anymore. Like when they realize a parent is addicted to drugs or going to jail because they committed a crime. Their world is turned upside down. Suddenly the people they love, and the people they thought would protect them forever are gone. The kids can't help but feel alone and even abandoned."

"I know the feeling," Tom whispered. "I just need to find the truth."

"Maybe Ignatius wasn't talking about you," Brooke said as she gently stroked Tom's hair. "Maybe he was talking about his life and people close to him who hurt him."

"But why would he tell me that? None of this makes sense. That's what scares me the most. The unknown."

"You'll figure it out. You always do. And I'll be right there by your side. Always."

Tom sighed as he wondered whether Ignatius deserved sympathy as an innocent bystander to the relationship between Cosimo Benedetto and BCC, or if he should be eyed with suspicion. Within minutes he was sleeping. Brooke slowly slid off the coach and placed a pillow under his head.

She placed a blanket over him and kissed his cheek. "I love you," she whispered.

Cosimo sat in the still salon of the *Vulcania* watching the scene play out in front of him on the large flat screen TV. Although the enormous yacht was sailing at 22 knots, the vessel was steady. The iced amaretto in the small tumbler barely swayed.

Cosimo was disturbed by what he'd just witnessed. Tom was confused and frightened. That's not how Cosimo planned it. The old man had said too much. He was getting weaker with age and was far too emotional. Cosimo warned him to stay strong. He assured the old man that, in the end, his plan would succeed. All he had worked so hard to achieve, and all he had built, would be preserved. He would see to it that his legacy would endure.

The authorities would fail in their pursuit of him just as they had failed in the pursuit of their promise to the people they governed. Cosimo was sure of it. Governments no longer held true to the values that led to their formation: to serve and protect the people. They no longer existed to provide safety, ensure prosperity, and promote liberty and justice for *everyone*. Governments now ruled to ensure their own survival and to protect a select few at the expense of many. Why were some allowed to wallow in poverty and death, while others were showered with opportunities that guaranteed fame and fortune? Yes, it was true the only man Cosimo knew as his father broke the law to provide for himself and his family, but why did the Americans have to hunt him down and kill him like a caged animal in a farmhouse in the countryside while others who had done worse lived and prospered?

Why did governments treat the rich and powerful one way, while others were left to die, alone? Why was he forced to abandon everything and everyone he loved? Cosimo longed to stop the tyranny of governments and to right wrongs that caused so many to suffer, including himself. But what he wanted most was to reclaim the one thing he valued most in order to ensure his legacy would live on forever.

Tom was part of those plans, but the *Ragazzo*'s emotional state was now in question. Cosimo was growing concerned.

He needed Tom to see things more clearly, to see things his way. Soon Tom would have a choice to make, and his decision would determine both their fates.

20

The package arrived at the office of Resjudicata.com on New York's lower east side in an unmarked yellow envelope. Inside was a thumb drive with no markings and nothing else.

LaShandra Johnson had been at her desk since 8:00 a.m. that morning waiting for a senate staffer to return her call about a story Resjudicata.com was ready to publish concerning the CIA's covert support for insurgent groups in Myanmar. Before going public with its accusation that a particular senator accepted gifts in exchange for quietly pushing the CIA to arm those groups, Rejudicata.com wanted to give the senator in question an opportunity to offer his side of the story.

Resjudicata.com touted itself as an investigative news organization, dedicated to transparency and exposing corruption and injustice wherever it occurred. It was especially adept at informing the public what its elected officials were up to. Its bread and butter was publishing whistleblower accounts of public corruption, and it routinely disclosed documents and information that government officials tried hard to keep secret. It was Resjudicata.com that had blown the lid off the Flint, Michigan, water contamination scandal, and it was Resjudicata.com reporters, including LaShandra Johnson, who had investigated two congressmen accused of receiving bribes for voting in favor of the oil sands pipeline from Canada to southern Texas.

Resjudicata.com had surreptitiously obtained hidden video recordings of the congressmen meeting with representatives of the oil companies where they happily accepted two briefcases filled with cash. Days after the article and videos were posted on Resjudicata.com's website, the congressmen resigned in disgrace and were later indicted. As a result of its work exposing the congressmen's graft, Resjudicata.com received the prestigious Langley N. Baker award for excellence in journalism.

Resjudicata.com also exposed the relationship between Florida's Governor and one of his young staffers, and the abortion she received that he paid for, despite the Governor's professed pro-life stance. After spewing vile epithets against Resjudicata.com and threatening to sue for invasion of privacy and assorted other bogus claims, the Governor resigned in disgrace two weeks after the article was published. Still, some years later, he was working as a lobbyist in the Florida statehouse, profiting from his connections to his former colleagues.

LaShandra Johnson looked at her watch. It was 9:30 a.m. and Resjudicata.com was publishing the story about Myanmar at noon whether she received comment from the senator or not. Her information was rock solid, supported by multiple sources and documents secretly obtained from an "official" within the CIA. Although all she really expected was a curt "no comment," journalistic integrity required she request a comment before publishing.

LaShandra had been with Resjudicata.com for eleven years. She began working there after graduating from Columbia University's School of Journalism, and had risen to Managing Editor, the job she currently held. She was good at what she did, and actually believed people were entitled to know what their government was doing behind closed doors. LaShandra wasn't a socialist by any stretch, but she was concerned about the growing gap between rich and poor and was cynical about big corporations' wealth and power. They couldn't sustain their accumulation of power and money for as long as they had, she believed, without some official somewhere looking the other way.

LaShandra learned long ago that the rich don't get richer unless they're given opportunities the average Joe doesn't have. It was Resjudicata.com's job, and LaShandra's mission in particular, to shed light on the power wielded by the top one percent, and to expose connections between corporate America and the elites on one hand, and lax oversight by government regulators on the other.

With some time to kill, she looked down at the thumb drive that had arrived at her office earlier that morning in the yellow package. Resjudicata.com received dozens of unsolicited packages every week containing all sorts of nefarious allegations of conspiracies, dark money plots, Ponzi frauds, sexual dalliances by the rich and powerful, and get-rich-quick schemes that turn out to be con jobs targeting poor and marginalized communities. Occasionally an amateur sleuth would provide information about aliens and UFOs, alleged serial murderers, or sleeper terrorist cells just waiting for the green light to unleash their fire and fury. Ninety-nine percent of the information sent to Resjudicata.com turned out to be off-the-wall nonsense that wouldn't even make it onto the back page of the trashiest tabloid.

LaShandra decided to spend a few minutes checking out the thumb drive. Her laptop scanned the contents which displayed a list of thirteen files all containing the initials AMX. She clicked on the first file. It toggled to over two dozen sub folders containing documents about AMX Corporation. LaShandra remembered reading a blurb in her morning news feed about a trial in New York involving the company. She began skimming the materials. There were charts, graphs, reports and memos stamped "Highly Confidential" and "Attorneys' Eyes Only." The documents had numbers on the lower left-hand corner, and they looked to be sequentially numbered from 101456 to 103892. LaShandra randomly clicked on document 101982 and began reading. The report detailed the carcinogenic effects of a chemical called centuron. The report appeared to be old, and the type looked like it was from a dot matrix printer. LaShandra scanned the page to see if she could find a date. She clicked backwards to get to the first page of the report. "6/75" was type-written on the upper left-hand corner of the page. June 1975, LaShandra surmised. She kept reading. The author, Dr. James Gail, a scientist of some sort, was advocating for the removal of centuron from the market because studies showed it caused cancer.

LaShandra picked up her smartphone and typed in AMX and centuron in the search box. Within seconds article after article popped up about the AMX trial. The company was being sued in a mass tort action by hundreds of plaintiffs claiming their cancer and other ailments were caused by centuron, the chemical manufactured by AMX, used in cleaning solutions the company sold. According to the articles, hundreds if not thousands of people had died from exposure to centuron. The plaintiffs claimed AMX knew the chemical caused cancer when they began manufacturing it as a degreaser for industrial use in the 1970s but hid the information from state and federal regulators. The article noted that depending on the outcome, scores of other plaintiffs across the country would be lined up to sue AMX claiming damages for their injuries. And family members would be suing to recover damages for loved ones who succumbed to the poisonous chemical and wouldn't be coming home. Unnamed sources quoted in the articles speculated the federal government was investigating AMX and that criminal indictments could soon follow.

LaShandra turned back to the document on her laptop. If 6/75 was indeed a date, then in June 1975, Dr. Gail concluded centuron was a carcinogen that should be banned based on the results of studies he conducted.

LaShandra clicked on other files. One particular file caught her attention. It was named "Economic advantages of centuron." She clicked on it. It was a memo authored by a Dr. Wilhelm Sonnenschein who held a master's in business economics and a Ph.D. in macroeconomics from MIT. The legend across the top of the memo read in bold print: "PRIVILEGED AND CONFIDENTIAL. ATTORNEY CLIENT COMMUNICATION." It was dated January 1976. The first paragraph indicated Dr. Sonnenschein wrote the report in response to a request by the law Firm of Rednick & Grimes in Cleveland to provide "an analysis of the projected economic feasibility of using the chemical centuron in manufactured products versus the potential, but yet unknown, risks associated with the chemical." Dr. Sonnenschein included an Executive Summary at the beginning of the report. LaShandra smiled. She wouldn't need to read the entire document, just the first four pages. She read quickly.

Dr. Sonnenschein concluded that AMX could realize enormous profits from sales of products containing centuron because no other product on the market matched its cleaning power. Multiple blind tests showed consumers would choose products containing centuron over other products. Based on Dr. Sonnenschein's analysis, AMX stood to make upwards of at least a hundred million dollars a year in profits. When LaShandra got to the last paragraph, she read it twice.

In view of studies the Company has conducted testing the effect of centuron on humans, which confirm the efficacy and safety of the chemical, there exists no impediment to the use of centuron as an ingredient in widely available commercial products.

The sentence contained a footnote. She scrolled down to it:

This author has not independently verified the results of the studies referenced above. The conclusion concerning the efficacy and safety of centuron is based on statements and representations made by representatives of AMX Corporation.

LaShandra clicked back to the report from Dr. Gail. She checked the date again. 6/75. She toggled to Dr. Sonnenschein's report. January 1976. If AMX knew as early as June 1975 that centuron caused cancer, why did Dr. Sonnenschein write six months later that AMX was claiming centuron was safe?

LaShandra kept clicking through other files containing names such as "Cancer and Centuron," "Centuron-the silent killer," and "The Truth About Centuron." An entire subfolder was entitled "Projected Economic Advantage and Nondisclosure." It contained several memos written by AMX's Vice President of Marketing at various times from 1977 to 1979. LaShandra selected a few of the memos and read through them. She couldn't believe what she was reading. Senior management of AMX in the late seventies was openly admitting the commercial success of AMX depended on concealing its suspected carcinogenic effects. The company was weighing the risk of cancer among centuron's users against the profits the company could earn from selling products containing the chemical. Several charts were included, entitled "Risk v. Reward." LaShandra quickly realized the charts compared the economic benefit of selling products containing centuron, against potential legal exposure and liability if death or illness resulted from its use. Other charts showed AMX's potential profits if it never disclosed to the public what it knew about centuron. The black line indicating profits steadily rose to the right until it literally went off the chart. The last article noted that centuron is used in at least a dozen cleaning products still sold today.

LaShandra kept clicking and reading. If this was all legitimate, the information would be explosive. For decades AMX knew, but concealed, that centuron was a silent killer.

She found another file named "Federal Grand Jury Evidence." Based on her prior work chasing crooked politicians and shady corporate executives, she knew grand jury minutes and the evidence considered by a grand jury are confidential, and it is against the law to disclose the information to the public. Yet here it was. All the evidence considered by the grand jury investigating AMX. The last document in the sub folder was marked "Sealed Indictment." Just two days earlier, the grand jury voted to indict AMX and its senior management on twelve counts including multiple counts of fraud, RICO violations, and lying to the FDA, EPA, FBI and other government agencies. The indictment was under seal and hadn't been publicly released.

Just as LaShandra was about to exit the sub folder, she noticed the asterisk. She scrolled down and began reading.

Important interests will be negatively impacted if the indictment against AMX Corporation is unsealed. If certain facts and evidence are revealed, several high-ranking members of the US Government will suffer embarrassment, at a minimum, while others may face civil and even criminal liability. Serious consideration must be given to suppressing the evidence and this indictment.

LaShandra's mind was racing. Who sent this to Resjudicata.com? What was the motive? Blackmail? Was he or she a whistleblower? Fame? Civic duty? Was this legitimate, and who was trying to conceal this damning information from the public? She looked for any evidence revealing the identity of the person who sent her the thumb drive.

The second to last file on the contents list might provide the answer, she thought. It was marked "personal communications of CTB." LaShandra opened the file. It contained various emails, letters and memos. She looked for a name, but all she could find were the initials CTB. One of the emails was named "To Whom It May Concern." She clicked on it. It appeared to be an email. No name was listed in the "To" box. LaShandra right clicked on the email and scrolled down to properties. It was written the day before, at 6:15 pm. She again began reading:

I can no longer remain silent and will not be part of an organized government effort to suppress the truth and hide information from the public. Since at least the mid to late 1970's, AMX Corporation knew the chemical it created in 1973, centuron, was a carcinogen that caused cancer and other serious ailments. Study after study the company commissioned confirmed these results. Yet the product worked so well in many daily applications, including in household cleaners, that no other product on the market came close to centuron's effectiveness as a cleaning agent. The company also commissioned economic studies forecasting profits that could be earned by selling products containing centuron. Those studies showed that in the first 10 years of sales, profits would exceed $15 billion dollars. In twenty years, profits would grow to $150 billion dollars. The company weighed the risks and rewards. It decided to bury the scientific evidence of the known health risks of centuron. It calculated that even if those health risks were uncovered many years later, the profits AMX earned in the interim would more than offset damages it may be held liable to pay to victims and their lawyers who sued the company. Beginning in the early 1980's, AMX corporation began mass producing multiple products containing centuron. It is estimated more than a million people have been injured or died worldwide from cancers and other conditions linked to their use of and exposure to centuron. The truth must finally come out.

The federal government has been investigating AMX Corporation for several years. It has uncovered incontrovertible evidence, including internal memos and studies commissioned by AMX itself, concerning the devastating health effects of exposure to centuron. The evidence was finally presented to a grand jury empaneled beginning four months ago. The grand jury considered all the evidence and returned a twelve-count indictment against AMX Corporation and its senior management. The indictment has been sealed, and I fear it may never see the light of day. There are forces within the US Government and Department of Justice who will go to great lengths to protect AMX. It took four months to present evidence to the grand jury because certain senior officials at the DOJ equivocated and raised one roadblock after another. AMX has powerful lobbyists on its side, as well as several members of Congress. It has also bought the protection of senior officials in the DOJ and White House. The only hope that the truth about AMX and centuron will be revealed to the public is if Resjudicata.com publishes this information.

LaShandra read the last paragraph of the email twice to make sure she hadn't missed anything:

I am a senior official in the Department of Justice and work closely with the Attorney General of the United States and senior members of the Administration. I previously worked in private practice and was one of several attorneys representing AMX Corporation for the past several years. I am fully aware that by disclosing this information to Resjudicata.com, I am violating my oath to protect the confidences of my clients, including my former client AMX, and my current client, the United States of America. But disbarment is a small price to pay to reveal the truth to the American people about centuron and the cover-up taking place at this moment at the highest levels of the US Government. In due time, I will reveal my identity. Until then, you are at liberty to disclose the contents of this thumb drive. And the contents of this email.

The email was signed "CTB."

21

Tom felt rested when he woke up the next morning. He'd been on an emotional roller coaster the last twenty-four hours. But he'd finally slept well. He was looking forward to his mother's visit next week. He hadn't seen her since he and Brooke left New York a month ago. Although he called her several times a week, he missed her and looked forward to her visit.

Sharing the little he did with Brooke last night also made him feel better. She was the one person he felt completely at ease with. He could talk to her about anything, and he loved bouncing ideas off her. He trusted her judgment, which was always spot on. He regretted that his work and his obligation to never reveal his client's confidences prevented him from sharing more. How ironic, Tom thought, the attorney-client privilege was intended to promote truth and candor, yet it resulted in him keeping secrets from the one person he trusted and loved as much as anyone.

Tom was still stunned at the vast reaches of the Syndicate's empire and the scale of Cosimo's crimes, everything from narcotics distribution to securities fraud to computer hacking and data theft for profit, not to mention scores of other smaller crimes that made the more brazen ones possible. He still couldn't wrap his head around the fact that the plane carrying Jacob Cartel to his untimely death was owned by Cosimo and the Syndicate. If what Tom suspected was true, that BCC helped facilitate the Syndicate's activities, and maybe was even complicit in its crimes, then the whole firm was in jeopardy. Tom worried about Ignatius. How much did he know? Did he willingly conspire with Cosimo and the Syndicate? Tom remembered what Brooke said to him last night: that Ignatius's comment about threats might be more about him than a warning to Tom. Time will tell, he thought. He was somber and pensive. There was so much he still didn't know and much work to do.

The meeting of the strike team began promptly at 11:00 a.m.

"Before we get started, any update on how Special Agent Bruce Young is faring in light of his mother's passing?" Tom asked. "Has anyone spoken with him?"

No one responded.

"I guess he's still in mourning. No doubt he has a lot of details to tend to and sort through. Ok, let's get going. Who wants to start?"

Madeline Kelly spoke up. "As you know, we've been working our sources in Afghanistan to try to develop additional information on the Syndicate and possibly find a mole. Earlier this week, our agents on the ground, working closely with the CIA, picked up communications between leaders of two Taliban factions of Afghani tribal forces who until that point had been engaged in a costly and deadly battle against each other. But this time the two men were discussing a truce, apparently negotiated by quote "the Sicilian."

"It appears the Syndicate is arranging to storm a warehouse in central Kabul," Madeline continued, "where vast amounts of munitions, weaponry, and equipment were stored by the US military, remnants of the war on terror. The Syndicate plans to sell the goods on the black market. But it also plans to share some of the spoils with the warring factions so long as the two sides cease fighting each other and instead join forces to protect the Syndicate's interests in the region, including the poppy fields and several processing depots the Syndicate is building. With the crackdown on illegal narcotics in the US, the Syndicate believes it will be easier to process poppy into heroin in that part of the world to supply new markets in Central Asia."

"So Cosimo's drug trade is actually leading to peace in Afghanistan," Tom said sarcastically, "will wonders never cease to amaze me. I guess we can add theft of US property to the long list of crimes we're going to charge Cosimo with.

Good job, Madeline. Keep us posted on the details of the theft and make sure our people and the CIA are in position to record and trace the munitions and weapons. With any luck, we can make arrests and convince some of those charged to give up more information about Cosimo and the Syndicate."

"Got it, Tom. We're on it," Madeline said.

"Who's next?" Tom asked.

Special Agent Ann Leonardo raised her hand. "At your request, a forensic team of FBI agents and I have been reviewing thousands of hours of audiotape and videotape the FBI collected over the last forty years on the Gambino crime family and their activities. The quality of much of the information has degraded over time, but with new technology we have, we've been able to digitize the information which allows for audio and video search capabilities. We've reviewed information through early 1993, when Cosimo Benedetto was deported to Italy. So far, we haven't uncovered any evidence linking Cosimo directly to any crimes, although we have been able to solve a few mysteries about the Gambino's involvement in a number of hits in Florida and New York around that time that no one had previously pieced together." Ann continued her briefing. "In the 1980s, the Gambinos imported a number of young men known as "zips" from the countryside around Palermo to act as enforcers. But the men spoke in their native Sicilian dialect which was indecipherable to FBI translators working on the case at the time. It sounded like gibberish to them, nothing like the Italian language itself. After Gotti was convicted in 1992, the FBI didn't bother to go back over the old tapes with the new translation software it now has. Coincidentally, my parents are both from Sicily and immigrated to America before I was born. Although my parents assimilated as well as they could into American society, they still spoke their native Sicilian dialect at home and with our extended family. During holidays and special events, barely a word of English was spoken, or Italian for that matter. It was all Sicilian. Anyway, I've spoken the dialect my whole life, so I was able to understand the recorded conversations that were never transcribed before. As a result, I was able to fill in some of the gaps the Bureau missed during its investigation. Just a little trivia I'm sharing in case any of you are interested."

"Isn't that something," Tom said, genuinely interested in Ann's story. "The FBI, the most powerful federal investigatory agency of the most powerful nation on earth, failed to invest in adequate resources to translate what targets of their investigation were saying on wiretap. Can you imagine if you were with the FBI in the 1980s, Ann? The success you would have had back then would have been astounding. Please let us know if you come up with anything directly tied to Cosimo."

"Well, there is one thing," Ann said. "Based on the data in our files, conventional wisdom is that Cosimo has no descendants or other living blood-line relatives. But that may not, in fact, be the case. We listened to some audio recordings from late 1988 or early 1989. Date ranges are missing from the tapes and much of the audio is garbled, but there was quite a bit of chatter picked up around that time because John Gotti had been indicted for racketeering. The order went out for every Gambino capo and soldier to report to the Ravenite Social Club on Mulberry Street, the Gambino's headquarters in Little Italy, in the days and weeks following his arrest to show their allegiance to the Boss. In one recording, we picked up a conversation between two wiseguys saying "Nino" wasn't around because his *commare*, or girlfriend, had just given birth to Nino's child. In another recording inside the Ravenite itself, Gotti asks about Benedetto's whereabouts and why he hadn't shown up to pay his respects. Someone in the room responded that Nino just had a baby, and he should be excused, which Gotti accepted. Based on that evidence, we now believe Cosimo Benedetto fathered a child sometime in the late 1980s."

"Very interesting," Tom said. "All these years we never knew Cosimo had a family, until now. Although it may not amount to much, Ann, please have your agents check the birth records of every hospital in the New York area from 1988 to 1990. I'm curious to see what you can find."

"Okay, Tom," Ann said with a quizzical look on her face. From deciphering wiretap recordings to looking up birth records, Tom was prepared to leave no stone unturned to bring down the world's most wanted criminal.

By 1:00 p.m. everyone had given their report. Surprisingly, no one brought up BCC's connection to the Syndicate. Tom debated whether to mention it. He decided now was the right time.

"I'd like us to focus on the law firm of Balatoni, Cartel and Colin," Tom said. "I've looked at a number of documents we've collected suggesting a relationship between the firm and the Syndicate. My assistant will circulate those documents to you this afternoon." Pointing to Rebecca Morse, Tom asked her to take the lead looking into BCC. Rebecca was still investigating the hacking of the Department of Veterans Affairs, but he knew she could handle the additional assignment. Rebecca was smart and tough as nails, and he trusted she would thoroughly investigate BCC.

"It may just be that a firm as big as BCC, with as many attorneys as it has, simply crossed paths with the Syndicate," Tom said. "Given the Syndicate's tentacles reaching into so many industries and companies, some of which are presumably legitimate, it may not be unusual and maybe this will turn out to be a dead end." Tom was still holding out hope BCC's connections to the Syndicate were just run of the mill dealings on behalf of a client, albeit one involved in perpetrating heinous crimes on a global scale. "But if there's something more to it, we'll need to know," Tom quickly added.

Tom decided to leave out the part about Jacob Cartel's untimely death when a plane traced to a company ultimately owned by Cosimo Benedetto, and a BCC client, exploded over the Mediterranean. There would be time to dig further into that later.

"Madeline Kelly looked up from her notes. "Tom, didn't you work at that firm before you came to the DOJ?" she asked.

"Yes, I did. But that doesn't matter. We still need to investigate it."

Madeline looked like she wasn't done asking questions.

"And isn't that where Attorney General Mitchelson practiced before he became a Senator?" Madeline asked hesitantly. "Is he aware of the potential connection between BCC and the Syndicate?"

"Yes," Tom said. "The AG was a partner at BCC for over twenty years and left in 2000. I was still in grammar school at the time and we weren't running in the same circles yet." Everyone chuckled at Tom's attempt at humor. "And no, the Attorney General is not aware of BCC's potential involvement, and until we're able to remove the word *potential* from that statement, there's no need to brief him on this. But if that changes, then the whole dynamic changes. Thank you all for your time and attention this morning. Good work. See you next week," Tom said before returning to his office to make some calls.

The phone in LaShandra Johnson's office rang at exactly 2:00 p.m. The caller clicked on the voice distortion icon.

"Is this Ms. Johnson?"

"Yes, who's this?"

"I hope you've had an opportunity to look through the thumb drive delivered to your office this morning."

"Yes, I have. I found it very interesting."

"As I thought you would," said the caller. "If and when you publish the information, I will provide you with additional material. About AMX, but also other information the US Government is trying to hide. I have enough material to keep you very busy for a long time."

"I see," said LaShandra. "Of course, we need to verify the information before we publish something like this. Tell me, are you CTB?"

"I am," the caller said.

"Can we meet? In person? I want to vet the information you gave me," LaShandra said in hopes of keeping the caller on the line and talking.

"Not now. Perhaps after you publish the information I sent you."

"But how can I be sure the information is accurate and authentic? We need to conduct our diligence," LaShandra said.

"Resjudicata.com has five days to publish the information. All of it," the caller said sternly. "If you fail to do so, I will begin selectively leaking it, together with evidence that Resjudicata.com was aware of it but quashed the story, no doubt because it is in the pocket of dirty politicians and lobbyists trying to protect AMX. Now that's hardly a reputation Resjudicata.com will want, especially since it touts itself as the voice of the people and purveyor of truth without fear or favor. Isn't that so, Ms. Johnson?"

"Resorting to extortion won't get you very far," LaShandra retorted. "In any event, why do you need us? If you're so certain the information is authentic, why don't you disclose it yourself? Why do you need Resjudicata.com?"

"Legitimacy. Your organization has done a good job to this point building its credibility, no one will question the legitimacy of the information, or the motives of the whistleblower. And I assure you the information *is* authentic, Ms. Johnson," the caller said.

"What's in it for you? Surely you can seek protection under the whistleblower laws and make lots of money with the information you have."

"I seek neither fame nor fortune. I simply want the same thing you want. For the truth to come out."

"You say you want to uncover the truth, but then why are you hiding and why are you still at the DOJ?"

"Ms. Johnson. The US government as a whole, and the DOJ in particular, have suppressed more truths and trafficked in more lies in numbers far greater than the world's population. The longer I remain on the inside, the longer I can uncover those lies and expose more truths."

"But If we disclose the information you sent us, and eventually your identity, you won't be able to continue to gather additional information from the inside," LaShandra said.

"Let me worry about that. In the short time I've been here, I've already uncovered more secrets than you can imagine, and I intend to uncover more. In due course, I will disclose every last bit of information I've gathered. The way the government operates will change dramatically after I disclose all I know. I look forward to seeing the information published in five days, Ms. Johnson." The line went dead.

LaShandra exhaled. She doubted the caller was CTB, a high-ranking official in the Department of Justice willing to throw away his career exposing AMX Corporation. But that wasn't the point. If the information about AMX was legitimate, it was damning. AMX would wind up paying billions. Heads would roll all over Washington if officials in the White House and DOJ were trying to suppress the information, protect AMX, and keep the indictment under wraps. And Resjudicata.com and LaShandra Johnson would become the most famous names in journalism.

But what mattered most to LaShandra was truth and transparency. That's what motivated her. She could blow the lid off one of the biggest scandals of the century. She needed to report what she knew no matter who CTB was. But first she needed to verify it. She turned to her computer and began her search to corroborate the information CTB gave her.

Agent Bruce Young clutched the cell phone tightly as he drove toward Chesapeake Bay. The FBI would never know it was missing from its cache of thousands of phones, computers, tablets, listening devices, voice distortion magnets, and every other high tech electronic gadgetry imaginable. The waste within the Bureau was sinful. He parked in the rest area near the drawbridge. He hadn't had a drink since early that morning and craved one badly.

He walked briskly up the incline of the bridge roadway. He was holding the phone in his right hand which was in his jacket pocket. He looked around to see if any bike riders or sightseers were out for a stroll. He saw no one. He was alone. It was cold and misty, and fog was rolling in across the bay. He glanced around one more time. When he was sure no one was looking, he took his hand, still clutching the phone, slowly out of his jacket pocket and as he turned, he allowed the phone to slip out, falling three hundred feet to the Chesapeake Bay below. "Fuck CTB," he said as he scowled, turned, and walked back toward his car.

Bruce Young had run out of things to lose in his life. He easily gave in to the demands of the men who approached him on the National Mall. Sure, he didn't want his secrets exposed for everyone to see, especially his daughter, but he would have done this, or something similar, anyway even without their sorry-ass threats—or the money.

"Who cares that those bastards think they're blackmailing me," he muttered to himself. "I'm finally getting what I deserve."

22

The *Vulcania* was still two days away from arriving in Port Hercules in Monaco. Cosimo was spending more and more time secluded in his gold-emblazoned study receiving encrypted updates from his network of hackers, bag men, dope dealers, and strongmen around the globe. Given the Syndicate's vast operations, and depending on the time zone the *Vulcania* was sailing in, Cosimo could be working at any hour of the day or night, fielding calls on the *Vulcania's* secure satellite telephone system or participating in virtual video meetings from the yacht's state of the art boardroom replete with electronic digital encryption technology. Cosimo was certain his communications were completely untraceable. Cosimo and Totto Nessa liked to joke that the person capable of intercepting communications from the *Vulcania* hadn't been born yet. The fact was, Cosimo thrived on secrecy and lived for outwitting those who spent their waking hours trying to capture him.

When he wasn't working, Cosimo made it a point to spend time with Fabiana. When the *Vulcania* was anchored, they'd snorkel, dive, or ride one of the three Polaris 2500 wave runners stored below deck in the garage. Fabiana and Cosimo dined together most evenings, unless Cosimo had a business meeting or call to tend to.

And after a long day plying his trade, after Fabiana retired for night,

Cosimo enjoyed playing *briscola* or *scopa* with Totto and Gino Terranova in the *Vulcania's* parlor. Occasionally the captain would join them when the radar indicated a clear radius of at least two hundred nautical kilometers.

Monaco was a favorite destination for Gino Terranova. A few years ago, he became enamored with a young Brazilian card dealer at the Monte Carlo Bay Casino. He arranged for her to live in a stylish apartment overlooking the harbor and provided her a nice monthly stipend to live comfortably during the long stretches when Gino was away. Of course, Gino also provided round the clock security for the young woman, even though she wasn't aware of it, to ward off any unsuspecting gigolos who might misinterpret her unwed status as a sign she was single and available. Gino's men intervened on more than one occasion to educate a few unsuspecting playboys whose libido emboldened them to make inappropriate requests of the young woman. It was unfortunate, but each year, it seemed, Monaco saw a number of male gamblers go missing, never to be heard from again. On occasion, Gino would arrange for the woman to travel to stay with him on the *Vulcania* for a few days, but only when Cosimo was ashore.

But there were no late-night parlor room card games tonight. The *Vulcania* was sailing full steam to Port Hercules and a rendezvous with destiny.

At a little past midnight, Cosimo dialed the old man's phone from his study. It was just past 6:00 p.m. in New York, and the old man would likely be sitting down for dinner in his palazzo penthouse overlooking Central Park. Gerard, the old man's butler, answered. He kindly asked Cosimo to hold the line while he brought the phone into the dining room.

"I need to speak with you about the *Ragazzo*," Cosimo said brusquely.

"Of course, Nino."

The old man sat motionless. Blood drained from his face, and he suddenly lost his appetite. A chill came over him. He hated speaking to Cosimo and did so only out of necessity and obligation. He would not be where he was today, not after the debacle of 2008 and 2009, were it not for Cosimo. The old man was overwrought with guilt and regret, but at the time he had little choice. He either accepted Cosimo's offer to salvage his reputation, his legacy, the firm he built, and the livelihood of thousands who depended on it, or lose everything he worked so hard to achieve causing so many to lose so much.

Although his downfall was not his fault, he would live with the regret of his resurrection for the rest of his life.

"Ignazio, when we spoke the other day, you did not mention you called the *Ragazzo*." Cosimo's voice was sharp. The line was crystal clear, and he could hear the old man wheezing on the other end.

"What's the matter with you? Waxing on about threats from those closest to him and becoming overcome with emotion? You're filling his head with confusion and making him doubt how strong he is and how powerful he can be. This is not what we discussed, and it is not part of my plan. Your role was to provide opportunities for the *Ragazzo* and allow him to be seated in a position of authority so when the time comes, he can learn the truth and provide the assistance that will be needed."

How did Cosimo learn what he and Tom spoke about? The possibilities were endless, and each one scared Ignatius beyond words.

"Nino, I did not betray any of your confidences," Ignatius said, his voice trembling. He was uneasy and uncertain about what to say next. "Perhaps I let my emotions get the best of me when I spoke with him, but I am certain he does not suspect a thing. Please understand I would never harm the *Ragazzo*. Or you. I care deeply for him. As if he were my own son."

Cosimo exploded in rage. "He is not your son! Do you hear me? He is not your son! Don't ever say that again. Your job is over, Ignazio. You did what you needed to do when you delivered him to the Justice Department. Now you will stand down. I prohibit you from having any further contact with him, do you understand me?"

Ignatius's chest tightened and he was having difficulty breathing. His head began to throb.

"Please don't shut me out, Cosimo. Please," Ignatius said in desperation. "Please…"

"You will cease any further communications with the *Ragazzo*. Do you understand me? I will give you instructions if and when I need your assistance again. Until then you are to do nothing. If you betray me Ignazio, so help me God, I will tear it all down. Every last bank account, financial arrangement, and client, and I will destroy you, worse than the fate that had befallen you when I came to your rescue. Do I make myself clear?"

"Yes, yes. I understand," he mumbled, his voice terror-stricken.

Cosimo slammed the phone on the desk.

The pain started in Ignatius's chest and radiated toward his left arm. He felt his airway constrict. A tingling sensation overcame him, and his vision blurred and narrowed. The room began to spin. The throbbing in his head was too much. He pushed away dishes set on the table in front of him and knocked over the glasses. Red wine spilled onto the white linen tablecloth. He dropped the phone which hit the marble floor with a thud.

Gerard ran into the dining room when he heard glass breaking. There he saw Ignatius slumped back in his chair, his eyes closed, gasping for air.

Fabiana walked by the study as she took a break from reading in her stateroom when she heard Cosimo yelling. She gently knocked on the gold-plated door and waited for Cosimo to answer. When he did, she turned the handle and nudged open the heavy ornate door. Cosimo was sitting behind his marble desk, his chair angled toward the glass wall as he stared into darkness.

"Darling, is everything okay?" Fabiana said softly.

"Yes, yes, bella. Why are you still awake?" Cosimo walked over to her and gently swept the bangs away from her forehead. At forty-five, with dark hair that naturally curled at the ends, Fabiana looked as radiant and beautiful as she did when she was twenty-five.

"I heard you yelling. I was concerned," Fabiana said as she gently kissed Cosimo's neck.

"Everything is fine, bella. It's just some business, that's all," he whispered, hoping to change the subject.

"Is it about the young man?"

Cosimo looked away.

"Why is he so important to you, darling?"

Cosimo had never lied to Fabiana in all the years they'd been together. He didn't have to. She was always discreet and never questioned him about his business. Surely, she knew his immense wealth did not come from legitimate interests. But she didn't care. She loved him deeply and trusted him completely. She also knew he was smart and driven to leave a legacy. But for whom?

Cosimo looked at Fabiana and smiled. He gently stroked her face. "Bella, all I do and all I have is for the future. One day, when the time is right, you will come to understand and accept. I promise you. But until that time, please, I ask for your compassion and your support."

She nuzzled her head into his neck as he turned his gaze toward the sea. One day the past will be the present, and those living in the present will be given the opportunity to protect the future, he thought.

Hours later, as Fabiana lay in bed sleeping, Cosimo finalized his plans for the future.

23

The drive back to Capitol Heights, Maryland, took longer than Agent Young expected. Traffic was backed up on the interstate for ten miles east of Baltimore. He tried shortcuts and drove the back roads in hopes of getting home quicker. He needed a drink badly.

His 2001 Toyota Camry had over 200,000 miles on it, and enough dents, dings, and scratches to make it look like it had been through a demolition derby. It was brown once, but after several cheap paint jobs to patch over mismatched parts, it was now a multi-colored hue of creams, browns and taupe. In the end, it just looked like shit. Literally. The agents in his office nicknamed the car the Pilgrim because it looked old enough to have been driven by the Pilgrims when they arrived at Plymouth Rock. But since he was woefully behind on child support payments, buying a new car, or even a newer one, wasn't in the cards. Not until the money came in. He had big plans for how to spend the small fortune he expected to receive as soon as Resjudicata.com published the materials about AMX. He'd already picked out the young companions he liked from photos he saw online.

When he arrived at his apartment, he poured a whiskey up to the rim of his favorite coffee mug. He missed the liquid nourishment, and these days he craved it more and more. He was hungry, but the whiskey would tide him over until he finished the next project on his to do list. He sat at his computer and connected to the Bureau's intranet via the encrypted link he wasn't supposed to have. After two decades in the Bureau, he had become somewhat of a tech wizard and knew his way around the Bureau's antiquated computer system. The databases he was going to access tonight, however, were off limits even to high-ranking agents such as himself.

Once he connected to the FBI internal network, he remotely interfaced with Tom's desktop computer. He accessed the imaging program tab from the system's drop-down menu and typed in the encrypted password. He then reconfigured the computer's internal timing and dating sequence to make it appear as though Tom had accessed the DOJ's and FBI's investigative file database approximately twenty-four hours earlier. After a few more clicks of the mouse, the download icon, a red and blue hourglass, appeared on his screen. It took several minutes for the virtual sand to pour through the pinched center all the way to the bottom.

The screen went blank except for the message in the lower left-hand corner that read *AMX Corporation data duplication complete.*

Because Tom could not be involved in the DOJ's investigation of AMX given his prior representation of the company, ethical guidelines required him to be walled off from all matters concerning the company. The Chinese wall, as lawyers called it, meant Tom couldn't access any files concerning AMX. So Agent Young first had to reprogram Tom's computer to make it look like Tom breached the ethical wall, and then he accessed the imaging program to make it appear as if Tom downloaded the same material that was delivered to Resjudicata.com's office earlier that morning. Among the downloaded documents were confidential internal AMX files the FBI obtained from an informant who was a former AMX executive, as well as minutes of the secret grand jury empaneled months earlier to hear evidence of fraud and other federal crimes against AMX.

With the download finished, Agent Young turned his attention to his second task.

He accessed the FBI's OPR incident database and typed in multi-factor authentication codes on separate screens. The Bureau's OPR, or Office of Professional Responsibility, was the internal affairs unit for both the FBI and DOJ. It was Big Brother in action. If the Bureau even had a whiff of suspected corruption or graft within the ranks of the DOJ or FBI, special agents from the OPR division would covertly descend on the suspected official and perform a detailed proctological exam, analyzing every orifice, electronic communication, bank account, and daily movements of not only the official in question but relatives within four degrees of lineage. The analysis was so thorough and aggressive that traces of dirt could be found on even the cleanest, most ethical employee.

OPR's success rate was the stuff of legend. It was OPR that was responsible for rooting out one of the most infamously corrupt FBI agents, John Connelly, a fellow Agent Young crossed paths with several years earlier. Connolly was the FBI handler for Whitey Bulger, the notorious Boston crime boss who went on the lam for sixteen years after Connolly tipped him off about an impending indictment. Connolly was eventually convicted of racketeering and spent time in federal prison and was later convicted of murder in Florida and sentenced to another forty years in state prison. The work done by OPR was so robust, it contributed to the historically low levels of corruption within the FBI and DOJ.

Agent Young's connections within OPR over the years came in handy, and from time to time he utilized his resources to nudge a colleague or two into seeing things a certain way. But he had never engaged in such a brazen attempt to hack into the OPR database to incriminate someone and destroy their career. He thought long and hard about his plan before putting it in motion. But what choice did he have?

The men who approached him on the bridge made it clear that if he didn't comply, his career would be destroyed, and he'd probably spend the rest of his life behind bars without the one thing he craved more than liquor. He knew full well men convicted of doing the things he liked to do didn't fare well in prison. The silver lining was that going along with the instructions he'd been given meant he wouldn't have to play second fiddle any longer to inexperienced paper pushers like Tom Berte.

Perhaps one day he would regret his actions. But not today. Today he gladly gave in to the demands made of him.

With a few more clicks of the mouse, the OPR database recorded that approximately twenty-four hours earlier the office desktop of C. Thomas Berte, Executive Deputy Attorney General of the United States, downloaded and duplicated 64 gigabytes of information concerning the AMX investigation onto a flash drive, in contravention of DOJ's operating protocols which prohibited anyone, from the most junior clerk to the Attorney General himself, from accessing confidential information and downloading it for export outside the DOJ's computer network.

Before he returned to his whiskey, he had to execute the final step in his plan.

He disconnected from the OPR's incident database and accessed the Wells Fargo internal computer banking network. Agent Young had been a lead investigator on the task force that investigated Wells Fargo when the bank was charged with fraudulently opening bank accounts in the names of unsuspecting customers so bank employees could earn credits and pocket higher bonuses. He managed to retain quite a bit of knowledge from that investigation, including the passcodes to open new accounts. After a few seconds, and with a few clicks of the keyboard, C. Thomas and Brooke Berte were now owners of an account at Wells Fargo Bank containing three quarters of a million dollars apparently transferred from a left-wing nonprofit organization named the First Freedom Foundation backed by leading social liberals and think tanks. And after surreptitiously accessing the Bureau's facial recognition database and remotely connecting to Wells Fargo's internal closed circuit video system, the bank's security logs would record a gentleman who looked exactly like Tom Berte walk into a Wells Fargo branch to access the account containing the ill-gotten gains.

Based on the electronic breadcrumbs he left behind, it wouldn't take OPR long after it noticed the surreptitious digital copying of AMX files from Tom's desktop to discover an electronic wire transfer into the account that occurred at precisely the moment the AMX files were downloaded. A few hours later, OPR would have possession of the video confirming Tom's withdrawal of funds from his newly opened bank account. Mission accomplished.

With his work done for the night, FBI Special Agent Bruce Young fell into his recliner, almost spilling his whiskey. He took a long gulp and savored it. He closed his eyes and mumbled the words he'd said to himself so often the past few days. "Fuck you C. Thomas Berte." After a second gulp he said, "Today wasn't even my best day."

24

The awesome powers of the Department of Justice can get things done very quickly when both the President of the United States and Attorney General push to bring down the world's most notorious criminal. One day after the strike team met to plot the course of its investigation, Tom received a link with an encrypted password that unlocked thousands of pages of reports and spreadsheets detailing the financial dealings of three companies with suspected ties to the Syndicate and BCC: CNB Limited, Cambridge Logistics, and Duce International,

Rebecca Morse was scheduled to brief Tom at 2:00 p.m., but he wanted to get a head start reviewing the documents himself in hopes of finding a smoking gun.

As he prepared to review the documents, he contemplated the enormity of the investigation he was charged with leading. Its outcome could potentially affect millions of people. Indicting and convicting Cosimo Benedetto would restore faith in the integrity of the securities markets, prevent confidential information from being accessed and held for ransom at the whim of the Syndicate, and help rid the country of the ravages of fentanyl and other illegal drugs that killed thousands each year. It wasn't lost on Tom that he was undertaking the most important and impactful work he would likely ever perform in his career.

The data was mind numbing. Each of the companies affiliated with the Syndicate generated hundreds of millions in revenues annually and spent the money twice as fast. Money was transferred to banks around the globe and to dozens of other entities. The Syndicate owned interests in everything from car dealerships on the West Coast of the US, casinos in Macau, oil fields in Kuwait, diamond mines in South Africa, and a fleet of cargo ships in Greece and China.

Companies with names like Synergy Industries, Talcon Mining, and Galactica Shipping received tens of millions of dollars monthly and wired tens of millions out. Then there were transfers of at least a million dollars each month to an entity called Legacy Fund, but with no indication where Legacy Fund was located or what it did. Other transfers of larger amounts were made to unknown accounts in unnamed countries. Vast amounts of money seemingly disappeared without a trace.

The spreadsheets also revealed something else. Every month various companies and funds associated with the Syndicate paid millions to BCC. Some of the payments referenced BCC invoice numbers, others had no reference at all. Some payments were as large as several million dollars every month for years, while others were as small as ten thousand dollars paid on a one-time basis. Whatever BCC's involvement with the Syndicate, one thing was certain: companies affiliated with the Syndicate paid the firm vast amounts of money.

Tom sat back and wondered how it was possible that BCC earned as much as it did from the Syndicate, and yet he had never heard of any of the Syndicate-affiliated clients when he worked at the firm. He rationalized it would have been difficult for him to have known of the firm's relationship with the Syndicate given that BCC has tens of thousands of clients worldwide. It's not like the companies advertised their connection with one another or to Cosimo.

After a few hours of analyzing, cross-referencing, and reading hundreds of pages of financial statements, emails, and bank statements, Tom felt numb. His head ached and his eyesight was blurry. Fortunately for his sake, Rebecca arrived for their meeting right on time.

"We've learned information that confirms your suspicions regarding BCC's relationship to the Syndicate," Rebecca said as soon as she entered

Tom's office. She was all business, just like he preferred. "And it's a disturbing picture."

"Do tell," he said, eager to understand BCC's role in the Syndicate's criminal enterprise.

"By all accounts, BCC was a highly successful and stable law firm throughout the 1990s and early 2000s," Rebecca began. "Its profits per partner grew each year as did the firm's revenue and the number of matters it was retained to handle. By 2005, the firm represented over half of the Fortune 500 companies and more than a third of the world's largest banks, brokerage houses, and insurance companies. The firm liked to flaunt its hard-earned success. It owned apartments in Washington, DC, New York, San Francisco, Chicago and in every other major city in which it had an office. Twenty-eight apartments in all by my count.

"It also owned real estate in Telluride, Colorado, the Swiss Alps, Grand Cayman, Bermuda, and on the Greek island of Santorini. These weren't rinky-dink time shares, but rather grand homes or condos with a full-time staff. BCC's partners also liked to travel in style. The firm owned a majority interest in at least four jets and a large yacht anchored in the Caymans. It paid for memberships in at least a dozen exclusive golf clubs around the world. The firm's partners and associates were paid extremely well, and the firm always topped the list of firms doling out the highest bonuses to its associates every year. But I assume you already knew the last part," Rebecca said with a wry smile.

Tom sat there expressionless.

"With all that money flowing and work pouring in, no one asked questions, and I assume everyone expected the good times would continue forever." Rebecca paused to take a sip of water.

"I know most of the information you mentioned, except maybe for the jets and the yacht in the Caymans. Do you have anything else?" Tom asked anxiously.

"I sure do," Rebecca continued. "The good times ended in 2008, threatening the firm's financial stability and its very existence. You'll recall the housing crisis and subprime mortgage debacle that occurred at that time. Well, it hit BCC hard. When the financial markets seized up in 2008 and 2009, BCC's revenues took a huge hit. By the middle of 2009, revenue was down over 50%, with fully a third of BCC's clients in free fall and defaulting on their obligations to the firm. Several of its largest clients, including brokerage houses and other financial institutions, went belly-up and declared bankruptcy, and the annual billables from those clients disappeared."

Rebecca opened a folder and flipped through some charts.

"While revenues were down sharply, BCC's expenses continued to rise. Mortgages on the properties it owned, which were at low adjustable rates, all reset at much higher rates at the end of 2008 due to the credit crunch. Banks started demanding that BCC increase repayments on its credit lines, and additional credit was impossible to get.

"With business drying up, BCC was left with dozens of guaranteed payouts to its top attorneys. Those without contracts that still had business headed for the nearest exit. That put in jeopardy covenants the firm had in place with several banks that provided it with credit. If more partners withdrew from the partnership, the firm would be in breach and the banks would have immediately called in the firm's loans. BCC was in dire financial straits and its survivability was very much in doubt. It began to default on rent payments on its offices around the world, and invoices from vendors and suppliers went unpaid and began to pile up. In short, BCC was desperate for cash. Could you imagine the stress Ignatius Balatoni and Jacob Cartel must have been under at that time, not to mention the embarrassment and humiliation at having the firm they built into a legal powerhouse be on the verge of collapse?" Rebecca asked.

"How could this be?" Tom said, surprised. "I was in college in 2008, but I knew about BCC, and I kept an eye on the legal market since I was considering going to law school. I never read anything about BCC being on the balls of its ass. By all accounts it was thriving, and we all know in the years after the recession BCC grew exponentially, with profits per partner increasing by double digits year over year. What happened?"

"BCC found its white knight, or at least its knight in shining armor, that's what happened," Rebecca said confidently. "His name was Cosimo Nino Benedetto."

"How?" Although he asked the question, Tom was afraid the answer would confirm his worst fears.

"From what we've learned over the past couple of days, Ignatius Balatoni, a.k.a. The Pope, made a pact with the devil. The nature and extent of his personal relationship with Cosimo Benedetto is still unclear, but what is clear is that Benedetto began bankrolling BCC's operations beginning in 2008 and it continues today. Some of the work BCC has done for Benedetto and the Syndicate was and is legitimate and above board, setting up corporations, handling deals, and representing them in litigation. But that was small potatoes. The revenue from that work, while significant, could hardly keep BCC afloat the way it was accustomed to operating. So BCC began providing additional services to the Syndicate. Illegal services."

Tom shook his head and closed his eyes.

"BCC assists with the creation of bogus bank accounts, sets up dummy shell corporations, exploits currency and securities markets with phony filings with the SEC and other regulatory agencies, and facilitates the laundering of billions in drug proceeds. It conceals the tracks of computer hackers, and gladly engages in scorched-earth litigation tactics, what it calls lawfare, against anyone who threatens the Syndicate's interests. BCC essentially is in-house counsel to the largest and most prolific criminal organization in the world and in doing so is an accessory to the Syndicate's crimes. Like a modern-day Bonnie and Clyde. Ignatius Balatoni and BCC, and Cosimo Benedetto and the Syndicate, are part of a criminal conspiracy. Everything else BCC does, all the work it performs for its legitimate clients, is just a facade to cover up the firm's illegal activities on behalf of the Syndicate," Rebecca stopped to let Tom absorb her presentation.

The words hung in the air while the two sat in silence. Even with the evidence before him, Tom was still having a hard time wrapping his head around what he'd just heard. He tried to collect his thoughts. BCC was revered. It had blue-chip clients and the finest attorneys among its ranks. Law books were full of landmark cases where BCC lawyers made precedent and improved the lives of scores of people, promoted individual liberty, and protected the rights of individuals and corporations.

Sure, from time to time, its clients' names appeared on police blotters or topped the list of worst companies to work for, but every law firm had clients like that. The US judicial system, the envy of the world, was designed with the ideal that attorneys should take on the representation of even the least deserving client. BCC was no different, but the vast majority of its clients were legitimate and happily paid top dollar for the advice and counsel of the best lawyers in the world.

All of that meant nothing at the moment. Based on the evidence Rebecca and her team uncovered, BCC was, at a minimum, a co-conspirator with Cosimo Benedetto and the Syndicate in the commission of some of the most reprehensible crimes ever prosecuted.

"Jacob Cartel," Tom mumbled. "He died in an accident involving a plane owned by the Syndicate in 2009. We need to investigate the crash and find out what happened."

"We already know. It was no accident," Rebecca offered matter of factly. Jacob and Ignatius clashed over Ignatius's plan to save BCC. Jacob wanted no part of Cosimo Benedetto's rescue of the firm and was prepared to walk away from BCC and allow it to collapse. But Ignatius's ego couldn't let that happen.

"Cosimo told Ignatius he would take care of convincing Jacob to see things his way. Ignatius gave in. When Jacob resisted and threatened to go to the authorities, Cosimo had him killed and covered his tracks to make it look like a leak in a fuel line caused the jet to explode. Cosimo Benedetto murdered Jacob Cartel."

Tom inhaled sharply. His eyes blurred again. He was living a nightmare. He'd never been through an out of body experience before, but he was sure he was having one now. Time was suspended. It was as if someone else was hearing the history of BCC's involvement with the Syndicate. It was the story of another law firm, not the one he had worked for.

"How good is your information, Rebecca? Are you certain?" Tom asked even though he knew deep down the information was rock solid.

"Do you know Kevin Pillsbury?" Rebecca asked.

The name rang a bell, but he wasn't certain where he'd heard it. He shook his head in confusion.

"Pillsbury was the deputy chief financial officer of BCC until last month when he quietly resigned. The reason for his untimely resignation was his arrest by the FBI a few days earlier for trafficking in stolen art. He'd made himself a nice little nest egg by the time the FBI caught wind of what he'd been up to. Facing years in prison and millions in restitution and fines,

Pillsbury made the FBI an offer it didn't see coming. He began spilling the beans on BCC.

"He gave us emails, memos, bank statements, audio recordings. Everything we could ask for, and more than we really need, to prove BCC's complicity with the Syndicate. He had it all stashed away in case one day he needed to barter for his freedom. When that day came, he was ready to make a deal. And a sweet deal is what he got in return. Pretty smart on his part. We have BCC dead to rights, Tom. We could get a grand jury to indict the firm today if we wanted to, along with Balatoni and the entire executive committee."

Tom was stunned by the confluence of events, including the investigative powers of the FBI and DOJ, and the raw good luck it took to gather evidence proving BCC's role in the Syndicate. He was thinking through the possibilities.

"We're not going to do that just yet," Tom said, his mind racing. "Not until we have enough evidence to take down Cosimo and the Syndicate for all the crimes they've committed. At that point, we'll shut BCC down. For good."

Rebecca smiled in agreement.

Tom knew he had to speak with Ignatius. But he needed to be smart about approaching him. He needed a plan. The warnings he received last time the two spoke began to make sense now. When Ignatius said it's those closest to you who can be most dangerous and betray you, he must have been talking about Cosimo Benedetto. When Ignatius warned Tom about learning things in this job that would shake his confidence and trust in his fellow man, he must have been talking about Tom discovering BCC's crimes at the hand of the Syndicate.

But some things were still murky and made no sense. What was the nature of Ignatius's relationship with Cosimo that caused Ignatius to sell his soul in exchange for financial salvation? And why did Ignatius recommend Tom for the position at DOJ? Surely, he knew Tom would find out BCC was nothing more than a shill for Cosimo and the Syndicate to conceal its global criminal empire. There had to be more to the story. It gnawed at him that he was missing something, but he had no idea what it was.

Rebecca broke the silence and interrupted Tom's thoughts.

"The good news is the Attorney General left BCC well ahead of the firm becoming aligned with Cosimo, and so his reputation is intact. He has nothing to worry about," Rebecca said, sighing in relief.

Tom and Rebecca looked at each other and both knew exactly what the other was thinking. C. Thomas Berte, on the other hand, worked at the firm when BCC had a front row seat as an accomplice to the Syndicate's most brazen crimes. Tom knew it would be an uphill climb to convince people he was completely in the dark about BCC's activities.

But he had no idea how steep the climb was about to get.

25

The AMX trial was in its fourth month, and Troy McDonald had just informed Judge Simons the defense would finally rest its case the following week. Judge Simons had been on the bench for thirty-nine years and had taken senior status ten years ago. That meant he pretty much got to choose which cases he presided over, and he was able to keep his docket relatively light. He no longer presided over criminal cases, and he turned down small negligence cases. He preferred to spend his time on weightier matters involving constitutional issues or questions of novel statutory interpretation of federal statutes. But what he enjoyed most was presiding over complex and lengthy civil trials. The longer the better, and the more at stake the more interesting he found them.

Over the years, Judge Simons developed a reputation for having extreme patience and for being a lawyer's judge. He allowed lawyers who appeared before him to try their cases without much interference. As long as they were experienced enough to know what they were doing in front of a jury, he allowed them to try the case at their pace. If a lawyer wanted to call more witnesses, so be it. If a lawyer wanted to make objections during cross-examination, he'd allow the lawyer the time to make as full and complete an argument as she could. He believed experienced trial lawyers could sense when juries wanted more or had enough, and he wasn't going to call the shots for them.

Some judges liked to showboat in the courtroom, letting everyone know they were the smartest lawyer in the room, and they ruled with an iron gavel and ran a tight ship. But not Judge Simons. He considered himself an umpire. He would rule when he had to, and otherwise remain silent and on the sideline. That was why trial lawyers loved trying cases before him. They knew the jury would be deciding their client's fate, for better or for worse, without Judge Simons' thumb on the scale.

Troy was examining one of six expert witnesses AMX was parading in front of the jury to dispute the toxic effect of centuron. This particular expert, who turned eighty-nine today, was explaining a study he conducted with lab rats that had been given low doses of centuron over a five-month period. The study showed 82.5 percent of the rats had no noticeable reaction to centuron, and only 2.7 percent developed some minor skin rashes or eye irritations.

"And Dr. Stanton, how would you characterize the 2.7 percent rate of rashes and irritations compared to the percentage of the population that develop such conditions idiopathically, meaning without a cause?"

It was a question Troy and Dr. Stanton had rehearsed a million times. It was an important point that could help AMX's case. If centuron only caused rashes and irritations at a rate no more frequent than occurred naturally, then centuron may be harmless after all. The question called for Dr. Stanton to testify that idiopathic rashes and irritations occurred in about 2.5 percent of the population, which was statistically insignificant compared to the 2.7 percent of lab rats who suffered similar reactions after exposure to centuron. But Dr. Stanton muffed the answer.

First, he said he couldn't hear the question. When Troy repeated it, he said he didn't understand the question. When Troy rephrased the question, Dr. Stanton said he wasn't sure he could give a reliable answer because unexplained rashes and irritations occur so frequently that most of the time they aren't diagnosed or reported, so any statistical sampling would be skewed by the unreported cases.

What the hell was Stanton doing? Generally steady and unflappable, Troy was losing patience. The jury started to squirm. The plaintiffs' lawyers sensed another strategic pitfall for AMX and were secretly pumping their fists under the table. Troy decided to change tactics. He would get back to that question after a break.

He was most worried about Dr. Stanton's cross examination. If he couldn't handle the softball questions they'd rehearsed in advance, how would he hold up to cross examination by the vultures sitting on the other side of the well in the courtroom? AMX's Achilles heel was that Dr. Stanton only tested centuron at low levels. Had he conducted the study using higher levels of centuron, the same levels at which plaintiffs claimed they had been exposed over several years, the results would look much different. It was a calculated risk AMX was willing to take because it had no other scientific data to challenge plaintiffs' experts. AMX decided to go with what it had because the alternative was to go with nothing at all.

Troy looked at his watch. It was 4:40 p.m. The courtroom was stifling. The rays of the late summer sun stabbed through the window blinds behind the jury box. The temperature in the courtroom steadily climbed throughout the day, and it was no match for the decades-old air conditioning system that groaned and clanked just to keep the packed room at a balmy seventy-nine degrees. Judge Simons was often heard saying the hardest part of his job was staying awake after lunch. Today was no different, even for everyone else in the courtroom it seemed.

By 4:45 p.m., Judge Simons put Troy and Dr. Stanton out of their shared misery. At a break in the questioning, the Judge said he needed to prepare for a conference call in another matter and adjourned testimony for the day. He told the jury and lawyers he would see them promptly at 9:00 a.m. the following morning and reminded them not to discuss the case with anyone.

Troy gave a quick glance of relief to the young blond female associate who had replaced Tom on the case. He saved his more hostile comments directed to Dr. Stanton for when they returned to the office.

As the courtroom emptied and Troy was collecting his notes and binders, LaShandra Johnson approached him.

"Counselor, may I have a moment?"

Troy noticed the "Press" credential on the lanyard around her neck.

"All press inquiries should be directed to the media relations office of AMX Corporation. I have no comment."

LaShandra looked around to make sure no one was within earshot of what she was about to say. "This isn't your typical press inquiry, Counselor. I'm certain you'll want to hear me out."

Troy again looked up from packing his briefcase. He had dealt with the press before and knew how to handle himself.

"Take the car back to the office with Dr. Stanton and the others," Troy told his associate who was standing at the railing separating the well from the spectators' gallery. "I'm going to hang back and will call you when I get to the office." The associate turned on her heels, tugged her wheeled litigation bag, and slowly walked out of the courtroom to meet Dr. Stanton and the other representatives of AMX who had made their way to the hallway. Troy clasped his briefcase shut and stood in front of LaShandra.

"My name is LaShandra Johnson. I'm managing editor of Resjudicata.com."

"Resjudicata.com," Troy said, furrowing his brow. Isn't that the radical, left-wing progressive website that publishes anything it can get its hands on no matter who gets hurt in the process?"

"That's one way of looking at us. The other way is that we fulfill the promise of the First Amendment. We believe everyone has a right to know what our government is doing with our tax dollars. We also believe everyone has a right to learn information that affects their health, wellbeing, and livelihood. And we believe that in order for lawyers to protect the rights of their clients, they need information. And right now, I have information."

Troy wanted to debate whether Resjudicata.com did more harm than good when it published information without regard to confidentiality and privacy laws, and whether that was really the purpose behind the First Amendment, but it was late, he was tired, and he had a lot to do to get ready for trial the next day. Besides, he realized long ago he learned more from listening than by speaking. The debate would have to wait.

"I'm listening," Troy said as he and LaShandra walked out of the courtroom and over to a corner of the wide hallway near a window overlooking Foley Square.

"I recently came into possession of information concerning your client," LaShandra began. "Some of it looks to be quite damning. It seems AMX knew as far back as the 1970s that centuron was extremely dangerous and could lead to serious injury. Even death. It also appears AMX made an economic decision to keep selling products containing centuron because its profits more than offset liability it might incur from people being injured or even dying from the chemical. It seems AMX took a calculated risk and gambled with people's lives."

"That's all news to me. I don't know anything about that," Troy said, trying hard not to flinch or show any emotion. "Even if it's true Ms. Johnson, what do you want from me?" Troy instinctively thought he was being set up and possibly even being recorded in hopes he'd say something damaging about AMX.

"Since you're AMX's attorney, I want to give you and your client an opportunity to comment," she said, staring directly at Troy. "Resjudicata.com is prepared to publish the information, including memos and reports from scientific experts AMX hired before it started selling products containing centuron, as well as reports from AMX's economic experts. They tell a compelling story, and I'm sure the public would be interested in learning what AMX knew back then."

"You need to consider the source, Ms. Johnson. If the information you claim to have is accurate, it could be very valuable to whomever had it. Why would they simply turn it over to you instead of leveraging it to get something from AMX?"

"Oh, come on. Maybe not everyone is in it for the almighty dollar. Maybe the person or persons or organization that provided Resjudicata.com the information about AMX truly cares about doing some good and saving lives and shining a light on one of the biggest corporate scandals of this century. It's not all about leverage and profit."

"Look, I don't know what information you have or think you have, or what kind of hit-job you're going to concoct, but before you publish anything about AMX, you better do your homework and double and triple check your sources because if there's even one falsehood in anything you publish, Balatoni, Cartel and Colin will slap Resjudicata.com with a lawsuit so fast it will make your head spin."

"You get defensive very quickly, don't you. I've done my homework and coming to you is just another step in that process." LaShandra paused and looked around to make sure no one was close by. "There's something else Resjudicata.com was given. And it relates to a grand jury."

Troy swallowed hard.

"You're treading into dangerous territory. You should know it's illegal to disclose information about grand jury proceedings. They're secret for a reason."

"Ah, but you forget I have the First Amendment in my corner. Besides, who said we'd publish anything about a grand jury? But the fact such information exists confirms the legitimacy of the other information."

Troy fought to keep his expression neutral. If a grand jury was empaneled and heard evidence against AMX, civil liability was the least of AMX's worries. Who the hell would give this kind of information to Resjudicata.com? And why?

"Please ask your client if they want to sit with me to answer a few questions," LaShandra politely asked. "I'll share what I can with them, and I'll include their version of the story in what we publish, along with the documents I have, and we can let the public decide who's in the right and what the facts are. How about that?"

If the offer was legitimate, it would buy AMX much needed time, maybe even enough time to get through the trial. On the other hand, if Resjudicata.com published a scathing story about AMX before the trial ended, Judge Simons would have no choice but to declare a mistrial. A mistrial now might not be the worst thing for AMX, Troy thought.

"I will take your offer back to my client and get you an answer," Troy said flatly. "But if AMX is going to speak with you, they're going to want more. I still think the information you have is contrived and fake news. You at least need to tell me how you came into possession of it."

LaShandra considered Troy's offer.

"Let's just say my source is a high-ranking attorney with the Department of Justice who previously represented AMX. He's willing to reveal himself, eventually, and put his career on the line so the truth can be exposed."

"Ms. Johnson, I don't know what's going on here, but it sounds to me like someone is setting you up. I've been AMX's lawyer for over 10 years, and there's no one who represented AMX who is now a...."

Troy stopped mid-sentence. Seconds passed that seemed like minutes. Troy was having a hard time processing what he'd just heard.

"What? What were you about to say?"

Troy stood there in a trance.

"Mr. McDonald, I don't know what you're thinking, but the source of my story isn't really the point. The only thing that matters is whether AMX knew centuron was a deadly poison when it started selling products containing the chemical and just didn't give a damn because it was staring at potentially billions in profit. Your client has seventy-two hours to decide if they want to meet with me, review the information I have, and give me their side of the story. After that, we're publishing the story and posting documents online. All of them."

Troy felt sick. A wave of nausea suddenly came over him.. Either LaShandra Johnson, if that was her name, was making this shit up, or someone was pumping her full of bogus information.

He looked at LaShandra. "Don't publish anything until you hear from me. Nothing."

When she didn't respond, Troy spoke through his clenched jaw. "Do you hear me?"

"You have seventy-two hours, Mr. McDonald."

The Amtrak Acela train arrived on time at Washington's Union Station at 6:10 p.m. Mary collected her roller bag from the overhead compartment and followed the line of weary business travelers down the platform toward the terminal. Mary spotted Tom standing just outside the doors to the gate.

Tom gave his mom a big hug and grabbed her bag.

"How was the trip, mom?"

"Very comfortable and relaxing. I finished one book and started another. I almost wished the ride was longer because I was at an exciting point in the book."

"I'm glad you're here. I'm so happy to see you. I missed you. Brooke is preparing dinner at the apartment. I hope you're hungry. I can't wait to show you around Washington."

As Tom and Mary got in a cab, Tom's Blackberry rang. Troy McDonald's name appeared on the screen. What a great surprise Tom thought, but he decided to let the call go to voicemail. He slipped the phone in his jacket pocket as he and Mary chatted in the back of the cab. Moments later, his phone vibrated and he heard the ping of an incoming text message.

Tom pulled out his phone and read the text.

911. Call me asap. Troy.

26

Brooke met Tom and Mary in the hallway in front of the apartment.

"I'm so happy to see you," Brooke said as she hugged her mother-in-law. "Come in and make yourself comfortable."

"This is a beautiful apartment," Mary said as the three walked into the living room. "I'm so glad we'll have a few days to spend together." Mary reached for Brooke's hand. "You both look wonderful. Are you enjoying Washington?"

"We love it here," Brooke said, as she grabbed Tom's arm and leaned into his shoulder. "Even though your son is working as hard as ever and hasn't slowed down one bit."

"Ah, no rest for the weary," Tom said as he looked nervously at his phone again. He was anxious to call Troy and find out what was so urgent.

"And apropos of that, I need to make a call. Brooke, can you show mom to her bedroom so she can get settled. I'll be out as soon as I can, and we can catch up over dinner."

"See what I mean?" Brooke said, as Tom hurried into the master bedroom. "Even having you here for a visit isn't enough for him to clock out of work."

"That's my son. Always putting work first. I see nothing's changed with you, Thomas. I guess you're still trying to save the universe," Mary said, loud enough for Tom to hear as he hurried down the hallway.

"Yeah, something like that, mom," Tom said, rushing to close the door behind him.

Troy answered the phone on the first ring.

"Tom is that you? Thanks for calling me back."

"Hey Troy, sounds like you have an emergency on your hands. What's going on, buddy? How've you been?"

"Tom, listen, I don't know where to start. I'm fine." Troy stammered and spoke haltingly. "Are you involved with AMX in any way?"

"What do you mean, Troy? At the DOJ? No, I haven't had time to think about AMX since I left BCC. I've been so busy with other things. What's going on? How's the trial?"

"I'm not sure. I mean, the trial is still going on. Maybe we have another week before it goes to the jury. You haven't spoken with anyone about AMX or...?" Troy hesitated for a moment, sounding unsure whether he should say more. "Or about centuron or what we may or may not know about it?"

"What the hell are you talking about? Of course I haven't spoken to anyone about AMX or centuron or anything related to the case at all. I have no idea what's happening with AMX." Tom paused. "But it sounds like you know something. What is it?"

"I'm not sure. After testimony concluded today, I was approached by a reporter. She's from Resjudicata.com."

Tom had heard of it. From what he knew, it was similar to the *Drudge Report* or *Wikileaks*, but focused on law and good government, and it touted itself as a scholarly alternative to traditional news outlets, with one hundred percent transparency for the American people as its mission. Tom didn't like where this was going.

"She claimed she received a document dump about AMX. Including some very sensitive memos dating back to the 1970s."

Tom didn't know exactly what Troy was referring to but wasn't surprised to hear about memos written in the 1970s. He had worked on cases involving AMX since his first day at BCC and heard rumors of some old secret memos, but AMX always denied their existence. He had reviewed millions of pages of documents but never saw any memos about centuron from the 1970s. If they existed, they would be the holy grail for plaintiffs' lawyers.

"But AMX has always denied the existence of such memos," Tom said.

"I know, but this reporter claims to have them, and Resjudicata.com is prepared to publish them and blow the lid off of AMX and centuron."

"Are you fucking kidding me?" Tom said. "That's going to be devastating to AMX if it's true."

"That's only half the story, Tom. The reporter also said she has grand jury material. If a grand jury was empaneled and has been hearing evidence against AMX and indicted the company or its management, its game over for AMX."

"Holy shit. Resjudicata.com is playing with fire. It's illegal to disclose grand jury information. Resjudicata.com must know that."

"I don't think this reporter gives a shit. Resjudicata.com will hide behind the First Amendment all day long."

"Troy, even if I knew something, which I don't, I couldn't comment on anything related to a grand jury, you know that. But the fact is I've been walled off entirely from anything having to do with AMX. I have no information about AMX, period. Do you think the reporter really has the information she says she has? I mean, where would she get it from?"

"That's the scary part. She says her source is a high-ranking official in the Justice Department." Troy uttered the next sentence very slowly. *A lawyer, who formerly represented AMX."*

"What? That makes no sense. What the hell are you saying?" Tom tried to steady himself. "Are you saying what I think you're saying?"

"Look, I'm not saying anything. I'm just telling you what the reporter told me. Her name is LaShandra Johnson. Do you know her?"

"Nice try." Tom thought of telling Troy to go fuck himself. "Of course I don't know her. And for the record, I'm not her source."

"I know, Tom, I didn't mean it that way. Actually, I don't know what I meant. I've gone over what she told me a million times. I know all the lawyers that worked for AMX over the last twenty years or so, and no one is a current high-ranking official with the DOJ. Other than you. At first, I thought it might be the AG, God forgive me. But he never so much as billed an hour of time on any matter for AMX. I just had my secretary pull up all the billing records for AMX since it became a client of the firm in the nineties. None of this makes any sense."

For a moment neither Troy nor Tom spoke. Finally, Troy broke the silence. "I hate to say it, but it sounds like someone may be trying to frame you to take the fall for this. The reporter told me her source wants to be revealed. If you're named as the source, Tom, you're fucked."

Tom fell back onto the bed. "There's no way, Troy. There's got to be a mistake here. Maybe the reporter got her wires crossed or maybe you misheard her."

"I didn't mishear her. For once stop thinking there's an innocent explanation for everything. The stakes are too high. For AMX. For BCC. And most of all for you. Take off the rose-colored glasses, Tommy, and consider, just for a moment, that not everyone in the world is out to praise you and that, maybe, just maybe, someone is trying to knock you off your fucking pedestal. Or maybe they're out to destroy AMX even if it means you're collateral damage. You would be the perfect fall guy. You've represented AMX and would know where the bodies are buried. And now you're at the DOJ and theoretically have access to grand jury material. Someone may be using you. The reporter said she's publishing the story in seventy-two hours. Actually, it's less than seventy hours now. You may have just under three days to salvage your career and save your ass."

Tom ignored Troy's comment about the rose-colored glasses. He had bigger things to worry about. "I'll figure it out," he muttered. "Maybe I can get the FBI involved. Does anyone else know about this? Did you speak to Balatoni about it?"

"No, I only called you and haven't mentioned it to another soul. And I won't until we know more. Besides, Balatoni had some kind of a breakdown yesterday. No one's heard from him."

"I had no idea," Tom said.

"Look, I know Balatoni is great and you're fond of him, but you need to think about yourself now and how you're going to get yourself out of this potential mess. Balatoni can wait."

If only that was true, Tom thought. The venerable Ignatius Balatoni and BCC were knee deep involved with the Syndicate, and now someone was going after AMX and possibly trying to implicate Tom for leaking confidential information. How the hell did he wind up in this mess?"

"I know. I'll figure something out. Sit tight until you hear from me. I'll get to the bottom of this."

Tom pressed the end call button and looked up at the ceiling. This couldn't possibly be happening, he thought. His mind raced with possibilities about who might be behind the plot to frame him and destroy his career. Was it even a set up? Something didn't feel right. He had to get to the office. He would think of a plan on his way.

Cosimo sat in his study aboard the *Vulcania* listening intently to Tom's conversation with Troy. Pangs of doubt came over him. He hated to see Tom hurting, but it was for the greater good, Cosimo reasoned. Just be patient. A few more weeks, maybe, and he would know if the plan he had been formulating for years would work. Certainly, there was risk. But what was the alternative, especially once the authorities closed in on him? At least this way, he was giving himself a fighting chance. A chance to preserve his legacy. Cosimo called Totto Nessa and asked to see him in his study as he watched Tom on the large monitor walk into the kitchen of his apartment where Brooke and Mary were standing.

"Brooke, mom, I'm sorry but I'm going to have to skip dinner. I was on the phone with people from my office and there's an emergency I need to deal with. I need to go to the office."

"Come on, really?" Brooke frowned. "Your mom just got here. Can't it wait until the morning, or can't you have someone else handle it?"

"No, sorry sweetie. I need to take care of this myself. Mom, I'm sorry, but this is important. Enjoy dinner with Brooke, and I promise tomorrow night we'll all go out for dinner to our favorite restaurant in Adams Morgan."

"Okay," Mary said, "but don't run yourself ragged."

Tom kissed his mom on the cheek, gave Brooke a quick kiss on the lips, and ran for the door.

"I swear, I think Tom's working more now than he ever did at the law firm, where he made a heck of a lot more money," Brooke said to Mary as she watched Tom race out of the apartment. "He is so damn determined and conscientious, which I love about him, but sometimes I wish he would slow down and just enjoy the moment. I'm sorry, I'm just upset he ran out like that," Brooke said as she threw the dish towel she had been holding into the sink.

"Oh, honey. You don't need to apologize. Tom has always been like that. Whenever he commits to doing something and gives someone his word, you can take it to the bank. He is loyal to a fault. Even when he was a little boy, he was always the responsible one and the one who volunteered to get things done, whether it was in school or in sports."

Mary continued. "One time, when he was seven or eight and playing little league, the coach asked for help the next morning to prepare the field for a game. Tom told the coach he would help. The field was down the block from our house. Tom was up at seven the next morning and left me a note saying he was going to the field. When I got up and noticed he wasn't in the house, I panicked. I found the note and ran to the field. And there he was, rake in hand, smoothing the infield dirt. When I yelled to him, he ran over and asked me why I was surprised he was out so early. 'Didn't you hear me say to the coach I would work on the field?' he asked. 'I gave him my word, mom, that I would do it and so I needed to be here.'

"He had committed to doing something and he was going to see it through no matter what. That's who Tom is. His word is his bond, and duty and commitment are everything to him. I guess he was born that way."

Brooke had never heard that story before, but it didn't surprise her. It's what she loved most about Tom. His determination. His ambition. His sense of responsibility. She fell in love with him because she knew if he wanted something, nothing and no one would stand in his way.

Cosimo sat back, staring at Mary on the large screen, listening to her speak about Tom. He was still, but something within him was stirring.

Totto Nessa walked into the study and jolted Cosimo, who wiped away tears that had welled up in the corners of his eyes as he cleared his throat.

"It's time to put the next phase of my plan into motion."

27

Tom directed the cab driver to take him to Main Justice. He didn't know what he would do when he got there, other than to review the DOJ's document database. He wouldn't be able to access any files about AMX if they existed, but if he was being used as a pawn and fingered as the source of leaks about AMX, his gut told him he might find clues on the DOJ's computer network.

After seven years at BCC, Tom knew his way around computers. There were days at BCC when he felt he was more of a forensic IT investigator than a lawyer. Associates were always being tasked with looking up information concerning clients, opposing parties and witnesses, and searching metadata, and Tom became an expert at mining the depths of the dark web for morsels of information that could help a BCC client. But it was Tom's hide on the line now. He needed to do a deep dive to find out if he was being framed for leaking AMX files.

He entered through the night entrance doors at Main Justice. He didn't recognize the guards manning the security checkpoint. As a senior member of the Executive Staff, Tom wasn't required to walk through the metal detector or empty his pockets into the plastic tray to be x-rayed along with anything else he was carrying. He displayed his ID badge and expected to walk through the turnstile next to the red sign reading "Executive Staff

Entrance," but instead one of the guards stopped him and asked to inspect Tom's ID badge. "Working late this evening, sir?" the guard asked, smirking.

Tom found the question odd, but he wasn't in the mood for small talk. He just wanted to get to his office. "Yeah, I forgot something in my office and need to retrieve it." The guard studied the badge and looked at Tom again. He jotted notes in a book. Tom was getting antsy. "Is there a problem? I'm kind of in a hurry."

"No, no problem. We're just following procedures." The guard handed back the ID badge and moved out of the way.

"Thank you for your patience," the guard said, as he followed Tom with his eyes all the way to the elevators.

Tom considered taking down the guard's name, but just then the elevator doors opened and he sprinted in, anxious to get to his office. He speed-walked down the marble corridor lined with large paintings of former Attorneys General on the walls. He was struck by the silence. All of the office doors were closed, and the only sound came from his shoes squeaking on the polished floor.

He glanced at his watch. It was 8:15 p.m. He grinned, thinking that at that very moment three quarters of the associates at BCC were still in their offices, with probably more than half just starting to draft memos or conduct research that would take them well into the wee hours of the morning to finish, while the other half were about to pull an all-nighter with no sleep at all. Working past seven, much less pulling an all-nighter, at the DOJ was a rarity. Maybe that's why the guard was surprised to see the Executive Deputy AG come into the building at such a late hour.

He swung open the door to his office and was about to reach for the overhead light switch when he was struck by the view out his window. The semi-darkness, silhouetted by the light in the hallway, cast a glow on the large window on the far end of his office. He noticed the lit dome of the US Capitol perfectly framed by the curtains. The late summer sun had just set over downtown Washington, and the western horizon was streaked with faint rays of red and orange as twilight gave way to darkness, with the lights of the Capitol twinkling in the distance. Tom had never noticed that particular evening view from the doorway to his office. It looked like a painting, and he could've gazed at it for hours. But he had work to do. Instead of switching on the light, Tom closed the door behind him and hurried to pull the chain on the lamp on the corner of his cluttered desk. It illuminated his desk just enough for Tom to see the folders and papers piled high covering every square inch of the leather blotter.

Tom pulled back his chair while he fumbled for the undermounted tray holding the keyboard. He typed in his password and leaned over to grab a legal pad and pen when the message *System Error: Invalid Passcode* appeared on his screen. He must have typed it too quickly, he thought.

Tom retyped his password, slower this time. The same message appeared on the screen. He typed the passcode a third time, slowly hitting each key, one at a time. Same result. Maybe his password expired, Tom thought, and he just hadn't seen the alerts to change it. He clicked Ctrl-Alt-Enter which brought up the Change Password screen. He typed in a new password, retyped the new password, and hit enter. He got the same message: *System Error: Invalid Passcode*.

"Fuck." Tom let out a grunt and threw the pen he'd been holding. He hated calling the IT helpdesk because nine times out of ten their advice was simply to reboot. He clicked the home button and clicked restart. The screen went blank momentarily and then started whirring back to life, scanning through several images as his computer rebooted. Finally, he was at the password screen again. He typed in the new password. *System Error: Invalid Passcode*. He scrolled back and typed his old password. *System Error: Invalid Passcode*. "Damn it," Tom yelled out to no one. He scanned his directory card next to his phone and reluctantly called the helpdesk.

After several minutes of explaining the problem, providing his employee ID number, and waiting for the technician to verify his identity, Tom was told that due to a system upgrade, the DOJ's computers would be down until at least 9:30 p.m. Tom looked at the clock on his desk and saw that it was barely 8:30. He looked at his Blackberry and noticed the last email he received was at 6:15 p.m. He asked the technician whether the upgrade also meant he couldn't send or receive emails or texts on his Blackberry, and he was told that since his phone was linked to the DOJ's servers, that was the case. Tom cursed himself for not having a second smartphone that wasn't connected to the DOJ network.

Tom considered going back home, but he decided knowing tonight if his DOJ computer was used to access information about AMX was worth the wait. He looked at the stack of documents on the table across from his desk. Tom hadn't yet combed those documents, and this seemed like as good a time as any.

Just as he was about to get up, he decided to check in with FBI Special Agent Ann Leonardo. Tom had a sticky note on his monitor reminding him that Ann was looking into hospital birth records from 1988 to 1990 to see if Cosimo Benedetto fathered a child at that time. Unable to send Ann an email or text, he called her.

"Ann, this is Tom, I hope I'm not disturbing you."

"Not at all. I just picked up take-out and am driving home. What can I do for you?"

"I'm at the office with a few minutes to kill while the computer system is being worked on, and I thought I'd follow up on the research you're doing regarding the child Cosimo may have fathered. Any luck with the hospital records?"

"Burning the midnight oil, aren't you?"

"Yeah, I guess. Something like that. You know, when I was in private practice, I wouldn't have thought twice about still being in the office at this hour, probably drafting a brief or doing research. Anyway, I'm getting out of here soon and just wanted to check in. Any update?"

"I came up empty. No records of a Cosimo Benedetto or any of the aliases we've associated with him in any of the birth records from 1988 to 1990. Looks like it's a dead end. Sorry."

"Well, it was worth a shot. Thanks for following up. By the way, have you heard from Agent Young?"

"Not a peep," Ann replied. "No one has. I guess he's taking his mother's passing really hard."

"Hmmm." Tom had no experience with colleagues going off the grid for such a prolonged period of time, without an email or message or some kind of contact, even just to check in. But then again, he'd never experienced the loss of a parent as an adult, so he wasn't sure how he'd react if he were in that position.

"His two-week bereavement leave is up Monday, so I expect we'll see him back in the office then," Tom said. "Enjoy dinner and have a good night."

"Yeah, thanks. You, too. And don't stay in the office too late."

Ann pushed the end call button on her steering wheel. As she looked down the road, she wondered whether Tom knew his birth records didn't identify his father. There was just a blank space. She came across his records when she conducted the search on Benedetto. Tom was born on January 25, 1989, in Roosevelt Hospital, Commack, Long Island. Anne wondered whether Tom ever met his father. Little surprised her anymore after five years at the FBI. You never know the crosses people bear, or the scars they carry, she thought.

Tom leaned back in his chair. There was nothing he could do about the AMX leak or the possibility that he was being framed for it until he accessed the DOJ's computer network. With about forty-five minutes left to kill until the system would be back up and running, he grabbed a *Yoo-hoo* from the small refrigerator, flipped the switch to the overhead light, and walked over to the table to review the stack of documents relating to the Syndicate. He pulled out one of the chairs around the table and picked up a folder marked "BCC Bank Records 2012-2016."

At that very moment, unbeknownst to Tom, in a secure room in the sub-basement of Main Justice, investigators from the FBI's Office of Professional Responsibility were reviewing data access and timestamp files from Tom's desktop. The OPR duty officer in charge received a notification that C. Thomas Berte's desktop computer had been accessed some twenty-four hours earlier and files had been duplicated onto a USB drive. The investigators were able to confirm that 64 gigabytes of data pertaining to the DOJ's investigation of AMX Corporation, as well as the FBI's investigative files on the company, had been copied without authorization. The present whereabouts of the duplicated data was unknown.

That information set in motion a series of operating protocols, including a complete assessment of Tom's computer use history, and a forensic examination of electronic banking records belonging to C. Thomas Berte and his relatives, as well as a review of C. Thomas Berte's office, home and cell phone communications, and tablet access usage.

This is where the power and might of the US government was at its best. The FBI could digitally access terabytes of information regarding any person in the world within seconds and no one, neither the courts, the information providers, nor, most importantly, the target of the investigation, would have a clue their private communications and financial affairs were being scrutinized from top to bottom. The Fourth Amendment be damned. If the FBI found something incriminating or that even hinted at a crime, that's when it would go to court for authorization to execute a search warrant for information they already knew existed. It was a game played out thousands of times a year against terrorists, fraudsters, and anyone else unfortunate enough to be caught in the crosshairs of the world's most powerful law enforcement agency.

FBI investigators from OPR quarantined several suspicious communications and transactions. At the top of the list was a $750,000 wire transfer into a Wells Fargo bank account in the names of C. Thomas and Brooke Berte made a day earlier, at about the same time the AMX data was duplicated and downloaded from Tom's computer. The source of the payment was the First Freedom Foundation, or Triple F, as it was known. Based on intelligence reports, Triple F was a left-wing activist organization, loosely associated with the ANTIFA movement, that raised millions of dollars each year from wealthy sympathetic donors and organizations, and provided grants to left-leaning think tanks, policy institutions, and first amendment advocacy groups. Triple F was registered in Mauritius, and its sole physical presence in the United States was a computer server located in a nondescript warehouse on the outskirts of Seattle. Among the recipients of grants from Triple F was Resjudicata.com.

The OPR duty officer immediately issued a Code Red, the highest alert used by OPR reserved for suspected rogue personnel within the Justice Department, and he notified the Assistant Director of OPR via encrypted transmission. An FBI investigative detail team was immediately dispatched.

While the investigation was active, every move and every communication made by C. Thomas Berte, his wife, relatives, and associates would be monitored by the FBI. For the time being, at least, Tom was the most closely surveilled person on American soil.

Tom waded through the documents in the BCC banking folder. A few minutes before 9:00 p.m., he heard footsteps in the hallway. It was the same squeaking sound his shoes made when he was walking to his office. The sound grew louder as the person got closer to Tom's office and then stopped. Whoever it was, was standing right outside his office. Tom noticed the door handle turn. He was about to get up when his chair creaked ever so slightly. The person at the door let go of the handle. Moments later there was the sound of a knock.

Tom immediately thought it might be the night cleaning crew, but he had glanced at his wastepaper basket when he sat at his desk earlier and noticed it was already emptied. Reflexively Tom shouted, "Who is it?"

"IT Department, may I come in?" Tom pushed back his chair and made his way to the door, cracking it open slowly.

"Good evening, Mr. Berte. I'm sorry to bother you, sir," a young man said, barely out of high school, wearing khaki pants and a white polo shirt with the DOJ insignia on the left breast pocket.

"Yes, may I help you?" Tom said, as he exhaled and opened the door farther.

"Sir, I'm from the Office of Information Technology. I understand you're trying to log on to the computer system from your desktop. Due to a system malfunction, we will need to reconfigure the hard drives accessed by computers on this floor. Unfortunately, that will take us several hours, so it's unlikely you'll have computer access until tomorrow morning, at the earliest. I wanted to let you know in case you were hoping to use your computer this evening."

In reality, there was no system malfunction, but OPR wasn't about to let Tom have access to the DOJ's files again.

"Shit," Tom mumbled. The clock was ticking, and he needed access to his computer if he had any hope of figuring out what was going on. Coming to the office tonight was turning out to be a waste of time.

Tom shook his head. "Even the DOJ is not immune to computer crashes, huh?" Tom said, knowing he sounded like an asshole. "Thanks for letting me know."

Tom shut the door and decided to just go home. He was about to walk back to his desk to turn off the lamp, clearly frustrated, when he remembered he wanted to mark his place in the banking records he was reviewing so he'd know where to pick up tomorrow. The investigation into the Syndicate could wait a day, Tom thought to himself, while he first dealt with the AMX leak.

Tom was about to place a sticky note on the edge of the page in the folder containing BCC's bank records when his eye caught an entry in the middle of the page. In August 2016, BCC made a $25,000 wire transfer to Harding & Glasgow, an accounting firm on Long Island. Tom flipped a few pages to a list of bank transfers made in September 2016. He saw another entry for $25,000 paid to the accounting firm. His eyes narrowed. Tom flipped several pages in and looked at entries for December 2016. That month BCC made a $50,000 transfer to the company. He kept flipping pages. Each month BCC paid Harding & Glasgow at least $25,000. His heart raced. He kept scanning the pages and saw that a few days before each BCC payment to Harding & Glasgow, the same amounts were deposited into BCC's account from companies associated with the Syndicate.

He thumbed through the stack of papers for prior years and saw similar entries every month from 2012 to 2016. Payments to BCC from Syndicate-related companies just a day or two before the same amounts were transferred by BCC to Harding & Glasgow. He looked around for a folder containing bank records for later years. He found a folder for BCC's banking records for 2017 to 2019. He leafed through them and saw the same entries. BCC paid Harding & Glasgow tens of thousands of dollars every month—and received payments from the Syndicate in the same amounts just days prior.

Tom took in a quick breath as his knees buckled. He grabbed the chair he had been sitting in and stumbled onto it. His chest tightened and his shoulders sagged. The information was mind boggling. BCC, one of the largest law firms in the world, was the middleman for payments from the Syndicate to a small accounting firm on Long Island.

But this wasn't just any accounting firm. It was the same one Mary Berte had worked at for the last thirty years.

28

Brooke and Mary sat on the living room couch after dinner having tea. Mary wasn't as upset as Brooke that Tom rushed back to the office. It gave her an opportunity to spend time with just Brooke, whom she loved like a daughter.

"Thank you for the delicious dinner, Brooke. I had almost forgotten what a wonderful cook you are. I really want the recipe for the risotto you made. It was so tasty."

"Thanks, mom. It's super easy to make. I'm glad you enjoyed it."

"Tell me honey, are you happy living here in Washington?"

"I'm really happy, mom. I love this city. My sister lives nearby so I get to see her a lot. And I love my job at the Children's Advocacy Group. I'm helping so many children who have had such hardships. Many of these kids come from broken homes, and some were orphaned at a young age. It can be sad and overwhelming at times hearing what these kids have gone through, but they are so grateful for any help they receive. Although it's difficult because we're constantly in fundraising mode, it's also inspiring to see so many organizations, companies, and individuals open their hearts and wallets with generous donations that allow us to do so much good. It's incredibly rewarding, and I'm truly blessed."

"I can't imagine what those poor, innocent children go through. I'm so proud of you and the great work you do."

"Every day, seeing so many kids across our country go to sleep hungry at night, and not having parents to hug them and tuck them in, makes me realize that parenting is the most important job in the world. Tom and I can't wait to start a family of our own and finally make you a grandmother."

"Ah, are you trying to tell me something, sweetheart?" Mary said, grinning.

"No, no. We're not pregnant. But Tom and I talk about it. A lot. I thought our move here and Tom's new job would make us less busy, which would have allowed us to start a family right away, but instead it's just the opposite. I actually think Tom works more now than he did when he was at the firm. He's certainly under a lot more pressure. You saw what happened tonight. And the work is so intense. I mean, he hasn't shared any details with me, but I know he's working on this extremely important criminal case and he's constantly getting emails and updates. Even the President is aware of what Tom is working on, can you believe that? Apparently, it's going to be big news when they bring indictments."

"Oh," said Mary, as she fidgeted with the crucifix on her necklace.

"I just hope it happens sooner rather than later because the stress he's under can't be good for him. And I really want him around a lot for our baby, whenever it happens. I don't want him working so much when we have kids or to rush back to the office at night, like he did tonight," Brooke said, taking a sip of tea.

Mary looked concerned and reached out for Brooke's hand. "Maybe things will slow down at work soon, and you and Tom will be able to spend more time together," Mary said, trying to sound reassuring.

"What was it like, raising Tom on your own as a single parent?"

Brooke noticed Mary stiffen at the question. She let go of Brooke's hand and grabbed her cup with both hands, taking a slow sip.

"It wasn't that bad," Mary said in a low voice. "Thomas was such a good boy growing up, he made it easy. He was responsible and cleaned his room and worked hard in school. He did everything I asked of him." Mary's voice trailed off.

"But you had to do it all on your own. Tom told me you attended all his sporting events and after school events, and on weekends you would drive him to games or to his friends' houses. You worked full time, but still found time to make dinner every night and go on vacations with him. You were amazing. It sounds so incredible. How did you have the energy and time to do it all?"

"You make it sound like I was mother of the year," Mary said, with a short, anxious laugh. "I did what I had to do to raise my son. It's surprising what people can do when it becomes necessary. I had no other choice. You set your mind to it and make things work." Mary took another sip of tea.

"Tom brought up his dad when we were talking last week. He had a difficult day at work," Brooke said.

Mary stiffened again, opening her eyes wide. She crossed her arms and sat up.

"What did he say about him?"

"He was just wondering what kind of man his father was. He was speaking about Ignatius Balatoni, you remember him, the founder of the law firm Tom worked at, and how respected he is and how brilliant he is, and I guess it got Tom thinking about his father."

Mary looked around the room, and then lowered her head.

"Mom, are you okay?"

"Yes, I'm fine. I'm just...I'm looking for my sweater. I guess I'm a little chilly."

"I really love your son. I worry about him, of course, but I love him so much. I just want him to be happy."

"I know you do, dear. And I know how much Tom loves you," Mary said, draping the sweater over her shoulders. "You two make a great couple. And you're going to make wonderful parents whenever that day comes."

They sat in silence for a few minutes. The light in the living room was dim. Mary was tired and her eyes looked heavy when Brooke's phone pinged.

"It's Tom," Brooke said, reading the text on her phone. "He says he'll be home in about an hour, and you shouldn't wait for him if you want to go to bed."

"That's good to know. It's been a long day and I'm getting a little tired.

Tom is so very lucky to have you. And I am too. I love you, dear." Mary yawned, while leaning slowly back and closing her eyes.

"Oh, mom," Brooke whispered softly. "I'm sorry I was complaining about Tom working so hard. All he ever wanted is to show you how much he appreciates all you've done for him his whole life. I think that's why he's worked so hard to get where he is. He just wants to make you proud of him."

"You have no idea how proud I am of him, " Mary said softly, as she rested on the couch, her eyes still closed. "He's the best son I could have asked for."

Moments passed. The room seemed darker now. Quieter. Still. Mary was slowly drifting off to sleep. "His father and I are so proud of him," Mary whispered gently.

Brooke froze.

After several seconds, Brooke said, "You mean Tom's father *would* have been so proud of him *if* he was still alive, right?"

Mary sprang upright. "Ah, yes, of course, that's what I meant to say." She was coming out of her stupor. She realized what she had said and shook her head, fidgeted with her necklace, and looked at her watch. Her voice quivered a bit.

"What I meant to say is that if Tom's father was still alive, I know he'd be proud of him. Just like we all are."

The words lingered in the still air of the darkened room. Brooke bowed her head and shut her eyes tight.

"It's getting late sweetie, and I'm very tired," Mary said, her voice still shaky. "I think I'll go to bed now. Are you going to wait for Tom?"

"Yeah, yeah, I have some reading to do, so I think I'll read until he gets home."

"Okay, dear. Thank you again for a lovely dinner. And thank you for letting me stay here."

They stood and embraced in a tight hug. After a few seconds, Mary turned and headed down the hallway to her room. "Good night, Brooke. I love you."

"I love you too, mom."

Brooke sat back on the couch. She closed her eyes again, unsure what to make of what she had just heard.

It was 11:00 p.m. when Tom arrived home. He noticed a light on in the living room and saw Brooke lying on the couch reading.

"I didn't expect you to still be awake," Tom said as he sat next to her, gently caressing her leg.

"I wanted to wait for you. Is everything okay? Did you put out the fire?" Brooke asked as she closed the book and placed it next to her.

"Listen, honey, I need to go to New York tomorrow morning," Tom said as he pulled away from Brooke.

"What? Why? What's going on? Your mom just got here *from New York*."

"I know, but I'll just be gone for the day. We're at a critical point in the investigation I'm working on, and I need to meet with people in New York to try to get some information."

After seeing the monthly payments to the accounting firm his mother worked for, coupled with the evidence he'd learned confirming BCC's connection to the Syndicate, Tom knew he had to confront Ignatius. He toyed with the idea of speaking with him by phone but ultimately decided it would be better to meet in person. If Ignatius was as frail as Troy said, this may be his last chance to see him. Tom needed answers no matter what dirty secrets they revealed. Even if it meant having to advise the great Ignatius Balatoni to hire a lawyer.

Tom also wanted to go to New York to meet with LaShandra Johnson and find out what she knew about AMX. If she believed Tom was the source of the leak, he needed to plug it right away. He considered telling Brooke the truth. But he was uneasy about sharing as much as he had with her, and didn't want her to worry about him. Plus, until he was certain he wasn't being framed, he didn't want anyone knowing what he was doing in New York, even Brooke.

Little did Tom know the FBI was already watching his every move.

"Tom, are you okay? Are we okay?" Brooke's voice trembled. "Does this have anything to do with your law firm and Ignatius Balatoni and what we talked about last night?"

"Oh, sweetie. Everything's fine. We're okay." He tried to sound reassuring. "This is just about the case I'm working on. We're at a pivotal point and we have a lot of questions we need answered. Those answers could be the key to blowing the case wide open. That's all. And the people in New York I need to meet with could provide answers to those questions. I promise I'll be home tomorrow evening, and the three of us will go out to dinner," Tom said, sounding more confident than he actually felt.

Tom leaned in to give Brooke a hug. His mind was racing. He wanted to ask his mother why BCC was paying the accounting firm she worked for tens of thousands of dollars every month. Was there an innocent explanation? Maybe the accounting firm did work for BCC, or for a legitimate company in the Syndicate's vast network, and BCC just paid the bills and was reimbursed?

Then Tom had another thought.

What would happen to Ignatius when the Justice Department indicted the firm for conspiring with the Syndicate as its long-time in-house counsel? And what would happen to him, and to Brooke, if the information about AMX became public and he was accused of being the leaker?

Tom's world was caving in on him, but he needed to stay strong, for Brooke's sake. He didn't want to worry her, and he couldn't tell her what he knew or suspected.

"Tom, I've been thinking of something," Brooke finally said, piercing the silence in the room as Tom slowly pulled away and looked at her. "What if...what if..." Brooke's voice trailed off as if she was afraid to say more.

"What is it, Brooke?"

"What if your father didn't die when you were young? What if he's still alive?"

On the large monitor in his study, Cosimo had watched Brooke and Mary speaking in the living room. The live feed closed-circuit cameras his people had secretly set up in the apartment were crisp and the sound static free. He could not stop staring at her. He was surprised at Mary's slip of the tongue and noticed Brooke's stunned reaction. And now he was watching Tom and Brooke. He watched as Tom looked at Brooke in disbelief. "Maybe she misspoke," Tom said. "Maybe she was tired and just meant to say that my father *would* have been proud of me *if* he was still alive."

But Brooke said she knew what she heard. She shared with him what her gut was telling her.

Cosimo watched Tom trying to shrug off Brooke's concerns, and joked that she was doing the same thing she did whenever they watched a crime show. But he also saw the look of concern on Tom's face when he finally turned away from Brooke and squeezed his eyes shut. Cosimo recalled what Ignatius told Tom, and he suspected Tom knew more than he was letting on.

Cosimo sat quietly in his darkened study aboard the *Vulcania*. The yacht would be docking in Monaco in a few hours, and Gino Terranova, Cosimo's trusted bodyguard, would be flying to the United States. Fate had determined Cosimo's destiny, as well as Tom's. What had taken years to plan would now play out in a matter of days.

Cosimo called Totto Nessa who was working in his office. "Has Gino been briefed?"

"He has. He will take the helicopter to Nice, where a jet will be waiting to take him to the United States. He'll arrive at Dulles Airport by midday tomorrow."

Cosimo sat stone-faced. "Grazie. Excellent work, as always. Please ask Gino to see me before he leaves."

"Of course. And the *Ragazzo*?"

"I will take care of him," Cosimo replied as he stood and walked to the window cradling the phone. "As I always have."

Cosimo looked out toward the horizon. He was concerned. Would the plan work the way he intended? Would Tom cooperate? These were sound questions. He knew there were risks, but some amount of risk was inevitable. He had considered the consequences. And his goals. His whole life was about taking calculated chances and mitigating risks. That's why he'd also planned for the possibility Tom would go rogue.

The final phase of his plan was underway. His questions would soon be answered.

PART III

29

Tom's flight to New York was scheduled to depart at 7:45 a.m. While still at his office the night before, he had called Ignatius's home and spoken to Gerard, his butler. He was told Ignatius was weak but resting comfortably, and occasionally taking visitors. Tom said he would visit the next morning, but not to tell Ignatius. He wanted to surprise him, Tom told Gerard, and thought Ignatius would welcome the visit. Gerard agreed, and Tom said he hoped to arrive around ten.

He was still rattled by what Brooke had said last night. She was one of the smartest people he knew, but even she could be wrong sometimes. Tom was certain she misheard his mother, or his mother misspoke. Tom's father died a long time ago and nothing was going to change that. He promised her he would raise the issue with his mother when he got back from New York. But ever since he'd spoken to Troy the night before, and later discovered payments by BCC to the accounting firm that employed his mother, Tom's father was the furthest thing from his mind.

Tom noticed the dark sedan parked across the street from his apartment building when he left for the airport. Although he had never seen the car before, he admitted he never took the time to notice such things. No one was sitting in the car and given the number of government employees living in Washington, DC, it wasn't unusual for dark sedans to be parked anywhere downtown.

He knew he was being paranoid. But if he was being framed for leaking confidential information about AMX, including secret grand jury materials, perhaps higher ups in the DOJ or FBI had found out, and maybe he was being watched.

Tom thought back to how suspiciously the security guard had eyed him the night before when he entered Main Justice. And he became suspicious of a tall, white-haired man, who boarded the plane right before the flight attendant closed the airplane door. The man took a seat two rows in front of Tom's seat. The plane was detained at the gate after the scheduled departure time due to "unsigned paperwork" the pilot announced, but it pushed back moments later, right after the white-haired man boarded.

Tom thought it unusual that the man had nothing in his hands. No carry-on luggage or briefcase. Not even a newspaper. The man stared straight ahead the entire flight and didn't make eye contact with anyone. Tom lost track of him in the terminal at LaGuardia after they landed, and he wasn't on the taxi line that Tom waited in for ten minutes while traffic in front of the terminal was at a standstill.

He'd been through LaGuardia a hundred times, and he hated it. Fortunately, it was undergoing a much-needed modernization project that would finally bring the airport into the twenty-first century, but the traffic and gridlock caused by around-the-clock construction was a nightmare.

The drive into Manhattan wasn't any better. The cab inched along in morning rush-hour traffic and arrived in front of Ignatius's apartment building on the corner of Fifth Avenue and 76th Street at about 10:25 a.m. It had already been a long day.

The doorman opened the door to the lobby and the concierge called up to Ignatius's apartment after asking Tom for his name. Tom looked up and down the street when he exited the cab and was now looking out the lobby's large plate-glass window onto Fifth Avenue. No white-haired man. And no dark sedan either. He felt relieved, thinking he was a knucklehead for suspecting the FBI was following him.

Unfortunately for Tom, he hadn't noticed the yellow taxi without a passenger in the back seat following the cab Tom was riding in from

LaGuardia into Manhattan, or the blue van with *Sid's Painting* stenciled on its side panels that began following Tom's cab when it came out of the Queens Midtown Tunnel. The blue van double parked in front of a fire hydrant halfway down the block from Ignatius's building on the opposite side of Fifth Avenue. Unbeknownst to Tom, the white-haired man was in the back of the blue van sitting in front of a bank of video monitors with a receiver in his ear and a transmitter in his hand.

Gerard was standing in the foyer as Tom exited the private elevator into Ignatius's apartment. He greeted Tom and invited him to follow him down a long hallway past a library with soaring ceilings, carved wood paneling, and shelves teeming with books, then past an elegant living room replete with tapestries and artwork lining the walls. Farther down the hallway, they passed a grand formal dining room on the left, visible through an alcove, that could easily sit twenty around a long, oval table centered under two large crystal chandeliers.

The apartment was immense, Tom thought, a suitable trophy befitting the man who founded and ran one of the most powerful law firms in the world. At least by appearances. Finally, they arrived at the covered loggia which opened onto an expansive garden terrace overlooking Central Park. Ignatius was sitting in a tufted pillow-backed chair in front of a glass table, a blanket covering his legs.

Gerard walked in front of Ignatius and gently announced he had a guest. Ignatius put down the *Wall Street Journal* and turned toward Gerard. His mouth fell open when he saw Tom standing behind Gerard's right shoulder. He quickly removed his glasses and fumbled with the newspaper as he tried to get up to greet Tom, but he was unsteady and didn't have the strength to stand. Tom rushed over to hold Ignatius's arm and coax him back into his chair. "Ignatius, it's okay, please don't get up."

"What a lovely surprise," Ignatius said, his voice raspy and weak and his breathing labored.

It pained Tom to see Ignatius so frail. It had been almost three months since Tom last saw Ignatius at his going away party, but in that time the decline was obvious. Ignatius looked older, gaunt, his skin pale, with dark circles under his eyes.

"Please, sit, I'm delighted to see you," Ignatius said, his voice raspy and the words slightly slurred. Turning to Gerard he asked him to prepare breakfast for Tom.

"No, that won't be necessary. I won't be staying long. Just coffee would be fine, thank you, Gerard."

"I wish you had called. We could have met for breakfast at the Pierre," Ignatius said.

For years Ignatius held a standing reservation for breakfast at the Pierre Hotel on Fifth Avenue. He had the same large table reserved every day, in the left corner of the main dining room, with a bird's eye view of everyone who came through the front doors. Even though he had breakfast there only a few days a month, and even fewer than that when he was traveling or spending time at his homes in Boca Raton or London, the table was always reserved for Ignatius Balatoni and his friends, with the tab generously paid by BCC, whether breakfast was served or not.

"No, no, it's fine. I didn't want to impose. I just wanted to see you."

Ignatius thought back to the conversation he had with Cosimo. He was to have no contact with the *Ragazzo*. But how could he have avoided this? Tom came to visit him. Surely, Cosimo would understand and allow this one exception.

"You look wonderful, Thomas. How have you been? Have the issues we discussed last time resolved themselves?" Ignatius was becoming more animated. Although his voice was still shaky.

"That's partly why I'm here. There are some questions I need answers to. Some sensitive questions."

Ignatius dreaded hearing those words. He knew this day would come. The day Tom learned the truth about BCC and pieced together the puzzle. It's why he opposed recommending Tom for the position at the DOJ. It was too soon, Ignatius had pleaded. He'd pushed back on Cosimo and tried to persuade him there was another way. But Cosimo would hear none of it. He had a master plan, Cosimo kept saying, and Ignatius just needed to do as he was told. Given the leverage Cosimo held over him and BCC, Ignatius was in no position to battle Cosimo.

"What do you want to know?" Ignatius asked hesitantly.

"Tell me about Cosimo Benedetto," Tom said sternly.

He braced himself for Ignatius's reaction.

But Ignatius did not react. There was no wide-eyed look of amazement, or jaw-dropping recoil in fear or embarrassment. It's as if Ignatius expected the question.

After a few seconds, Tom repeated his question. He spoke firmly and deliberately.

"Ignatius, tell me about Cosimo Benedetto and his organization."

Ignatius bowed his head and slowly turned away from Tom, as if he couldn't stand to look at him. His eyes glistened with tears and his hands trembled. In a frail voice barely above a whisper he asked, "What do you know?"

"I know enough," Tom said, bristling. "I know BCC was on the verge of shutting its doors in 2009 when Cosimo Nino Benedetto and his Syndicate bank-rolled BCC and saved it from collapse.

"I know you and BCC have essentially been in-house counsel to the Syndicate ever since, having a seat at the table while Cosimo and his people committed heinous crimes and perpetrated brazen frauds that allowed him to steal hundreds of billions of dollars."

Tom spoke slowly, his voice steadily rising.

"I know you and the firm helped the Syndicate form dozens of dummy corporations while exploiting stock markets by perpetrating fraudulent pump and dump schemes.

"I know you and BCC were accessories to the Syndicate's cybercrimes, including hacking public and private computer networks and hijacking them until huge ransoms were paid.

"I know you and BCC facilitated the Syndicate's global narcotics distribution operation that has led to the addiction and death of thousands of people around the world. I know you conspired with the firm to secrete and launder the Syndicate's dirty profits while it helped finance Afghani warlords. We have documents and emails and all the evidence we need thanks to a confidential witness within BCC who's cooperating with the Government to save his own hide."

Tom paused for a moment to catch his breath.

"I also know Cosimo is the mastermind behind the Syndicate, and you and BCC helped him every step of the way to grow the Syndicate into one of the world's deadliest criminal organizations.

"And, Ignatius," Tom said, pausing again and inhaling deeply, "I know Cosimo Benedetto killed Jacob Cartel, your best friend since law school, and your brother-in-law."

It was all too much for Ignatius to handle. Blood rushed from his face, and he broke down sobbing. The sight of the old man, The Pope, ashen, his head thrashing from side to side, made Tom sick to his stomach. Ignatius was trying to catch his breath, but it was Tom who sat there breathless.

Gerard, hearing his boss sobbing, came running to the threshold of the loggia and was about to enter when Tom waved him away. Tom wanted to call the FBI to have Ignatius arrested on the spot and BCC's offices raided and bank accounts frozen, but first he wanted to hear directly from Ignatius. An admission, an explanation, a rationalization, an excuse. Anything. He wanted to hear it directly from The Pope himself.

Slowly, Ignatius regained his breath and wiped away his tears. Gone was the vicious fighter Tom saw when he first joined BCC, when Ignatius Balatoni, ever the gentleman lawyer, could make opposing counsel quake in their Gucci loafers with a well-timed glare, conveying the threat of the full weight of his behemoth law firm raining down on anyone who dared challenge a BCC client. Gone was the scholarly, bespectacled lawyer who counseled presidents and corporate titans, and who judges respected because they owed their positions to his patronage. Gone, too, was the founder and named partner of BCC who ran the firm with an iron fist, and who could make or break an associate's career, or the career of any BCC lawyer for that matter, with just one phone call.

Tom met Ignatius's gaze. "Tell me, Ignatius. How could you let this happen? Why would you make a pact with the devil?"

"You don't understand," Ignatius began after a long pause, his voice trembling. "Judge Colin, Jacob, and I, we devoted our lives to building a premier law firm, one that we hoped would last for centuries, and would promote justice and the rule of law." He was wheezing but took a deep breath and continued.

"We founded our firm on the belief that being a lawyer is a noble calling. That being in the service of others in order to protect life, liberty, property, and the rights the Almighty bestowed upon mankind is a solemn undertaking of God's work. We were his foot soldiers." Ignatius appeared to regain his own footing and began to look steadier. "We were conscientious and determined and diligent and proud and eager. We hired the brightest legal scholars whose commitment to the highest ethical standards was beyond reproach, and whose desire to fight for their clients, no matter the cost or sacrifice, knew no bounds."

Ignatius paused again to wipe tears from his eyes. Even at eighty-eight, and despite being frail and weak, Ignatius Balatoni still maintained his oratorical gift that commanded attention.

"Based on sheer perseverance and grit and old-fashioned hard work, we produced unmatched results and enjoyed successes the three of us could have never imagined when we opened the doors of Balatoni, Cartel and Colin."

Tom shifted his weight. He wanted Ignatius to get to the point, but almost reflexively understood he needed to give him the opportunity to state his case. At his pace.

"As our clients grew in number, so too did BCC. After many years of dedication and toil, BCC was lauded as the most respected law firm in the world. Thousands of families relied on BCC for their own financial well-being, to pay for homes, education, and vacations. They relied on BCC for their livelihood and for their children's comfort and happiness. BCC was responsible for providing for those families, to allow them to pursue the American dream. BCC made it possible for its employees' children to enjoy all the wonders that our world has to offer, and all the wonders that I as a child wanted but never had."

Ignatius sighed and wiped the corners of his mouth but maintained his composure. His voice grew slightly louder, and he sat more upright in his chair.

"And then one day, because of the ruthless avarice of so many, but through the fault of no one at BCC, it all almost vanished. Yes, BCC spent lavishly, and perhaps foolishly, on its employees and partners for many years. Yes, BCC got caught up in the race for the exposition of material wealth so we could demonstrate to our clients, and those we coveted as clients, that they would become stronger and richer if they retained our lawyers. And yes, our largess was excessive and extravagant, but we justified it by believing that our firm was serving society's needs and embodying the work of our Creator."

Tom was growing impatient listening to Ignatius's sermon.

"Until it all stopped," Ignatius said. "The cases, the referrals, the deals, the money. It just all stopped. The phones stopped ringing. Our lawyers sat idle. All those families that depended on BCC for their financial security and happiness were about to be crushed under the weight of BCC's debt and extravagant spending that had gone on for decades. Some would become homeless. Children would go hungry. Our employee's lives and the lives of their families would suffer."

Tom jumped in. "Is that how you justify what you did? That you were playing Robin Hood and saving lives? They would have been better off without BCC's complicity in all the crimes Cosimo and the Syndicate perpetrated that killed so many more people than you saved," Tom growled through clenched teeth, barely able to contain his rage at the man he once considered a mentor.

"You wanted your law firm to be revered, but it should have been reviled," Tom snapped. "You did it to protect yourself and your reputation. You were afraid of what would happen to you, and to your wealth, your power, your ego, and to your place in history. You were selfish. You craved adulation and just cared about you." He wanted to ask about payments to the small accounting firm on Long Island, but he noticed Ignatius's eyes filling with tears again and his hands trembling wildly. Ignatius began speaking even before Tom stopped.

"Perhaps, Thomas. Perhaps you are right," the sound of anguish evident in his voice. "I'm not immune to the fear of failure. My pride and hubris are my downfall. I was presented with an opportunity to save BCC, and to save myself. Jacob Cartel wanted no part of it. He was a good man. A stronger man than I was. He said it was better to die poor and with dignity, than to live in wealth but with shame and humiliation. He was right, but I wouldn't listen. I was stubborn. We did not speak for three months before he died."

"You mean before Cosimo Benedetto killed him in cold blood," Tom snapped. As soon as he said those words, he regretted it. Ignatius was already suffering, and Tom just twisted the knife. Ignatius was sobbing now, cradling his head in his hands.

Tom paced. He walked over to Ignatius and thought of trying to comfort him, but he was seething and too overcome with resentment and disgust. Ignatius Balatoni threw away a storied career after reaching the pinnacle of the legal profession, and he put in jeopardy the well-being of thousands of lawyers who dedicated their careers to BCC. All Tom could think of was that Ignatius Balatoni was going to spend the rest of his days behind bars.

"Was it worth it?" Turning around and spreading his arms out he asked again, "Was all of this worth selling your soul?"

Ignatius's voice was small now. He was quaking. "I didn't know, Thomas. You must believe me. At first, I didn't know the extent of the crimes Cosimo would commit," he said, trying to regain his breath. "I didn't know the power the Syndicate wielded. I didn't know Cosimo was a murderer. I didn't know he would kill Jacob." Ignatius hung his head and let out a guttural cry. "I should have known. I know now I should have understood better, but I was blinded by the possibility of saving the firm. When I discovered the truth, it was too late. Cosimo owned me. He owned BCC. I am overwrought with remorse. I should have..."

"You should have put a stop to it." Tom lashed out. "You should have stopped it when you had the chance."

Both men fell silent.

Tom had enough. Rather than ask any more questions, he decided then and there that Ignatius should be in custody.

"I'm calling the FBI. Your involvement and BCC's involvement with the Syndicate ends now."

Tom pulled out his cell phone and began dialing the number for the FBI's New York Field Office.

Ignatius tried clearing his throat. He looked down at his lap and at his trembling hands. Then, in a low, hoarse voice he said: "He is my brother. Cosimo Benedetto is my half-brother."

Tom heard the words but couldn't process what Ignatius just said. "What?" Tom's hand, which still held his cell phone, fell to his side before he finished dialing. "What did you say?"

"Cosimo is my half-brother."

Seconds passed. The room was spinning.

"There's something else you need to know, Thomas."

Ignatius's head fell back, and his eyes rolled back. His knees hit the glass table, knocking over cups and saucers. Ignatius stopped breathing.

"Gerard! Gerard!" Tom screamed as he tried to lift Ignatius to keep him from falling out of his chair.

"Call 911! Call 911!"

30

The wail of sirens could be heard before the ambulance and police cars arrived in front of Ignatius's apartment building and came to a screeching halt. The paramedics, pushing a stretcher and carrying medical bags, rushed into the building with the police following closely behind. The white-haired man knew they were coming because he'd listened to the wiretap on Ignatius's phone line. An eighty-eight-year-old male apparently suffered a heart attack, according to the 911 call.

Less than ten minutes later, the paramedics pushed the stretcher out the front door of the building and into the waiting ambulance that was left idling with its emergency lights on. The white-haired man did not see the person lying on the stretcher with an oxygen mask strapped to his face, but he assumed it was Ignatius Balatoni.

A few minutes after the ambulance sped away heading south on Fifth Avenue, Tom walked out of the building. He was confused and still reeling from what he had learned. Never in a million years would he have imagined that Ignatius and Cosimo were related. But it explained Ignatius's comment weeks earlier that it is those closest to you who pose the gravest threat and can hurt you the most.

He squinted in the midday sun. Ignatius's final words still replayed in his head. "There's something else you need to know..." Dozens of possibilities raced through his mind. He wanted badly to know what Ignatius was about to say before he lost consciousness.

By the time the paramedics raced Ignatius out of the apartment, his pulse was weak and the look in their eyes told Tom they didn't think he'd make it to the hospital. Tom shuddered at the thought of Ignatius passing. He was emotionally conflicted. He respected and revered him, dreaming that his own father possessed some of the same qualities he so admired in The Pope. But as the same time Tom was angry felt betrayed. The man he respected had gambled away his legacy, not to mention the rich history and prestige of his law firm, in a bid to salvage his ego and reputation. The image Ignatius Balatoni worked so hard to curate for so many years would forever be tarnished by his decision to join forces and protect the world's most notorious criminal—who, Tom had just learned, also happened to be Ignatius's half-brother.

Tom again considered calling the FBI's New York Field Office, this time to file a report, but given Ignatius's condition, he wasn't going anywhere, and Tom didn't want the FBI devoting resources preparing to arrest a man who may already be dead. And since it was a Friday in August, there were likely almost no partners in BCC's New York office, most of whom "worked" remotely on summer Fridays from their beachfront McMansions in the Hamptons or lakeside retreats. A raid on BCC's offices could wait until Monday.

Given the commotion that morning, Tom almost forgot the other reason he came to New York. The seventy-two-hour deadline LaShandra Johnson gave Troy was now down to less than sixty hours, and Tom was no closer to learning who leaked the AMX files to Resjudicata.com, or if he was being framed.

Tom hailed a cab and directed the driver to the downtown address of Resjudicata.com. As the cab maneuvered down Fifth Avenue in midday traffic, the blue *Sid's Painting* van with the white-haired man sitting in the back followed close behind.

Some twenty minutes later, Tom arrived in front of the nondescript, six story brick building on East Fifth Street, off Avenue C. He entered the building and looked at the directory. There was no front desk and no security. Tom walked up two flights and down the hallway until he found the door with the name Resjudicata.com stenciled across the frosted glass. How ironic, Tom thought, that a 21st century new media company that harnessed the power of the internet to disclose secret information about corporations and governments, housed itself in a nineteenth century brick and mortar walk-up building. For all the advancements in publishing, and the advent of the twenty-four-hour news cycle, Resjudicata.com still held the appearance of a backroom news operation from a long-ago era.

After knocking on the door and being buzzed in, Tom approached the young man sitting behind the counter enclosed in bullet proof glass.

"I'd like to speak with Ms. LaShandra Johnson."

"I'm sorry, but she is out in the field working on an assignment." The man didn't look up from his computer screen or pay much attention to Tom. It was quiet and it didn't look like anyone else was in the office.

"Do you know when she'll be back?" Tom asked, more than a little annoyed that the receptionist wasn't very receptive.

"I don't expect her in the office today, but you can take one of her business cards. It has her cell number on it. She usually answers her phone." The young man looked up long enough to point to the business card holder on the ledge adjacent to the small opening in the glass in front of him, and then returned his focus to his computer screen.

Frustrated, Tom walked downstairs while debating whether to call LaShandra Johnson.

The man with the white hair knew exactly where Tom was. He suspected Tom would visit the office of Resjudicata.com. As soon as Tom exited the cab and headed for the building's entrance, he pushed the talk button on the console in front of him.

"The canary has entered the coal mine. Execute the search warrant."

At that moment, six agents from the FBI's Washington headquarters pushed open the rear doors of the unmarked black van that had parked behind the dark sedan in front of Tom's apartment earlier that morning shortly after Tom left for the airport. Their plan was to search Tom's apartment if, as the FBI suspected, Tom was going to New York to meet with Resjudicata.com.

The agents rushed the lobby, announced they were with the FBI, and flashed their credentials. Two agents remained in the lobby with the doorman to make sure he didn't call up to Tom's apartment to announce their visit, while the other four agents headed for the stairs and climbed to the seventh floor. Once outside apartment 7L, one of the agents knocked hard on the door. "FBI, open the door."

Brooke and Mary had just sat down for an early lunch of cobb salad and roasted vegetables when they heard the loud knock. Startled, they looked at each other. The FBI agent knocked again, harder this time, and yelled even louder: "FBI. Open the door."

The residents of two other apartments on the seventh floor opened their doors slightly and stuck their heads into the hallway to see what the commotion was about. The agents quickly motioned for them to get back in their apartments.

Brooke ran to the door and looked through the peephole. She saw two men and two women wearing blue jackets over what appeared to be bullet proof vests. The jackets had a gold patch on the left side of the chest area emblazoned with the letters *FBI*. They were holding guns.

The lead agent heard footsteps and knew someone was standing on the other side of the door.

"This is the FBI. We have a search warrant to enter your apartment. Open the door now."

For a moment Brooke thought Tom might be playing a trick on her. What if the Executive Deputy Attorney General had sent FBI agents to deliver flowers to her? What a sick joke, she thought. But the guns looked all too real.

Within seconds the lead FBI agent yelled again. "You have five seconds to open the door or we're knocking it down."

This was no joke. Brooke stood back trying to protect Mary who rushed over and was standing behind her.

"How do I know you're really from the FBI?" Brooke demanded from behind the locked door, her voice loud but trembling with fear.

"Ma'am, I am Special Agent Douglas Aronson of the FBI. I am holding my ID up to the door for you to see. There are three other agents with me in front of your apartment, and two more in the lobby of the building. We have a warrant to search the contents of your apartment, including electronic communication devices. I am slipping a copy of the warrant under the door. Pursuant to Court order, I am directing you to open the door now and allow us entry to your apartment."

Brooke looked at the ID through the peephole. She had no idea what a legitimate FBI ID looked like, but the picture on this one resembled the person at the door, and the FBI logo was visible and clear. She knelt and picked up the copy of the search warrant. From what she could tell, a magistrate judge of the Federal District Court for the District of Columbia had issued the warrant at 12:30 a.m. this morning.

It entitled the FBI to search the apartment of C. Thomas Berte and Brooke Berte and seize electronic devices, financial records, cash, jewelry, the contents of any safes, as well as any other paper records or documents relating to a Wells Fargo account and AMX Corporation. The warrant referenced an investigation into C. Thomas Berte and Brooke Berte for obstruction of justice and stealing and mishandling government and classified information among a laundry list of other crimes, and included an alphabet soup of italicized references to statutes with the letters U.S.C.

"My husband is the Executive Deputy Attorney General of the United States," Brooke shouted, while motioning for Mary to remain quiet and back away from the door. "This must be a mistake. What is this about?"

"Ma'am, we know who your husband is. You and he are being investigated for violations of the laws of the United States. You are free to contact your husband or your attorney, but we're coming in in five seconds with or without your compliance."

Brooke had to act quickly. She thought of calling Tom on his cell, but it would take too long, and the agents were about to break down the door and barge in with guns blazing.

"Two seconds," the lead FBI agent said.

Brooke lunged for the doorknob and unlocked it. She intended to open it slightly as a sign of good faith, but the FBI agents weren't playing games. As soon as the door was slightly ajar, one of the agents thrust a short, thick metal pry bar into the opening to prevent the door from being shut. Within seconds they thrust hard against the door, practically tearing it off its hinges, shoving Brooke backward into the closet in the small vestibule before she fell to the ground. Three agents charged in, their guns aimed straight ahead, as Agent Aronson, gun in hand, stood over Brooke and asked about Mary. The other agents began making their way through the apartment and were quickly joined by the two other agents from the lobby.

"She's my mother-in-law. She does not live with us. She is staying with us for a few days," Brooke responded quickly, her heart pounding and eyes filling with tears.

"Okay, thank you ma'am," Agent Aronson said as he helped Brooke to her feet. "We'll make sure not to search her belongings, but we'll be going through all the rooms in the apartment. We're going to be here a while, so you might as well take a seat and try to relax." When he and the other agents were satisfied that Brooke and Mary posed no threat, and that no one else was in the apartment who could interfere with their search, they holstered their weapons.

Mary was shaking but appeared relieved the agents would not search her bags. Just to make sure, she took a seat on the chair in the corner of the living room with a view into the guest bedroom so she could keep an eye on the agents when they entered her room. She hadn't uttered a word since the agents rushed into the apartment.

"What is this about?" Brooke demanded, her voice quaking. "We've done nothing wrong. This must be some kind of mistake."

"There's no mistake ma'am," Agent Aronson replied. "As I said, you and your husband are under investigation for violating the laws of the United States and accepting a payment of $750,000 for disclosing confidential information. We have videotaped evidence of your husband accessing the bank account and withdrawing a large sum of money, and we have wiretap evidence. You are under suspicion as an accessory before and after the fact. It's all set forth in the search warrant. You're free to contact your lawyer if you'd like."

"I'm going to call my husband instead." Brooke dashed into the living room and picked up her cell phone.

Agent Aronson turned his back and raised his left hand to his mouth. With his thumb he pressed the button on the radio transmitter in his palm and whispered, "smoke signal two." The agent who remained in the unmarked black van clicked on the receiver to record Brooke's call.

Tom's phone rang as soon as he exited the building housing Resjudicata.com's office. He saw Brooke's name on the screen and clicked the talk button.

"Hi, Brooke."

"Tom, the FBI is in our apartment! They have a search warrant to search our computers and take our documents and jewelry. They came in with guns, Tom, guns! They're turning the place upside down. They said we're under investigation for taking money in return for disclosing confidential information. What the hell is going on? I'm scared. Please tell me this is all a mistake!"

Tom expected Brooke to be her cheery self when he answered the call. He couldn't believe what he was hearing.

"What the fuck! Are you serious?" Tom stopped dead in his tracks. "A search warrant? They have guns?"

"I'm dead serious. They've put away the guns now, but I'm really freaked out. What is going on? Tell me!" Brooke screamed.

"I, I don't know." Tom stammered. He tried to collect his thoughts, but his brain was in a fog.

"How many agents are there? What are their names?"

"Ah, Agent Aronson, or something like that. There are six of them, I think. What's this about?"

"Where's my mother?"

"She's here with me. She's as freaked out as I am. Will you please tell me what the hell is going on!"

"Brooke, listen to me very carefully. This call is likely being recorded. Stay in the apartment and keep an eye on the FBI agents. Stay off the phone and the computer. Do not say anything to the agents, do you hear me? I will contact you so we can talk. Don't call anyone. Wait for me to contact you. Stay off the phone. I love you. We'll be okay. I promise. I give you my word."

Tom hit the end call button on his phone. He looked around and saw a blue van with *Sid's Painting* written on its side. Was that the same van he saw earlier? He looked up and down the street and noticed at least four other similar vans. He was getting paranoid. He needed to think. He needed a plan. He walked in circles for a few seconds, and then looked down the street again. This time he noticed a man with white hair walking quickly toward him. Tom thought he'd seen the man before. The airplane! Earlier that morning. The white-haired man. He was the same man who sat two rows in front of him. Trailing the white-haired man as he made his way toward Tom were two other men in khaki pants and what looked like flak vests. Tom began to walk backwards. After a few steps, he turned and ran for the corner. When he was almost at the curb, he looked over his shoulder. The white-haired man and his goons were in full sprint running toward Tom.

Cosimo glared at the monitors in his study aboard the *Vulcania*. The terrified look on Mary's face when the agents raced into the apartment waving their weapons made him sick. He called out for Totto Nessa. He clenched his fists, and momentarily questioned his plan. He threw the remote control which crashed against one of the monitors.

As Totto approached the study, he heard the smashing glass. He opened the gold-plated door to see Cosimo standing in front of the flat screens. One of them was shattered, but the feed showing people with blue jackets scurrying around was still visible. Totto saw Brooke talking to one of the men in blue jackets, tears streaming down her face. He also saw Mary and the look of terror in her eyes.

Cosimo turned to Totto Nessa. "The time has come to bring in the *Ragazzo*. He must learn the truth."

31

Tom ran as fast he could south on Avenue C toward Houston Street. For once he was glad for gridlock. He weaved in and out of traffic to evade the white-haired man and his presumably armed buddies. Tom was in good shape with strong legs that allowed him to run fast, but his leather-soled dress shoes kept slipping on the sidewalk, slowing his pace. Fortunately, the extra adrenaline made up for his lack of traction, and he kept putting distance between himself and his pursuers.

At Second Street he turned left and headed west. The F train subway stop was a few blocks away, and he just needed to get to the station without getting caught so he could disappear among the maze of Friday afternoon commuters trying to get an early start on the weekend. He looked back and saw the white-haired man had slowed and was running behind the two goons. They were no match for Tom, though, given the extra weight they carried around their mid sections.

As Tom approached First Avenue, a police car with its siren blaring and lights flashing sped north. Tom thought the police would try to cut him off. As he turned south to run past the speeding car, he noticed it wasn't slowing down. The police blew past the red light and continued to head north, oblivious to Tom and his pursuers.

Tom continued his sprint, wondering if it was the FBI chasing him, or someone else. He didn't have time to consider the possibilities. He dodged cars and ran in between two buses stopped at a red light. He glanced back and saw only one of the goons following him. Had they separated, or did the other one fall back? The sidewalks were teeming with pedestrians, which gave Tom even more cover as he finally reached the subway station.

He raced down the steps two at a time. He looked back but didn't see any of the three men chasing him. As he passed a garbage can on his right, he grabbed his Blackberry and thrust it into the opening on top of the can, allowing the phone to drop onto a pile of garbage. If someone was tracking him based on the location of his phone's cell signals, the trail would run cold at the bottom of the trash bin.

As he sprinted for the train, he realized he didn't have a metro card. The station was jam packed and waiting in line to purchase one wasn't an option. Through the metal bars separating the crowd from the passengers getting off the train that had just pulled into the station, he noticed a homeless man pulling a shopping cart containing all his worldly possessions. Tom assumed the man would be exiting through the emergency metal gate because the cart was too bulky to slide under the turnstile. He walked over to the gate and held it open while pretending to help maneuver the cart. As he did so, he slipped through the open gate and ran twenty feet into an uptown F train just as its doors closed behind him.

Tom's eyes darted around as the subway car started moving. No sign of the white-haired man or the two goons. He decided to stay put instead of illegally walking between subway cars. One misdemeanor for fare jumping was enough. He didn't want to add to his rap sheet.

The cool air felt good. Tom's shirt was soaked with sweat. He lost the jacket he was carrying when he walked out of Resjudicata.com's building, dropping it somewhere as he raced through traffic. He tried to control his breathing. Pain radiated through his lower back from the adrenaline rush, and his knees felt weak. The subway car was crowded so he had to stand. Just as well, Tom thought, because if he sat, he might never get up. He needed to get in touch with Brooke and calm her. He also needed to find out who was chasing him and why. Tom couldn't believe what had happened in just the last few hours. He looked at his watch. It was almost

1:00 p.m. Tom looked up at the subway map above the doors and counted the stops to Penn Station.

Tom made sure he was the first person to exit the train as it pulled into the station so if anyone was following him, he'd spot them first. He hadn't figured on the immense crowd, though, standing shoulder to shoulder on the platform, with hordes of commuters trying to get on the subway as an equal number were getting off. Within seconds, Tom was lost in a sea of people. Even if someone was following him, there was no way they'd get close to him. He lowered his head and led with his shoulder, cutting and weaving to get through the crowd. He followed signs for Penn Station and walked briskly down the long tunnel. The air was stale and steamy and smelled of piss and body odor. New York in the summer.

He finally arrived on the Seventh Avenue side of Penn Station. Tom had been in Penn Station only a handful of times and still needed to check the overhead signs to get his bearings. He remembered an Irish pub on the second floor he'd been to a few times with friends after a Rangers game upstairs at Madison Square Garden. He found the escalator and ran up the steps toward the pub.

It was packed with a young crowd looking to catch a buzz before boarding the Hampton Express for the two-hour ride to the playground of the rich and famous. He made his way over to the bartender, a young, pretty brunette wearing cowboy boots, a cowboy hat, and a red flannel shirt tied-off at her slim waist.

"Excuse me. I seem to have lost my cell phone. Can I borrow your phone to make a quick call to my wife?" The bartender seemed interested in Tom until she heard the word "wife." She lifted the handset off the cordless phone by the cash register and handed it to him. "Make it quick. And buy a beer."

Tom smiled and asked for whatever was on tap.

Instead of calling Brooke, Tom called his favorite pizza shop near his apartment in Washington, DC.

"Antimo, this is Tom Berte. I need a big favor. I can't explain right now, but I need you to deliver a pie to my apartment. But here's the thing, I need you to include a note for Brooke in the box. Grab a pen. Ready? Here's what I want you to write: 'Go to Antimo's at 5:00 p.m. and use his phone to call me at our regular Friday night spot in NYC. Bring mom.' Got it, Antimo? When she gets there, please let her use your phone. Okay? What? No, I don't want any toppings on the pizza. Deliver an empty box for all I care, just get the note to Brooke! Thanks, Antimo. I owe you one. Gotta go."

Tom thought about calling Mary's cell phone to deliver the message to Brooke but reconsidered after remembering what Agent Young had told him about the FBI's advanced technological capabilities. For all Tom knew, the FBI was able to intercept radio and cellular frequencies into and out of his apartment, even without tapping the phone line directly. He couldn't risk it, and so on the fly he came up with the idea of calling Antimo to deliver the message to Brooke.

Tom had a few hours before he needed to get to the little Vietnamese restaurant on Second Avenue and 73rd Street where he and Brooke had dinner almost every Friday night when they lived in New York - if Tom got out of work before nine. A few years back, when Tom started at BCC, he had taken on a pro bono case for the owners of the restaurant and helped them adopt a little girl from Costa Rica. They were so grateful they tried to pay Tom for his work. Tom declined every time, and the couple insisted he and Brooke have dinner at their restaurant, on the house, as often as they wanted. It became their regular Friday night spot. The food was so good, they would have eaten there even if it wasn't free. They left a large tip for the wait staff every time they went, which made them feel better about not paying for their meals.

Tom kept looking around to see if he was still being followed. No sign of the white-haired man or anyone else. As he waited for his beer, he decided to make another call. The bartender wouldn't mind, Tom thought, since she was now preoccupied with a Wall Street type, probably hoping to cash in on a big tip. Tom called Special Agent Ann Leonardo.

"Tom, where are you? Are you okay?"

"I don't know, Ann, why don't you tell me? Why the hell were armed FBI agents knocking down the door to my apartment today?"

"Look, you need to turn yourself in. Things don't look good, but running isn't the answer and won't help your situation. You and your wife are in serious legal jeopardy. Tell me where you are, and I'll send someone to pick you up and bring you in."

"The hell I will!" Tom snapped. "What's this all about?"

"We know about the AMX files you copied, and we know about the three quarters of a million-dollar payment. Make this easy on yourself and your wife. Please surrender. We'll see if we can work something out, especially for your wife. The FBI Director and Attorney General have been briefed. A warrant for your arrest has been issued, and it's just a matter of time before your wife is arrested too. Please Tom, do the right thing and turn yourself in."

"Are you insane? Do you hear yourself? I haven't done anything wrong. I'm being set up."

"Tom, please, just come in and we can talk about it. Just tell me where you are."

"No. This is crazy. I had nothing to do with any AMX files and have no idea about a $750,000 payment. There's a man, tall with white hair. Is he with the FBI?"

"Yes, he's the Agent in Charge working under Agent Young. I know he's surveilling you. It won't be long before he finds you. I don't want this to get out of hand."

"Call them off, Ann. I've done nothing wrong, dammit! And I'll prove it!"

After more than two hours, Agent Aronson and his team were wrapping up their work, cataloging items they had searched and handing Brooke receipts for what they confiscated: the contents of Tom and Brooke's desks, a desktop and two laptop computers, two tablets, and Brooke's phone and her jewelry box containing her engagement ring. Brooke had managed to slip off her wedding band when the agents first stormed the apartment and knocked her to the floor, and she managed to hide it in her shoe without anyone noticing.

Mary remained silent while the agents searched every corner of the apartment. She fidgeted with her hands and tugged at the crucifix on her necklace. She tried to console Brooke, who alternated between stomping around the apartment in anger and sitting on the couch crying. Brooke kept asking no one in particular, "Why is this happening to us?"

As soon as the agents left the apartment, Brooke let out a sigh and hugged Mary. "Mom, I don't know what this is about, but I'm really scared. Tom said we should wait for him to contact us. My head is pounding, and it feels like it's about to explode."

"Oh, sweetheart. There has to be an innocent explanation for all of this. I'm sure Tom can clear it up. I'm so sorry this is happening to you. Why don't you lie down for a bit until he calls. It'll make you feel better."

"That's a good idea, mom. I feel nauseous and my head hurts." Brooke slowly made her way to the master bedroom and closed the door.

After a few seconds, Mary tiptoed to the guest bedroom. Her purse was in the same place she left it earlier that morning. Her hands were trembling, and her heart was pounding. She closed her eyes, tried to control her breathing, and whispered the Lord's prayer, a technique she started using a long time ago to soothe her nerves.

She reached for her purse and pulled out her cell phone. She pressed the numbers she knew by heart but had only dialed a handful of times in the last dozen years. She waited for her call to be answered.

32

"Nino, is that you? Something terrible has happened. I am in Washington visiting Thomas and Brooke. The FBI barged in with guns and searched the apartment and took computers and papers and Brooke's jewelry. They kept saying something about Thomas having leaked classified information and getting paid $750,000. And they say Brooke is an accomplice. Thomas would never do that. He never would. Brooke is hysterical. Thomas is in New York. Nino, you need to do something. We need your help!"

"I know, Bella. I know what is happening and I'm as upset as you are. Please try to remain calm. Do you know exactly where Thomas is right now?"

"How do you know what's happening? How can you possibly know? It all happened just in the last few hours. Nino, how do you know?" Mary's eyes widened and her voice was breathy.

"Bella, please, try to remain calm. I've always told you I'm aware of everything and I will always protect you and Thomas. Listen to me, please. I know Thomas is in New York. He went to see Ignazio earlier today. While they were meeting, Ignazio had a heart attack and was rushed to the hospital. He's alive, but barely. Bella, the time has come for Thomas to learn the truth. I can help him. He's being double-crossed by the very government he's working for. I need to speak to him. I need your help to get in touch with him."

Mary was flustered. Her mouth was dry. Her heart was racing. "What can you do? How can you help him?"

"I have a plan. But I need to speak to Thomas. I need you to persuade him to contact me."

"Huh, what? How can I do that?" Mary was trying to think and speak at the same time. She was too scared to cry. She felt queasy, as if she was about to faint.

"You need to tell him. Tell him everything. Tell him the truth. But most importantly, tell him I can help him. Tell him I can save him."

Mary was silent for several seconds.

"I don't know. I can't tell him over the phone. He'll never believe me."

"Listen to me," Cosimo shouted into the phone, but quickly caught himself, realizing that raising his voice was the last thing he should do. "I'm sorry, Bella. Please, listen to me. Thomas is in danger. He knows that. He will listen to you. He always listens to you. Tell him I have proof of his innocence, and I can help him. I can clear his name and protect him and his wife. All he needs to do is contact me. He'll listen to you. He always has. He won't want to disappoint you. He loves you. Tell him to do it for you," Cosimo was speaking softly and sounded reassuring, knowing Tom always did what his mother asked of him.

Mary relaxed a bit hearing Cosimo tell her he could help. He was always able to reassure her and make her feel secure, ever since the first day they met. Mary was young then, in her mid-twenties. She'd been out to dinner with her girlfriends in Manhattan's Little Italy, when a young Cosimo Benedetto, wearing a shiny suit with black slicked-back hair, a gold bracelet, pinky ring, and a diamond encrusted gold watch caught her eye. He was standing at the bar, holding court among a group of similarly young, well-dressed men who looked like they had nowhere to be and plenty of time to drink, laugh, and spend their cash.

After a few minutes of harmless flirtation from across the restaurant, Cosimo made his way over to Mary's table. Her girlfriends had noticed the good-looking guy at the bar with the shiny suit glancing in their direction, and each of them secretly hoped he would be making his way toward her.

But Cosimo set his sights directly, and only, on Mary. He held out his hand as he approached her. "Good evening. My name is Cosimo Benedetto, but my friends call me Nino. What's your name?"

That was the first night of a whirlwind, magical romance that would change Mary's life forever. From that moment on, the two became inseparable. Cosimo doted on Mary, showered her with gifts, and catered to her every desire. He called her multiple times a day just to say he loved her. Every night was an adventure. Dinner at the best restaurants, dancing at the finest clubs, and front row seats at movie premieres, sporting events, operas, and Broadway shows. Money was never an impediment, and the huge bulge in Cosimo's pants pocket, a wad of hundred-dollar bills, guaranteed that whatever Mary wanted, and wherever she wanted to go, he'd make it happen.

She heard whispers among her friends and family that Nino's professed job of comptroller for a construction company obscured his true calling, but by then she had fallen madly in love with the young, handsome Cosimo Benedetto and didn't care what he did for a living. He was smart and sophisticated, and she loved that he spoke French and Italian and even Latin. They had a fairy-tale romance and all she knew was that he treated her with respect and made her feel like she was the most important person in his life.

But despite her deep love for him, her father would never approve. He was a police captain who was overbearing and protective of his daughter. She knew anyone she brought home would have to live up to his impossibly high standards. He began steering conversations at the dinner table to gangs, especially of the ethnic variety, railing against their crimes and saying they were tearing apart the fabric of society. He was openly critical of gangsters like John Gotti who found themselves on the cover of New York's tabloids more often than his fellow police officers who worked hard to clear the streets of thugs and wiseguys. Mary was certain her father knew Cosimo's true profession, and he soon forbade Mary from seeing the love of her life. Talking to her father about a future with Cosimo was of no use, and she knew she could never defy him.

That was a lifetime ago. As Mary heard Nino's voice on the phone, all those memories, and the pain and hurt and the love, came rushing back.

She still loved Cosimo Benedetto and wanted so much for him to protect her. She snapped back to the moment.

"Please, Bella, tell him to contact me. I will protect him. I will take care of everything."

"Okay. Brooke spoke to him when the FBI agents were here, and he said he would get in touch with us. When he does, I'll…I'll…I'll tell him he needs to speak with you. I'll tell him the truth. I'll tell him you can help him. He'll finally learn the truth."

Mary didn't hear the door to her bedroom open or the footsteps behind her.

She felt a hand on her shoulder. Startled, she jumped.

"Mom, who are you talking to?"

33

Special Agent Bruce Young checked the Resjudicata.com website hourly. When the hell were they going to post the information about AMX and finally destroy Tommy's career?

His sham bereavement leave was coming to an end Monday, but he was in no condition to return to the Bureau. His drinking had increased, and he was drunk more often than he wasn't. He hadn't seen his daughter in several months and was sinking into a deep depression. He slept little and ate even less. His only sustenance came from the bottle of third-rate whiskey that was always within reach, and the fantasies that played in his mind that he'd soon actually be able to indulge with the money he'd been promised. It would arrive as soon as Resjudicata.com published the information. He kept checking the website.

The window air conditioner unit was on the fritz, unwelcome news in the late August heat. It kicked on with a loud thud that sounded like cinder blocks tumbling from the sky, but barely blew enough air to move a feather. And the air it pushed was damp and lukewarm. Just another item to add to the growing list of expensive things he needed to replace but couldn't afford. Not yet anyway. Even the trusted Pilgrim finally crapped out. The battery died when he returned from his trip, and he couldn't even afford to get a jump.

The stifling heat caused him to doze while sitting in front of his computer. The occasional thud of the air conditioner grinding to life jolted him awake just long enough for him to wipe sweat from his brow before he dozed off again. He never heard the large black SUV with tinted windows pull into the driveway and park behind the Pilgrim.

Gino Terranova wrestled his large frame out of the truck. Anyone bothering to look would have been shocked to see such a hulk of a man, wearing an overcoat on one of the hottest days of the year, heave himself out of the SUV and lumber purposefully to the rear of the house. Luckily for Gino, the block was deserted, with most of the houses abandoned and boarded up.

Gino assumed Agent Young would be armed, or at least have access to weapons, so he came prepared. The long overcoat concealed the laser enabled Remington ACR assault rifle with silencer. The Glock in his shoulder holster was locked and loaded, as was the Beretta in his drop leg holster strapped to his massive thigh which, although difficult for him to grab quickly given his girth, would come in handy as a weapon of last resort if necessary. He didn't really need the ten-inch hunting knife in its sheath at his side, but Gino didn't feel comfortable without it.

He trudged around to the back of the house and hoisted his body up the three brick steps to the weathered green door which was open. A flimsy screen outer door was the only thing separating him from his prey. He peered in and spotted his target slumped in a chair. He was either asleep or dead. The computer monitor in front of him was in screen saver mode, with colorful geometric shapes and designs bouncing across the sides of the screen, indicating his target had been in that position for a while. Maybe this would be easier than he expected.

Gino turned the knob to the screen door which squeaked as it opened, but Bruce Young remained still. Gino slowly walked into the dimly lit kitchen. The floors beneath his 375-pound frame creaked with every step, but his target, who was sprawled out in a chair in the adjacent living room, didn't wake. Gino noticed dishes piled high in the sink, and dry, caked-on splatter all over the stove and counter. The chairs in the kitchen were mismatched, and the walls were a dingy yellow. The tattered and peeling linoleum floor looked like it hadn't been swept or washed in years, and the sun-faded orange shag carpet in the living room was frayed and stained. "What a shit hole. I guess the FBI doesn't pay that well," he said to himself.

Gino held the assault rifle loosely in his hands as he slowly made his way through the kitchen and into the living room. The five-pound weapon was like a feather in his oversized hands. The drawn shades blocked out most of the sunlight, except for a few wisps of light casting a darkish shadow. As Gino inched closer to his target, he noticed Bruce's chest rising. He was alive.

When Gino was about two feet away from his victim, he leaned in. His massive right hand gripped the handle of the rifle nestled under his right arm, his index finger wrapped around the trigger. Gino pressed the muzzle end of the barrel into his target's forehead above the bridge of his nose and put his left hand on his throat, shaking him awake. "Don't make a sound motherfucker. Today is the day you meet your maker," Gino growled.

Bruce Young opened his eyes wide. He grunted under Gino's suffocating grip, unable to speak. His legs and arms flailed as he tried to wiggle his torso and push Gino off him, but he was no match for Gino's brute strength. Gino hoisted him up from the chair by his throat. With each move he made, the muzzle of the rifle dug deeper into his forehead, tearing his skin and causing blood to run down his face.

"Calm down, asshole. Stop moving or I blow your fucking head off."

Fully sober now, Bruce realized he was in no position to fight. His forehead blistered with pain, and he felt his windpipe crack. He was on the verge of losing consciousness.

Bruce stopped moving but remained wide-eyed. Gino loosened his grip on his neck just enough to allow Bruce to suck in a huge gulp of air, and he coughed when he exhaled.

"Who are you? What do you want?" Bruce stuttered, trying to catch his breath.

"I'm your worst enemy, Bruce Young." Gino sneered, confident his target was subdued, and he wouldn't have to spill any more of the man's blood.

"I'm with the FBI," Bruce tried to say as he coughed some more. "The people I'm working for will cut you into pieces. Do you know who you're dealing with?"

Gino swung the butt-end of the rifle hard across his victim's face and mouth. At least two of Bruce's teeth sailed clear across the living room. Blood poured from his nose and mouth. He doubled over in pain and let out a shriek.

"See what you made me do," Gino said, scowling. "Now, you won't look so good for the little girls." Gino moved back toward the kitchen and grabbed a dirty dish towel off the table. He threw it at him. "Now shut the fuck up and stand up. We're going for a little ride."

Tom took two big gulps from his beer. He had to get to the Vietnamese restaurant on the upper east side by five. He looked at his watch. It was 4:00 p.m. He decided to call LaShandra Johnson with the few spare minutes he had. The phone rang five times before going to voicemail. Tom debated leaving a message, but he hadn't figured out what to say. He'd call again when he got to the restaurant.

As he walked out of the pub and toward the main waiting area of Penn Station, he noticed a utility closet with its door open. Looking around to make sure no one was following him, he peered into the closet. It was empty except for two cleaning carts and dozens of bottles of cleaners, mops, and brooms stacked along the walls. For a second, he wondered if any of the cleaners contained centuron.

He noticed two blue shirts on a hanger with the name "Becker Cleaning Service" stitched on the left chest pocket and on the back, part of the uniform used by the janitors who tried in vain to keep Penn Station tidy for the thousands of commuters who marched through its doors daily. Looking around once more to make sure no one was lurking outside the closet, Tom walked in and closed the door behind him. He quickly removed his shirt and put on one of the blue shirts. He looked down and noticed a pair of well-worn sneakers, a better option than the dress shoes he'd been wearing since he left his apartment almost twelve hours earlier. He peered in to see if he could find the size. Nine-and-a-half. They'd have to do. He placed his shirt and shoes in a black garbage bag he found on a shelf. Hanging on the back of a door was a Knicks baseball cap. It completed the look, Tom thought.

Within seconds he was back in the main concourse. His eyes searched left and right. He flinched every time he saw a man with white hair, but luckily there was no sign of the agents who had chased him earlier. With the cap pulled low over his eyes, Tom headed for the subway that would take him east to the Lexington Avenue line, where he would switch to a northbound train to get to the Vietnamese restaurant.

The subways were running extra slow for a summer Friday afternoon rush hour, as workers spilled out of their offices. Tom got to the restaurant at about 4:45. Van Nam and Mai were setting up for the dinner crowd.

"Mr. Tom, is that you? So nice to see you again," Van Nam said in broken English, hesitating as he noticed Tom's blue work shirt and cap. He called out to his wife Mai to come greet Tom.

"Huh, Mr. Tom, are you okay?" Van Nam asked. Mai rushed over but looked confused to see Tom dressed the way he was. She was so accustomed to seeing Tom in a suit and tie every time he and Brooke dined there on Friday evenings.

"Mr. Tom? Welcome back," Mai said in English, which was only slightly better than her husband's. "Ah, you move back to New York? Is Ms. Brooke with you?"

"No, no," Tom said. "I'm just back for a visit. It's a long story. Look, Van Nam, can I use your office for a few minutes? Brooke is calling me here at five and I'd like to take the call from your office."

Van Nam had a confused look on his face. He turned to Mai who nodded her head. "Yes, yes, Mr. Tom." Mai said. "Follow me. You want dinner?"

"No, thank you, that's not necessary." Tom followed Mai and Van Nam to the back of the restaurant and into the tiny office. "I just need to use your office and telephone. I'll explain everything later."

Tom sat in the chair behind the small desk that essentially filled the entire space. He looked at Van Nam and Mai and asked them not to answer the call that would be coming in at five. He thanked them again, and after an awkward silence, they closed the door to the office and made their way back into the dining room.

Tom still had a few minutes to spare before Brooke would call, so he tried LaShandra Johnson again. Tom couldn't believe it was just about twenty-four hours since he first heard her name and the possibility that he was being framed for leaking secret information about AMX to Resjudicata.com. Information that Ann Leonardo had since confirmed, and which made Tom a wanted man. The call to LaShandra went to her voicemail. This time he decided to leave a message. Tom took a deep breath.

Ms. Johnson. My name is Charles Thomas Berte. I'm the Executive Deputy Attorney General of the United States. I understand you spoke to my former colleague yesterday, Troy McDonald, an attorney at Balatoni, Cartel and Colin, about information you have concerning AMX Corporation. I was told you may believe I am the source of information that was provided to you. I am calling to tell you, in no uncertain terms, that you are 100% mistaken. I have not leaked any information to you or anyone else about AMX. I will call you again this evening. Please do not publish or disclose any information until we have a chance to speak. Thank you.

Tom hung up, hoping the message would at least cause LaShandra to hit the pause button. Part of him thought it was crazy that he was being framed for the AMX leak. But then he thought back to the words Ignatius said to him—*sometimes the biggest threat comes from those closest to you.*

Moments later, the phone rang. Tom looked at his watch.

It was 5:00 p.m.

34

"Brooke is that you?"

"Yes, Tom. Thank God you answered. Are you okay?" Brooke's voice quivered.

"Are you using the phone from Antimo's?"

"Yes, yes. It was really clever how you sent me that message. Are you okay? Where are you? What the hell is going on?"

"Oh, babe, I'm so sorry you have to deal with this. Did they hurt you or mom today when they searched the apartment?" Tom was anxious and on edge, but mostly enraged.

"I'm okay. I was scared to death. Especially when I saw the guns. So was your mom. She's here with me. The FBI agents pushed me to the floor when they barged into the apartment, but I'm okay now, just still freaked out. Not knowing what's going on is the worst part. The FBI agents said we received a $750,000 payment for leaking information about one of your former clients. I can't imagine that's true. Is this some kind of mistake?"

Tom was seething. The thought of armed agents forcing their way into his apartment, knocking Brooke to the ground, and scaring her and his mother nearly to death infuriated him.

"Yes, that's exactly what this is, Brooke. I don't know anything about any leak, or any pay off. The first time I heard about this was last night when

Troy McDonald, the partner at BCC that I worked with on the AMX trial, called to tell me a journalist approached him yesterday to say she'd been given a thumb drive containing confidential documents and suggested that I'm the person who sent it to her."

"Apparently the FBI thinks so too. And that I'm involved. None of this makes sense!" Tom heard the fear in Brooke's voice. She was practically yelling into the phone. "Why the hell do they suspect you as the source of the leak?"

"I don't know, babe. A couple of guys, who I later found out were FBI agents, were following me today, and one of them was even on the flight with me to New York this morning. We were in a foot race, but I managed to evade them. Right after you called me today, I spoke to someone from my team who told me I'm essentially on the 'most wanted' list, and the FBI has a manhunt out for me. This is fucking crazy."

Brooke began crying and screamed, "Oh, my God, what is happening to us? Why is this happening?"

"I'm going to turn myself in," Tom said almost without thinking. "I can prove I'm innocent and didn't leak the information. I'll just take my chances with the criminal justice system."

"How can you do that?" Brooke said, sobbing. "I heard the agents say they have wiretaps and confirmation for a Wells Fargo bank account you opened where the money was deposited, and one of the agents said they have video of you withdrawing some of the money. They also said they have evidence you accessed classified information from your office computer and downloaded documents and that I'm an accomplice. I heard them say they have us dead to rights and we'll spend the next twenty-five years in prison." Her voice was trembling.

"This is insane. All of it. I'm innocent. Whatever evidence they have is fake or doctored. I never opened a bank account at Wells Fargo, and never withdrew money or downloaded any damn documents, and I've never leaked anything. Sweetie, you have to believe me." Tom was shouting and his voice reverberated against the walls in the tiny office.

"I do. I never for a moment doubted your innocence. But I'm not the one you need to convince. I'm scared."

He was scared too. He thought back to something Agent Young told him. *This isn't your grandfather's FBI. The technology the FBI has today would make your head spin.*

"There's something else you need to know. But I think it's better if you hear it from your mom."

Tom sat in silence waiting for his mother to come on the line.

"Thomas, are you okay?"

"Yes, mom, I'm fine. I'm sorry about what happened today. I'm sure it's the last thing you imagined would happen during your visit with us. I'm sorry." He tried hard to hold back tears.

"Shh, it's okay, son. I'm okay. I was a little shaken. Brooke and I both were, especially when Brooke fell to the floor and we saw the guns, but we're okay now. But I'm afraid of what the government will do to you. Those agents today, they had venom in their eyes. They won't be satisfied and won't stop until they capture you."

"Please don't worry, mom. I'm going to figure a way out of this. There's got to be a way, and I'll think of it. I'll handle it, and I don't want you to worry. You've had enough to deal with in your life. I don't want you to be frightened."

"Thomas, you need to listen to me. Please be quiet and just listen to me." Mary raised her voice. Her assertiveness stunned Tom for a moment. She sounded stronger than he ever remembered hearing. "There are some things in life you can't handle on your own. This is one of those times."

"What are you talking about?"

"There are things that have happened to me, to you, that I never told you about. Partly, it was because I was ashamed. And partly because I was scared. And because I wanted more for you. I always wanted to protect you and shield you."

Tom's heart raced and his palms were sweaty. He braced himself for what his mother was about to tell him.

"There's someone who can help you. Help prove your innocence. He's done some terrible things. And I wanted to protect you from all of it. But the time has come for you to know the truth. And to save yourself and your family."

"Mom, does this have anything to do with monthly payments from BCC to the accounting firm you work for?"

Tom heard Mary gasp.

"You know about that?" she asked. "What else do you know?"

"Before I answer that, there's something you need to answer."

He debated whether he should ask the question. But the events of the last twenty-four hours whirled in his head. He thought of the conversation he had with Brooke last night and Brooke's suspicion that his father was still alive. He thought of how scared Brooke sounded when the FBI executed the search warrant. He couldn't rid his mind of the image of armed agents rushing into his apartment and pushing her to the floor.

He hated himself for putting her through this, and for not being there with her. His career was on the line, not to mention his and Brooke's freedom. Everything he'd worked so hard to achieve was crumbling before his eyes. He had to know the truth.

"Do you know Cosimo Benedetto?"

35

"He's your father."

The words hung in the air. Tom's mouth fell open, but no words came out. He gasped for air but was too stunned to breathe. He was hot and sweaty. The brick walls of the small office closed in on him as the room spun. He was about to pass out. Sounds were muffled and darkness obscured his vision. He must be having a dream. The events of the past twenty-four hours hadn't really happened. The last three months hadn't happened. He was still an associate at BCC. He and Brooke were happy, living in New York and thinking about starting a family. Ignatius was alive and well and basking in the twilight of his career at having founded a preeminent law firm that would continue to thrive long after he went on to his just reward. None of what he learned was true. None of this was happening. Thoughts were crashing in his head. The pain was too much. He just wanted everything to stop.

The sound of his mom's voice thrust him back to reality. This *was* happening. It *was* true.

"This isn't how you were supposed to find out. I don't know how, or when, or even if, you would have ever learned the truth, but I didn't want you to know. Cosimo did, though. He always said he had a plan. He wanted you to know you were his son. You are his son. He wanted to tell you. When the time was right. But I didn't. I wanted to protect you."

"Thomas, are you there?" Mary asked after a long silence.

"He's...my...father?" Tom said slowly, letting each word sink to the same bottomless pit where his heart now sat. "How is that possible? You told me my father died when I was young." He was trying to make sense of the nightmare he was living. "You said Charles Berte died in a motorcycle accident. You lied to me all these years?"

"I wanted to protect you. I had to protect you. Cosimo always wanted you to know the truth. He's loved you since the day you were born."

Tom was searching for words but couldn't speak. He was suffocating and clenched his jaw.

"I was young and naive," Mary continued. "I fell in love with him the moment I met him. He was smart and strong, and he cherished me. He loved me. We were together for a long time, and it was the happiest time in my life. He was my rock and told me how much he adored me. We talked about the future. I wanted to marry him, and he wanted to marry me. But I couldn't. Grandpa Jack wouldn't hear of it. He forbade me from marrying him."

The crush of memories and flood of emotions came rushing back. Cosimo was her first lover and there would be no one else. She gave in to her desires and willingly lost herself in him. It was heaven. He was passionate and she was insatiable. But it was never about sex between them, but rather love in the making. Mary never doubted Cosimo's love or his fidelity. They had a rock-solid relationship built on respect and trust, and there would never be another man for her. Cosimo made sure of that, even after he was deported. The landscaper working at Mary's house who made a pass at her learned that the hard way.

"We spoke often about raising a family. And when I became pregnant with you, I was overjoyed. It was a dream come true." Mary left out the part about secretly considering having an abortion, but ultimately deciding she couldn't go through with it. "Cosimo was devastated when I told him I wouldn't marry him. He wanted to plead with Grandpa Jack and promised to do whatever it took for us to be together. But grandpa would never allow it, and I couldn't defy him. And then, almost in a flash, just a few years after you were born, Cosimo was arrested. I didn't see him for three months while he was in detention before he was sent back to Italy."

Tom was listening to his mother but hardly heard her.

"I knew about the life he led. And I hated it," Mary said, sobbing, "but I loved the man. He didn't choose that life as much as it chose him. It was the only life he knew. He had such anger and hatred for the government and for authority. When they deported him, they'd robbed him of the only family he had left." Mary sounded distraught.

Tom's gut wrenched in pain. The veins in the side of his head throbbed. He was soaked in sweat and breathing hard. He wanted to put his fist through the brick wall of the office.

"You can't be serious, mom. He's a criminal. A gangster. A wiseguy. He's a goddamn thug and a mass murderer. He's killed people with his own hands, personally ordered the deaths of others, and he and the organization he controls are responsible for the deaths of tens of thousands of people around the world with the drugs they deal." His voice escalated into a yell. "I know all about Cosimo Benedetto. He was a two-bit street hood working for the Gambino Crime Family in the eighties and nineties. You make him sound like he was some kind of saint. He's a sociopath. He's ruthless. He's the leader of a worldwide criminal organization that has left behind a trail of death and destruction a mile high and runs deeper than any of us know. Cosimo Benedetto is a stone-cold killer. I can't believe you're telling me he's my father."

"And I loved him," Mary snapped. "He is the only man I've ever loved. And he loved me and cherished for me. And he loved you. He adored you. It destroyed him when he left you."

"It apparently didn't completely destroy him because he's still alive and he's more dangerous now than he's ever been. Do you have any idea how much destruction that man is responsible for? He's the man I've been investigating for the last three months. He's the man the United States Government is hell-bent on catching and imprisoning for the rest of his life."

"The very same government that wants to put you in jail and stormed into your apartment today with guns blazing and ransacked it," Mary screamed. "The same government that is ruining your life. For thirty years I've denied myself my one true love to protect you!

"You want to hate what the man does for a living, hate it," Mary said. "I do. But you need to know the payments you found going to the accounting firm I work for are the least of what your father has done for us. Everything we have, everything you have, you owe to him. The house we lived in, the vacations we took. Your awards, your achievements, your trophies, the grades, Harvard, Harvard Law School, the clerkship, the law firm, none of it would have happened if not for your father. He made it all happen."

"Bullshit. It's all blood money. I worked for all of that. I earned it. I achieved all of that on my own," Tom yelled, furious his mother was suggesting otherwise.

Mary considered telling Tom the entire truth. That all he had accomplished in his life, his privileged resume, all his triumphs, and how and why things always seemed to fall in his lap, were the result of Cosimo pulling strings and orchestrating Tom's life, even manipulating it. It wasn't based on his own merit. He had little to do with it and wouldn't have achieved half of what he accomplished without Cosimo's help. He didn't have the grades, test scores, or the good fortune. Cosimo arranged it all. Just like when Tom was an undergraduate at Harvard and almost missed out on a perfect 4.0 GPA when he got a C- on a final exam. He appealed, but the professor refused to change the grade, until Cosimo interceded on Tom's behalf. After Gino Terranova had a chat with the professor, Tom received an A on the exam. The professor quietly retired at the end of that semester and was never heard from again. One of the many casualties of Cosimo's enormous reach. It was vintage Cosimo. He used his influence and resources and, when necessary, brute power to ensure Tom always came out on top. But now was not the time for *that* truth. Mary had a job to do. She needed to persuade Tom to call Cosimo. It was the only way to save him.

"I don't want to argue with you," Mary said. "All that matters now is you clear your name and protect Brooke and the two of you get out of this mess you're in. I know you're innocent. Brooke knows you're innocent. Cosimo can help you. He's been following your career and has vast resources. I spoke with him today. He knows who's trying to frame you and Brooke. He wants to help you. You need his help."

Tom was reeling from what he'd just heard. How could he turn to Cosimo for help?

"Ignatius Balatoni is my...?"

"He's your uncle. He is your father's half-brother. His mother returned to Italy after Ignatius's father died right before he started law school at Yale. She was young and beautiful. And when she returned to Italy she had another child. She gave birth to Cosimo and quickly put him up for adoption. Ignatius adored you from the time you were born. I know he had a massive heart attack earlier today, but he's still alive.

"You need to think of yourself, and Brooke. The government won't stop until they destroy you both, just like they want to destroy Cosimo. He can help you. Let him help you."

Silence.

"I want to speak with Brooke."

"Babe, listen to me. This is all crazy. I can't believe any of this is happening." Brooke spoke fast and was jumbling her words. "I just knew, when your mom said your father was proud of you last night, I just knew he was still alive. I've had a feeling for a long time that something wasn't right. But you didn't want to hear it. Something never made sense, but it makes sense now. He says he has evidence to clear you and me. He said he can help us. He wants to help us." Brooke started crying again. "I don't know how, or what he knows, but it sounds like he's the only person who can help us prove we're innocent. I think you should speak to him. Just hear what he has to say.

"Your mom is really hurting. She hates that this is happening to you. To us. And I'm scared. I'm afraid, for you and for me. Our lives and our careers will be destroyed. This will kill my parents. They won't be able to handle it. Please, call him, just talk to him. Listen to what he has to say. Promise me you'll call him."

Brooke's words hit hard. He hated hearing her sound so afraid and helpless. She didn't deserve what was happening to her and neither would her parents. But he was torn. "Brooke, do you understand what you're asking me to do? My father is a criminal. He's a goddamn murderer. The

Justice Department is investigating him. I'm investigating him. He deserves to rot in jail. And we're going to catch him. I want nothing to do with him." Tom squeezed the phone, his knuckles turning white. He couldn't believe Brooke didn't get it, and that he needed to spell it out for her in such elemental terms.

"You're not investigating anyone. You don't work for the Justice Department anymore. You and I are being hunted right now. Someone is trying to ruin us. They're trying to destroy our lives. I heard them today. I saw them. They won't stop until they ruin us. And your father says he can help you. For once, stop fighting other people's battles and just focus on your own. Protect yourself. Protect me. Then you can start saving the world again."

The sound of Brooke sobbing was too much for him to bear. He was in disbelief and overwhelmed. She begged him to take down Cosimo's number and, before she hung up, made him promise he'd make the call.

Tom was confused and in shock. He was wanted for crimes he didn't commit. He just learned the man he'd been pursuing, the world's most wanted criminal, was his father. His head was spinning. He was physically sick and mentally exhausted. He was about to puke. He needed time to think. The two most important people in his life wanted him to do something that went against every fiber in his being. He'd never asked for help—from anyone. This was a legal problem he was in, and he was a lawyer. And a damn good one. He could figure out how to get himself out of the hell he was in. He just needed to come up with a plan.

Tom stared into nothingness, his mind taking him back to simpler days, when the knock startled him. Van Nam slowly opened the door. Standing behind him was Mai carrying a tray of bun rieu, thit kho to, and bun thit nuong, Tom's favorite dishes from when he and Brooke ate at the restaurant on Friday nights. The aromas made Tom nauseous, but he tried hard not to show it. He realized he hadn't eaten anything since a bagel on that morning's flight, but he wasn't hungry. He felt sick.

"Mr. Tom, this is for you. We don't want to know what is the matter, we just hope you and Ms. Brooke okay." Van Nam said in halting English that was difficult to understand. Please eat—on house—like always."

"Thank you, Van Nam, Mai. You shouldn't have." Tom hoped talking would prevent him from dry heaving. "This looks delicious."

Mai cleared the small desk and set the dishes in front of Tom, and Van Nam put down silverware and a glass of Tom's favorite lemon tea. As he did so Isabella ran into the cramped office.

"Mr. Tom, you remember Isabella?" Mai asked.

Tom looked at her. Her brown eyes were big and beautiful. She had thick dark hair, dark skin, and a smile that lit up the dingy office. She was not shy at all and came right up to the desk and held out her hand.

Mai turned to Isabella and said in Vietnamese, "This is the lawyer who brought you into our lives."

Van Nam translated for Tom what Mai said to Isabella.

"I was happy to help, Mai. You and Van Nam deserve to be parents to this beautiful little girl," Tom said as he reached to shake Isabella's hand. "How old are you, Isabella?"

"I'm six, a whole hand and one finger," Isabella said, holding up her hands.

Everyone laughed. "You've taught her to speak Vietnamese?" Tom asked Mai.

But before Mai could answer, Isabella spoke up. "And I speak English and Spanish too."

"What a beautiful, precocious little girl," Tom said.

Then Isabella spoke again, "Thank you for giving me my family." Isabella walked around the desk and held out her arms to give Tom a hug. "I love my family," she said. Mai's eyes welled up with tears, and Van Nam puffed out his chest as only a proud daddy could. A lump lodged in Tom's throat.

"I'll just eat a little and will need to leave in a few minutes," Tom said, his voice cracking. Turning to Isabella he said, "Thank you, Ms. Isabella, for being who you are and for making your parents so happy."

Isabella smiled and grabbed her parents' hands. The three of them left Tom alone in the small office and closed the door behind them.

Tom looked down and shut his eyes. He forced himself to focus. He had to consider his options. He needed to devise a plan to save himself and Brooke. A plan that would get him out of this mess and defeat the powerful forces seeking to destroy him. Barely fifteen minutes passed. The rough outlines of a plan were coming together in his head, helped by meeting little Isabella. Through shuttered eyes he began to see glorious light pierce the gloom.

He grabbed the phone on the desk and dialed Lindsay Crutcher's number in London. He knew it was almost midnight there and he'd probably be waking her, but time was his enemy.

"Lindsay, I'm sorry to be calling so late, but I need to ask you something. Tell me about MI 6's Project Sana."

36

Before leaving the restaurant, Tom pulled Van Nam aside. He needed a favor but was embarrassed to ask. He left that morning with forty dollars in his wallet, credit cards, and his bank card. The cash wasn't enough for what he needed, his bank account was likely frozen, and his credit card was certain to leave an electronic trail Tom couldn't risk. He asked to borrow $500. Without hesitation Van Nam walked into the small office Tom had been using, went to the safe in the footlocker in the corner, and pulled out five crisp one-hundred-dollar bills and handed them to Tom. "If you want more, I give you more."

"No, Van Nam. This is enough. I'm sorry to ask you for this. I promise I will pay it back in a few days," Tom said, uncomfortable he even had to ask for the money in the first place.

"No mention it. After what you do for my family, this is least I can do. Good luck, Mr. Tom. If you need anything, you call me." The two men embraced, and Tom promised he would see Van Nam again soon.

On his way to the restaurant earlier that afternoon, Tom had passed a sign advertising prepaid cell phones in the window of a corner bodega, the kind of place that doesn't ask questions or require identification. After shelling out $175, plus $75 for prepaid international cellular access, Tom finally had a means of communicating without fear of being traced, as long as he didn't call the wrong people. Now all he needed was a quiet, out of the way place to conduct his business. Tom thought for a second. Central Park was just a few blocks west. Tom was certain he could find a hidden spot to make. He had an important call to make.

Cosimo was sitting in his study aboard the *Vulcania* with Totto Nessa. It was almost one in the morning, and the two were enjoying amaretto on the rocks and smoking Cuban cigars. The *Vulcania* had docked in Port Hercules in Monaco a few hours earlier. Cosimo was expecting visitors the following morning, old friends from Sicily who were interested in expanding heroin processing facilities they recently established in the remote, mountainous region north of Licata. They wanted to share a proposal with Cosimo for how to deal with the newly elected *Presidente della Regione di Sicilia* (President of the Region of Sicily) who was yet unschooled in the extensive powers the Syndicate wielded throughout the island.

The President, a northerner who only recently moved to Sicily, had campaigned on a promise to rid Southern Italy of the mafia's influence. Cosimo considered intervening prior to the election, but he concluded it would be better optics to have an anti-mafia candidate win the vote initially in order to quell cries from Rome that Palermo wasn't doing enough to stifle the mafia's power. Cosimo knew he could *persuade* the President to see things his way after the election, and the two would co-exist in an arrangement that would benefit both men: the Syndicate's interests would continue uninterrupted, and the new President would live to see another year.

Mary called Cosimo after she spoke with Tom. She relayed that she begged Thomas to call him. She explained she told him that Cosimo had evidence that he was being framed by his former colleagues in the government and that Cosimo could help prove his innocence. Mary said she told their son everything. That Cosimo was his father. That Ignatius was his uncle. That Cosimo had supported Mary and Thomas their whole lives.

Mary also told him that Cosimo could protect him now, and that he needed his father's help. Even Brooke implored Thomas to call.

Cosimo was pleased. His plan was coming together. All he wanted was an opportunity to speak to his son and tell him how much he loved him and prove he could help him.

And all he would ask in return was for Thomas to protect *him*.

Cosimo sat silently, waiting and hoping for the phone to ring.

"Nino," Totto said as the wait dragged on. "I've always been loyal to you. And I've never questioned you about the merits of your plan. Your successes, time and again, have proven your instincts correct. But this time I must ask you. How could you be certain that allowing the *Ragazzo* to take the position with the Justice Department would result in him protecting you? He could have just as easily used his position to persecute you. Even now, with this development, are you certain your plan will work?"

Cosimo took a sip of amaretto. The smoky sweetness lingered in his mouth as he considered Totto's question.

"I have no assurances, Totto," Cosimo said when he finally spoke. "For thirty years I've thought about how I would reunite with my son. With each success he achieved, our destinies separated further. But I could not deny him his path in life. I could just ensure that his path was made easier, straighter. Above all else, I knew Thomas loved his mother and would do anything to protect her and ensure her happiness.

"He would listen to her and do whatever she asked of him. And I knew Ignazio would nurture him and care for him. I hoped that given the opportunities I created for him, when the time came for Thomas to learn of me, that he would accept his fate. My only hope for the future is the possibility of regaining what I've lost in the past."

Cosimo stood and walked to the large windows overlooking the city of Monte Carlo at the foot of the harbor. "I have lived a long life, Totto. Who knows how much longer I have. The authorities are getting closer. They're getting wiser and more sophisticated. The end could come sooner than any of us know. I may be running out of time to save myself and reclaim my son."

He turned to Totto. "By having someone on the inside—by having my son on the inside—I could learn what they know and how they plan to attack me. That's why I devised my plan the way I did. It may be my last chance to protect all I've built against tyranny and oppression by the world's authorities. By creating the need Thomas would have for me, I could save him and save myself in the process. If my son accepts my plan, all that I have will be his. I love him dearly," Cosimo said as he became emotional. He took another sip of the cold amaretto and gazed at the crystal blue waters of the Ligurian Sea.

Even though Totto was his most trusted confidant, Cosimo hadn't shared all the details of his plan with him. Cosimo understood there was a possibility his son would accept his assistance but reject his love. He also understood that Thomas might turn his back on him and attempt to betray him, like so many others before him tried to do. But Cosimo was prepared for that. If Thomas refused to execute the plan, Cosimo would use the resources at his disposal to *persuade* his son to give up all he knew about the government's investigation into the Syndicate's operations. After manipulating his son's life and orchestrating his successes and accomplishments, Cosimo would have no qualms turning on him and falsely claiming that Thomas had hustled and cheated his way to the top. That, along with the felony conviction that would certainly befall him and Brooke for disclosing secret grand jury minutes and confidential information about the government's investigation into AMX, would surely be enough to convince Thomas to fall in line and comply with Cosimo's demands.

Cosimo shuddered at the thought of having to invoke the nuclear option against his son. But if Thomas was going to be a threat, he would have to be neutralized. Cosimo hadn't survived this long by allowing threats to exist. He understood that bringing Thomas in was the end game. Either his son would embrace him, accept him, and protect him, or else. His plan would allow Cosimo to know for sure whether he could trust his only child. Time would tell.

The phone ringing jolted both men. Totto glanced at Cosimo who reached over and slowly raised the receiver off the cradle.

"*Pronto.*"

"Cosimo Benedetto?" Tom said, hesitating just a bit, but trying to sound confident.

Totto Nessa checked his laptop. The call was coming in on an untraced, prepaid international line that had been activated just a few minutes earlier. The phone was a burner. Tom was smart. The apple hadn't fallen far from the tree. Totto nodded toward Cosimo.

"Yes, this is Cosimo. Is this Thomas?" Cosimo said, betraying an accent that Tom barely discerned.

"Yes." Tom took a deep breath, trying hard to recall the precise words in the script he prepared for himself before calling Cosimo. "I never expected to speak with you. I was told you died when I was very young."

"I know. I wish things had been different. Your mother is not to blame. It was out of her control. She wanted what was best for you. We both did." Tom heard Cosimo's voice crack.

"You care for her?" Tom asked.

"More than you will ever know. She is the only woman I have ever truly loved, and I would give my life for her."

Tom thought he would vomit.

"I'm sorry. For the way things turned out. This is not how I wanted things to be. But I was always there for your mother. And for you."

"I know," Tom said. He was angry with himself for interrupting Cosimo. He planned to listen more than talk, but he was nervous and couldn't contain his emotions. "My mother told me you provided for her, and for me. Thank you for taking care of us," Tom clenched his fist.

"I did it out of love. For you and your mother." His voice cracked again.

Tom couldn't stand the emotional shit show. He wanted to scream. He wanted to yell. He wanted to wake up from this nightmare. But he had a job to do. He steeled himself for what was to come.

"My mother tells me you can help me and my wife. Can you?"

"Yes. I have followed your career closely. And I owe a debt of gratitude to my brother." Hearing Cosimo mention Ignatius infuriated Tom.

"I'm aware of your government's efforts to destroy you and your wife. Don't ask me how. There will be time later for me to share the details with you. I trust you are not entirely surprised."

"No, I'm not. Although there's still quite a bit I don't know, I'm aware you are a powerful man with many friends. And I know that with power comes knowledge and the ability to control things." Tom said, trying to sound sincere and appreciative of Cosimo's offer to help. "My mother tells me you have evidence that proves I'm being framed."

"I do. I can prove your innocence. I know who is framing you. I can protect you. If you let me."

"The FBI will stop at nothing until they put me behind bars. I have my suspicions of who's trying to frame me, but I have no proof. And without proof I have nothing."

"I have proof," Cosimo said, sounding excited. "You have enemies in the US Government. They've made it appear as if you copied files relating to your former client, and they arranged for a payment into a bank account with your name on it to make it look like you were paid off. I have everything you need to clear your name. Evidence of the hacking, the altered facial recognition images to make it appear that you opened the bank account and retrieved the funds. I have evidence that will prove you were not the source of the leak. I can protect you. Let me help you."

"Cosimo. I can't believe this is happening to me. My wife is terrified. The FBI is searching for me as we speak. There's a national manhunt for me. If they catch me, they'll…"

Tom allowed his voice to fade away.

"I won't let that happen. Listen to me. I won't let them capture you. Let me send my people to you so I can protect you."

Tom let out a guttural sigh. "I'm scared, Cosimo. My wife is scared. Scared of what they'll do to me and to her. And I'm scared of what will happen to her, and to my mother."

The words pierced through Cosimo. He hated putting Tom through this, but he was proud that his son's first instinct was to protect those he loved. "I won't let anything happen to you or them. I can protect you, and your wife, and your mother. I have the power to protect all of you."

"I don't know. If what I believe is happening is actually happening, then I'm being watched very closely by the FBI, and my movements are being tracked. We need to be careful and smart about this. I want you to help me, Cosimo. I need your help."

Cosimo finally exhaled. He had held his breath for what seemed like an eternity waiting for his son to accept his offer. His plan was working. The end was in sight. There would be no need for Cosimo's *alternate* plan. He would finally be able to help his son in plain sight, without hiding it like so many other things he had done. He would be able to demonstrate his love and loyalty, and this time, for the first time, Thomas would know his father was behind it.

"Where are you, so I can arrange to come to you?" Tom asked.

Cosimo flinched. He hesitated. His instincts told him to avoid the question. His whereabouts were a state secret. But he didn't want to be evasive. He wanted his son to trust him, to feel comfortable. If he pushed him away now, he worried Thomas would turn and run.

"I am in Europe," Cosimo said, refusing to engage in the debate going on in his mind. It was his son he was speaking to, after all, dammit.

"The past three months have taught me things about my government that I would never have imagined," Tom said. "The government's power and might is broad and limitless. I need to make sure I'm not being followed. I need time to cover my tracks. I will contact you tomorrow and we can arrange to meet."

Cosimo didn't like the idea. It wasn't how he'd planned things. He didn't like not being in control, but he could hear the fear in Thomas's voice. His son was smart and knew what he was doing. Yes, he was afraid, but he wanted to protect his wife and mother, just as Cosimo would. He didn't want to risk alienating his son by demanding that he follow his orders. Not now, not after everything he had done to get this close.

"Ok, I will await your call, and then I will have my people bring you to me. And Thomas, know that I love you. I have always loved you." Cosimo's voice trembled as he held back tears.

"I know Cosimo. I know," Tom said, as he pressed the end call button.

Tom bowed his head, closed his eyes and let out a deep breath. His mouth was dry and his skin clammy. His pulse raced and his eyes twitched. He'd just spoken to the man he wondered about his whole life, but someone who hadn't been real until this moment.

He looked through the clearing in the trees to make sure he wasn't being watched. A young mother pushed her sleeping baby in a stroller, while two small children tried in vain to corner a squirrel as it raced up a tree. It was just a normal late summer evening in the park for so many people, Tom thought, except for him. He was scared. Sweat poured down his face. But just as he was getting choked up, he caught himself. He sat up straight and wiped his face while clearing his throat. This was no time to give up or give in. It was no time for gloom. He had a job to do.

He pressed the numbers slowly on his burner phone. This call might just be the most dangerous call he'd ever made.

37

"Mr. Attorney General, this is Tom Berte."

"Tom, Jesus, where the fuck are you? You need to come in. Look, I don't know what happened here, or why you did what you did, but this isn't good for you or your family. You can't run. You need to turn yourself in."

"Mr. Attorney General, please listen to me. I did not leak any AMX documents. I would never do such a thing. I have never violated the oath I took when I became an attorney, and I never will. You must believe me, sir. I am being framed for crimes I didn't commit. And I can prove it, sir. But I need your help. I need you to trust me."

"Tom, listen, I don't know...."

"Sir, please, just hear me out," Tom blurted, stopping the Attorney General in mid-sentence. "Three months ago, I swore an oath to defend the Constitution and the United States against all enemies. I solemnly swore I would faithfully discharge the duties of the office you appointed me to. I gave you my word, sir, that I would do everything in my power to help capture Cosimo Benedetto. I intend to deliver on that pledge and fulfill the oath I took. I am in a position to do that. Now. And I will prove my innocence. But I need your help. Sir. Will. You. Help. Me?"

There was a long pause. Tom knew the call was being recorded on the AG's end. He instinctively looked around to see if he was being watched. He half expected a hit squad to bound out of the tree line and take him down. The call was a mistake. Just as he was about to disconnect, he heard Attorney General Mitchelson speak up.

"What do you need from me, Tom?"

At precisely 9:30 a.m. the following morning, Tom called Cosimo again.

It had been a long night and Tom didn't get much sleep. But he'd done what he needed to do. His own plan was in motion now. Today would be the first day of the rest of his life.

For anyone who was watching or listening, Brooke and Mary had been picked up by an Uber fifteen minutes earlier. They were ostensibly headed to run errands at the mall. Brooke had to get a new pair of reading glasses, she said, after the FBI agents rummaging through her desk when they executed the search warrant broke hers. Then she and Mary would head to the supermarket and arrange for the groceries to be delivered to the apartment later that afternoon. In the meantime, they would have an early lunch in Georgetown, followed by a mani/pedi and a relaxing massage, which was desperately needed after the stress they endured the past twenty-four hours. All of this was arranged by Brooke and Mary the night before at the kitchen table in the apartment, where they purposely used the landline to schedule their appointments.

But the driver of the car with the fake Uber placard in the window intentionally missed the exit for the Crystal City Mall in Arlington, Virginia, and kept driving south. About an hour later he exited the highway, and eventually turned on to a restricted access road leading to an unmarked gate at Marine Corps Base Quantico. Brooke and Mary would remain there until Operation Eradicate Aifam concluded one way or another. Tom had reached out to Brooke and Mary when they were still at Antimo's the night before, after speaking to the AG, and laid out his plan. She was fearful, but ultimately agreed to follow his instructions. There was no other way.

Tom also finally connected with LaShandra late Friday night. She wasn't surprised to hear Tom's side of the story. She doubted "CTB" was the source of the leak. Something just didn't smell right from the outset, she said. If the source was so willing to reveal his identity and what he knew about AMX, why did he need Resjudicata.com? Why didn't he just disclose the information himself? A government insider blowing the whistle on a corporate scandal, coupled with a cover-up that extended to the highest levels of government, was certain to lead to a feeding frenzy by the press, with or without Resjudicata.com as the mouthpiece.

Tom begged LaShandra to hold off publishing any information about AMX for a few more days. While he could no longer protect AMX from the truth, he could ensure the public would have accurate facts. He also suggested to LaShandra that by waiting a few days, he might be able to provide secret details about another, more explosive story, that would surely be front page news around the world.

Resjudicata.com would be given an exclusive, Tom offered, and given behind-the-scenes information that no other news organization had. The information would be cataclysmic and would propel LaShandra and her team into the pantheon of journalism history and put Resjudicata.com on the same plane as the most venerated news organizations in the world.

LaShandra was intrigued. Although she was prepared to publish what she had about AMX, the fact that she didn't know the identity of the leaker concerned her. By waiting maybe she would learn who CTB really was since it wasn't C. Thomas Berte. And getting an exclusive on a related headline-grabbing story made the wait worth it. She agreed to push the deadline by an additional seventy-two hours.

Tom hoped it would be enough.

He was tired and his head still throbbed, but it was a small price to pay to salvage his career and protect his family.

When Tom called Cosimo that morning, he confirmed he had tied up loose ends, made sure his tracks were covered, and was now ready to finally reunite with his father so he could be protected.

Tom listened to Cosimo's instructions carefully, and by 11:15 a.m. he arrived at the heliport on 34th Street and the West Side Highway in Manhattan. The pilot walked over to Tom and motioned for him to climb aboard the helicopter. Within a few minutes, the Sikorsky 800 was high above Manhattan and headed for the General Aviation Terminal at JFK

International Airport. Cosimo's men made sure Tom wasn't being followed and whisking him out of Manhattan by helicopter ensured no curious interlopers would get in the way.

Eight minutes after leaving Manhattan's west side, the helicopter touched down at JFK. Tom was escorted off the chopper and taken to a hanger where a Gulfstream G650 awaited him. Tom wondered whether BCC also arranged for the purchase of this jet through one of the Syndicate's dummy companies. As he boarded, he thought of Jacob Cartel and how he was at the pinnacle of his career when he was pulverized in the skies over the Mediterranean. He was betrayed by the same two men who had played an outsized role in Tom's own life. Tom had already placed his own future in the hands of Ignatius, and now he was about to place his fate in the hands of Cosimo Benedetto, the person who so callously orchestrated Cartel's death. Pangs of doubt washed over him. His hands trembled and the nausea he had been experiencing for the last twenty-four hours left him short of breath. But his own plan was in motion now and he wasn't about to stop it.

By noon, the jet taxied to the far end of the runway and was waiting for clearance from the control tower. At exactly 12:04 p.m. on that fateful Saturday afternoon in late August, the private jet carrying the man who was once the Deputy Executive Attorney General of the United States roared down the runway headed for a meeting with the world's most wanted criminal.

Cosimo monitored developments throughout the morning and into the afternoon, first from his stateroom and then from his study.

Totto Nessa made all the necessary arrangements with the help of the Syndicate's friends in New York. It was his idea to have Tom travel by helicopter to JFK and then board the jet to Nice. His men first spotted Tom when he exited the cab in front of the heliport on the Westside Highway. From that moment, he was under continuous surveillance and in a protected bubble, including a two-thousand-yard security perimeter around him. Dozens of men with high powered weaponry were stationed up and down the Westside Highway and on the sidewalk in front of the heliport, inside the terminal, and on rooftops of nearby buildings, offering an unobstructed view of the heliport and its flight path. High radio and cellular frequency scanners were activated. Any communications concerning Tom would have been picked up by the surveillance teams. Just in case, two more Sikorsky helicopters occupied by men carrying automatic assault weapons circled high above the west side of Manhattan to ensure there would be no attack from above. The same precautions were taken in and around the General Aviation Terminal at JFK. Totto couldn't risk Tom being captured, or worse, followed, bringing his pursuers to Cosimo's doorstep. If either occurred, the army of men stationed around the heliport had their orders.

Cosimo slept little the night before. He was full of conflicted emotions. Part excitement, part apprehension, and part anxiety. He had not gotten where he was in life by being careless. Cosimo replayed the plan in his mind several times. He didn't want the joy of reuniting with his son after some thirty years to blind him to the risks he was taking.

Cosimo ate little at breakfast and lunch. He canceled the meeting with his friends from Sicily and told them to return home and await further instructions. The fate of the President of the Region of Sicily could wait a bit longer.

Fabiana sensed Cosimo's tension. He told her a special guest would be arriving on board later that evening and suggested she might enjoy the night in the casino in the company of Gino's girlfriend.

Gino Terranova did as he was instructed and sent Totto the video of the "confession." It was a pivotal piece of the plan, and one that hopefully would convince Thomas that his government was his enemy. The collateral damage that lay in its wake was unfortunate, but Cosimo spent little time concerning himself with such trivialities and had no regrets. All his life he had done what he needed to do. If people were weak enough to be extorted by greed, and their dark, hidden addictions, it was their fault Cosimo rationalized to himself.

As the sun set over Monaco, Cosimo stood on the aft deck of the *Vulcania* taking in the refreshing breeze and trying to soothe his nerves. He noticed the yachts moored on either side of the *Vulcania* preparing to depart. Port Hercules was buzzing with activity, not unusual he thought, given that it was the last weekend in August.

Two large yachts slowly sailed into the harbor and dropped anchor about a thousand meters from the pier. They would eventually maneuver onto either side of the *Vulcania* once the berths were vacated.

Unbeknown to Cosimo and Totto Nessa, two days earlier, an employee at the private dock in Rhodes where the *Vulcania* had been moored was arrested and charged with possession and intent to distribute fifty kilos of pure cocaine that had arrived in Rhodes earlier that morning in the bowels of a commercial fishing boat. The drugs had a street value in excess of five million dollars, and the young man, originally from Athens, was facing up to twenty years of hard labor in a Greek prison camp. He offered to trade the only information he possessed in hopes of reducing the charges against him.

The young man worked on the *Vulcania* while it was in Rhodes, he told the authorities. Word among dock workers spread quickly that aboard the yacht was the head of an international criminal organization. When the yacht departed Rhodes, it was rumored to be heading to Monaco. Interpol was alerted and its personnel, as well as agents from the DGSE, France's national intelligence agency, and the CIA, were dispatched to Monaco where they spotted the *Vulcania* in Port Hercules.

The massive yacht's stealth technology prevented authorities from monitoring on-board communications, and infrared optical diffusers made it impossible to remotely capture images of the vessel's passengers. As a result, overnight, the decision was made in Washington to keep the *Vulcania* under constant visual surveillance and to monitor everyone going onboard and coming ashore.

When Fabiana arrived at the Monte Bay Casino and met Gino's girlfriend, agents from Interpol were nearby. As the women ordered champagne and caught each other up on their lives, one of the agents, dressed as a waiter, who started working at the casino's bar just hours earlier, overheard Fabiana tell her young friend how happy she was to leave the *Vulcania* for a few hours because Nino was preoccupied with a business meeting he was having later that evening with a young American and he was behaving oddly. The comment was picked up by the waiter's recording device, and the agents in Washington let out a sigh of relief. They had guessed correctly when they went all in on preparing to execute their counter strategy in Monaco.

The Gulfstream G650 touched down at Cote d'Azur airport shortly after 10:00 p.m. local time. Tom had finally fallen asleep during the flight and felt rested. He was the only passenger on board and had the run of the place. The young Swedish flight attendant was very attentive when Tom boarded the plane and said she was willing to provide him with anything he needed, but he made it clear as soon as they were airborne that he wasn't interested in anything she had to offer. He just wanted to be left alone.

Before she left, though, Tom asked where they were headed. Nice, France, she replied, and then he would be taken by helicopter to Port Hercules in Monte Carlo. The agents in Washington let out another sigh of relief.

Tom awoke minutes before the jet landed. He tried to think whether he had dreamt of anything, but his mind was blank. He was still tense, and the side of his head still tingled, but he felt comforted by rehearsing what he was going to say when the time came to meet Cosimo.

Tom needed to put him at ease and get him talking. He had to persuade Cosimo he was willing to start a relationship with him. The entire strategy turned on Cosimo opening up to him, believing they were alone and that their conversation wasn't being recorded.

Tom trusted the plan he put in place. The nightmare that started when Ignatius first brought up the idea of Tom working at the DOJ would soon be over. He prepared as if he was going to trial. With Cosimo Benedetto as his star witness.

Moments after taxiing to the private hanger, where the G650 came to a stop next to several other jets, each as large and luxurious as the jet he had just flown on, Tom deplaned and was escorted to a waiting helicopter. He wouldn't be going through passport control on this trip. The helicopter looked familiar, and Tom thought it was similar to the one he had seen in the photo of the *Vulcania* on the first day he started at the DOJ some three months earlier.

Within minutes, the blades of the Augusta Westland AW 109 whirred to life. Tom was on his way to meet a man he didn't know, but whose power, corruption, and manipulation had made this moment possible.

38

The lights of Monte Carlo bay became visible as the helicopter, still at the edge of the horizon, made its way toward the *Vulcania*. Humidity hung in the air, enshrouding the city set between the sea and mountains in a gauzy haze.

For the last hour or so, the Augusta Westland AW 109 cut through the night sky without so much as a sway or bounce as it made its way to its destination. To Tom's surprise, for all its power, the engines and rotor blades emitted a gentle hum and were much quieter than the helicopter that ferried Tom from Manhattan to JFK.

As the chopper approached the harbor, Tom looked out at the twinkling lights. Port Hercules was dotted with hundreds of vessels of various shapes and sizes, some docked at piers, others moored in the harbor, sprinkled like glow-in-the-dark confetti against the blackened waters below. The brighter lights of the casinos and clubs of Monte Carlo rose from the harbor toward the mountaintop encircling Port Hercules, creating a yellowish halo in the moon-lit sky. Because of its immense size, the *Vulcania* was docked at the far end of the pier, farthest from the shoreline and close to the entrance to the harbor. The two yachts flanking it, although large in their own right, were dwarfed by the massive *Vulcania*. Their passengers disembarked as soon as the vessels were secured, no doubt excited to gamble the night away in the city's casinos. Their interiors were dark.

The *Vulcania*, on the other hand, was glittering with a necklace of sparkling lights along the top ridge of its tallest deck from stem to stern. A silhouette of warm, soft interior lighting radiated through several windows and portholes. As the helicopter closed in on its target, the helipad on the ship's topmost deck lit up the nighttime sky, revealing a red X where the pilot would touch down.

Totto Nessa was standing at the bottom step of the landing pad as the helicopter came in for a smooth landing. He waited while the pilot powered down the engines and the rotor blades came to a halt. After a few minutes, Totto made his way to the helicopter's door. He opened it and greeted Tom.

"Good evening. I am Totto Nessa. Welcome aboard the *Vulcania*."

Totto offered Tom his outstretched hand and guided him out of the helicopter. Tom didn't know who or what to expect but appreciated the greeting.

"I hope you had a pleasant journey," Totto said, as he motioned Tom toward the stairs outlined with perimeter lighting.

"Yes, it was very pleasant. The helicopter ride was smooth, as was the flight from New York."

"Excellent. Please, right this way and I will escort you to the salon. Mr. Bene—" Totto caught himself. "I'm sorry, Cosimo is waiting for you."

Tom followed Totto down a few steps and through a door into a large foyer with marble floors and linen-covered walls. The cool conditioned air felt good, a welcome relief to the humid, warm night air that engulfed Tom when he stepped off the helicopter.

Unbeknown to Tom, as he entered the foyer, sensors built into the walls scanned Tom for weapons and listening devices, and sensors on the handrails scanned Tom's handprints for metallic residue that might reveal recording devices. Since sirens didn't blare and lights didn't blink, Totto wrongly believed Tom was clean.

"Do you need to use the facilities?" Totto asked.

"No, I'm fine, thank you."

"Well, then please follow me."

The men walked down a long corridor with plush carpeting underfoot and softly lit sconces on the walls to a waiting elevator. As the doors opened, Tom took notice of the dark wood paneling, gold-plated handles and button panel, and crystal chandelier. For a moment, Tom thought he was back at BCC's offices. After working at the DOJ for three months, he almost forgot what opulence looked like. The men rode down two decks in silence.

As they exited the elevator and proceeded down another corridor that was wider and brighter, with paintings lining the walls, Tom looked out through the large plate glass windows and saw the lights of Monte Carlo in the distance at the edge of the harbor.

"Have you visited Monte Carlo before?" Totto asked.

"No, this is my first time." His hands were cold, and his temples throbbed.

"Well, perhaps tomorrow we can arrange for you to explore the city a bit."

"Yes, that would be nice. We shall see," Tom responded, trying not to show any emotion.

After what seemed like a ten-minute walk down long corridors, around corners, past marble statues, gold-framed artwork, and large urns brimming with flowers, Totto and Tom arrived at a set of tall, intricately carved wooden double doors with frosted glass inserts and gilded hardware.

Tom's heart was pounding. He was headed for a meeting that marked the culmination of an almost thirty-year journey. He felt dread and fear, but there was no turning back now.

He had given his word.

39

Totto opened the massive doors to the salon. Tom noticed red and gold everywhere. Large picture windows lined both sides of the cavernous room overlooking the two yachts that had berthed on either side of the *Vulcania*. A grand piano sat in one corner, next to the fireplace, its raised top supported by the lid-prop. More paintings lined the walls, and two large palm trees sat in each of the far corners. Several cream-colored leather sofas were arranged around mahogany side tables, across from high back armchairs covered in red silk with gold piping. Two enormous crystal chandeliers, dimmed, provided warm, subtle light. The opulent decor and gilded accents would just as easily have been at home in the palace at Versailles, Tom thought. Soft music, just audible, played in the background. The room had a scent of lavender and vanilla, fragrant without being noxious.

Tom did not see Cosimo until he rose from the wide white leather chair tucked in the corner of the salon beside the piano. The sight of Cosimo stole Tom's breath. The man he had wondered about since he was a young boy was standing before him.

Tom froze.

Wearing white linen pants, a pale blue untucked satin shirt, and leather slippers, Cosimo was shorter than Tom expected. His fine, grayish white hair was combed back and barely covered his squarish forehead and scalp. He looked older than Tom imagined, but distinguished and handsome with a bronze glowing tan that highlighted his deep blue eyes. His prominent Grecian nose looked sculpted and gave him an air of stern authority. He slowly took a step toward Tom, held out his arms, and gently embraced him, kissing Tom first on one cheek, then the other. When he stepped back, Tom could see Cosimo's eyes fill with tears.

"I've waited a long time for this moment," Cosimo said, his voice cracking, just as it had when the two spoke on the phone. "Thank you for coming," he whispered, his lips quivering, as he wiped away tears.

Tom was numb and remained stoic. He'd turned his head and offered his cheeks but did not return Cosimo's kiss. When Cosimo embraced him, Tom raised his arms a bit, but only briefly brushed Cosimo's back. He had a faint memory of having seen him before, but not in person. Tom thought back to one of the photos he saw when he was briefed about Cosimo and the Syndicate by Agent Young on his first day at the DOJ. He noticed a resemblance between those photos and the man standing before him now. Seeing him in person forced Tom to focus intensely on Cosimo's eyes. In them he saw a vague reflection of himself. The similarities were nuanced, but they were there. The deepness of his eyes, framed by an expansive brow and receding hairline painted a portrait of Tom forty years from now. Tom was staring at his future self.

Tom also immediately thought back to the woman in one of the photos he saw during his initial briefing at the DOJ. She was pregnant. He had thought there was something familiar about her, Tom remembered. He realized now the woman was a young Mary, his mother, pregnant with Tom. He shivered at the realization. It was as if he was hovering above, watching the scene unfold before him.

Cosimo motioned Tom to sit on one of the leather sofas arranged around a glass-topped coffee table. As he did so he turned to Totto. "Thank you, Totto. I'll call you if we need anything."

Totto nodded and closed the doors to the salon as he walked out.

Cosimo offered his son a drink, but Tom asked only for water. His breath was stale, and his saliva was sour.

"How's your mother?" Cosimo asked.

"She's fine. I mean she was well, before the events of the last few days. I think she's just frightened now. We all are," Tom said, taking a gulp of water from the glass Cosimo handed him.

Cosimo sat on the smaller sofa to Tom's left. "It's despicable what the government can do to a man. I'm sorry you and your wife are going through this."

"Which part?" Tom asked, as he took another gulp of water. "It's as if this has all been a dream." Tom lowered his head and looked at his shoes. "A nightmare, really."

"I know. If I could change all of it, I would," Cosimo said. "I hope you believe me when I tell you I never stopped loving your mother, or you."

Tom nodded.

"I have been so proud of all your accomplishments. I want you to know I was there, with you, every step of the way, ensuring you and your mother never wanted for anything. I tried to give you everything I could and everything you ever wanted."

Tom nodded again and offered a faint smile. "I know. I know all you did for me and my mother."

In reality, Tom didn't know the half of it. All that he had achieved, in high school, in college, at Harvard Law School, his clerkship, the job at BCC, the position at DOJ, none of it would have happened without Cosimo's "assistance." He had opened doors, leveled the playing field, and rewritten the rules all to benefit his only child.

"Your brother, Ignatius, has been very generous to me." Tom said. "Do you know anything about his condition?"

"The last update I received is that he is in grave condition. My brother is a good man. Very smart and very proud. An excellent lawyer. He built a fine law firm," Cosimo offered while turning his head as if trying to brush off the subject.

"But even he needed your help," Tom said, willing to show Cosimo he had done his homework.

"I'm sure you learned a lot about me in the last few months. My brother was the victim of circumstances beyond his control. The United States Government allowed things to get out of hand, and when things came crashing down, it was good people like Ignazio who were left suffering the consequences. I always told him to trust no one except family. I will do anything to help my family. In the end, it is always those closest to you who will protect you."

Tom stiffened at hearing those words. It was the exact opposite of the warning Ignatius gave him. I guess it depends on your perspective, he thought, and who's wielding the power. But the ultimate power play was still to come.

"And now I'm the one in need of help," Tom said. "My wife is devastated. The people I worked with and trusted are out to ruin my career, and what they've done could land her and me in prison for a long time. I feel like my life is slipping away and I'm losing control." Tom allowed his voice to rise in anger.

"Thomas, you could have never seen this coming. You are a brilliant and talented lawyer, but I'm afraid you placed your trust in the hands of the wrong people. Based on what I've discovered, there are forces around you who are envious and fearful of what you would accomplish. They have their own agendas, and their own interests to protect, and you are standing in their way. They've taunted you and set you up to take the fall. You were expendable in their eyes, and they've gone to great lengths to destroy you." Cosimo sat back on the sofa as his words hung in the air.

"I feel like such a fool. I never expected this." Tom fidgeted with his hands. He paused and looked out the window. "I was always curious what you were like," Tom said, softening his voice. "I imagined the type of man you were, and the type of father you would have been. All my friends had dads to take them to games, play baseball with, go fishing or camping with, and to teach them life lessons. I missed not having a father around. I wished I knew you when I was growing up." Tom caught himself and abruptly stopped speaking as if he were trying to hold back tears, but he knew no tears would flow.

Tom noticed Cosimo's eyes glisten again at the sight of his son becoming emotional. Tom wondered how long he could keep up the charade.

"I'm sorry," Cosimo said, appearing to try hard to regain his composure. "I've spent my entire life protecting my family and those I love. I wished I could have been there for you, physically present, to help you, to teach you, to support you. I wanted, desperately, to be a part of your life, but I understood why your mother and her family were against it. I didn't blame her. And when they caged me like an animal and exiled me, they prevented me from being with you. I have carried that anger with me for the last thirty years. So much time has gone by. But I desperately wanted to reunite with you. I have always loved you. I'm sorry, my son."

Tom shifted in his chair. Both men sat in silence for what seemed like an eternity. The music continued playing in the background.

Finally, Tom looked up and cleared his throat. "Cosimo. If I'm to regain my life, I need your help."

Cosimo sat up straighter.

"I can help," Cosimo said, sounding eager. "I want to help you and protect you. I want to share my life with you. I want to give you everything I have." Cosimo reached over and cupped Tom's hand.

"I don't care about money," Tom jumped in quickly. "I'm not looking to get rich, I'm looking to get even. I'm looking for power to protect me and my family, and to destroy those who are trying to ruin me."

Cosimo's eyes narrowed and he smiled. There was no doubt Thomas was his son, he thought. Cosimo saw in him the same passion, energy, and loyalty he had when he was Thomas's age. "We can help each other." Cosimo said excitedly. "I can help you and you can help me. I have a grave mistrust of the same government that is out to destroy you. I have always hated institutions of power. From the time I was a young man and learned that my father was killed by those in power, and then when they exiled me and prevented me from being with my family, I vowed I would never bow to those whose only credence is their own self-preservation."

Cosimo continued. "Whether it was institutions of government in Italy or in the United States, or anywhere else in the world, I've come to learn they are all led by men and women who are lustful of power and money. They govern to benefit themselves, not to serve the people. The only goal of those in power is to destroy unity and sow divisions, so the powerful can retain their positions and control the divided masses."

Tom was listening, but his stomach was churning. The hypocrisy was almost too much to bear. He reminded himself he was staring at his father, although the man in front of him was someone he didn't know and could never love.

"Cosimo, the power of the United States Government is extraordinary. I'm afraid of what comes of all this. I'm not sure I'll be able to overcome what they've done to me."

"Your whole life you've played not to lose, Thomas. But you can't play that game anymore. You've got to risk losing in order to win everything. I will help you." Cosimo paused. "Ignatius came to learn that lesson when he finally asked for help. He had no choice."

"But what about Jacob Cartel?" Tom asked. He wanted to say more but decided to gauge Cosimo's reaction first.

Cosimo shook his head and sneered. "Poor Jacob was foolish. He too played the game not to lose, and in the end, he lost everything. He didn't care about the thousands of others he would have brought down with him. He was given a choice and made the wrong decision. Sometimes, for many to survive, and thrive, one must be sacrificed."

"So you sacrificed Jacob Cartel?"

"Jacob was standing in the way, and he had to be eliminated."

"Did Ignatius agree?"

"Not at first, but eventually he acceded to ensure his success and the success of his firm," Cosimo said. "As I said, Ignazio had no choice."

"What choice do I have?"

Cosimo let out a sigh. "You can choose your family. You can choose to be with me. To protect me. To protect the empire I've built, and in return all that I have will be yours."

Tom closed his eyes and let out a sigh of his own. "How can you help me? How can you help me prove I'm innocent?"

Cosimo reached over and grabbed the remote off the coffee table. He pressed a button. A large television monitor rose from the top of the credenza on the far wall as lights dimmed further and shades lowered until the salon was almost completely dark. Cosimo pressed another button on the back-lit remote. Within seconds, the bloodied face of a man sitting in a chair appeared on the screen. He was grotesque. His hands were bound behind him, and his legs were shackled. His was bruised and battered, and one eye was swollen shut. The man's lips were cut and torn. He was missing several teeth and was panting heavily. His head flopped to one side and then the other. His left ear lobe dangled, nearly touching his shoulder. A devilishly large man stood over him. His face was long and narrow. The large man grabbed the hair of the man sitting in the chair and pulled it back, lifting his pulped head toward the camera.

Tom recognized him. The man in the chair began to speak in slurred words.

My name is FBI Special Agent Bruce Young. During the past week, I accessed the computer systems of the FBI to download secret and confidential information concerning AMX Corporation. I also accessed secret material concerning a federal grand jury empaneled to hear evidence against AMX. I manipulated the FBI's computer systems to make it appear as though Executive Deputy Attorney General Thomas Berte downloaded the data. I then provided the materials to Resjudicata.com, and again made it look as though Mr. Berte was the source of the information.

Working with others within the Department of Justice, I opened a bank account in the name of Tom Berte at Wells Fargo Bank and arranged for $750,000 to be transferred into the account to make it appear as though Mr. Berte was paid for the information provided to Resjudicata.com. I also used doctored facial recognition technology to make it appear as though Mr. Berte withdraw some of the money. Mr. Berte was not involved in this and was not aware of my actions and those of my colleagues. He is innocent.

The screen went dark. Tom sat on the sofa in stunned silence as the lights slowly brightened and the shades rose. He looked at Cosimo. "It was Bruce Young who framed me for the leak?"

"And he wasn't alone," Cosimo said. "He was working with others at the highest level of the FBI. This is what I mean, Thomas. You cannot trust your government. They are out to destroy you."

Tom did not react.

"But how did you learn this?"

"I have vast resources. I have experts in computer technology in Tel Aviv that work for my organization. They were able to gain access to the FBI's servers and traced the source of the duplicated materials to a computer belonging to Agent Young. It wasn't difficult at all."

"What will happen to Agent Young now?"

"He had to pay for what he did to you. For what he put you, and Brooke, and Mary through. He was a foolish man, weak, and he has paid dearly."

"You had him killed?"

Cosimo turned to him. "Yes, to protect you. I will always do everything in my power to protect the people I love. That pig will never hurt you again."

Cosimo slowly stood. "Will you protect me now, Thomas?" he asked in a voice that sounded oddly gentle. "Will you protect me and everything I have created?"

Tom, too, stood up and made his way to the window. The haze had lowered, but he could still see lights of the casinos and buildings that sprawled up the mountain side in the distance.

He gazed in silence, allowing the past few moments to sink in.

"I want to destroy the people who are destroying me and my family," Tom said when he finally spoke. "The hatred I have for the US government knows no bounds, Cosimo. I want to work with you, and to learn from you. I can tell you what they know about you and your organization, and how they plan to attack you and take you down. I can tell you the intelligence they have on you, and the methods they're using and who their sources are. We can fight them. Together."

Tom saw Cosimo's shoulders relax as he exhaled.

"Thomas, you and I can achieve things that no one has ever dreamed of. The Syndicate I control is even more powerful than the FBI and the Department of Justice." Cosimo was becoming animated and spoke quickly. "The United States government is ruthless, but stupid. We can outsmart them. With the technology at my disposal, and the loyalty of people who work for me, as well as your friends at the law firm, we can fight and win. And we will make them pay. Just like your government paid $500 million dollars to protect the information of thousands of veterans when my people hacked the computers of the Department of Veterans Affairs." Cosimo cocked his head and let out a gruff laugh.

Tom shut his eyes. Allow him to keep talking, he said to himself.

"Just like they pay every time I undermine their financial systems and stock markets. In fact, tomorrow, the stock of a company called Amtel, which I control, will rise fivefold after the markets open, but will plummet before the trading day ends." Cosimo was giddy with excitement and couldn't contain himself. "It will be like Cambridge Logistics, only bigger. I have wreaked havoc on the economy of the United States and saddled it with billions in costs to care for an addicted society. I control all of that, Thomas.

"They pay to fight wars against enemies I finance in the Middle East and elsewhere. I will always make the United States pay for what it has done to me and my family. The Syndicate will triumph over the gutless men and women who run the United States, and together we can rule our destiny and take what we deserve."

"I want to be a part of it, Cosimo. I want to be a part of your life," Tom said, stiffening his back and holding his head high. He, too, sounded excited. "I want to punish the United States for what it has done to me and Brooke."

Cosimo strode toward Tom and stretched his hands, eager to hug him.

After a short embrace, Cosimo continued. "All that I have is yours, Thomas. Together, we will make our empire stronger and governments around the world will have no choice but to bow to our demands. Our power will be unmatched."

Cosimo kept talking and making damning admissions about the industries he controlled and the empire he ran, but Tom no longer heard him. Cosimo's voice became fainter as the thoughts in Tom's head grew louder. Tom's entire life had come down to this moment. He was finally awakening from his stupor to escape the sinister darkness. Glory was about to overtake gloom. He waited for Cosimo to pause. He inhaled deeply and turned to him.

"I want to be a part of your life. You are my father and…I. Am. Your. Son."

The initial blast rocked the *Vulcania* at the same time the power was cut, plunging the massive vessel into total darkness. Cosimo fell to the ground.

"Thomas, where are you?" Cosimo screamed. "Are you alright? Thomas!"

40

Armed militia from the DGSE along with CIA tactical units exited their armored vehicles and approached the pier in darkness. As soon as the order was given, they sprinted toward the floating fortress. Security agents guarding the *Vulcania* had no time to react. By the time they realized what was happening, it was too late. Some of the security agents grabbed their weapons and indiscriminately fired at the incoming paratroopers, but their shots missed wildly. One by one they were picked off by sharpshooters stationed across the pier. At that same moment, sixty special-force marines stowed in each of the smaller yachts that had been commandeered by the DGSE and berthed next to the *Vulcania* hurled flash bang grenades toward the bridge and forward decks and launched two rope lines onto the *Vulcania's* decks. Amid acrid smoke and thundering noise, the marines hoisted themselves onboard.

Seconds later, sirens raged from Interpol police vans racing up the pier. Dozens of armed officers leapt from the vans and ran up the forward and aft gangplanks. Three Apache helicopters flew low over Port Hercules and hovered over the *Vulcania*, while French soldiers rappelled down static ropes and made their way onto the yacht's decks. The forces had clear orders to kill anyone who resisted.

Satellite-enabled video drones circling above provided real time feed of the attack taking place below. The scene played out on large screens in the Vault, the underground command bunker built deep into the bedrock below a remote unused airstrip at CIA headquarters in Langley, Virginia. The Directors of the FBI and CIA each wore headsets, along with a dozen intelligence officers, listening to instructions given by commanders on the ground and aboard the surveillance plane circling the skies over Monaco. The plane, a modified Cessna Triple 8, was equipped with a "dirty-box" and picked up communications from the implanted micro resin synthetic chip. As soon as Tom uttered the code words "I Am Your Son," the senior operations commander in the Vault, a seasoned military veteran in a prior life and now the CIA officer in charge of the ambush, gave the "go" order to storm the *Vulcania*.

In the salon, waves from grenade blasts knocked Cosimo to the ground next to the piano. The whirling and thumping of Apache helicopters hovering above grew louder. Cosimo staggered to his feet and looked at the security monitors on the wall to the left of the starboard windows. Flashing lights raced toward the pier. Screams could be heard from decks above and below the salon. The stampede of running footsteps grew louder as armed paratroopers swarmed the vessel.

The *Vulcania's* captain heard the approaching sirens moments before the computer monitors toppled over from the thundering grenade explosions. Despite the *Vulcania's* massive size, the bridge's floors and walls vibrated and buckled from repeated blasts as dark smoke engulfed the bridge. He was thrust against the main control panel when the power cut out. The concussion grenade pierced his ears, and he landed hard on the slate floor. The last thing he saw before losing consciousness were multiple beams of white light blinding him.

Totto Nessa was in the engine room re-coding software for the bow thrusters when he too was thrown hard by the blasts. The engine room was plunged into darkness. He managed to regain his balance and ran toward the wall-mounted intercom. After multiple attempts to reach Cosimo, he tried the bridge. He heard only static. He ran toward a small porthole and saw armored vehicles racing toward the *Vulcania* with dozens of armed soldiers in camouflage, some clad in body armor, storming the vessel.

Instinctively he reached for the Glock in his waist holster and raced toward the sentinel quarters to engage the vessel's defense security system and unlock the armory cabinet containing Russian-made assault rifles and machine guns. He heard the pounding of footsteps and muffled screams. Within seconds, voices directed him to stop, but he was trained to ignore such commands. He turned and raised the Glock to his chest. The blast came instantly, and the flash lit the room. Totto Nessa slammed backwards, crashing into the bulkhead stanchion. Blood splattered across the walls. "Target neutralized" squawked through the headsets in the Vault at Langley.

Twelve decks above the engine room, Cosimo crawled on the floor of the salon and made his way to the phone, yelling at Tom to stay low and crouch behind the sofa. Cosimo rushed to lift the handset and shouted for the captain. No response. He shouted Totto's name. Still nothing. He yelled out. "Don't worry! My men will protect us." He scrambled to a wooden cabinet with gold inlays behind the piano and pulled open the door. He turned the dial several times to the right, and then to the left. He opened the inner door to a steel safe and pulled out an AMP-69 rifle. He checked the magazine and racked the charging handle. He turned toward Tom.

"Thomas, slide behind the sofas."

Hearing nothing except the thumping of footsteps growing louder making their way toward the salon , Cosimo raised his head and peered over the edge of the piano. The room was dark and filling quickly with turbid smoke. He could barely see the rifle he was clutching.

"Thomas, come here!"

Tom fell to the ground when the first blasts rocked the *Vulcania*. Although he expected mayhem when he uttered the code words, he wasn't prepared for the grenade explosions. He lost his balance and sense of space. Everything went dark as acrid odor filled his nostrils and stung his eyes. He thought he blacked out for a moment. His ears were ringing, and the salon was spinning. But he managed to regain his bearings and made his way to the enormous doors.

Flood lights suddenly arced across the decks. Pilots in the Apache helicopters circling above trained their nightscope halogens into the windows of the salon, illuminating it like a stadium at night. Through the haze and smoke filtered by the bright lights Tom could see Cosimo crouching low behind the piano. He slowly stood and glared. He saw Cosimo's chest heave with every breath, the look of terror and desperation on his face.

"Thomas! Come here! I will protect you!" Cosimo screamed.

Just as Cosimo uttered those words, the battering ram blew open the massive doors to the salon, nearly ripping them off their hinges. One of the doors hit Tom in the back and knocked him to the ground as etched glass shattered across the floor. A dozen paratroopers in full protective armor aiming assault weapons with lasers stormed the room.

"Get down! get down!" they demanded, with others yelling "gun! gun!"

Cosimo indiscriminately discharged his AMP-69 in rapid succession with deafening claps. Muzzle flashes sparked as crystal shattered and wood splintered and shredded into a million fragments. Bullets pierced the salon walls, ceiling, and chandeliers as multiple rounds of ammunition ricocheted off the paratroopers' protective armor. The barrage of gunfire set off a fury of bursting flashes and concussive explosions. Beams of red light from the paratroopers' laser-armed rifles targeted Cosimo in concentric circles and intersecting blurring lines. Almost instantly hundreds of rounds of ammunition riddled the piano and wall behind Cosimo in perfect precision, disintegrating everything in their path.

Four armed troopers made their way to Tom and fell onto him, crushing him under their weight, but shielding him from the gunfight. Tom squeezed his eyes shut and winced in pain. He willed himself to remain conscious while thundering sounds of explosions from the firefight surrounded him. More paratroopers stormed the salon, shouting and spraying the room with munition shells and grenade blasts as they took cover behind anything that hadn't yet been destroyed. Tom held his breath as the smell of gunpowder and burnt smoke penetrated his airways.

In the Vault, live feed from body cameras blazed across large screens. Hazy, grainy images of paratroopers running in formation into the salon cut across the monitors. Flashes of fiery sparks blurred in and out of focus. Sounds of explosions engulfed the command center, intermittently pierced by static and howls from air horns and sirens. The intelligence officers sat at the edge of their chairs, many of them cupping their mouths. The FBI Director appeared to be praying as the CIA Director focused intently on the blurry video feed from thousands of miles away.

The gun fight continued for what seemed like interminable minutes with sounds of metal, glass, and wood shattering amid an ear-popping rampage.

"Target down! target down, target down," finally echoed in the Vault.

Crackling and static grew louder as the blasts and explosions grew fainter. The salon became quieter, except for sirens still blaring in the distance. Several of the officers and paratroopers, with their lasers focused on the target, made their way to Cosimo.

"Salon secured," said the lead agent, as others formed a perimeter around the room standing guard in front of the windows and the entrance where the massive doors once stood.

Paratroopers who had fallen on Tom scrambled to their knees.

"Sir. Are you okay? Sir, have you been shot?"

While managing to regain his breath, and with the sound of gunfire still ringing in his ears, Tom blinked at the bright lights still arcing in the salon. The smell of gunpowder hung in the hazy air. He tried to focus and began to sit up, regaining his balance. He felt pain in his sides from being thrust to the ground and tasted blood in his mouth. Pangs of nausea came over him. "I want to see him," Tom mouthed. After a few seconds he screamed: "I want to see him!"

Blood drenched Cosimo's white linen pants and satin shirt and trickled down his forearms and legs. He had been shot in both legs and left arm, but he was still alive. Breathing hard, his hair was disheveled, and his clothes were torn. His eyes looked cold and dark. He sat with his back against what was left of the piano, bullet holes riddling the wall behind him. At least seven paratroopers trained their assault rifles with beams of red light targeted on the world's most wanted criminal.

Hearing Tom's voice, Cosimo raised his head and glared at him.

"You told me you are my son!" He was panting heavily. "You betrayed me! You said you would protect me!", his voice steadily escalated into a scream. "I gave you everything you have! I made you who you are! You would have accomplished nothing without me. Nothing!" Blood mixed with saliva spewed from his mouth the sound of fury in his voice. "All your successes. All your achievements. All the glory, and awards, and victories. It was all me. You would have never made it to Harvard fucking law school without me. You would have never been where you are without me! I made it all happen, not you. It was me. I made you! You're nothing! You're nothing without me! You're a traitor!"

He thrashed his head wildly, tears and sweat streaming down his face. "I made it all happen! I made you! I gave you everything! Everything you have, you have because of me. You're nothing! Nothing!" Cosimo screamed before letting out a long shriek. He doubled over. He heaved and clutched his chest trying to catch his breath.

Tom rose slowly, raised his head, stood ramrod tall and squared his shoulders. He narrowed his eyes and stared intensely at Cosimo. His nostrils flared. He took a deep breath and set his jaw. For the first time in several days he felt no fear.

"I may be your son because of circumstances I had nothing to do with and had no control over, but I'm no traitor." He was covered in sweat. His lips were bloodied and the pain in the side of his head was sharp. He wanted to keel over and puke, but he had one final message to deliver.

"I took an oath to support and defend my country against all enemies. And you Cosimo Benedetto are an enemy. I gave my word that I would find you and bring you to justice. Today, I fulfilled that promise and kept my word. To my country. To my family. And to myself!"

41

"Tom, the nation is indebted to you. I know I speak for all Americans when I say you have our gratitude and thanks for the tremendous work you've done and the personal sacrifices you've made for our country." President Tayla Ferguson offered Tom her outstretched hand.

"Thank you, Madam President. It was an honor of a lifetime to work in the Department of Justice on behalf of the American people."

The President had called a hastily arranged press conference in the Rose Garden scheduled to begin in a few minutes. For now, Tom, Brooke, AG Mitchelson and President Ferguson were enjoying a private meeting in the Oval Office.

"Tom, the past several days have been nothing short of extraordinary. The Attorney General told me you actually had a microchip recording device implanted under your scalp to record Cosimo Benedetto's admissions," President Ferguson said to Tom. "That's astounding. Your courage is incredible. You are a national hero."

"Thank you, Madam President," Tom said as he blushed, uncomfortable with his fifteen minutes of glory. He looked at Brooke, who tightened her grip on his hand.

"At some point during the progression of the investigation, I learned of this nanotechnology developed by the UK Intelligence Service in conjunction with the FBI and CIA that is virtually undetectable," Tom said. "We knew from confidential sources that using traditional surveillance equipment was impossible. The subdermal microchip was the only means we could use to record Cosimo Benedetto. When the opportunity presented itself for me to meet with the target, I contacted the Attorney General and he immediately agreed to arrange for the procedure to take place."

Tom left out the details about the AG arranging for Tom to be clandestinely picked up late that Friday evening in New York City and taken to a military hospital at Joint Base McGuire-Dix-Lakehurst in New Jersey, where Tom underwent the procedure to implant the microchip, and then was driven back to New York City before daylight so he could call Cosimo the next morning. He also omitted details about the late-night appearance by Department of Justice lawyers before a magistrate judge to obtain legal authority to surreptitiously record Benedetto in coordination with the ministry of justice for the Principality of Monaco that greenlighted the plan to storm the *Vulcania* in Port Hercules. Tom was certain President Ferguson was aware of the mission, and likely even authorized it.

Tom paused for a moment and then held his head high. "But Madam President, if I may, the real heroes are the men and women who risked their lives capturing Cosimo Benedetto. They displayed true courage and are the ones deserving of recognition and praise, along with the fine men and women of the FBI, CIA and Department of Justice, who work tirelessly each day to protect and defend this great nation and its people."

The group nodded in agreement and sat silently for a moment.

"Are we still being recorded now, Tom?" President Ferguson asked, smiling. "Perhaps we can have the chip implanted in the First Gentlemen, so everything I say to him is recorded and he can't deny I said it." The four of them laughed, lightening the mood and allowing everyone to relax a bit.

Brooke then chimed in. "Maybe I should have made sure the chip remained implanted," as another round of laughter filled the Oval office.

"Much to my wife's disappointment," Tom said, "the chip was removed yesterday morning at Walter Reed Medical Center. I'm no longer a walking tape recorder." He turned to Brooke and put his arm around her waist.

"It is incredible, isn't it, when you think of the brazen plan Cosimo Benedetto devised to try to manipulate you into joining his ranks. First, he succeeded in blackmailing FBI Special Agent Young into delivering confidential information to Resjudicata.com while making it look like you were responsible for the leak, and then he tortures Agent Young into claiming that officials in the FBI were behind a plot to frame you and Brooke. What happened to the two of you is tragic. Cosimo Benedetto is positively despicable." The President suddenly stopped. "I'm sorry, Tom. I know he's your father."

Tom was still reeling from the events of the last few days. He sat up straighter and took in a breath. He knew this subject was coming and he was ready for it.

"No need to apologize, Madam President," he said as he inched closer to Brooke and moved toward the front edge of the couch.

"Being a lawyer has taught me some very important lessons," Tom said. "First is that guilt exists. I have seen it with my own eyes." Speaking confidently he continued. "Second is that people are responsible for their own actions. And third is that the law can be a powerful weapon to achieve justice. In this case, like in so many others led by the courageous women and men of the Department of Justice and the FBI, justice has prevailed." Tom paused and looked at Brooke. "I know Cosimo Benedetto is guilty of the heinous crimes he committed, and he alone is responsible for his deeds. While the sins of parents are often visited upon their children, I will not bear shame for being my father's son. The shame is his alone."

Tom was still processing the information he learned since Cosimo's arrest, which his mother hinted at when they spoke after the search warrant was executed at his apartment, that all of his triumphs resulted from Cosimo's manipulation. He now knew Cosimo pulled strings that provided him privileges others didn't have and allowed him to accomplish things he never would have achieved on his own. He knew Cosimo bribed, blackmailed, threatened, and intimidated everyone in a position to judge him in order to guarantee his success. But learning Cosimo put his thumb on the scale, and his mother was aware of it and didn't stop it, crushed Tom. He had been cheated out of the truth and robbed of the dignity of knowing whether his efforts alone would have been good enough to achieve the same successes.

He would never know if he was smart enough, or had worked hard enough, or had learned well enough to succeed on his own merits. He'd never know if he could have done it alone—without Cosimo Benedetto's maneuvers and schemes. His abilities, his worth, and his confidence were shaken. Had he received false praise his whole life? Did it matter that Cosimo and his mother were motivated by love and wanted the best for him? Or did wanting too much for their son deprive him of the opportunity to know who he was? Ignatius was right, after all, Tom thought. It is those closest to you who can hurt you the most. It would take time for Tom to come to terms with all of it and heal.

As for Mary, it was the discovery that Cosimo was ultimately behind the plot to frame their son and Brooke that led her to accept the punishment that would eventually befall him. She recoiled at first, when she learned Tom double-crossed Cosimo into believing he would accept his help, only to lure Cosimo into making damning admissions that would seal his fate and result in the multiple life sentences he eventually would receive.

But in the days since the events on the *Vulcania*, Mary came to understand the evilness and cruelty that she always knew existed within Cosimo. She could never forgive him for putting Tom and Brooke through the unthinkable pain they had endured, and for the devious plan he formulated to deceive Tom in the hope her son would form an alliance with him that would ultimately benefit only Cosimo. Mary finally accepted that Cosimo could no longer be a part of her life. She returned home when Tom made it clear she was not welcome at the White House ceremony.

The President turned to Attorney General Mitchelson and congratulated him not only for the successful mission, but for recognizing that Tom was the right person to lead the investigation that ultimately brought down the world's most wanted criminal.

The Attorney General was eager to pick up where the President left off. "Thank you, Madam President. When I first hired Tom, he gave me his word he would do everything in his power to help capture Cosimo Benedetto. Not only did Tom keep his word, but he did so with honor and integrity. When Tom contacted me Friday evening, he reminded me of his commitment and was adamant that he was being targeted for crimes he didn't commit, and he explained the plan he devised to deceive and capture Benedetto and bring down the entire Syndicate. Believing in Tom and his allegiance to the rule of law, we sprang into action and helped him execute his plan.

"As of this morning, we've raided multiple offices and safe houses connected to the Syndicate and shut down everything from computer hacking operations in Tel Aviv and Russia, to heroin refining plants in Sicily, Turkey, Afghanistan, Greece, and Syria. We've frozen bank accounts around the world containing over ten billion dollars and seized assets worth hundreds of billions more. Over three hundred people are in custody around the globe, including Cosimo's right-hand man Totto Nessa who, although gravely injured, survived the raid on the *Vulcania*.

"Many of those arrested are cooperating with authorities. Nessa included. Fifteen countries in addition to ours have filed charges against Benedetto and the Syndicate's leadership. Although Cosimo Benedetto was defiant till the end as agents took him into custody, given the damning admissions he made to Tom, and the other evidence we have in hand, I am very confident Cosimo Benedetto will spend the rest of his life in prison. He'll never harm anyone again."

After a short pause, AG Michelson continued. "And if allowing Tom and Brooke to pay the price for crimes they didn't commit weren't enough, in the last twenty-four hours we also learned that Benedetto had a back-up plan in the event Tom didn't agree to protect him and betray the government. If Tom wouldn't comply, Benedetto was prepared to extort him by unloading a cache of doctored evidence showing that Tom had lied and cheated his way to get to where he was, all but ensuring Tom's life and career would be ruined forever. Benedetto was prepared to give his son a choice: have everything or lose it all."

Tom shook his head and looked down. He still could not grasp the lengths to which Cosimo would go to destroy his life. Learning about Cosimo's manipulation was painful enough. Learning the truth about the kind of man his father was made the pain much worse. In the end, though, it justified the ultimate manipulation of Cosimo that resulted in Tom's salvation.

"But thanks to Tom and the tremendous efforts of the men and women who worked on Project Eradicate Aifam," AG Mitchelson quickly added, "none of that will come to pass. We finally achieved our goal that was decades in the making. We have eradicated the notorious Benedetto Syndicate, saving our nation and its people from untold crimes the Syndicate would have continued to perpetuate against them, and we've literally saved the lives of countless people around the world. We did it. In the end, getting close to his son got Cosimo Benedetto burned."

The Attorney General grinned and took a sip of water. After a moment, a solemn look fell across the AG's face.

"The collateral damage left in the wake of Cosimo Benedetto's capture, however, is immense," he continued. "After we arrested Benedetto's bodyguard as he was about to flee the country, we recovered the body of FBI Special Agent Young.

"And beyond the loss of life and treasure, is the loss of one of our nation's greatest law firms," AG Mitchelson said as he turned to President Ferguson. "Both Tom and I started our legal careers in private practice at Balatoni, Cartel and Colin, as you know Madam President. Last evening all of the firm's offices were raided by local police and intelligence agencies. We expect indictments to be handed down within the hour, and I suspect the firm's partners will vote later today to dissolve the partnership and close shop."

Tom's mind turned to Troy for a second. He was a good lawyer who got involved with the wrong firm.

The AG cleared his throat. "Ignatius Balatoni, the last remaining founder of the firm, will escape punishment, however. At least earthly punishment. He passed away overnight after suffering a massive heart attack last Friday morning." He paused and looked down as his eyes glistened. "I'm aware that you and Ignatius Balatoni were friends, Madam President, and you took counsel from him, as we all did. All I can say is that he had us all fooled."

Tom had learned of Ignatius's passing when he arrived at the White House. He choked up when he heard the news and struggled with how to react to it. He was the last person Ignatius spoke to before he died. He had respected Ignatius and cared for him, but couldn't get past his complicity in Cosimo's crimes, or his responsibility for the death of Jacob Cartel. He would need time to mourn and time to reflect. In the end, though, Tom knew Ignatius Balatoni was responsible for his own actions and he, too, had to suffer the consequences.

After regaining his composure, the AG continued. "In a million years I would never have thought the great Ignatius Balatoni was capable of doing what he did, or that his law firm was complicit in Cosimo Benedetto's evil deeds. But the one positive that has come out of this whole ordeal is that our nation is richer for having had the privilege of Tom's service. His legacy will not be the crimes perpetrated by BCC or by Ignatius Balatoni or even by Cosimo Benedetto, but by his professionalism and the judgment he exhibited during his time as Executive Deputy Attorney General. I have witnessed firsthand what everyone else who knows and worked with Tom has seen over the years: tremendous courage, unwavering commitment to the common good, dedication to the rule of law, integrity beyond reproach, determination, someone who is always willing to give credit to others before himself, and someone who truly cares about everyone he meets."

Turning to Tom, Mitchelson said, "You are a true patriot. I am proud to have hired you, and humbled that you accepted, but I'm even more proud to count you as a friend. I am in your debt."

A lump formed in Tom's throat, and he felt himself becoming emotional.

Seeing Tom uncomfortable with the well-deserved praise, Mitchelson shifted gears.

"This morning, Resjudicata.com published the documents concerning AMX, including Agent Young's involvement and Cosimo Benedetto's plot to frame Tom. It laid out in detail Agent Young's fabrications and lies, at Benedetto's direction, that the DOJ and this Administration somehow tried to thwart the investigation into AMX. But the truth has prevailed. In fact, later today, the Justice Department will be announcing a forty-two-count indictment against AMX and its executives, something the Department has been committed to doing since it first learned of the potential criminal conduct engaged in by the company.

"Resjudicata.com also agreed to refrain from publishing the secret minutes of the grand jury so as to not compromise the integrity of proceedings. Having said that, however, the Department is in negotiations with AMX's *new* lawyers, and I expect the company and its senior management will plead guilty to the indictment, and it will admit the civil claims against it and settle the litigation. As part of the deal, AMX will fund a one-hundred-billion-dollar trust to pay those victims who have been injured or killed by centuron."

"I'd say we've had a good day at the office, wouldn't you?" President Ferguson said, smiling and nodding her approval. "Seriously, we have many blessings to celebrate," President Ferguson continued. "Tom, your work has been extraordinary, and the praise you have received and will continue to receive from this moment forward is richly deserved. The nation is grateful for your service. And Brooke, thank you for sharing Tom with us. And please accept my apology for all that you've endured."

Tom and Brooke leaned into each other. "Thank you, Madam President," they both said. Tom added, looking at Brooke, "It's all part of the job," and they all laughed again.

"Tom," President Ferguson said after a few moments, "there is one more thing I'd like to discuss before we move into the Rose Garden. Attorney General Mitchelson shared with me last evening that he wishes to step down at the end of the year. He has served this administration and our country brilliantly over the last two years, and as a superb Senator before that. He deserves to spend time with his family and savor his accomplishments." The President turned to AG Mitchelson and the two clasped hands briefly.

"Tom, after speaking with the Attorney General, and based on his highest recommendation, we both think you would make an excellent Attorney General. I would like to nominate you for the office of Attorney General of the United States. Any doubts about your inexperience or age will be erased as soon as people learn what you've done in your career and how you helped capture the world's most notorious criminal." The President paused as Tom allowed the moment to linger.

"I've already taken the liberty of having informal conversations with leaders of the Senate Judiciary Committee, as well as Senate leadership from both parties, and I'm certain your nomination will receive bi-partisan support from a vast majority of Senators. How would you feel about leading the men and women of the United States Department of Justice?"

Tom smiled and looked at Brooke. He wasn't shocked or surprised, and there was no false modesty. Just serenity and resoluteness.

"Madam President, I am honored that you and the Attorney General would consider me for this position, and I thank you for the offer. I am truly grateful and humbled.

"The events of the last few months have taken their toll on me, and on Brooke as well. I've learned things that I need to grapple with, not only about my family and my past, but about myself. When I was younger, I often wondered if I would give up everything I had for the opportunity to have my father by my side. Now, I'm faced with the reality of wondering if everything I was given was worth having the father I had." Tom paused and looked at Brooke. "I promised Brooke last night that I would take a break from the law. We have long talked about moving to upstate New York and becoming ski bums for a while. This seems like the right time. And maybe we'll work on starting a family of our own," Tom said, as he kissed Brooke's forehead.

"That sounds wonderful, Tom. I'm envious," President Ferguson said, smiling. "Not about having a newborn again," she quickly added as everyone laughed. "But about your future and the life you will have together."

"I wish you much success, Madam President, because your successes are our nation's successes. Brooke and I will support you in every way we can. But at this time I cannot commit to working again in government or even as a lawyer in the future. I need to step back and deal with the events of the past few months, and just enjoy time with my family. I hope you understand, Madam President."

"I do, Tom. And I wish you and Brooke much peace and happiness. While there will always be a place for you in my administration if you change your mind, in the meantime, I pray you will find solace and the comfort you deserve." President Ferguson stood and shook Tom's hand, and then embraced Brooke.

"Now, let's spend fifteen minutes in the Rose Garden telling the world all that you've accomplished."

The Winter Verdict
Book 2 in The Tom Berte Legal Thrillers

Lawyer Tom Berte's bucolic new life is about to be shattered by a threat he can't ignore.

Tom Berte, a former Department of Justice lawyer, thought he'd left his past behind when he moved to Castle Ridge with his family. But when a brutal attack leaves him fighting for his life, Tom and his family find themselves at the epicenter of an unfolding conspiracy that stretches from the local ski resort to a desert compound on the other side of the world.

At the heart of the mystery is Phoenix Holdings Group, a shadowy international conglomerate with its sights set on Castle Ridge Ski Resort. When a catastrophic "accident" at the resort claims dozens of lives, Tom uncovers a chilling connection to his own assault and a ruthless plot that could endanger millions.

With his wife and daughter's lives hanging in the balance, Tom must navigate a treacherous path of legal intrigue, corporate espionage, and looming revenge.

Get your copy today at
severnriverbooks.com

ACKNOWLEDGMENTS

Like any journey worth pursuing, the one that culminated in this book being published would not have been possible without the help, support, and encouragement of some amazing people I have the good fortune of knowing and loving.

I'll begin with a special group of friends who were beta-readers of an early draft of this story when it was still rife with typos, run-on sentences, and grammatical errors. They provided invaluable advice and insight, while graciously ignoring misspellings and some sections that were plain gibberish: Carrie Benevento, Pam Divino, Trina Foltz, Rosemarie Kushnir, Julie Shell, Mary Stout, and Brett Underhill are members of a book club with my wife, Justine. A second book-club crew of beta-readers includes Joanne Bujalsic, Sally Langa, Linda Manabat, Ann Marie McKool, Betsy Ricker, Carol Clancy Silver, Mirian Stokes, Sharri Thompson, Gayle Trulli, and Lori Uffer. A huge thanks to each of you for your time and willingness to indulge the fanciful thought that I might one day become a published author. Your commentary, criticism, and suggestions made this story better. Whatever faults remain lie entirely with me.

I also imposed on a few others whose judgment and opinions I value and trust: Sinquen Hawkins, Jeremy Garfield, Rose Grimaldi, Loreto Grimaldi, and Dr. Michael Castellano. I asked each of them for their unvarnished critique and assessment, and they assured me they could be objective and would shoot-straight. Their suggestions and comments helped improve this story immeasurably and for that I will be forever grateful.

Any aspiring writer who's tried to "find an agent" to represent them knows how daunting and challenging that can be. I was blessed to have found two.

A special heartfelt thanks goes to my "first" agent, Carol Woien, of the now-closed Blue Ridge Literary Agency. At the time she took me on as a client, Carol was the only person who satisfied the following two criteria: (a) she had no previous relationship with me or my wife and therefore had no reason to be complimentary about my work; and (b) she read the entire manuscript and still liked it. Her immediate enthusiasm and excitement for this project was inspiring and a comforting balm after so many other agents passed on it after only reading a 250-word query letter. Carol, thank you for believing in this project and for taking a flyer on me.

After the untimely passing of Dawn Dowdle, owner of Blue Ridge Literary Agency, and the closing of the agency, Carol decided to pursue other interests. That's when I was blessed for a second time with my second agent, Terrie Wolf, of AKA Literary Management, who agreed to represent me. Her enthusiasm and good cheer from the start were infectious, and her unwavering support for my work was the fuel needed for this book to become published. Terrie, I owe you much, and the words 'thank you' don't begin to express the depth of my gratitude and appreciation for all you've done.

To the amazing team at Severn River Publishing, especially my copy editor Amie Swope and publisher Cate Streissguth, thank you for your invaluable advice and guidance. This book is better because of your brilliant work.

To my author friends, Jamie Lynn Hendricks and Paula Munier, I am in awe and admiration of your talents and the wonderful and amazing stories you create. In particular, Jamie's input and advice at a critical stage in the process were instrumental in helping me move this project forward.

To the readers of this book, I thank you from the bottom of my heart. I take none of this for granted, and I am humbled and honored that you have devoted your precious time to reading the words I've written. I hope you found some modicum of enjoyment in it. Without you there would be no books, and without books, there would be no wonder, amazement, and joy in this world. You are responsible for my dream coming true as much as anyone.

To my parents, immigrants from Italy, who gave me every opportunity I could ask for, and who instilled in me at a young age the importance of education, the value of knowledge, and the virtue of realizing that hard work and determination are the necessary building blocks to achieving success, I am who I am because of you. I hope I've made you as proud of me as I am to be your son.

None of this would have been possible, or frankly worth the time and effort that goes into writing a book, without the unyielding love and support of my beautiful wife and three amazing children. Michael, now in college, and smart and filled with knowledge beyond his years, was my first informal editor who provided insightful feedback and suggestions. I am in awe of his creativity and genuine goodness, and his excitement about this project kept me going even when I began to doubt my ability to complete it.

In early 2020, just as the covid-19 pandemic was beginning to ravage the world, my oldest son, Anthony, now in medical school, brought up the subject of a book I had started writing when I was still in law school many, many years ago. With his encouragement, I dusted off the three chapters I wrote when I was in my early twenties and set out to finish writing the story I started then, fulfilling one of my cardinal rules about life: always finish what you start. He was the spark I needed to continue this project.

To my daughter Elizabeth who's in high school, I stand in amazement at the young woman you've become, and your many talents and the joy and smile you bring to everything you do. You completed our family, and you will forever be my baby girl.

Whatever other accomplishments I've had in my life, they pale in comparison to the joy and happiness each of you has brought me. My proudest moment will always be when I introduce myself as your dad.

To my beautiful wife, Justine, your unwavering support and encouragement throughout our marriage has meant the world to me and allowed me to dream that I could one day write a book. You are the greatest gift God has given me, and I thank him every day for allowing me to be in your life. You make everything we do worth it. You are my rock. *Con te partiro* to live the dreams we create together.

ABOUT THE AUTHOR

Dan is a litigation partner in a national law firm with over 1,100 attorneys, and a mafia aficionado. His series is inspired, in part, by a fascination with all things mafia and an actual case where he worked closely with the Department of Justice and FBI. After several years, Dan's team succeeded in recovering over $240 million on behalf of thousands of innocent investors swindled by foreign nationals. He is a graduate of Tufts University and Fordham Law School. In his spare time, he enjoys traveling and skiing with his wife and three children. He is also a volunteer firefighter in his hometown of Colts Neck, NJ.

Join the reader list at
severnriverbooks.com

Printed in the United States
by Baker & Taylor Publisher Services